JOHN ELLISON

TIMES CHANGE

BEFORE THE CHILDREN ACT

A NOVEL

Copyright © 2016 John Ellison

The moral right of the author has been asserted.

Apart from any fair dealing for the purposes of research or private study, or criticism or review, as permitted under the Copyright, Designs and Patents Act 1988, this publication may only be reproduced, stored or transmitted, in any form or by any means, with the prior permission in writing of the publishers, or in the case of reprographic reproduction in accordance with the terms of licences issued by the Copyright Licensing Agency. Enquiries concerning reproduction outside those terms should be sent to the publishers.

This is a work of fiction. Names, characters, businesses, places, events and incidents are either the products of the author's imagination or used in a fictitious manner. Any resemblance to actual persons, living or dead, or actual events is purely coincidental.

Matador
9 Priory Business Park,
Wistow Road, Kibworth Beauchamp,
Leicestershire. LE8 0RX
Tel: 0116 279 2299
Email: books@troubador.co.uk
Web: www.troubador.co.uk/matador
Twitter: @matadorbooks

ISBN 978 1785892 639

British Library Cataloguing in Publication Data.
A catalogue record for this book is available from the British Library.

Printed and bound in the UK by TJ International, Padstow, Cornwall
Typeset in 11pt Aldine by Troubador Publishing Ltd, Leicester, UK

Matador is an imprint of Troubador Publishing Ltd

'The times they are a-changing' – Song by Bob Dylan

1

A Newcomer to the Legal Department

A diverse crew of solicitors, legal assistants, clerical assistants, typists, someone called a muniments officer, plus the Borough Solicitor himself, Mr. Edward Shimble, and his secretary, made up the staff of the legal department of the London Borough of Haringey in September 1979. They were dispersed around the two upper floors of a three storey building, in a dusty and dirty road, exhausted by vehicular traffic, leading off Wood Green's High Road. Its grey, modern façade curved round to the side, faintly resembling a quarter of a large orange, and had much exterior glass. In appearance it was more modest than the blander but grander, wide-fronted Civic Centre, where the borough's councillors – 'the members' – met, took refreshment, talked and made decisions. This was to be found around the corner and uphill a few hundred yards away, set back from the road.

The legal building in Station Road had a touch more individuality than the Civic Centre. Its substantial window volume had caused one inmate extravagantly, possibly after lunch in the adjoining public house, to declare that the place had 'almost exclusive entitlement to the sun.' Furthermore, the rear upper windows had access, on a clear day, to a distant view of the roof of the borough's own Alexandra Palace (whose title exaggerated its splendour), planted majestically on a height beyond which lay the prosperous shopping streets of Muswell Hill.

The London Borough of Haringey extended – and, as I

write, still extends – from Tottenham in the east to Highgate and beyond in the west, nudging Enfield's borough boundary to the north and Islington's to the south. It was and is one of more than thirty such municipal structures gathered together seamlessly in a giant jigsaw, forming just one dimension of England's capital city.

A relatively autonomous section of the legal department (to which Edward Shimble generally paid limited attention), consisted of two solicitors who bore primary responsibility for work for the borough's Social Services Department, mainly in relation to children. The two solicitors were Melanie Cusack, who had been unenthusiastically in post for almost two years, and just-qualified Robert Fordham, who had taken up his duties at the beginning of the week. Robert Fordham's doings occupy much space in this narrative.

He had not yet sized up the lack of devotion to the task of his partner-in-social services-work, but his own eagerness was unquestionable. Yet his only relevant experience was as a trainee – then entitled an Articled Clerk – within a rural county council in the south-west. There for some three months during his two years of training he had dogged the heels of fully fledged practitioners, and he was hopeful that this would be enough to fit him for the times ahead.

His main links were to be with 'fieldwork' social workers based in each of the borough's area offices, located chiefly in the north and south of Tottenham, in Wood Green and in Crouch End. Less frequently he would be dealing with the senior management, headed by urbane and eloquent Social Services Director Michael Stone, whom he had met at his interview and who was stationed in what had once been Tottenham's own Town Hall.

So Robert Fordham, a clean-shaven young man of middle height and more on the side of good looks than the alternative, and the owner of a friendly, open personality, was no longer just the shadow of a proper lawyer. He was the person responsible for advising and representing a Social Services department – which meant, in practice, guiding and being guided by individual social workers and their supervising 'seniors', each of whom managed a small team.

On his second working day, Robert Fordham drove his not very new Ford Escort car to the north Tottenham Social Services building where a child protection case conference concerning a three-year-old child called Amy was programmed to take place.

He had with him a typed request for a legal representative to attend. The author was the family's social worker, whose name – typed below her large and legible signature – was Jessica Palmer.

The North Tottenham office, a detached and ageing building, looked on to a shop-adorned high street close to a well-known football stadium, and was advertised by a large sign, imprinted high on the building's wall. Robert managed to park his car without difficulty in a side road, relishing the summer-autumn sunshine during a short walk before he entered the reception area. This was sparsely but not badly furnished with a mix of upright chairs, armchairs and even a plastic-covered sofa which tolerated a freshly committed rip on one arm-rest, apparently the work of a sharp blade. A worn carpet filled most of the room. A middle-aged black female receptionist sat behind a desk.

He told her why he had come, and was in friendly fashion advised that he would be collected shortly. Minutes later a young woman, perhaps in her mid-twenties, slim and well-formed, with flowing auburn hair expressed in a simple pony tail, her oval face bearing a slightly upturned nose and dark brown eyes encompassed by much light, emerged. She identified herself simply as 'Jessica' and welcomed him and, indeed, several other visitors, to whom he had paid scant attention, but who had secured seats before his own arrival. Robert was immediately taken with her.

Stairs were climbed and he and the others were ushered into a large room with grey walls. There was little furniture save a long wooden table, scratched and battered from much use, hemmed in by metal-framed chairs, with more of the same in reserve stacked against a wall. He sat down. Within minutes, after a late-comer had joined the group, almost all the chairs were occupied, leaving a single place vacant at one end of the table.

This was where the chairman would sit, and this seat was soon filled by a middle-aged man. He had a large and kindly face and was wearing, Robert noticed, thinking of his own smart dark pin-striped suit, brown corduroy trousers and a sky blue sports jacket which failed signally to match the trousers.

The chairman identified himself by name and as the Area Manager. He had a soft unhurried voice and avuncular manner, and used both to welcome the various visiting professionals: a health visitor and her supervising manager; a male, middle-aged and bespectacled consultant paediatrician from a local hospital – the North Middlesex; the manager of a day nursery which the child Amy attended; two police officers in civilian garb and Robert himself. The procedure to be followed, said the Area Manager, was that Dr. Alan Pearson would contribute first, followed by Jessica Palmer and others. The conference had to consider whether Amy was a child at risk, and if so, whether there should be an application to the court for a protective order, or whether some other plan should be followed. But before any verbal contribution, those present introduced themselves, one by one, in their seated sequence.

One of these, not mentioned by the chairman so far, and sitting next to him at the table corner, was a young woman who spoke her name swiftly and quietly – Robert heard only 'Beth' – and who said, during this introductions process, that she was taking the minutes of the meeting. She kept her head, from which flowed a mass of blonde hair, mostly well down, and kept a biro pen busy, while doing so. She had an indisputably beautiful face, and had given her name and function without any hint of a smile. Robert forced himself to take his eyes away from her and to listen to what was being said.

He started to take his own notes. The household was four strong, the parents were married, and little Amy had an eight-year-old sister. Over the past six months Amy had been taken by her mother to the hospital three times with symptoms of drowsiness – semi-consciousness at best – and her mother was suspected of causing this condition by giving her medication prescribed for herself but not for Amy. Amy's mother, however, had denied doing any such thing.

The most recent occasion was some ten days earlier, and clinical tests had now confirmed that Amy had been inappropriately – excessively, even dangerously – medicated with the drug 'phenergan' ('inter alia, a sedative'). The mother herself had over these months more than once self-harmed through cutting her own wrists. The father was violent.

The paediatrician, Dr. Alan Pearson, put Robert in mind of a university lecturer addressing a small tutorial group in a restrained manner, without haste or heat. In his clinical, remote way, he expressed considerable concern for Amy's welfare. His nose was sharply defined, and seemingly had an objection to being straddled by spectacles, as he removed and replaced them two or three times over a minute or two, and said that the consequences of this kind of mistreatment were potentially life-threatening. He said too that no absolute proof of this abuse could be obtained. Amy, he said, had recovered from the latest incident, had now been discharged from hospital, while the parental denial of responsibility had been sustained. He added that she showed signs of emotional deprivation.

These concerns were unreservedly accepted by Jessica, who, with a crisp northern accent, expressed compassion for the mental health of Amy's mother, and spoke too of a threatening stance towards herself on more than one occasion by the father. She recommended Amy's urgent removal. Seated next to Jessica was her 'senior' or supervisor, a man a few years older, who had introduced himself earlier, but whose self-identification had been muffled, and who had remained silent save for expressing one-word support for Jessica's recommendation. No-one at the table disagreed.

The chairman turned to Robert.

'Is there a strong enough case to go to Court?'

'Could I clarify one thing?'

'Of course,' said the chairman benignly.

'If Amy were considered to be at risk while still in hospital, why didn't she stay in hospital? Couldn't a place of safety order have been applied for to secure her situation before going home? Or couldn't the police have been involved?'

The paediatrician, removing his glasses again for a few moments, answered, in his even tones: 'You're right to ask that. The parents came to remove her, and unfortunately there wasn't enough inter-professional communication at that point for a protective plan to be in place to inhibit discharge.'

'So you' – Robert's eyes were fixed on the doctor – 'would have supported a place of safety order to prevent Amy's discharge from the ward.'

'Indeed.' Dr. Pearson's spectacles were now in place again.

The avuncular chairman repeated his question to Robert.

'Is there a strong enough case to go to Court?'

Robert pointed out that ideally he needed to know what the parents said about it.

'Allowing for that,' said the chairman patiently, 'do you have a view?'

Robert removed his eyes from the chairman's sky blue jacket and glanced over at Jessica Palmer, whose skirt and blouse colours matched, as did everything else about her. She was looking at him expectantly, and he was conscious that she was not the only one. Unable to credit that there could not be a strong enough case, he declared that in his opinion there was. He added, self-consciously, the word 'provisionally', immediately feeling he was not being as brave as he ought to be.

The minute taker raised her eyes momentarily to Robert's – she had large blue eyes presided over by long eyelashes as well as an abundance of blonde hair – and added something to her notes. The meeting was soon over. Three-year-old Amy was decreed 'at risk' and there would be a request for court permission to remove her from her home.

This meant in practice, Robert knew, that the social worker Jessica would be seeking out a magistrate that day for authority to place Amy with foster parents for up to a month, both making her safe from misguided medication administration, and rendering out of order any mad attempt by her parents to abduct her. While others were rising to leave, Robert confirmed with Jessica he would visit the office again soon to read the file on the family. He then managed to catch the minute-taker before she left the room.

'I'm sorry to bother you,' he said, 'but would it be possible to have a draft of the minutes the moment they're typed?' He explained that it would help him to prepare the case for court, as his own notes of the meeting were not perfect. He had been listening more than writing. He asked, not having had a reply, when the notes would be ready. 'I don't want to put you under pressure,' he said, with a smile he hoped was engaging.

'But you've succeeded,' she said. She was looking straight at him and smiling slightly. She had candid eyes of such clear blue. He was mesmerised by her. He gave her his direct telephone line, and said the case was difficult. 'I'm sure it is,' she said, but without matching these words with any commitment to complying with his request and without troubling to look at him again.

It was lunch-time when Robert arrived back at the legal department offices, having bought, from a nondescript nearby café, sandwiches which he intended to consume at his desk in the comforting company of his *Guardian* newspaper. Sunshine had now departed the scene, donating a menacing aspect to the sky. As Robert, on the ground floor, was about to enter the lift, aiming to return to his second floor office, George Ballam, the office manager, who had just descended from the upper levels, taking the stairs, walked past him towards the building entrance. Robert had met George earlier in the week, and they had since exchanged greetings when passing each other in the corridors. George had then been in a genial mood. Now, he looked sombre, resembling the sky outside, and passed Robert without meeting his eyes or producing a word of salutation.

In his own small but sufficient room, after making himself a large mug of tea in a corridor niche dedicated to the production of hot drinks, and after divesting himself of his suit jacket, Robert bit into his lunch and read his newspaper.

He hadn't got very far with either when his colleague Melanie Cusack entered his room without troubling to knock. 'I've got a problem,' she said.

Melanie was a woman of slight build, well into her thirties, with a thin face and narrow nose and, Robert had already guessed correctly, equipped with a sharp tongue ever-ready for sudden release when owner authorised. She spoke quickly, unhesitatingly.

'The barrister I'd fixed up to do a beyond parental control case in Tottenham court next Wednesday,' she said, 'has dropped out, and it's yours if you'd like to do it. I know you want to get more experience of advocacy in court. It's not a difficult case.'

Robert expressed interest. It didn't occur to him to ask why Melanie couldn't book a replacement barrister or, for that matter, couldn't manage the hearing herself.

'I'll have a go,' he said, and added, more foolishly than he intended: 'You've got to prove the child is out of control, haven't you?'

'That's it.'

'Will the brief to the barrister tell me more?'

'Oh I hadn't actually got to the point of doing a brief.' She was speaking rapidly, without pauses. 'I would have done one if the barrister I'd booked hadn't let me down. The social worker's report is in the file. And there are some notes and what–have–you. I think the file should speak for itself.' She paused and continued. 'It would be weird for me to send you a brief when the file can tell you what you need to know.'

'Fair enough,' said Robert.

Melanie Cusack turned, saying nothing more, and withdrew to her own room. Robert sat in his chair musing, wondering what he had let himself in for. He took a long draught of tea. It was no longer hot, and he abandoned it. It occurred to him that he should telephone Jessica Palmer. Outside the window, he could see, rain was falling, and falling heavily. He was put through.

'I wondered if you'd made progress with the place of safety order on Amy.'

'Unfortunately, no. I was hoping to get down to the magistrates' court right away, but I've had to see the mother in another of my cases which is in court next week.' Jessica spoke briskly, and he guessed that she hailed from Lancashire or Yorkshire.

'That's not a beyond parental control case, is it?'

'Yes, that's right. It is. A 15-year-old girl. Melanie must have spoken to you about it, I imagine.' Robert was increasingly conscious of Jessica as a woman with confidence and clarity in her use of words to match his own, if not in advance of it.

'Yes.'

'I'm sorry, but the mother's waiting for me. I'm waiting for the court to phone me back to fix up a magistrate appointment about Amy. Goodness knows when I'll finish today.' She said this without a trace of annoyance or even resignation in her voice. 'And I haven't brought an umbrella,' she added cheerfully.

'It would suit me if I could come over to read the file tomorrow,' said Robert, as the rain thrashed his own office window. 'I should get a clearer idea of what needs to be done. I could come around twelve thirty.'

'That will be fine. I'm sorry I must go now. Thank you for your help.'

Robert put out a hand towards the substantial legal work in three weighty volumes with sky-blue covers – Stone's Justices Manual – stolidly upright in front of him on his desk. He selected the volume he wanted. He located the Children and Young Persons Act 1969, liberally annotated with footnotes, and read through the list of statutory grounds which had to be proved for a court to be able to consider making either a care or a supervision order. A care order, of course, implied the ability of the local authority to place a child away from home. A supervision order permitted welfare monitoring only. Refreshing his memory was reassuring. He told himself he should do it daily. It would set him up for the day, rather like having a regular morning swim.

The foundation for court action for the fifteen-year-old was that a child 'is beyond the control of his parent or guardian'. Another, rather wordy condition, applicable to phenergan-drugged little Amy, made 'avoidable' prevention of 'proper development' or neglect or impairment of health or ill-treatment a basis for proceedings. Yet another ground was that a school-age child was not attending school. All these, declared the Manual, were the 'primary conditions' for care proceedings. They were comfortingly immovable.

But though the strict words could not be altered, the 'proper development' condition, when linked with the impact of reported decisions in the higher courts, contained, Robert knew, traps for the unwary local authority lawyer. These could be sprung by well-prepared advocates acting for parents. A seemingly strong case could be blown away by a single cold legal submission. And strong evidence could fail through fielding weak witnesses or not fielding the right ones. Or through confusing the magistrates.

He rose to his feet and proceeded a short distance down the corridor to Melanie Cusack's room. He knocked and went in. Melanie was sitting at her desk, looking through the window at the driving rain. She turned to face him with an unwelcoming facial expression, as if she imagined that he proposed to return the wretched 'beyond control' thing to her.

'I've just spoken,' he said, 'to Jessica Palmer, who I gather is the social worker in this beyond parental control case.'

'That's right.'

'I wondered if I could have a look at our file.'

'I was just looking at it myself. Do you need it tidied up or are you happy to take it as it is.'

'I don't mind.'

'Well, here you are then.' She pointed to a grey file, where it sat on the rear of her desk, unopened.

'Thank you, I'll have a look.'

'You've taken a load off my mind,' she said with obvious relief. 'I can get on with other things now.' Despite feeling he had been landed with Melanie's work for reasons of her personal convenience, Robert felt sympathetic.

'By the way,' she added, 'you may find that Jessica Palmer gets above herself a bit.'

'In what way?'

'I'll leave you to discover that,' she said tartly. He reached forward. Inside the cardboard outer cover was a mixture of loose pages and pages pinned together. The file was not bulky and Robert took it back to his own room.

Once there, the internal telephone on his desk rang. The caller was the litigation manager, Bill Bowman, whom Robert had met a couple of times already, and whose office was situated on the floor below. He spoke with a working class London accent.

'Can I come and see you about something?' he asked.

'Of course,' said Robert.

'I'll come right away then.'

He was as good as his word. Bill Bowman was large and square, though not above middle height. Even his face was square. He spoke with chummy assurance.

'How are you getting on then?'

'Fine so far. I've got a lot to learn, I know.'

'The important thing here,' said Bill with slow emphasis, 'is to get on with the Man.'

'Mr. Shimble?'

'That's right, Eddie. You don't want to fall out with him.'

'Do people fall out with him?'

'Some do. He likes things done his way. Not everybody understands that. I know his ways. I worked with him before he got the job here.'

'You followed him here then?'

Bowman grunted. 'In a way. He sort of invited me.'

'I'm sure you have to set an example of good work and to have expectations of good work from your staff if you're the Borough Solicitor.' This Robert delivered with a degree of pomposity.

'I don't know about setting an example, but he is particular. Anyway, what I came in about was whether you could do a consumer protection case for us – dodgy curry prosecution. Indian restaurant. In court the week after next.'

Robert, already encumbered with Melanie Cusack's beyond parental control case, was cautious.

'Dirty saucepans is it?'

'Dirty everything. Important to win it. There's a punishment if you lose.'

'Punishment?'

'Punishment. If you lose, Eddie will make you eat there.' A grin spread across Bowman's square face.

'I'm not sure I can do it. I've been appointed chiefly to do Social Services work, and there seems to be quite a lot of that coming in my direction already.'

'Eddie said you would be up for it. He said you want to do advocacy.'

'I'd better say no to this one, because I could be up to my eyes in children stuff. Better to say no now, than find myself double-booked on the day. Isn't the general litigation solicitor your first option? That tall chap…?'

Bowman homed in.

'Colin Masson? He's on a NALGO union representatives course on the day of the hearing.' He spelt out the union's full name – 'National Association of Local Government Officers' – as if he were introducing Robert to a piece of local government life about which Robert was ignorant.

'Yes. He's the trade union rep for legal?'

'And a half. That doesn't give Eddie much pleasure, but he can't really complain. Colin Masson dots all the i's and all the t's, even when there aren't any to be dotted and crossed. He takes his union rep role seriously, too seriously some might say, between ourselves.'

'Have you asked Melanie if she has space for this restaurant hygiene case?'

Bill Bowman grinned and spoke bluntly.

'Melanie never has space for anything apart from time off for herself. The last time I asked her to do something she tried to palm me off with something she already had. And I finished up with that, too. She went off sick and I had no choice.'

'You can't do this one yourself?'

'Course not. I'm not qualified for court. That's your baby.'

'Hm. Well, sorry I can't help out at the moment.'

Bill Bowman left, waving one hand affably at Robert, who decided to make himself another mug of tea. He visited the electric kettle and mugs in the corridor and waited patiently for the kettle to boil.

The 'pens and pencils' manager, George Ballam approached, looking preoccupied but then snapping out of it. 'A watched kettle never boils,' he said, with an attempt at friendliness, and asked Robert how he was settling in.

'All right,' said Robert. He glanced both ways down the corridor and said to George:

'I've just been told that not everybody gets on with Mr. Shimble.'

'Was that about me?' The amiable expression disappeared from George's face.

'I didn't know that you didn't get on with him. I was only told that it was a good idea to keep in with him. He's been pleasant enough to me so far, but I've only been here a couple of days.'

'You'll learn then,' said George. The kettle steamed angrily and Robert added hot water to a tea bag.

'I'm sorry if I said something I shouldn't.'

'No you haven't. It's just that I had a bit of a barney with him this morning. I'd better not say more.'

Robert explained that Bill Bowman was the person who had warned him of the importance of getting on with Eddie.

'I expect,' said George, 'Eddie told him he'd had a bust-up

with me. They're like this,' he said, putting the fore-fingers of each hand together.

He smiled again for a moment before departing, his smile departing first, with the coffee he had made for himself.

Back in his office, Robert saw through the window that the rain had finally given up falling. He sat down to read the 'beyond parental control' papers passed to him by Melanie. The 15-year-old had a name – Michelle. Michelle West. She had run away from home months ago and had refused to go back, though whether her parents wanted her back at the moment was not obvious. Her own story was that her father had repeatedly hit her. She was said to have dropped from a first floor window at the family's council flat to get away from her parents.

This incident had led to the magistrate's place of safety order months before. After a series of time-limited 'interim' care orders, she remained lodged with foster parents, and the court was to be asked to make a full care order on her, thus passing parental responsibilities indefinitely to the council.

Robert gathered all this from a typed document labelled 'Social Enquiry Report' of which Jessica Palmer was named author. The rest of the file consisted partly of photocopies of case notes of visits and interviews, though the authorship of these was not always stated. Jessica's full and coherent notes, Robert noticed, were distinctive in that they always carried her initials at the end. There was also a report by an educational psychologist, and a medical certificate from a Dr. Elaine Abrahams, paediatrician, which stared out of a transparent plastic folder. This detailed minor cuts, bruises and marks due to the fall from the window, or, in some cases, consistent with an alleged correction with a leather belt. So Robert now knew the names of two local paediatricians.

A thought struck him and he picked up the file and strode down the corridor. Melanie was sitting at her desk, locked in thought, though this time an opened file did lie on the large, rectangular white blotting pad, which sat on her desk, as a twin did on Robert's.

'Sorry to trouble you Melanie,' he said. 'I'm getting an idea of this Michelle West case. I couldn't see right off from the papers which witnesses you were going to call.'

'Oh yes, witnesses. I thought that was obvious, but maybe it isn't.'

'The social worker, no doubt, but who else?'

'Do we need anyone else?'

'There's a medical certificate from a doctor about the cuts and bruises.'

'Yes. I sent him that to sign and send back to me.'

'I thought the doctor was a she. Dr. Elaine Abrahams.'

'Yes, correct. But if we've got her certificate, we don't need her in the flesh. The injuries were trivial, weren't they? The main thing is that the parents just can't control her.'

'According to the notice of care proceedings, it's also a case of over-chastisement,' said Robert. 'The notice does allege ill-treatment.'

Melanie looked at him coldly. 'Ill-treatment? Wasn't it just a wallop or two on the spur of the moment when she went bonkers? Six of one and half a dozen of the other? Anyway, ill treatment is more difficult to prove. My experience is that they give you a care order when you ask for one whether or not you bother with all the detail. I think the whole family should be shot,' she added without raising her voice. 'That would be the perfect form of chastisement. We'd be better off without the lot of them.'

Melanie spoke with conviction, and there was an inference from her words that she had had enough of this conversation, if not of her job.

Robert, though taken aback, held his tongue, saying instead, deliberately but not argumentatively 'I'd say we do have a duty to put across the best case we can.'

She threw the ball back at him, her face expressing developing irritation.

'Do you have your own suggestions for witnesses?' She made an effort to smile. 'I'm sorry, I've put it out of mind and it's an effort to get it back.'

It was as though Robert should be apologetic about raising such stress-creating and time-wasting questions.

'There doesn't seem to be a statement as such or a proof of evidence from the social worker,' he said.

'No, but there is her social enquiry report.'

'Yes, but it doesn't set out fully or chronologically the pattern of events which led to the proceedings.'

Impatience was now to the fore in Melanie's voice. 'I think that you can deduce that from the notes of visits and what-have-you.'

'Were you thinking of calling the educational psychologist?'

'I remember his report now. I assumed we could do without him. But please act as you think best.'

'OK. I get the picture.' Robert did not sound entirely satisfied.

Melanie looked at him with raised eyebrows.

Suppressing his own frustration, Robert thanked her for her help and left the room. She clearly considered him punctilious to a fault. Was he being like Bill Bowman's description of Colin Masson, dotting i's and t's even if there were nothing to dot and cross?

Back at his desk he extracted from the folder contact details of the possible witnesses. He decided that the educational psychologist, as well as Jessica, must give evidence. He completed his reading of what could be read and phoned the North Tottenham office. It was now after four thirty.

The receptionist told him that Jessica had gone out. He guessed that she must be on her mission to a magistrate to make a plea for a place of safety order on the three-year-old, and gave up on the call. He would see her next day anyway.

For more than a few moments he thought of the girl with long blonde hair and large blue eyes who had taken minutes at the case conference.

As recently as the previous week Robert had driven up to London, from his parents' home in rural Somerset, his car loaded with some of his belongings – mostly clothes, bedding, some items connected with food management, and a few precious books. He had toted these into the semi-furnished rented ground-floor flat in Crouch End he was to share with another young man whose previous flat-mate had moved out and who had advertised for a substitute.

If Harold Road was too modest a suburban double row of houses to be called 'an address', the accommodation would do: there was enough space for two to share in reasonable comfort, even if there was not enough light or recent decoration to give the place a particularly joyous appearance. London, as a place to live, was new and exciting to Robert, and he felt very much a stranger, and even a bit lost, in its vast unfamiliarity.

He left the office and drove to the flat, spending the evening watching television, after cooking himself a simple meal using the few utensils which had moved in with him. His flat-mate, inconveniently for the purpose of answering telephone calls without risking confusion, was another 'Robert'. He had seemed friendly enough, and was out somewhere. He had announced himself, when asked what he did, as a civil servant, or, more exactly, as 'a faceless bureaucrat with an inflation-proof pension'.

Already his flat-mate's failure to attend promptly to his washing-up in the kitchen was offending Robert Fordham's hygienic and tidy nature. With a feeling of virtuousness and trusting he was not setting a self-destructive precedent, Robert washed the other Robert's piled-up and dirty pans, plates and dishes. Two saucepans were extremely resistant to the process. If the flat were a restaurant, he thought, his co-tenant could be in danger of prosecution for hygiene crimes, and Bill Bowman might be asking him to prosecute.

Most of Robert's own effects were still at his parents' home in Somerset, and could stay there for the present. He would have dearly liked to set about buying his own place, but the first step would have to be to save for a deposit. For the time being he would make the best of renting and sharing. But he could do with a replacement bed. The one he was sleeping in was an ancient contraption, convenient for one person possessing an austere cast of mind or not able to afford a replacement. It would be all right for the moment, but how could he bring a girl-friend back for the night? If and when he found one.

2

Tranquillity Disturbed

It has already been disclosed that on the morning when Robert Fordham attended a case conference in the North Tottenham Social Services office, there had been an unpleasant clash in the legal building between the office manager, George Ballam, and the Borough Solicitor, Mr. Edward Shimble.

Shimble, in his late forties and boss of the legal department, had a good-sized room, tucked behind a smaller room occupied by his secretary, rather than a small piece of the open–plan areas occupied by many of his subordinate staff. 'Eddie' to senior staff, 'Mr. Shimble' to the rest, was answerable, though he preferred to downplay or even to deny the fact of his answerability, to the council's Chief Executive, 'Smiler' Roland Trask. Trask, who had a legal background of some vague kind himself, was based in the Civic Centre with the secretariat which registered the sayings and doings of the members.

Shimble was not at all satisfied with George Ballam. Trouble had broken out early that Tuesday morning, the day after Shimble's return from three weeks' holiday with his wife and two children in Devon. On the Monday Shimble had been caught up in a succession of meetings. He had not felt driven to ferret about in the desk-based wire basket tray holding his recent incoming post to consider which items should be prioritized for action. On the Tuesday, free of appointments, he was brought up sharp by something in that wire tray. It was a letter, an important letter, received while he had been away, marked for his attention by George Ballam, and telling him of a meeting which was scheduled to take place before, not after, Shimble returned to duty.

It was no less than an inter-boroughs letter – a letter giving notice of a meeting of representatives of London boroughs – and it concerned a question of transfers of housing accommodation from the Greater London Council to its junior municipal brethren. Obviously any personal attention he could give to the letter would have to take the form of an after-the-event inquiry.

In summary, without anticipating any possible adverse consequences for himself, George Ballam had seen the inter-boroughs letter amongst the daily deluge of incoming post, and had simply marked it for Shimble's attention, although the meeting was undeniably due to take place on a date before Shimble returned to the office. That was in Shimble's eyes a demonstration of first degree ineptitude. Shimble had reddened in the face, even begun to purple, as he weighed in the balance the magnitude of this misjudgment. On top of that, in Shimble's view, immediately after seeing the letter, Ballam should have organized copies for the solicitors assigned to housing problems. He had not done that either. Unforgiving words began to pile up in Shimble's head.

So, that sunny September Tuesday morning Edward Shimble was on the warpath, and as close as he usually got to brandishing a freshly sharpened axe; and George Ballam was on the receiving end.

It did not matter that the solicitor with first line responsibility for housing law had, within twenty-four hours after the letter's arrival, gone into Shimble's room for the purpose of a peek into his in-tray, and had pounced on the letter. He had proceeded without more ado to the photocopying room and had taken a copy for himself. He had gone on to attend the important inter-boroughs meeting, and his typed note of the meeting's highlights and lowlights had been placed snugly next to the invitation letter in Shimble's in-tray.

The meeting, which had been venued in a central London, and therefore architecturally more impressive, Town Hall than Haringey's Civic Centre, did not have earth-shaking or even London-borough-shaking consequences. It had generated discussion of a not very rigorous, vigorous or controversial nature and nothing in the way of resolution, save for the setting down of a further meeting a month or two hence.

Of all this Edward Shimble was aware when he called George Ballam in for a dressing-down. Ballam himself did not know – and Shimble did not disabuse him – that his mechanical response to the letter had caused no damage or adverse implications whatsoever for the council. Shimble was simply making unpleasant waves in a calm sea, as, at times, he was prone to do.

Ballam's second floor office was two doors along from Shimble's and the partition walls, like others in the building, were thin, causing any noisy exchange to be instantly deprived of privacy. Between the two offices was that of Shimble's secretary, Mary, whose surname was rarely uttered within the building. Her duties included keeping the Borough Solicitor supplied on demand with teapot-brewed tea in an immaculate bone china cup and saucer (members of a set bearing a blue and cream flower design), together with a matching bowl of sugar and a small silvery spoon, and troubling him as little as possible with incoming phone calls. Shimble particularly disliked speaking to Chief Executive Roland Trask unless it was unavoidable or to his own personal advantage. Mary typed Shimble's letters, while the letters dictated by others were the responsibility of the typing pool.

Mary's central role, for which she had a special gift, was to keep Shimble as tranquil and as free of local vexations as possible. She had a soothing voice and was able to deploy this frequently and effectively. Shimble was noted for devoting painstaking attention to letters and reports to members, but not necessarily to all other correspondence commissions. Mary coaxed him to attend to these lesser matters when otherwise delay seemed likely to follow.

Called in summarily by his own grey internal telephone to see his boss, George Ballam, a short, thick-set, bespectacled, man in his late thirties, had stood quietly facing the older Shimble, and watched him rocking back comfortably, as he did many times every day, in his well-padded maroon leather chair.

Shimble was marked by a 'job lot' physical make-up. He was entirely bald. The pink, duneless desert of the crown of his head, sat above a long, thin face in which a remarkably small triangular nose was affixed. A short neck led down to a long body from which his rotund stomach stood forward like a declaration of war. His lips were little more than short upper and lower horizontal lines – rather like a close-together equals sign – hiding even white teeth. His voice was as neat and as even as his teeth. He produced the smoking gun letter which had, when he had read it and considered the full reach of Ballam's folly and failure, threatened to raise his own blood-pressure, for which he was prescribed daily tablets.

'What do you say to this?' said Shimble, mildly enough, indicating the letter on his blotting pad with the palm of his hand.

Said Ballam, guardedly:

'Well, it's a letter.'

'Of course it's a letter. What do you say about it?'

'Well, it's dated...' George Ballam peered at it – it was upside down – but he managed to state the date accurately.

'Anyone can see that. What do you say about it?'

Ballam peered closer and turned the letter round so that he could read it more efficiently.

"It's about a meeting …on…oh yes, Wednesday last week. Something about housing."

'Rather late to spot that, aren't you?'

'Has there been a problem?'

Shimble considered, easing himself into a more stable position in his leather chair, and placing the fingers of his hands together, pointing upwards.

'There certainly would have been if someone else hadn't voluntarily been doing your job for you.'

'I'm pleased there wasn't a problem. But what are you saying I should have done?'

'Your job. It's for you to mark out post with a degree of acumen.'

Shimble, despite underlying frostiness, was continuing to speak quietly.

George Ballam squinted again at the letter.

'I can see I marked it out to you.'

'Quite. You marked it out to me when I was on holiday although the meeting was due to take place before I returned. What were you thinking of?'

'I apologise if I've upset you.'

'It's not a question of my being upset.' Shimble's exasperation was mounting. 'It's a question of your doing what you're supposed to do. My perception of your role, George' (here Shimble paused to use Ballam's forename and the pause in order to give his concluding phrase greater impact) 'is not quite the same as yours.'

He paused again, as Ballam said nothing, ending the interview with bubbling anger added to exasperation in the dismissive words 'You'd better go now.'

Shimble's face had been pink at the beginning of this exchange, and was now nearer purple, as George Ballam made his silent exit. Appreciating Shimble's need at a glance, Mary now set about making him a cup of tea with the help of the electric kettle standing by on a table in the corner of her room. Gradually, as he stirred and sipped his tea, pinkness returned to his face.

Back in his own room, George Ballam was angry – more so than he had been during the interview, and he realized that he had not handled it at all well. He could have said:

'You didn't tell me before you went on holiday how you wanted your incoming post dealt with. You didn't say whether I should leave it to the solicitors to check your in-tray, or whether I should mark it out, when it arrived, to those next in line. I only pass out the post. I don't allocate work.'

Had George been of a subversive turn of mind, he could have said this and added for good measure, perhaps also placing his own fingers together, pointing upwards: 'I have to conclude, Eddie, that my perception of your role is not quite the same as yours.'

Too late.

3

The Newcomer Digs In

The next morning, autumn was again pretending to be summer, and for a time the sunshine could have been called brilliant. Robert Fordham, on the other hand, was not in a position to take from this more than fleeting pleasure. Barely five minutes after he had lowered himself into his chair in the legal building, and had begun to look again at the material concerning the fifteen-year-old girl estranged from her parents, his desk telephone rang. He answered and Jessica Palmer greeted him.

'News,' she said. 'The magistrate made the order on little Amy.' Jessica was about to add something but Robert's response pre-empted her.

'Excellent!' He was curious. 'Did you have to go the magistrate's home?'

'Yes. Not the first time, though this was quite a plush residence in Highgate. Drive way leafy and long. Room for three or four cars to park plus two very wide garages. I had to admire the wallpaper to get the order. William Morris patterns. Plenty of ornaments lying around, and none of them were cheap and nasty.'

She had spoken more lightly and outside the 'strictly business' conversation than he had expected, was definitely now more matey with him. Was it possible she felt already he was someone with whom she could be natural? In the far away county authority where he had served his training period, Robert had met with more guarded, more impersonal social workers, often a lot older than he was.

'Were you grilled – apart from about the wallpaper?'

'Not really. Once I'd said it was lovely she asked me a few questions about Amy and she got her pen out. But we had problems later.'

'Problems?'

'I went round to the family home with Derek, my senior, to collect Amy. We had a foster home fixed up for her. They let us in but the dad got very stroppy. He said he'd physically resist Amy being taken away, even if the police came.'

'The police weren't with you?'

'No, that was Derek's idea. He thought we should play it low-key without the boys in blue.' She sounded dissatisfied with Derek.

'Anyway, we decided not to risk a violent scene.' Having blamed Derek for his misjudgment, she was now accepting his decision was irreversible. 'We did see Amy, and she looked all right. Derek' (she hesitated before continuing) 'just put the place of safety order back in his pocket.'

'So where does that leave us so far as going to court is concerned?'

'Can you fix a court date as soon as possible?'

'I'll do my best. Any dates impossible for yourself?'

Jessica told him that the following Wednesday she would be in court for a teenager.

'We may have to take that day anyway,' said Robert.

'I can't give evidence in two cases the same day. That would be too much.'

'That would mean leaving Amy unprotected for yet another week.'

'I don't think that's a good idea either. Wednesday will have to be a busy day for me then,' she said with stoicism.

'By the way,' said Robert, 'I've taken over the teenager's case.'

'Michelle West? Taken it over from Melanie?' There was disquiet in her voice.

'Yes.'

'Melanie was going to get a barrister to represent us. She said she'd get a good one.'

'She didn't manage that, so I've agreed to stand in at court.'

'Don't you think we need a barrister?' Jessica sounded more worried than critical.

Robert stood his ground, managing, he hoped, to avoid a tone of defensiveness. 'Leaving that aside, can we discuss who will be the witnesses for our case, apart from yourself?'

'Well, there's the ed psych?'

'Educational psychologist? Graham Townley? I've seen his report on our file. Who else?'

'There's Dr. Abrahams, Elaine Abrahams, who examined her. I can't think of anyone else.'

'What about Derek?'

'If you think so,' she said. A query in Robert's head never reached his mouth. Was Derek, professionally, an unreliable agent, even a waste of time and space? He asked a different question.

'I don't know at the moment if the ed psych has been lined up to attend. Do you know?'

'As it happens I spoke to him yesterday. He rang me and he seemed to assume he'd be needed, but I don't think he'd had any request from legal.'

'You mean from Melanie?'

'Yes, from Melanie.'

'Do you know if Dr. Abrahams has been asked?'

'No. But I think she might be on holiday from what I heard someone in my team say a couple of days ago.'

'I'd better make some calls. As you know, I'll be coming over in a bit to see Amy's file. I can update you then about the witness situation regarding Michelle's case.'

'Right.'

The call ended.

Robert considered what he had just been told. Why on earth, he thought, had Derek the 'senior' not asked for police back-up when they had the removal order and were visiting with the object of collecting Amy? Wasn't the father supposed to be violent?

A police presence would probably have overawed the Dad into giving up Amy, whatever he blustered when the police were off the scene. And by not following the thing through, wasn't the impression given that the risk to Amy was less than it was supposed to be? The case he had declared at the conference was a strong enough one was losing muscle tone already.

Robert had arranged to donate an hour that morning to a reconnaissance of the Tottenham magistrates' court, and he was to be accompanied by a guide who was familiar with the terrain and some of the actors. Godfrey, a trainee solicitor in the office who had just qualified, and had in recent times been working with Melanie Cusack, would be leaving the legal department for pastures new at the end of the week, and had offered to show him round.

Shortly after ten the pair headed downstairs for Robert's car, which was parked in an asphalted area reserved for staff at the back of the legal building.

The magistrates' court was roughly a mile away, across the road from Bruce Castle museum and park, and it proved to be a not stately but extensive building, set back from the main road. An angular semi-circle of a drive way, one-way in for vehicles, was entered through unlocked and open gates, and parking space around the court building was reserved for the privileged – those disposing of police cars and vans, not to mention magistrates and court officials. One side of the main road outside the court building was lined with the parked cars of the unprivileged, leaving no space for one more.

Robert parked in a nearby side street. He walked with Godfrey into the building, abandoning the sunshine behind them. They paused to satisfy a police officer marooned in a cubicle behind a glass screen that they were fit persons to proceed further. A pin-striped suit was not in itself a passport.

Once inside, a modest square foyer without seats of any kind, lay ahead. On the left side of this square waiting area, Court 2 sat at a right angle to Court 1, which was directly in front of them. Along a corridor to the left was to be found Court 3, beside which a public telephone booth patiently awaited users. Godfrey took Robert on a tour. A corridor to the right, after a few yards, met a dog-leg turn leftwards into remoter depths. Here was to be found Court 5, far more modest in size than its rivals; and here too a mysterious additional court carrying the number 4 was hidden away and further back, accessible only through an unmarked, curtained doorway. That morning all the Court rooms except Court 2 – where an adult prosecution was under way – were given over to juvenile court appointments.

It was now half past ten, and quite a lot of people, adults and youngsters, were standing around. In the case of Court 3, several were, in the absence of any seating, sitting on the floor outside. One of these, a young woman of striking, even glamorous, appearance, was handing a cigarette to a boy of sixteen or seventeen. She lit up for both. Godfrey said hello to her in a timid fashion. She responded brightly, standing up and introducing herself to Robert as Emily Frost. She seemed to take for granted that he knew she was a social worker. 'Your pin-stripe tells me what you do,' she said, looking him up and down, 'but who are you?' He told her. She was dressed smartly for court activity, and her facial expressions were animated. That she had a full-lipped mouth, capable, perhaps, of much laughter, and a figure to be envied, was not a debating issue. Godfrey stood by, wordless and ill at ease.

The boy, she said, her voice dropping to a whisper, was being done for stealing a sheepskin jacket. He was in the council's care and resident at a children's home.

Godfrey broke in clumsily, as if embarrassed, to point out to Robert a 'next door neighbour', by which, soon clarifying the obscurity, he meant a solicitor for the adjoining local authority, Enfield. Emily Frost rejoined her young client, first exchanging a smile with Robert.

The Enfield solicitor had stepped over to join them. Godfrey began to introduce him to Robert, but was overtaken by a breezy self-introduction. Jack Parnell was carrying a navy blue case, rather like a rectangular handbag, in which the three sky blue volumes of Stone's Justices Manual fitted snugly. Parnell, a tall young man, with receding fair hair, showed signs of restlessness, and was immediately loquacious, speaking rapidly.

'I've just come out of Court 1,' he said. 'It's been a scream of a morning; well, entertaining. It can be like a circus here.' He exchanged hellos with nearby Emily, who who was now stubbing out her cigarette and insisting that her teenage charge did so too, as they were at that instant being called into court.

Robert was struck by his Enfield opposite number's attachment to the three blue volumes, each weighing almost as much as, or perhaps more than, a brick.

'Do you really need those,' he asked mischievously, 'or are they worn like a carnation for recognition purposes.'

'That deserves a laugh,' said Parnell, without laughing or animosity. 'The latter, of course.' He went on to talk about his morning's 'fun'.

'First,' he said, "the social worker went into the witness box and took the oath. She can't have done it before, because after she read the words on the card in front of her, clutching the Bible in one hand, she ended the rigmarole by holding up her other arm and saying 'So help me God.' She must have seen it done like that in the films."

Robert, shaking his head, said he supposed that everyone had to be a beginner some time.

'The Clerk was a bit snooty about it,' said Parnell. 'He said' (and Parnell put on an affronted official voice): 'This isn't a Western court, madam.' Parnell went on. 'He got her to take the oath a second time. Properly. But nobody laughed. We were in front of Lady Feverel. She's a terror. You want to watch out for her. You should keep on the right side of her.'

That made two such advices in two days.

'After the messed up oath came the messed up report,' said Jack Parnell with a droll look. 'This same social worker had done a social inquiry report – it was a school attendance case – and the report was four paragraphs long. I did tell her before we went in that it looked a bit sparse. It didn't get to grips with the family situation and background. She told me the courts don't like long reports. Anyway, Lady Feverel gave her short shrift. She declared in her stately English home voice, that' – here Parnell continued with lush mimicry – 'if the report doesn't explain the family background, how can the court be expected to produce a solution?' His voice normalised. 'She told the social worker she'd better produce a report that showed a social inquiry had been conducted. She adjourned the thing for a week. The social worker was beetroot red when she went.'

'I'm looking forward to getting to grips with the realities here,' said Robert.

'You need to remember one thing,' said Jack Parnell. 'There are two different sorts of justice. One sort is Tottenham justice. The other is what happens everywhere else.'

He changed subjects, without changing speed. 'Do you play cricket, by any chance? Our second team is short of players.'

'Not really,' said Robert, though unsure why he was hesitant, since he enjoyed playing the game.

Jack Parnell said he would collar Robert about cricket when the spring came and wished him good luck. He went off with his three blue brick-heavy volumes in their rectangular handbag in one hand, and a large brown briefcase in the other.

As Tottenham's Court 2 was not at that moment in session, Robert pushed open the double doors to look inside. It was of traditional design. The magistrates' podium was set high, with the clerk's perch directly in front and below, while the rows facing resembled parish church pews. Dark wood and a Victorian ambiance prevailed. To one side, narrow steps discreetly descended towards basement cells.

Godfrey next showed Robert the office where the listing officer had a home, and then suggested that they could pay a fleeting visit to the county court. They drove northwards for a few minutes before parking near an unremarkable building on a corner of the main road connecting Tottenham with Edmonton. This was on three floors – a more compact building than the sprawling institution they had just inspected.

Once inside Robert could see that the Edmonton county court had less of the harsh feel of the small criminal justice factory he had just viewed. Its lists of civil cases for each court were affixed to a wall. An upper floor supplied two traditional lay-out civil courts, and between them was a rectangular public waiting area. This centre ground contained seats for at least a dozen people, and more than half were occupied.

The permanent resident judge, Godfrey told him, was Judge Madder. 'You want to keep on the right side of him.' Robert thus registered a named third person to whom this warning applied. How many more to come?

'He's very traditional,' said Godfrey. 'He is supposed to be neutral about whether witnesses take the oath or affirm, but I've heard him say to a solicitor that he was glad to see the solicitor take the oath. Personally, I like that.'

By now the sun had said farewell, and rain was falling again, though not with any sense of urgency. Robert deposited Godfrey back at the legal building near which he bought sandwiches before setting off for Jessica's office. On the way he passed the magistrates' court he had earlier inspected.

Moderately wet on arrival – he had determined to buy an umbrella as soon as he could, but had not yet succeeded – he was soon escorted upstairs by Jessica, whose natural warmth of manner only enhanced, he thought, her physical attractions. She took him into a large open-plan area sprinkled with desks and social workers. An empty desk and chair were waiting for him. Jessica's file on the little girl wrongfully dosed up with phenergan – allegedly – was already laid on the desk.

'Would you like tea or coffee?' she asked.

'Nice of you to offer. Tea, please. By the way, are you Lancashire or Yorkshire?'

'Lancashire, obviously. Where were you brought up?' she responded with spirit.

'I thought you would have registered my Somerset accent.'

'Not exactly.'

'That makes us quits then,' said Robert, though something in his voice implied he was points ahead in the exchange. If pressed he would have to admit that a rural west of England burr was something he had failed to acquire. Jessica looked at him quizzically, then made tea in a corner not far away, while Robert glanced through the file. She brought the tea to him. He noticed for the first time she was wearing a wedding ring, and mentally and regretfully crossed her off his list of possible future girl-friends. He took out his lunch.

'When I've had a proper read-through,' he asked, 'will you have time to discuss the case?'

'Unfortunately not. I have to do a home visit.'

'Michelle West?'

'Not this time. I have a caseload of thirteen families. I should say that I'm still a bit troubled you're not sending a barrister for the court hearing next week. Melanie always sends barristers. They're usually quite good. That's to say I'm not implying you're not.'

'I'm not Melanie either.'

'No.'

'I'll think about it some more. But it looks a fairly straightforward case to me. Is a court going to send back home a 15-year-old desperate enough to exit from a first floor window after a beating?'

'I see that. Trouble is, I never know which way the magistrates are going to jump. One of the women chairing the Bench at Tottenham – not Lady Feverel, I should say – always believes the parents, even when everyone else knows they're telling porkies. Sometimes they don't want to see what's in front of their noses. A good lawyer – sorry, I'm not trying to do you down – gives them less room to manoeuvre. Or it sometimes seems like that.'

'Don't the witnesses count more than the lawyer?'

'Maybe, but a good barrister can give witnesses like me confidence. Asks the right questions. And somehow steers the magistrates into the right state of mind as the hearing moves on.' Jessica, Robert decided, was trying to steer him into the right state of mind so that he would re-think his decision to manage the beyond control case without a barrister.

He was listening, and she continued.

'I had a court hearing, Robert, a couple of months ago. Another teenage girl – another runaway. The court insisted on sending her home against her wishes.' She stressed the word *against*. It was obvious to me she was going to run again, and was at risk. The parents were delighted and told the magistrates they were going to celebrate with a party. The lady chairman –

not Lady Feverel, she's too sensible – said it would be nice if I would celebrate with the family.'

'And did you?'

'Certainly not. The last thing the family wanted was to see my face again. Predictably, it all broke down a couple of weeks later and then we were back in court. The Dad then said he was washing his hands of his daughter. It was the same magistrate, who looked at me the first time as if I'd messed it up, and the second time as if she'd been right the first time. But this time a full care order was made.'

'Tottenham justice?'

'Yes, Tottenham justice.' Jessica sounded resigned, and as if she had heard Jack Parnell's axiom before. She continued.

'Anyway, I must go. You can have photocopies from Amy's file if you want. Ask Beth.' She pointed to a young woman who occupied a desk in a far corner. It was the girl with long blonde hair and blue eyes, the minute taker. 'And when you've finished with the file, give it to Beth if I'm not already back.'

Robert thanked her and she went. He glanced round the open-plan area. Several desks were unoccupied. Almost belonging to the big room were two separate cubby-hole offices, in one of which Robert could see Jessica's 'senior' Derek, who held a telephone close to his mouth.

He went over to Beth.

'You're Beth, aren't you?'

'Yes.' He assumed she remembered him.

'Sorry to bother you, but I need to.'

She looked up at him. 'You want those conference minutes. On Amy Stewart.'

'If they're ready.'

'They're nearly ready. How long are you going to be here?' She spoke to the point, without much friendliness of manner.

'I don't know. I've got to read the file and make notes. And I expect I'll need photocopies.'

'You're cluttering up my life,' she said, looking at him as if marginally amused.

'I wish I could clutter it up some more,' said Robert quietly. 'If I had your phone number, I could.' It was the ridiculous best he could do on the spur of the moment.

'Oh.' She paused and looked at him for two or three seconds.

'I'll think about that,' she said. 'In the mean-time, I must get on with these minutes.'

Robert, telling himself he had been over-eager, as on other occasions in his past, retreated to the desk which he had been lent, and buried himself in notes of visits, phone calls and the rest. The papers included several letters from the paediatrician – the unstably bespectacled and donnish Dr. Pearson – who had spoken persuasively at the conference. It seemed that the strength of the case rested almost entirely on the medical view.

On one occasion only, though, was there definite evidence that the drug phenergan had been found in excessive quantities in the child's urine, and that was some days after Amy's most recent admission to hospital. For the other two occasions a damning inference could be drawn from her semi-comatose condition. Could. But that was about it. And if the parents were involved in giving such a drug to Amy, why would they do that?

And what would Beth say, he speculated, the next time he asked for her phone number? And should he have prejudiced his professional position as early as this by unveiling his interest in the prettiest woman in the vicinity, and of whom he knew nothing but her stunningly attractive exterior and a certain detached composure when faced with that interest.

Over the next hour or more Robert filled several pages of a lined pad with notes and made a list of pages in the file – there were a lot of them – for copying. He took the file together with his list to Beth, who was typing briskly. She stopped and looked up at him with a faint smile.

'Have I got to copy all that?'

'Afraid so, if you can bear it. Can you send it on to me with the draft minutes? I have to go now.' He added, dropping his voice: 'Have you been doing this job long?'

'Eight months,' she said precisely. Unexpectedly, she opened up more. 'Before that I was a Town Hall committee clerk in Bedfordshire. Well, an assistant committee clerk. What about you?'

'This is my third day on the job. But I must go,' and he did, without resurrecting his earlier request for her telephone number. At least she had asked him a question. At that moment he noticed Emily Frost entering the room, immediately settling at a desk from which she dialled a number.

As he prepared to leave, he told himself again he had been too forward with Beth. At least, on the other hand, he had refrained from making a separate approach to the attractive, if not impossibly beautiful, Lancastrian Jessica, though such an approach would hardly have been compatible with his professional role in not one but two of her cases, even if she had not been wearing a wedding ring. He could hardly congratulate himself on his restraint with regard to Jessica.

Walking to the exit door from the large room, he passed by the desk tenanted by Emily Frost, who was engrossed in her telephone conversation and had not seen him. Yet another attractive, even exceptionally attractive, woman. She was facing away from him.

Back at the legal building by early afternoon, Robert telephoned Tottenham magistrates' court and asked to speak to the juvenile court listing section. In those days the court jailer was in charge of juvenile court lists as well as of any prisoners in the basement cells.

'I've got a case down for final hearing on Wednesday next week.'

'Yes?' said a male voice which betrayed no special commitment to conversation.

'It's a beyond control case – Michelle West.'

'Yes?'

'As it's for final hearing, it could take a while to get through as I understand the parents are contesting.'

'Contesting, are they?'

'I just want to make sure enough time is set aside.'

'That's asking a lot. There's a lot going on in this court,' said the listing officer woodenly.

'But is there anything else in the list that could get in the way of our having a full day set aside?'

The listing officer made a grunting noise, roughly equivalent to a sigh.

'I'll have to get the book out.' Robert waited, while the man at the other end of the phone got the book out and turned pages without hurry. Finally he spoke.

'Nothing else in that Court at the moment. That's court 5. But there's no saying what might get in between now and next Wednesday.'

'Can you mark it for a full day?'

'But you've just said you don't know how long it will be. I'll put it down for half a day. Their worships usually only sit for the morning.'

'We probably need a full day.'

'You'll have to take that up with their worships.'

The listing officer was about to put the phone down, when Robert injected another cry for help.

'I've got another case that needs listing. A place of safety order was made yesterday on a little girl.'

'Have you issued a notice of proceedings yet?'

'I'm about to.'

'Well, you're too late for next Wednesday,' said the voice with a note of finality and even of satisfaction.

'But you just said there's no saying what else might get in before then.'

'Yes, but we're full up, apart from emergencies. It'll have to be the week after.'

'Isn't this an emergency?'

'Not really.'

'The magistrates only sit on Wednesdays?'

'Only on Wednesdays. You've got a place of safety order for 28 days, haven't you?'

'28 days, yes. But the child hasn't actually been removed.'

'What's the point of having a place of safety order if the child isn't removed? Doesn't sound as if you think an order was required.'

The listing officer had now taken command of the conversation and was showing signs of enjoying having done so. Robert hadn't expected such a reasoned response. He was himself bothered by the same question. He persisted.

'Well, the order's in force, and we need a date.'

'Wednesday week then. Even better, the Wednesday after that.'

'Wednesday week please.'

'You'll lose the date if you don't send in the notice double quick. What's the name?'

'Amy Stewart.'

'It's just pencilled in at the moment. I'm doing you a favour.'

Robert didn't feel as if he was on the receiving end of anything that could, borrowing the lawyers' measure, be interpreted by the hypothetical 'man on the Clapham omnibus', as a favour. He now devoted time to dictating letters into a hand-held device that looked like a telephone receiver – letters to each of little Amy's parents, a memorandum to Jessica and a letter to the Court, which would enclose the notice of proceedings, high-lighting the 'proper development' basis to be relied on. Surely the evidence that would be counted out in front of the magistrates' eyes would enable a care order to be made in Amy's case. Or would it?

He looked over his handiwork to check that he had completed the notice correctly and stamped it at the bottom with the facsimile signature of Edward Shimble. There followed a visit to the typing pool supervisor, whom he asked that his letters be typed right away.

'You're taking a liberty,' said the supervisor, a middle aged woman who tried to give the appearance of being more obstructive than she ever managed to be.

He grinned broadly. 'Sorry, but child care cases do have to have priority.'

'I hope we're going to see eye to eye,' she said, despite her best efforts, letting the beginnings of a smile escape her.

Back in his room Robert made more calls before his typing came back. He then telephoned Jessica to let her know the date of first hearing for little Amy's case and to say she should expect to receive the notice next day. He also wanted to confirm that she would be able to deliver copies to the parents personally. Jessica was now in the office to receive his call.

'You're very efficient,' she said.

'But I'm giving you even more work,' he said sympathetically.

'I'll cope. If all goes well and we get a care order, I'll buy you a drink.'

'I'll look forward to that,' he said. Her friendliness, he surmised, was an expression of professional camaraderie, not of any wish to enter his personal life.

Outside it was sunny once again, and he looked out of the window, pleased that summer was still making occasional re-appearances. He had an evening ahead that he was not sure how to fill. Once in the flat he put the television on after getting something to eat, and then selected an additional evening companion. This was his well-thumbed copy of a 1940 novel by Eric Ambler, *Journey Into Fear*, about an Englishman abroad in mortal danger from Nazi agents. The title, he thought, symbolized nicely his entry into the world of courts and advocacy in which his mettle would soon be tested. His flat-mate was out again. More washing-up had been left undone. Robert navigated his way around it.

4

More about the Legal Service

That same Wednesday afternoon the Borough Solicitor commanded – through Mary – both George Ballam and Bill Bowman to his room. Each of them in turn over the internal phone asked Mary the purpose of this summons. She told them she thought it was something to do with making savings.

Edward Shimble thanked them for coming in, not excluding George from his cordial manner. 'The Leader of the Council,' he said, 'has asked all heads of departments to look into possible ways of making savings and to report back to him. He has asked me to do this as one of the heads of departments.'

This was technically true, save that the request had actually been made to Shimble, not by the Leader of this Labour Party-run council, but by the Chief Executive, 'Smiler' Roland Trask. Trask had passed on to Shimble what the Leader had said to him. So far as Shimble was concerned, Trask in this and in other such affairs was no more than a messenger boy, whose role in the enterprise was sufficiently nominal to require no attribution.

Shimble went on with precision, placing his hands together on his cannon-ball stomach, addressing the ceiling more than Ballam and Bowman as he floated backwards in his flexible maroon leather chair:

'You may know of the new government's wish' (he interrupted himself briefly to smile, indulgently, revealing his even white teeth) – 'Mrs. Thatcher's wish – to sweep away old wasteful attitudes and practices, to be more prudent with taxpayers' and rate-payers' money. This naturally applies to Haringey as much as anywhere else.'

He paused, floated forward to a more upright position, glanced at his audience and continued: 'I will be calling a meeting of solicitors and managers with this on the agenda, but I thought it would be helpful to have a preliminary discussion with you two – you, George, as Administrative Services Manager and you Bill, as Litigation Services Manager. This is not an academic exercise but will have practical implications. So, I am wondering what your preliminary thoughts might be. George, as admin supremo (Shimble had a habit of calling his senior staff 'supremos'), 'what do you say?'

George, hoping that the onslaught of the previous day was not to be resumed, replied in what he imagined was a constructive way.

'I'm wondering what the scale of savings to be made might be.'

Shimble scrolled back again on his chair, placing his hands on the back of his hair-free head and producing half a smile through his flattened equals-sign mouth.

'We should look at it,' he said, 'as if the Council has said we must make actual cuts of 5 per cent.'

George then asked Shimble if the Council had actually said this.

It was the wrong thing to ask. Shimble's face reddened and the fingers of his right hand began drumming on his desk. He said, obscurely, that for someone in George's position to say that, he must be living on the equivalent of a desert island which had just issued a unilateral declaration of independence. His expression recorded complacency with the illustration he had employed, but not with the 'pens and pencils' supremo. His finger tapping on the desk slowed to a halt.

George spoke up again.

'Perhaps we should no longer proceed with appointing a filing clerk.'

'How do you justify that?' asked Shimble, leaning forward, his scepticism suggestive of a spider who has decided to act decisively and without compassion against the interests of a very foolish fly.

'Well, the legal service has managed without one, or at least it has in recent times. The person who'd been doing a lot of the filing sadly died just before you took up your post here.'

Shimble, his chair tilted backwards to a degree disturbing for anyone solicitous about his welfare, considered the ceiling and said slowly that he was amazed George should even consider such a suggestion. 'You are interviewing for the filing clerk post next week, as you well know. It may be a burden you could do without, but we need a filing clerk, as you ought to know better than anybody.'

He gestured George, who was about to speak again, into continued silence, but George spoke up again anyway.

'I was about to suggest,' he said, 'that money might be saved by copying documents double-sided.' That suggestion fell on stony ground too. Shimble's thin lips tightened.

'I think you need to put your thinking cap on, George. Your first thoughts, I'm afraid, don't begin to address the issue.'

Shimble turned to Bill Bowman.

'What do you think, Bill – as litigation supremo?'

'I was turning over whether we should produce figures of work being done. Maybe we're carrying some dead wood, maybe not. If every section has to produce a list of the numbers of cases on the go, it would help to bring to light whether in some areas we are over-resourced or not.'

'An idea with potential, Bill.'

The meeting ended soon after that. George left the room before Bill Bowman, who Shimble asked to stay for a minute.

Bill's square face had assumed an apologetic look. "I hope you didn't mind me making the suggestion about producing figures of cases, Eddie. I was only feeding back to you what you told me was one option yesterday. I like using your word 'over-resourced' too."

Shimble chuckled. 'I didn't mind, Bill,' he said. He added his view that although necessary and overdue cuts had to be made in other departments, he wished to ensure that the legal department was not unduly affected.

Said Bill: 'And we've only had this government in power since May.'

'Not before time,' said Shimble, ending the conversation with the back of his chair safely vertical. 'I think we're going to see a few much needed changes for the better as time passes.'

The next day, Thursday, with sunshine actively, if not intrusively, installed for a third morning in succession, Robert Fordham was early into the office and almost collided with Bill Bowman at the tea-and-coffee-making niche in the corridor.

'Settling in all right?' Bowman asked Robert, as he poured hot water over instant coffee.

'Fine so far. Why don't you drink your coffee in my tent.'

The large and square Bowman assented, helped himself to a generous quantity of sugar, followed Robert into his room and took the chair in front of the desk, on a corner of which he placed his coffee mug.

Said Robert: 'How long have you been working here then, Bill?'

'Over a year. Eddie had just started here and he phoned me up and said the litigation manager post was vacant. He said why don't I apply? So I did. And I got it.'

'You both worked for the same borough?'

'Yes. Camden. I had the same job there as I have here. I thought I'd be there all my life. But I don't mind being here. After all, I'm paid more.'

'You were saying yesterday it's a good idea to get on with Eddie.'

Bowman looked uneasy. 'After all, he is the Borough Solicitor.'

'So does he fall out with people much?'

'You just need to know his ways and not cross him. I'll tell you a story. Just before he set off on his holiday in Devon he had a do with the garage seeing to his car.'

'How did that happen?'

'He had a nice Rover, quite a new one. But it broke down and the garage said it would be ready by noon on the day he was setting off. I collected him and his missis and kids. I had to lug dresses and a couple of suits into my car and a few cases as well. There was just about room for all of it. Then we drove to the garage. But the Rover wasn't ready, and it was well past noon.'

'He wasn't pleased?'

'Steam was coming out of his ears. They'd said it would be ready and it wasn't. They said it was taking longer than expected, and asked him to come back in a couple of hours. So I took the four of them for a cup of tea and a calm down, and then back to the garage we went. Car still not ready. He went absolutely potty, lightning and thunder at the same time. He threatened to sue them. I thought he was going to have a stroke. They agreed to lend him another car. That didn't help much.'

'Didn't help?'

'The only car they had spare was a Japanese job. A little one. It was like a washing machine on wheels. You should have seen his face. He had to take that instead of his classy Rover. We got most of the dresses and suits and stuff into it – I had to look after a couple of things there wasn't room enough for – and off they went to the sea-side. He was pretty choked.'

Bowman swallowed a mouthful of coffee.

'Does he often threaten to sue people?'

'Quite often. He threatened to sue people at his last job at Camden.'

'Really? That can't happen very often in local government.'

'He wanted respect.'

'Kow-towing?'

Bowman didn't like the word.

'You could call it that if you want.'

'Maybe kow-towing is the wrong word,' said Robert on reflection. 'Under the Chinese emperors it did mean prostrating yourself on the floor. Licking it as well.'

'He doesn't ask for that,' said Bowman, with no trace of irony in his voice. 'Anyway,' he went on, 'somebody lower down the rankings told him more or less to fuck off, and Eddie had him up on a disciplinary. Then some other people signed a letter of protest saying the charge was trumped up and he went berserk, threatening in writing to sue them all for libel. They backed down.'

'You weren't one of those signing the complaint letter?'

'Not me. Then he came here. Then I came here.'

'I hear he's fallen out with George Ballam.'

'That's nothing to do with me,' said Bowman quickly.

'What about the litigation solicitor – Colin? Does he get on with Eddie?'

'Colin Masson?' Bowman seemed to have forgotten that he and Robert had already exchanged a few words about Masson.

'Yes.' Robert had not so far had a conversation with that tall, angular and solemn faced young man, a few years his senior, though they had met and had exchanged greetings when passing each other. 'Does he get on with Eddie?' Robert asked again.

'Up to a point,' said Bowman cautiously. 'After all, he is the trade union rep, and he takes it seriously. More seriously than Eddie would like. They call him Mr. Thorough.'

Robert's telephone rang. 'I must be getting on,' he said. 'Nice to have company and a gossip, though.'

Bill Bowman strolled out, taking his half-empty coffee mug with him. Robert seized the telephone. The call was from the Civic Centre, from one of the clerks who serviced council committees.

He gave his name to the caller, who wasted no time explaining his mission.

'They tell me you're the man who'll be doing a report to the Social Services Committee about parental rights resolutions. One or two members have got hot under the collar about resolutions, saying the procedure isn't fair to parents.'

'Who said I'd be doing the report?' asked Robert, curious.

'Mary, Eddie Shimble's secretary. She says Eddie told her you'll be doing the report.'

'He hasn't told me yet,' said Robert.

'That's Eddie for you.'

'What do you want me to do?'

'Can you come over for a chat about it? No rush. Tomorrow if you like.'

They fixed a time for the next morning.

Robert continued to work on the beyond parental control case, writing out a list of events chronologically, and tying the list to particular witnesses, and deciding on the events to be given importance. The morning went quickly and so did the afternoon. Against likelihood, the sun stayed to shine though the sky had grown darker.

The day had been enlivened by another conversation with George Ballam, whose face was active when he joined Robert in the lift. Robert was returning to the legal building bearing an umbrella purchased from a clothes' shop in one hand and a doner kebab from a kebab bar for lunch in the other.

'Taking a chance with that?' asked George humorously, glancing at Robert's lunch.

'I hope not.'

'Did you hear about the scrap between Colin Masson and Eddie this morning?'

'No. A scrap?'

'Colin was in the county court first thing. Doing applications to evict squatters in front of Judge Madder. Four of them. But he had to withdraw in embarrassing circumstances. So Bill Bowman told me.'

'What was the embarrassment?'

The lift had arrived at the second floor, and talk was curtailed until both were in Robert's room.

'Bill had told Colin the evictions would be a piece of cake, and Eddie wanted to tell councillors that the evictions would go ahead. There's been some sneering publicity in the local press about the council letting squatters walk over the public. Spineless Labour and so on. So Colin gets to court and just before being called on, the housing officer who'd sworn the affidavits shows him letters to each of the four squatters from the Borough Secretary, who'd been guided by the Chief Executive.'

'Trask? Letters saying what?'

'Letters giving the squatters an extension of time, until the end of October, in fact. Colin was upset about being told to get evictions of squatters who actually had a right to occupy. Until the end of October. Although the squatters didn't produce the letters – in fact only one of them turned up – he said he'd have to disclose them to Madder and withdraw. Which he did. Said it was the only proper course. Then he told Eddie what he'd done and when Eddie complained he'd let the side down, he played the solicitors' ethics card.'

'So Eddie wasn't happy?'

'Eddie wasn't happy. Not a happy bunny at all. Said Colin should have pressed on. If the squatters didn't bother pursuing their case, why should he put their case for them?'

'Is Colin on the carpet then?'

'I think it's a stand-off. Eddie has met his match. But Eddie was scathing about Trask. Told Bill that Trask's a namby-pamby idiot for letting squatters rule the roost.'

'Are you friends with Eddie again?' Robert ventured.

'Better not ask,' said George.

'Bill was telling me this morning,' said Robert, 'about Eddie threatening to sue people for libel at his last posting, and threatening to sue a garage that didn't produce his car on time for his summer holiday.'

'I've heard all that. You may not know,' said George carefully, 'that Bill and Eddie are as thick as thieves.'

'I think you said something like that before.'

'Did I?'

Sunshine abruptly gave way to rain as Robert left the legal building, and made for his car. He now had every reason to use his new umbrella. Others, in the street, umbrella-less, could be seen running for shelter, any signs of happiness on their faces bullied off by the suddenly truculent weather.

Robert was beginning to think of the flat in Crouch End as home, and was pleased when he reached the kitchen to find the other Robert attacking his neglected washing-up with energy if not thoroughness. 'My girl-friend's coming round,' was the reason given. In these circumstances Robert decided to retreat to his bedroom, where he transferred his books from the floor to neat orderliness on the mantelpiece. This done to his satisfaction, he sallied out for a solitary Chinese meal, during which he resorted to the early chapters of his favourite Eric Ambler novel – *The Mask of Dimitrios*. It was almost as good as human company. On his return he was met with another surprise when he entered the kitchen. His fellow tenant's washing-up from the evening's hosting was already done, and done impeccably. Next day an explanation was proffered: it had been actively shared in by the visiting girlfriend, who had signed it off as acceptable.

5

The Newcomer's First Week Ends

The next morning, Friday, rain clouds shut out the sun decisively and Robert was not the only member of legal department staff whose umbrella was dripping on arrival at work. He was pleased to see arrive the draft minutes of the Amy Stewart case conference, with a covering compliment slip. This carried the simple message: 'I hope these are of assistance to you. Regards. Beth.' They were neatly typed, detailed and precise, according with his memory and his own sketchy notes, and were accompanied by the photocopies he had requested from the family's file.

Robert's opened post had been brought, soon after he had sat down at his desk, by Bill Bowman, who divulged that he had been in the post room and that George Ballam had asked him to bring it up. Bill had not been able to resist adding, glancing down at Beth's compliment slip and pretending he could smell perfume on it: 'Nice scent. I see you've got a message from Beth. Hm, Beth. So is it in code and means something else?' He looked hard at Robert. 'Are you playing Jack the Lad already?'

Robert resisted playing Bowman's game. 'In code?' he queried, as if he had not understood.

Bill Bowman went away, shaking his head, not troubling to translate the innuendo.

Robert thought of phoning the area office where Jessica Palmer worked, wishing he could find an excuse to speak to Beth, but failed to find one. Instead, while still thinking on these lines, he received a call from the same office. It was Jessica.

'How are you today?' he asked.

'I can't complain,' she answered. 'At least I don't have to see Amy's parents again today. I saw the mother yesterday afternoon.'

'You delivered the notices of proceedings?'

'I did. She was angry, but she let me see Amy, who seemed OK. There was one concerning thing. Mum had bandages on her wrists.'

'More wrist-cutting?'

'I would guess so. I asked her but she was elusive. She also said they were going on a week's holiday and so wouldn't be at the court hearing on Wednesday week.' She paused for a few moments to let Robert comment, but he said nothing, so she went on.

'I told her the court would expect them to be present. Do you think we should keep the hearing date?'

'Yes. If they don't turn up, it could be adjourned for a short time. Such as a week. I could, of course, serve a summons on them. It compels their attendance. Theoretically.'

'I'll ask Derek about that,' said Jessica. A short time later she rang back to say Derek was against summonses. 'He said it's too punitive, especially if the family is going to be on holiday.'

'You don't think they're just saying that, pretending to be on holiday and staying put?'

'I daren't guess.'

'And the risk to the child from delay and an absence of close monitoring?' asked Robert.

'Derek's the boss,' she said.

'You're going to do more home visits to check Amy's OK?'

'I've arranged to alternate with the health visitor. She's more acceptable to the family.'

'Pro-parent?'

'If she gets anxious about Amy, I'm sure she'll report it. So will the nursery. Both will.'

Later that morning Robert, who had spoken to Edward Shimble to confirm he should be preparing a report about parental rights resolutions, walked a few hundred yards to the Civic Centre, memorable for white stone and much glass at one end, and brown brick and small windows at the other, his umbrella hoisted again in protest against the resolute rain. The committee clerk to whom he had spoken over the telephone was on the first floor.

This person was no older than Robert, amiable and his fair hair was all over the place. His homely features, Robert noticed, were strewn with freckles in an equally random pattern. He sat at a desk which was at least as disorganised as his hair and his freckles, buried under heaps of papers. A half empty cup of tea sat perilously on one of the smaller paper collations. The office was cramped, with just enough space for the extra chair on which Robert positioned himself, first removing from it a weighty parcel and adding this to the chaos on the desk.

'I think the subject is a parental rights resolutions report to the Social Services Committee,' said Robert.

'Spot on. Remind me of the reason why we have these resolutions. Some councillors seem to think they contravene civil liberties.'

Robert spoke in lawyer-like fashion.

'When a child is in the council's voluntary care, with parental agreement, the council has no definite legal right to make decisions concerning the child or to resist the child's removal if the parents want the child back.'

'I know that bit. Go on then!'

'Sometimes there are good reasons for giving the local authority the rights of the parents. This can be done through a resolution passed by the Committee. It's under the 1948

Children Act. It's like having a care order without going through the courts, though parents have a right of review by the court.'

'That's what I thought.' Had the committee clerk's eyes glazed over? Robert's explanation rolled on.

'It's an essential remedy when the Children and Young Persons Act is not applicable for care proceedings because of the narrow terms in which the conditions for care proceedings are worded.'

'Weird.'

'Weird it may be, but that's the law. So what do the councillors want me to explain?'

'I'll brief you as best I can,' said the committee clerk. 'I know a recent resolution, a few months ago, got a couple of them bristling.'

Robert pulled out a notepad, ready to scribble.

'There are two issues. Number one, they want to know the procedure, to have some written guidance about it. They haven't got anything on paper at the moment. The second thing is that they have doubts about the fairness of the procedure.'

'How many resolutions go to Committee per year, on average,' asked Robert?

'Maybe four or five. And we've got one coming up soon, Mike Stone, the Director, tells me. But as I mentioned, a recent resolution – a dodgy one – muddied the waters, unsettled a couple of our masters and mistresses.'

'The practical problem is,' said Robert, 'putting it another way, that care proceedings aren't available because of risk to a child who's been in voluntary care for a while and who the parent wants back home. You can go to court on neglect or injury that happened yesterday, but not because of things that happened a year ago before the child came into care.'

The committee clerk yawned.

'You could put that in the report if you like,' he said. 'But make sure it's all clear and simple. Some of the councillors are pretty thick, and not all of them can read.'

'You're kidding me.'

'Only up to a point,' said the tousled haired committee clerk.

The discussion had come to a natural conclusion. Robert had already made up his mind to look into the circumstances of the recent resolution which had caused councillor unease. He made his way out of the Civic Centre, passing the high ceilinged rooms with long polished dark wood tables where council committees held their meetings, and the larger Chamber allocated for full Council get-togethers.

Descending the grand central staircase that wasn't particularly grand (though the red carpet made a valiant attempt at magnificence), he was startled and intrigued to see the minute-taker from the case conference, blonde Beth, descending the stairs below him, her arms folded in front of her as she walked.

'Hello Beth.'

She turned, releasing her arms from their folded position.

'Oh hello. Robert, isn't it?'

'That's me. Thank you for the draft minutes about Amy. They will be very helpful. I could say – do you come here often?'

She didn't smile. 'Only for job interviews. I've just had one.'

'I hope you get it.' She said nothing.

He glanced at his watch. 'What about lunch or even a cup of coffee, before you go back to the office. If you are going back there.'

'I am going back there. Coffee would be nice.' It wasn't an answer Robert would have dared to predict. So far Beth had kept him at a distance. Could that change?

It was not good municipal behaviour, Robert knew, to take

a coffee break in office hours, but he could not pass up this opportunity. Out they went into a still drizzly day. Nearby was a snack bar on a corner with seating room for eight or nine customers. They sat at one of three small tables. Robert ordered and paid for coffee, and asked about Beth's interview. This had been, she said, for the post of assistant committee clerk for the Housing Committee.

'Did it go well?'

'I think so. But you never know about the competition. I had a similar job before, in Bedford. And I have local government qualifications.'

'Did you move to London just for the excitement of the big city?'

'Is there excitement?' She hesitated. 'I moved partly to get away from unpleasant memories.'

Robert took the plunge. 'I'd like it very much if you were free to come to a film or the theatre with me. If you're not too busy.'

She considered. 'Have you got something specific in mind?'

As it happened, Robert had the previous day by telephone acquired theatre tickets for that very Friday evening – for himself and his flat-mate. He now took the chance of upsetting the latter by disposing of the second ticket elsewhere in a good cause. A first-rate cause.

'What about this evening? A Tom Stoppard play in the West End. *Night and Day*. It's supposed to be good. The play of the moment.'

'I've heard of it,' she said. 'I'm free. Can I meet you at the theatre? I'd like to pay for my ticket.' Robert resisted this, suggesting she reciprocate another time. She did not argue, and to his relief did not ask how he came to have a spare ticket.

It was settled. They fixed a time to meet. And when he

arrived, punctually, outside the theatre, Beth was already there. 'I hate being late for things,' she said.

The play proved, so far as Robert was concerned, to be stimulating, but over-cerebral, cumbrous in structure and too long. Beth, at the end, said simply that she had enjoyed it. Before, and during the interval, she did not ask Robert much, but was remarkably communicative about her own life.

She was in her late twenties, a couple of years older than Robert. She volunteered having been let down, when working in Bedfordshire, by a boyfriend who'd gone to the United States on the mutual understanding that she would join him. He had changed his mind. This was the unhappy memory that had precipitated her move to London. She added that there was no-one serious around at the moment.

'I hope you'll come out with me again,' he said, when she refused his offer to accompany her home. They parted to find trains on different underground lines. She had given him, though, her home telephone number. He had kissed her on the cheek.

She was truly beautiful, he thought, thinking of her large blue eyes among other advantages, but seemed more burdened by her past than he had experienced from past girl friends.

When Robert had telephoned his flat-mate with apologies, the other Robert had been unimpressed about having his theatre ticket confiscated. 'I see your motive,' he said, 'but question your morals.'

Robert was contrite and in no doubt that if similar circumstances arose in the future he would repeat the crime of transferring into Beth's hands his flat-mate's ticket.

He used up part of the next day, Saturday, investigating furniture shops, but bought nothing. He was earning around double what he had been paid as a trainee, but had little money until his first salary payment at the end of the month.

On the Sunday, at lunch-time, he made for a nearby

public house with the other Robert, who was himself at a loose end and had forgiven him, at least in part, for the ticket misappropriation. They each drank several pints of beer (all paid for by Robert, as was just), and on their return to the flat Robert fell asleep in an armchair until evening, when he tidied the kitchen sink by washing up and drying dishes and pans they had both neglected.

6

George Ballam Under Pressure

On the Monday morning Robert, who had travelled to work from his gloomy flat in dark, gloomy weather – rain just held at bay – found Edward Shimble's secretary, Mary, looking troubled. The door to Shimble's office was closed.

'Mr. Shimble has had a phone call from the Civic Centre,' she said. 'Albert Clack has collapsed. A heart attack, I think.'

Albert Clack, Robert learned, was employed in the legal department as a messenger and odd-job person, though was classified officially as 'a clerical assistant'. He had been transferred several months before from the Parks Department, where his job had routinely involved moving sports equipment, some of which was not light-weight, and over two or three years he had suffered several heart attacks. He had then, because of his poor health, been given a nesting place in the legal department with not a great deal to do. He was a friendly, cheerful man in his early fifties, and Robert had exchanged hellos with him, while not knowing his name.

The door to George Ballam's office was open, and George was standing by his desk, putting down his own internal telephone receiver as Robert went in.

'I hear Albert's had an attack in the Civic Centre,' said Robert.

'He has. Though at home, not at the Civic Centre. I've spoken to his wife. It sounds bad. And Eddie Shimble is blaming me.'

Robert could see that George was upset. 'What could you have to do with that?'

'He's just told me over the phone that I should have been more considerate of Albert's health. I don't know what more I could have done,' he said, shaking his head. 'I told Albert he mustn't lift anything heavy or do anything at all that his doctor had advised him against. Albert is stubborn. He is an active man, always busting to go and do things.'

'Sounds to me as if Eddie just wants to knock nails into you,' said Robert.

'Albert's collapse was nothing to do with his work here,' said George, 'but in Eddie's mind it's linked with the question of collection of post from this building and taking it to the Post Office.'

'Why should that be?'

'Exactly. There isn't a connection.'

George went on.

'For several months now Eddie's been grumbling at me about the fact that there is no direct collection of post from here by the Post Office, and about my having failed to make an arrangement for direct collection.'

'So what actually happens?'

'The system is that our outward post goes to the Borough Secretary's up at the Civic Centre and is then brought back in this direction to the Post Office.'

'The same for incoming post?'

'The same in reverse. Incoming post goes from the Post Office up to the Civic Centre and then back in this direction to us. It sounds Alice in Wonderland, but that's how it is.'

'But why?'

'It's because although we are based in two different sites, the Civic Centre for the Borough Secretary's and this place for Legal, Legal is still one leg of the Chief Executive's responsibility. As Bill Bowman would say, the legal department is in Trask's manor.'

'Weren't we once all in the same building?'

'That's the point,' said George. 'We were shoved out of the Civic Centre a couple of years back. Before Eddie Shimble arrived. But the post arrangements stayed the same despite our moving here.'

'So Eddie has a point, doesn't he? Shouldn't we be dealing direct with the Post Office on our own account?'

'Whose side are you on?' George went on, after producing a wry smile. 'Yes, you're right and Eddie's right, but I don't have the power. The power lies within the Borough Secretary's, just as it is responsible for money for postage, just as it is for supplying us office furniture, stationery and the like. And Eddie should have taken it up direct, instead of leaving it to me, and if need be he could have taken it up with Roland Trask. Eddie's got clout; I haven't. But he doesn't like acknowledging Trask is his boss. Or getting his hands dirty. He likes to delegate what can't be delegated, and then he complains to the delegate – such as me – that I'm not doing my job properly.'

Robert was perplexed. 'So what can you do?'

George put his hands out as if seeking help from the world. 'I have repeatedly asked the senior person in the Borough Secretary's for permission to pay the Post Office fee for a direct collection of our sack of post, and each time it's been refused. Eddie can't accept, for some reason, that the legal service is not autonomous. He keeps on telling me to ask again for permission to pay the fee. I'm about to do that. For the fiftieth time.'

Robert reverted to the issue of Albert Clack's collapse, which had got lost in this discussion.

'So if you managed somehow to charm the Borough Secretary into agreeing to a rational post collection and delivery system, Eddie Shimble wouldn't be putting Albert's collapse on to your shoulders?'

'Maybe.' George Ballam opened his hands again to indicate his helplessness. He continued: 'Of course, he's worried about his own heart at the moment, Mary's had to double-check his pulse.'

Robert returned to his own office, thankful that he was not under siege from Shimble.

On the Monday evening, he telephoned Beth. She was slow to answer, but when she did, she seemed pleased to hear from him. He suggested a meal out, later in the week. 'What about Thursday?' he ventured.

'Yes. Instead of eating out, I can cook you a curry.'

Startled as he was at this invitation, he responded with alacrity.

'I'll bring a bottle of wine. What wine do you prefer?'

Dry white wine was her preference, and she gave him her Tottenham address. She suggested seven thirty. Thursday, to Robert, seemed a long way off. But it was something to look forward to. And a half.

7

Into the Highgate Juvenile Court

Robert's baptism in forensic fire in the Highgate juvenile court took place on the Tuesday morning. Highgate was illustrative of the prosperous end of the borough, just as Tottenham represented the poorer end. In accordance with this scheme of things, Highgate magistrates' court was lighter, airier and less congested with humanity than Tottenham's, and blessed with fewer court rooms. It was discreetly located a short distance away from the prodigal production and carriage of pollution on the Great North Road, better known in recent times as the A1.

Each of the two magistrates' courts in the borough had a juvenile court day – Tuesday was Highgate's and Wednesday was Tottenham's. It was in the Tottenham court that the cases of Michelle West and Amy Stewart were to be heard, Michelle's as early as the next day.

Robert was worried as to whether he had done enough to prepare for Wednesday's traumas, but in the mean-time was primed to represent the borough at Highgate in two care proceedings cases triggered by omissions to attend school, or at least to attend school frequently enough to satisfy a beady-eyed education welfare unit. In these cases, the Education department rather than Social Services was giving Robert his orders; and he had risen early in dull, dry, colder weather, to make notes from two slender folders before driving the short distance to the court.

Entering the foyer in his three-piece, pin-striped uniform, Robert spotted Emily Frost in the waiting area with a teenage boy, and greeted her. With her wide, attractive smile, she was asking the boy to have a seat, a request he took up with reluctance. She told Robert they were waiting for his solicitor – someone, she said, from Slash & Co. She went on, her face sparkling – there was something surely Mediterranean about her features, he mused – to tell him what the case was about.

The boy's offence was that he had, one evening, stolen a warning lamp from the road works street location where it had been winking redly on and off. He had been arrested on his way home by a passing police officer, who had observantly noticed that something was making an enormous bulge under the boy's jacket. Soon after, he discovered the nature of the not very secret secretion and escorted the boy home, where, Emily told Robert, not much of a search of his bedroom was needed to reveal a dozen more such lamps, a couple of which were still flickering. As she spoke quietly to Robert, her face was alive and alight with zest for life, and he was much drawn to her.

Two events occurred simultaneously: the red lamp case was called on and the solicitor from Slash and Co, an elderly, conventionally if untidily dressed, man arrived. Emily, the teenager and the solicitor all advanced into court, followed closely by the prosecuting police officer.

Robert now inquired for, and found, a middle-aged education welfare officer whose forename was Shirley, and whose use of make-up seemed to him more than generous. She was responsible for both cases, each of which concerned boys, one aged eleven and the other fourteen, and she displayed a marked tendency to make moralistic remarks about the necessity of school attendance.

Robert spoke in turn with each of the two defence solicitors involved to clarify the extent and nature of any dispute; but there was no drama or much to discuss outside court, and soon the case of the eleven-year-old was called on. Mother, solicitor, son, Shirley and Robert all found their places in the plain, modern court room. Before long, the chairman, a small man with a small moustache and a pleasantly informal manner, addressed the mother simply. 'The question is,' he said, 'is Stephen going to school?'

The solicitor for mother and son, also agreeable in manner, informed the court (so quietly that he was asked to repeat himself) that the matter was contested, and Shirley went behind the witness lectern to give evidence. She produced, as requested by Robert, school attendance certificates, which were handed to the Bench, revealing long waves of absence. Shirley spoke of her visits to the family to encourage improvement and of her deep disappointment. 'I have to confess failure,' she said.

The mother gave evidence. She said, anxiety inscribed on her face, that the noise from traffic near the flat where they lived was very great, both from lorries and trains, that her son had a tendency to leg cramps and that he had not gone in to school during one week, having accidentally sustained a nasty burn on his back. She said too that an older son in his twenties did not help, as he sometimes ate Stephen's breakfast, leaving him to go hungry.

Robert asked the mother if it were true that during school days she had often taken him out. She agreed, adding that these outings were usually with Stephen riding a bike, as his legs got tired walking. He asked also if she felt she had cooperated with the education welfare officer. She replied that she couldn't complain about Shirley, who'd done her best to get her son to school.

Robert heard – as others must have heard – the chairman breathing to his colleagues 'Over-protective mother', and the whispered back jesting reply: 'Maybe there should be a care order on the big brother.'

The upshot of this first case, after a ten minute retirement by the magistrates, was that the 'primary condition' – that the boy was not attending school and in need of care and control – was proved, and the court ordered a social worker's report to assist with 'disposal' to be prepared in readiness for another hearing in four weeks' time.

Said the chairman to the mother: 'You and Stephen can go now, but it would be a jolly good idea if you make sure he goes to school over the next four weeks if you don't want him sent to boarding school.' Mother and son left the court without fuss, and the magistrates rose to their feet and moved off. Robert and the other solicitor also rose, bowing incongruously towards the private doorway through which the magistrates were already disappearing. The clerk told him in an undertone that the Bench always took their morning tea at this time.

Waiting outside in the foyer, as this discreet tea interval became protracted, Robert saw Emily speaking to the police officer who had prosecuted the 'red lamp' teenager, and went over to her after the conversation ended. 'Just a conditional discharge,' she said. 'But there was a good moment,' she added, with laughter in her eyes, "when the policeman giving evidence was asked by the chairman why he became suspicious about what the boy had under his coat. He just said: 'He was flashing on and off, your worships.'"

Robert was now greeted by his Enfield counterpart, Jack Parnell, remembered from the previous week at Tottenham, and who this time came over with a long-legged stride, saying hello both to Emily and to Robert.

'How are you adjusting?' Robert was asked.

'Slowly but surely getting there. Do you have anything special on today?'

'In a way,' said Parnell, 'or at least the background was unusual. We snatched a baby under a place of safety order a few days ago, but unfortunately when the social worker was about to leave the foster home by car the mother turned up and bent her windscreen wipers…'

'The social worker's?'

'The social worker's…and marked her bodywork…'

'The car's bodywork?'

'I think you are being deliberately unhelpful to Jack,' said Emily impishly to Robert, moving away to speak to her teenage client and to leave the building with him.

'The car's bodywork…with a coin,' Jack went on. 'The social worker drove off, reporting the damage at the police station. The mother was arrested for criminal damage.'

'How did she know where the foster home was?'

'That was our blunder. The social worker gave away the foster home address to the mother. She thought she had to write it on the place of safety order that she served on the mother. She didn't have to do that, of course. It wasn't a good idea either. The magistrates today were sympathetic to the social worker. Maybe that helped us get our interim care order on the baby today. Have I asked you about playing cricket?'

'Was it,' Robert asked, 'the same social worker you told me about before who took the oath raising her hand and saying *So help me God*?'

'No, this was a different one. Nice woman. By the way, do you ever make children wards of court in Haringey?' An answer from Robert was forestalled by the calling on of his second school attendance case of the morning. The answer would have been that he did not know.

The older boy, the fourteen-year-old, whom the friendly chairman addressed by name, answered questions in a bold manner. An overly bold manner (illustrated by the use of the word 'mate', when 'sir' would have been more acceptable), and Robert saw one of the side magistrates purse his lips. It became plain that the Bench considered this school non-attender too cocksure for his own good – and for their peace of mind.

Having heard from Shirley, who when giving evidence shook her head in exasperation with the boy, in short order they found 'the primary condition' abundantly proved. So abundantly, indeed, that they made an interim care order to the local authority, anticipating that a place for the boy would be found right away at the council's residential assessment centre in Hertfordshire, with a view to a comprehensive report to the court.

'You're a very lucky boy,' said the chairman, nodding his head benevolently. Robert's eyes were at this moment fastened on the kindly chairman's moustache, which was so small that it might have been a shaving oversight.

If intended to be a gift to mother and son, the outcome came as a nasty shock to both of them – and was unexpected by Shirley and Robert. The usual protocol required a social enquiry report to be considered by the Bench before major outcomes were pronounced, and such a report had not yet been requested or tabled. Instead the justices had made their own instant diagnosis of what was required to teach manners and responsibility to this upstart youth.

'I didn't think they'd do that,' Shirley said in a hushed voice to Robert, 'but on the other hand it may be for the best. If my reputation with the family before was mud…'

An urgent phone call was made to the assessment centre by a duty social worker unobtrusively present and a place was confirmed as available. Though the boy had been a confident, even a brash, speaker, vis-à-vis the magistrates, he was now in tears and in pieces – a condition which caused his mother to weep too. The plan of the duty social worker, together with a colleague, to escort the young person to the assessment centre, was held up until emotions had calmed.

Robert turned over whether he could or should have done something to make the capricious outcome less likely, or at least should have discussed the risk in advance with Shirley who, curiously, seemed pleased that the justices had exercised their authority with such casual self-belief.

But his job was done. He left the court room, waving across the foyer to Jack Parnell, who responded with the stroke of an invisible cricket bat. Shirley was still speaking to the distressed mother, whose teenage son was now angry. The Bench, previously 'mates' were now 'fuckers'. Returning to the office, the sky having brightened without actually producing sunshine, he was told that Albert Clack was still in hospital and in a critical condition.

The next day Robert was due to face up to his self-imposed obligation to present the case of teenager Michelle to the Tottenham justices. It was to be a long day, for which a long chapter is necessary.

8

The Newcomer's First Big Test

That Wednesday morning, between waking and arrival at the magistrates' court for the less prosperous end of the borough, Robert Fordham denounced himself over and over for having rashly accepted the role of the council's advocate in this case in which it was asserted that Michelle West was beyond the control of her parents, and had been the victim of unacceptable corporal punishment. Today was his journey into fear, and the fear had already begun.

At the same time he was psyching himself up to behave as a cool, clinical and persuasive lawyer. He possessed two three-piece dark pin-striped suits, and was wearing what he thought was the better of the two: the newer one, which also sported the narrower pin-stripe. The outdoor temperature had dropped like a stone overnight, and the only consolation was that the sky was largely free of cloud. Robert did not need his umbrella, but needed to keep persuading himself that he was up to the task for which he had volunteered so impetuously.

On the far side of the main road outside the court building a short line of parked cars was already in place as his own vehicle slowed to a halt behind another which was adding itself to the stationary queue. His own vehicle then became the penultimate car in the line as yet another slid into position behind him.

He soon saw that the driver of the car behind was Jessica Palmer. She had a passenger, a girl. So this was Michelle, the reason for his being at court. He glanced at her as she stood on the pavement with Jessica, preparing to cross to the other side, dressed neatly for school. She was slight of build, pale of face, and looked more like twelve than fifteen. She had a brace on her teeth. Jessica had told Robert that Michelle was short-sighted, but refused to wear the glasses prescribed for her. He walked up to join them.

Silently they crossed the road together before Jessica, hitherto occupied more with safety considerations than courtesies, introduced Robert to Michelle as 'the lawyer for Social Services'. Robert said hello and decided to leave the rest of the talking to Jessica, who, moments later, ushered her charge into a small side building through a door marked 'Probation Department'.

A number of people were standing about in the corridors of the court building, though it was early yet. A black gowned elderly male usher stood in the central square foyer, holding a clipboard. Fastened to this were the court lists: a sheet of paper for each court. In answer to a question Robert was given the information he wanted.

'Court 5. You're in the little court,' said the usher. 'Have you been in it?'

'No.'

'It's small. You could put two Court 5s in a telephone kiosk,' said the usher, who was a wag of a kind.

Robert drifted down the corridor to the right, then along the dog-leg corridor which led to the hidden-away Court 4, and more directly to the more accessible Court 5. No-one was yet hovering near these two numbered rooms where life-changing decisions were made in impersonal fashion. He opened the door to Court 5. It was empty of human life; tiny for a court, but with space enough for a slightly raised platform which supported the wide desk behind which the magistrates would sit. The clerk to the justices would, he could see, occupy the seat and table close to them. In front were light-wood tables forming three sides of the tiny square around which other participants would be positioned. The three blue volumes of Stone's Justices Manual were to hand at the rear of the clerk's little desk.

It was a plain, functional, court setting, and not in itself intimidating – very different from Court 2, which he had entered the previous week, and which resembled the interior of a dark-furnitured chapel of severe aspect, with the magistrates' platform substituted for an altar area. A box-sized court room should make things easier for him: at least the furniture did not glower at him with affronted authority.

'Michelle West? The escape from the balcony affair?'

A man somewhere in his thirties in a regulation pin-striped three piece suit, replicating Robert's own attire – even the pin-stripe-widths were identical – was approaching him.

'That's me,' said Robert.

'I represent Michelle's parents. Jonathan Spratt.'

'Counsel?'

'Counsel.'

'I represent the local authority. Robert Fordham.'

'Solicitor?'

How does he know? Robert asked himself.

'Solicitor,' he said. 'Do you have instructions?'

'I will have, when my clients arrive,' said Jonathan Spratt. He was a slim, small, dark-haired man, who compensated for slight stature with a large voice. The darkness of his hair extended to his neatly trimmed moustache, which sat above a large, but evenly distributed mouth, revealing correspondingly large teeth.

'You've not met them?'

'Oh yes, I've met them, a couple of days ago. But I must confirm their position today. They weren't at all happy when I saw them. That was clear enough. What witnesses are you calling?'

'I'll kick off with the educational psychologist. His report was sent to your instructing solicitors a few days ago. Have you read it?'

'Not seen it. My solicitors are hopeless. Spare copy?'

Robert fished out a copy from his briefcase.

'Thank you. It's not admissible as evidence, of course.'

'Not even when the man is in the witness box?'

'Not even when he's in the witness box. Is he here?'

'Not yet, so far as I know.'

Robert was inwardly cursing. He was starting to panic: to conclude that he was out of his depth and should have briefed a barrister. Someone with the easy, pushy confidence of Jonathan Spratt. He adopted a disinterested stance.

'The report may help your cross-examination.'

'You'll excuse me while I read it,' said Spratt. 'Ah – my clients are here.'

Along the corridor trooped a well-dressed couple in their forties. Mr. Spratt led them off towards the front entrance. There were no interviewing rooms, and Robert guessed they would find a fairly private corner somewhere. As he watched them retreat, a black-gowned usher, this time an elderly female member of the species, approached.

'Case of West?'

'Yes,' said Robert. 'I represent the local authority.'

He gave his name, which was laboriously written down. He assisted by slowly spelling it aloud.

'Are you ready to go on?'

'Not yet. The parents' barrister is taking instructions. Are the magistrates ready for us?'

'We haven't got a full Bench yet – unless you're happy with just two.'

'I doubt it,' said Robert, who had met with the problem of a shortfall in magistrate numbers during his training observation experience. What was to happen if a Bench of two – unlikely as it might seem – disagreed with each other?

'Is a third justice expected to appear?' he enquired.

'I'll let you know when I know more,' she said charitably.

It was almost ten thirty when Jonathan Spratt stepped steadily, without haste, along the corridor to speak to Robert, his clients not far behind, pausing some yards away. Mr. and Mrs. West sat down on the hard and low bench running alongside one dull grey-blue wall of the corridor for a part of its length.

'We're opposing a care order,' said Spratt firmly. 'We want Michelle home today.'

'Thanks for letting me know. Suppose she goes home and runs away again?'

'She won't run away. She'll know what's good for her this time,' said Spratt with assurance. 'Are the Bench ready for us yet?'

Robert told him that a full complement of justices was awaited.

'We can't manage with two,' said Spratt. 'We can't risk a hung jury at decision time.' He went off to speak to Michelle's parents and came back after a minute or two.

'Hello again. They want to know where Michelle is.'

'She's on the premises,' said Robert guardedly. 'She's here to be seen by the magistrates at the start.'

'I know,' said Spratt. 'Her parents want to see her now.'

'Surely we can't risk a blazing row between them at this moment.'

Jessica Palmer now joined them, first greeting Michelle's parents politely as she passed them in the corridor. 'Don't say hello to us,' said Mrs. West, stony-faced, wearing a dark skirt with a matching jacket outside a demure white blouse. Jessica, whose attire was rather similar, was expressionless as she joined Robert.

'An assistant social worker is sitting with Michelle,' she said. 'I've also had a phone message from Graham Townley, the ed psych. He's on his way.'

'Good,' said Robert, relieved.

Spratt, standing near, cut in: 'Might you be Jessica Palmer?'

'I am,' she said, without her customary warmth.

'Mr. and Mrs. West are asking to see Michelle. Any reason why that can't be facilitated? It may be a while before we get on.'

'On a previous occasion in my office,' said Jessica, 'a meeting between them was explosive. I doubt if it's a good idea to chance a repetition.'

Said Robert to Spratt: 'I suggest discussion from this point on is between advocates. Perhaps you would leave me to take instructions.'

'Very well,' said Spratt, his large mouth drawn tight, accepting the boundary line set by protocol and insisted upon by Robert. He rejoined Mr. and Mrs. West, exchanging words with them. Robert heard Mrs. West say 'Now' with exaggerated firmness. Spratt returned a few moments later and spoke to Robert.

'Mr. and Mrs. West insist on speaking to Michelle now.'

Jessica was forming words with her lips, but was overtaken by Robert. He spoke with what he hoped was authority in his voice:

'I'm sorry, but Michelle at this moment is subject to an interim care order which enables the local authority to make decisions overriding any made by her parents. We would wish in any event to take Michelle's views into account about a meeting at this sensitive juncture.'

The elderly female usher interrupted them loudly. 'All parties to come into Court.'

'All parties', save for Michelle herself, were soon in their places under the usher's direction. But no justices were to be seen. Instead their clerk was in his place, observing the arrivals.

The clerk was a curly headed, overweight, young man, who had somehow entered the court room without Robert noticing. Robert sat alongside Spratt. Jessica sat on a chair against the wall behind Robert, and Mr. and Mrs. West sat behind Spratt, with an empty chair separating them from Jessica.

'Are we all here?' asked the clerk, somewhere between business-like and welcoming. 'What about the child?'

'Michelle is on the premises,' said Robert, 'and can be brought in to be seen by the magistrates when they wish to see her.'

'We still have a difficulty,' said the clerk with a wry smile. 'Only two magistrates so far. Are you willing to accept two?'

Spratt responded. 'This is a contested application. There should be three justices in case of a conflict of positions, and there is most definitely a conflict of positions.'

Said Robert: 'I agree with that.'

Said the clerk: 'If we can start later this morning, are you ready with witnesses?'

'I can certainly start,' said Robert.

'The case is stood down until eleven fifteen,' said the clerk, immediately immersing himself in papers. All others left the room.

Once in the corridor, Spratt renewed his demand for the parents to see Michelle. 'If you don't arrange it pronto, I shall have to raise it when the case comes on. This is outrageous. Committed and caring parents not able to see their own daughter!'

While hardly raising his well-oiled voice, his words had been increasingly underscored by measured wrath, and had ended with a little surge. His moustache and manner were beginning to irritate Robert.

'I'll take instructions,' he said, wishing that Spratt would remove himself to a great distance, if not further. He steered Jessica towards a point in the public area near the court's main entrance, now mostly deserted.

'So, what's your view about the parents seeing Michelle?' he asked.

'I don't think it's a good idea. They're angry. They'll pressure her.'

'On the other hand,' said Robert, 'they must know it's important for them to behave themselves at court. If they behave badly it won't get them brownie points from the justices.'

'Yes, they may know that. But their history is one of losing their rags, especially Mrs. West. And supposing Michelle runs away? We're surely here to protect her from that.'

'My concern is that if we say no, the court may be more sympathetic to the parents' case. Can't we at least ask Michelle what she thinks? If she's unhappy about seeing her parents now, and refuses, we can tell the court that.'

'I'll ask her – but I won't put pressure on her,' said Jessica.

'Fair enough. I'm not putting pressure on you to put pressure on her,' said Robert, who suspected that was what Jessica might be thinking.

'No,' she said, 'of course you aren't. You're right. Before we make a final decision, we should ask what Michelle wants to happen.'

Robert was relieved that so far Jessica had shown no sign of being dissatisfied with his out-of-court performance. But he also suspected that if he made a hash of the job ahead he would be considered cavalier for not employing a barrister. Melanie had said that Jessica could get above herself, while declining to elaborate. Had Jessica complained about Melanie?

While Jessica walked over to the probation building, Robert stationed himself near the court's main entrance. As he stood there, the sun began to shine without doing much to mitigate the cold. A man in a brown suit and probably in his mid-thirties, his hair, neat beard and moustache, all brown too, walked into the court's drive-way from the road outside and up to the building.

It proved indeed to be Graham Townley, the educational psychologist, whose manner had something diffident and unassuming about it. Robert told him where Jessica Palmer and Michelle were. He added that discussion was going on about whether Michelle should meet her parents before the hearing started.

'We're waiting for a Bench to constitute itself,' added Robert. 'Michelle's parents seem hostile to Jessica.'

'Not easy people to deal with,' said Mr. Townley. 'I expect Mrs. West is spitting fire. Will you be asking me questions about my report?'

Robert explained that the intractability of the rules of evidence meant that Mr. Townley's testimony might need to be heard without the justices having the report in front of them.

Jessica soon returned with the news that Michelle would prefer not to meet her parents at this time, saying too that she, Jessica, would ring her 'senior', Derek, to get his view on whether or not she should agree to a meeting.

She was soon back from the telephone kiosk. 'Derek agrees with me,' she said. 'No meeting now, better to have one, he said, when today's storm is over, though that could be another nasty clash, and I may need to argue with him about that. They haven't asked to see her before today, you know. They do blow hot and cold.'

Robert reported this outcome to Spratt, who said, stiffly: 'I'll place the matter in the court's good hands.'

As he said this, a portion of corridor outside Court 5 was cleared of its small population by the now harassed-looking usher, who roped off the corridor mouth to allow unimpeded passage to the magistrates. They emerged from behind a curtained door in single file and proceeded to enter the court room in dignified fashion. In this under-sized court room, the magistrates had no private access and escape route. The case was called. It was already close to mid-day, and for Robert, hours of polite warfare seemed inescapable before his first day in Tottenham juvenile court was over.

Present in court, to be discreetly stared at, were a lady chairman in the middle, another woman on her left and a man on her right. Robert observed that Bench were by accident ranked according to size: while all roughly of the same height, the woman on the chairman's left was decidedly thin, the lady chairman herself was more stoutly constructed and the man on her right was unhealthily large.

A third magistrate had plainly been requisitioned from somewhere. The curly-headed clerk read a few introductory words from the notice of proceedings, identifying the child and the 'beyond control' basis of proceedings, and overlooking the fact that ill-treatment was also alleged. (Robert was too slow to react with a corrective interjection.) The clerk went on to say that Michelle was subject to an interim care order due to expire that day, and that this was the final hearing.

'Any reports?' asked the lady chairman briskly. For such a small room she spoke loudly, with a cut-glass upper class accent, which put Robert immediately in mind of mimicry performed by Jack Parnell. It's her, he thought correctly.

'No, Madam,' said the curly-headed clerk, with a short laugh which produced a frown from the lady chairman. 'This is the final hearing of the first stage in care proceedings. The local authority has to prove its case before reports can be produced. Mr. Ford, he went on...'

'Fordham,' interposed Robert.

'I'm sorry. Is Michelle here to be seen by the justices?'

Giving no time to Robert to reply, Spratt was on his feet. He announced, toothily, that he had a preliminary application.

'What is it?' asked the lady chairman curtly.

'Michelle is elsewhere on these premises, I've been told, and although her parents are anxious to see her and have asked repeatedly to see her, their request has been denied for reasons that are not clear or satisfactory to me or to them. They naturally want to build bridges between themselves and their daughter, especially as they consider that the council has created a gulf between them and their daughter.'

More ice from the lady chairman: 'Is this so, Mr. Fordham?'

Her question contained a note of displeasure, but was this due to her agreement with Spratt or for some other reason?

'Yes, Madam. It's felt by the social workers that a meeting at this sensitive moment would be more likely to be problematic than beneficial.'

'You can't be sure of that, can you?'

'I can't be certain – I mean the social workers instructing me can't be certain – but the history is one of a difficult relationship between Michelle and her parents.'

'I appreciate that. Is Michelle absolutely refusing to see them?'

'I understand she has said she would rather not.'

'How old is she?'

'Fourteen,' said Spratt.

'Fifteen,' said Robert.

'So which is it?'

Spratt had turned to his clients.

'She's fifteen,' said Mrs. West.

'I think that settles it,' said the lady chairman, with impatience controlled.

First obtaining supportive nods from her colleagues to the left and right, she went on to declare definitively: 'Well, she should see them, if only for ten minutes. We'll rise for that to happen.'

Said the clerk instantly, tolerating no foolishness: 'You can't direct that a meeting takes place.' He had stressed the word 'direct', and did not make the effort to add 'Madam'.

'Perhaps not. But that is our wish,' said the lady chairman, glowering at the clerk. She added, making a request he could not lightly refuse: 'Please join us for a few minutes.'

'Stand please,' said the usher. They all stood, and the lawyers bowed to the about-to-leave Bench.

Spratt whispered to Robert: 'I take it you'll arrange for mum and dad to see Michelle now.'

'I'll take instructions.' The Bench withdrew, and the curly-headed clerk followed them, expressionless.

Robert walked to the front of the building with Jessica. On the way he passed the elderly female usher, who had been present during the short hearing, and who was speaking to her male colleague – 'the wag'. He heard her say, obviously with reference to the lady chairman: 'She's a caution, isn't she?' He also heard the reply: 'One of these days she'll give a clerk a horse-whipping as a warning to the others.'

'Did you know our chairman today is Lady Feverel, the number one juvenile court magistrate?' Jessica asked Robert.

'I know now. The name matches the voice very nicely. I've heard it imitated,' said Robert.

'Why do magistrates have to be so idiotic?' she queried rhetorically. 'Are they deliberately wanting to ignite an almighty bust-up?'

Before she continued, a faint smile appeared on her face. 'About a month ago,' she said, 'I was here about a teenage runaway – a girl on an interim care order who had absconded from a children's home. I was in court with your colleague Melanie. It wasn't this chairman, it was a different one, a man. The girl's whereabouts had been unknown for weeks, but the mother then had a phone call from her. The call was from Paris. Anyway, Melanie told the magistrates the girl had been in Paris for at least a week, but was believed now to be back in London. The chairman couldn't believe it.'

Jessica proceeded to mimic the chairman's plummy voice and to repeat Melanie's exchange with him.

"*Where did you say she's been?* – His voice was high with disbelief.

Paris.

Paris? – He still couldn't believe it.

Paris. It's in France.

We know where Paris is.

'That was it,' said Jessica. 'Priceless.'"

Robert observed, as if drawing from a repository of lawyer-like wisdom: 'Yet he was entitled to be surprised. I wouldn't have thought, to be fair, that an adventure in Paris is generally thought of as being a rite of passage for a deprived London girl. I think,' he said, looking at his watch, 'we'd better get back to the business of today.'

During this commentary Jessica looked at him, without saying anything. It then occurred to Robert that he was being pompous and missing her point, which was that the magisterial reaction had contained the assumption that Paris was not for the likes of ordinary Tottenham people. Was Jessica being fair?

He moved on. 'Although they have no power to insist a meeting takes place,' said Robert, 'I suggest we allow it. If it goes badly, it won't be our fault. On their heads be it.'

Jessica agreed. She went into the probation building, spoke briefly to Michelle, and returned. 'Michelle isn't saying no,' she said, 'but she wants me there.'

Robert told Jonathan Spratt that the parents could see Michelle, but with Jessica present. Spratt replied that Mrs. West had guaranteed that Jessica would pull Michelle's strings. 'Your Miss Palmer is not a neutral person.' He added, with a superior air: 'I'd like to be there too.'

'If you're going to be present,' said Robert, 'I'll be present too.'

But it was soon conceded that the meeting between Michelle and her parents would proceed, with Jessica and an assistant social worker (who had been sitting with Michelle), as the only other persons in the room. Jessica took Michelle's wordless parents to the probation building, where their silence was broken noisily. The meeting was over in minutes. Michelle was left alone with the assistant social worker, a woman in her fifties.

Jessica reported back to Robert: 'It was even worse than I expected. Not much love lost, even at the beginning, and it never got beyond the beginning.'

'As bad as that?'

'Mrs. West told Michelle she was making them look stupid, forcing them into court. They started shouting at each other. Mrs. West went over and grabbed her by her shoulders and Michelle pushed her away and I stepped in between them and took her out.'

The elderly female usher, moving almost at a trot, black gown flapping, face in a frown, was now calling all parties back into court. The ritual inside the diminutive court room resumed. The magistrates were already in their places when Robert and Jessica joined the others. If the clerk had been the victim of a rebuke (or even a horse-whipping) for insufficient deference, he gave no sign of it.

Robert stood up. 'I have to report, Madam, that there was a verbal and even a physical altercation between Michelle and her parents when they met in the probation office, and evidence will be given in due course about it by Miss Palmer.'

'Very well,' said Lady Feverel, 'we feared that would happen. We'll see Michelle now.'

Jessica whispered to Robert that Michelle was upset and he passed that information on to the Bench.

'The child should be produced at the commencement of the hearing. That's right, isn't it Mr. Clerk?'

'That's the practice, madam,' said the curly-headed clerk.

Lady Feverel (looking at Jessica): 'Please now speak to Michelle, tell her there's nothing to worry about and bring her here just to be seen by us. She'll only come in for a minute or two. Too much time-wasting has taken place already.'

Whose fault is that? thought Robert.

Jessica left the court room. Minutes later, she was back with Michelle and the assistant social worker. Nothing was said to Michelle, who stood waiting for several seconds. Robert looked at her again. She had a slightly bulbous nose and a brace on her teeth, and a guarded facial expression. The magistrates were only yards away, so perhaps she could see their faces clearly. Robert thought of Dr. Pearson, who wore his glasses only in short bursts.

'We're very glad to meet you, Michelle,' said Lady Feverel graciously. 'We're sorry you haven't had a peaceful morning so far, but we are concerned about your relationship with your parents. You can go back to school now. I assume someone's going to take you?'

'Yes,' said the assistant social worker, replying on Michelle's behalf in a London accent, and not encumbering herself with much deference. 'I'll do that.' Michelle said nothing, and left the court room with her escort.

Lady Feverel, glancing at her watch, exchanged whispers with each of her colleagues on the Bench – known widely among the legal profession, it should be said, as 'book-ends'. 'We have a difficulty,' she announced, 'in that it's now almost one o'clock and the Bench has not planned to sit this afternoon.' She paused and continued. 'If we do sit this afternoon, we must rise at four o'clock at latest. One of my colleagues has an appointment which cannot be cancelled. What is the estimate of time now for this case?'

'In the light of the history of this morning,' said Robert, 'another full day.'

'Two full days,' said Spratt.

As things turned out, Robert's estimate was closer.

'Mr. Clerk,' said Lady Feverel, 'during the lunch interval,

please make inquiries about dates for completing this matter. We will rise now and the court will sit again at 2 p.m.'

Robert found the educational psychologist on the bench in the corridor, his back firmly pressed against the grey-blue wall, turning over the pages of his own records. Robert told him the case would re-start at two and that his evidence would be needed soon after that.

'I haven't done this before,' confessed Mr. Townley.

Robert repressed a desire to echo him. 'I'm sure you'll have no difficulties. I'm sorry you've been kept hanging about.' Content to have more time to look at his own notes and think his way ahead, Robert strolled off to a café not far away (identified for him by Godfrey during his reconnaissance the previous week) where he downed, with devotion to the task, a plateful of bacon, fried eggs, sausages and tinned tomatoes, joined by two slices of fried bread. Jessica, meanwhile, made a series of telephone calls from the public phone in the court building, and managed to buy a roll at the café where Robert was finishing his own meal.

Ten minutes later than earlier promised, the magistrates filed in, and were again in their seats before others of the party were in theirs. An exchange of bows with the lawyers had to be postponed.

'You'd better start,' said Lady Feverel to Robert, pre-empting the clerk, who had been about to say something similar.

Robert outlined the history unemotionally and succinctly. "Your worships,' he began… "As the notice indicates, the local authority relies on two primary conditions, both the 'proper development' ground and the 'beyond parental control' ground in the Children and Young Persons Act, to establish the threshold for a possible order."

'I think you can take those matters as known to us,' said Lady Feverel sharply. Robert, manifestly, was being tedious. He carried on bravely.

'Mr. and Mrs. West's household, I understand, consisted, before Michelle was the subject of a place of safety order, of the parents, Michelle and her six-year-old younger brother.'

'I shall summarise baldly the history, with a few dates, which will be reflected in the evidence. The first witness will be Mr. Graham Townley, an educational psychologist who has been involved with the family over the past year or more. I shall also call Mr. Derek Ivins, senior social worker, who was directly involved in the run-up to these proceedings. If the primary conditions are made out, I will call the present social worker, Miss. Jessica Palmer, at the disposal stage.'

'Michelle has been placed with foster parents, Mr. and Mrs. Patrick, for the last four months, that is since the 1st of June. This was on the authority of a place of safety order granted that day, and since then there have been interim care orders every four weeks. Over this time her parents have not asked to see Michelle and she has not recently asked to see them. That pattern was broken today with further shouting and physicality.'

Mrs. West: 'That's a lie.' She spoke with emphasis, impatience touched with anger.

Said the clerk: 'Your time will come, madam.'

Robert continued. 'They have, however, been speaking to each other over the telephone from time to time. Serious difficulties in the relationship have been known to Social Services over the past seven months. At the beginning of March Michelle was seen with a black eye, due, she has claimed, to a fight between herself and her mother.'

Mrs. West: 'That's a lie.'

Lady Feverel intervened serenely. 'Please don't interrupt, Mrs. West. Your barrister will be able to speak for you later, and you will be able to give evidence yourself. Please carry on, Mr. Ford. Please also keep an eye on the clock.'

Robert let the abbreviation of his name stand. At least, unlike Mrs. West, he had not been told not to interrupt.

'A month later, on 1st April, there was another physical confrontation, which caused Michelle to refuse to return home, while her parents refused to have her back at that moment.'

Mrs. West: 'That's a lie.'

Lady Feverel spoke more assertively this time: 'Please be quiet, Mrs. West.'

Robert continued: 'After a few days with a foster family, she was willing to return and her parents were willing to have her back, and she did return home.' Mrs. West this time did not intervene.

'The final incident, which triggered the application for a place of safety order, was on 1st June. On that date what appears to have been a severe physical correction of Michelle by her father, led to her decamping from a first floor balcony and going to a friend's for the night. A medical certificate signed by Dr. Elaine Abrahams – which I now hand in – confirmed not only minor abrasions from her fall, but found some marks possibly inflicted by a leather belt.'

Mrs. West murmured something inaudibly.

Lady Feverel, glancing first at the certificate now before her, asked, leaning forward slightly: 'Are we going to hear from Dr. Abrahams?'

'I understand she is on holiday, Madam.' Robert began to summarise.

'In the local authority's view,' he said, 'Mr. and Mrs. West have had unrealistically high expectations of their daughter – who Mr. Townley describes as having lower than average intelligence. Further, in seeking to insist on the fulfilment of these expectations, when Michelle has been resistant and perhaps could not meet them, their anger has spilled over into physical chastisement of a harsh and unacceptable nature, while Michelle herself is at a stage where she is increasingly ready to meet violence received with violence returned, and resolute against a return home.'

Mrs. West muttered audibly: 'What does he know?'

Lady Feverel: 'Thank you, Mr. Ford.' There was no sign of gratitude on her face.

Robert obstinately continued. 'She has sustained physical harm which must amount to ill-treatment. This, together with rejecting behaviour from her parents, must also give rise to emotional harm which must adversely affect her development. She has therefore been ill-treated and is also beyond her parents' control.'

Spratt rose. 'All this, of course, your worships, is very much disputed.'

Mrs. West (louder this time): 'It's a pack of lies.'

Lady Feverel: 'The Bench understands your feelings, Mrs. West. I've asked you more than once to stop interrupting. If you persist, I'm afraid you'll be asked to leave the court. Your interruptions are not assisting progress.'

Spratt spoke quietly to Mrs. West and she nodded.

Robert continued: 'Mr. Townley, the educational psychologist, is just outside and ready to give evidence. With your permission, Madam, I will call him now.'

The brown haired and suited ed psych was brought in. He stood behind the witness stand, took the oath in a firm voice, a hand holding the card on which the oath was written betraying a slight tremor. He identified himself and his qualifications. Robert began with scene-setting questions.

Little by little the picture of Townley's involvement came into the light, flattened to two dimensions by his highly diplomatic translations of the parental anger and frustration he had observed. His nervousness soon went. He came over as moderate, self-effacing, low-key.

He said that he had been drawn in originally, more than a year before, on the request of Michelle's father, to see her in school, in consequence of the concern of both parents about what they regarded as Michelle's under-achievement. He had found her friendly, chatty, rather young for her age, and lacking in confidence. An intelligence test produced a result – in the mid-seventies – suggesting her to be below average intelligence. He found her lack of academic motivation unsurprising, and commented that this was evident from conversation with her.

'That wouldn't be unusual, would it?' asked Lady Feverel, demonstrating her experience and understanding.

'No.'

He went on. Early in March this year he had met Michelle's parents to discuss his preliminary assessment.

'Was this meeting helpful?' asked Robert.

'It was difficult. Each parent interrupted the other repeatedly. Mrs. West expressed discontent with Michelle on several fronts – she pointed to her behaviour at home as well as to her indifference at school. She expressed concern about what the neighbours thought as a result of overhearing Michelle's hysterical reactions to being corrected. She was particularly abrasive about the company Michelle kept, and mentioned ethnic minority children in particular.'

'Did she use the term ethnic minority children?'

'So far as I remember she used the term "blacks".'

'Did you make any recommendations?'

'Not at that stage. Mr. and Mrs. West had their own proposal. This was to transfer Michelle to a single sex Roman Catholic school – St. Margaret's – and indeed they had already arranged this. It was not what Michelle wanted – she didn't want to lose her school friends and make new ones – but they were determined to go ahead with this transfer.'

'Was this in your view a sensible solution?'

'Possibly,' he replied enigmatically. But his discussion with the parents, coincidentally had taken place a day after a physical confrontation between Michelle and her mother.

'The black eye incident?'

Spratt cut in. 'I must protest against the flagrant leading of the witness.'

'I don't believe I did lead the witness. I'll approach the question in another way,' said Robert. 'Did Mr. and Mrs. West tell you anything about an altercation when you saw them in early March?'

"Yes. Mrs. West said something about it. She said Michelle had gone wild – she used the word 'mental' – and that to avoid her running out of the home, they had shut her into the lounge. She had then gone on to the balcony and screamed continuously."

'Did you see Michelle at some point?'

'Again I protest at the leading of the witness,' interjected Spratt.

'I don't think this question is unacceptable,' said the clerk. 'The answer could be either yes or no.'

Robert nodded to the witness, who confirmed he had seen Michelle later that day and had noted a bruise under her eye.

'Which eye?'

'I can't remember.'

'Did you ask Michelle about it?'

"No, she volunteered. She said she was fed up with getting thumped by her parents. She pointed to her eye and said 'My mum punched me.' She said her Mum had wanted to kill her. She said also that her mother had always preferred her younger brother to her."

'That's a lie,' fulminated Mrs. West.

This time Lady Feverel was silent.

Robert paused for a moment, peering at the large lined notebook below him, where he had listed a series of questions and areas of possible questioning. He had turned two pages instead of one and realising this, went back a page to find his place.

'Did you see any sign of injury in addition to the bruise under the eye?'

'No.'

'Did you reach any general conclusion about the relationship between Michelle and her parents?'

'Not more than provisional. I had the sense that Michelle couldn't do much right in their eyes. I thought that the problems at home were likely to contribute to the problems at school. I did suggest help from the Child Guidance Clinic.'

'Was this suggestion taken up?'

'Not so far as I know.'

'When was your next contact with the family?'

'I had a routine chat with Michelle about three weeks later, towards the end of March. Problems at home seemed to have died down. I had a call from Mrs. West. She asked me to put pressure on Michelle to work harder at school.'

'And did you?'

'I didn't consider that to be my role.'

'Not your role?' Lady Feverel had stepped in, with doubt embedded in her question.

'Not my role,' repeated Mr. Townley.

Robert glanced at Lady Feverel, who had resumed simple watchfulnesss, and noticed that the unhealthily large man on her right seemed close to nodding off. He spoke louder, not looking directly at the target of his increase in volume. 'You saw Michelle again at the beginning of April?'

Robert registered that the eyes of the large bookend had opened more widely, as Townley replied.

'That would be right. I saw her in the late morning at school, on 2nd April. There had been problems the previous day…'

'Your understanding about that was what?'

'I object,' said Spratt, loudly, mouth billowing out below his dark moustache. 'Evidence of the witness's understanding is not evidence of anything…'

Robert said patiently he was seeking only to clarify the

order of events and what was in Mr. Townley's mind to influence his views.

Said Lady Feverel: 'Please continue, Mr. Ford.'

Robert asked what the educational psychologist understood had happened.

Townley continued. 'My understanding was that Mrs. West had left Michelle at the police station – in effect handing care of her over to the police – and that Michelle herself was refusing to return home. That was my understanding.'

Spratt rose and intervened at this moment. 'I object to the approach adopted by my learned friend. Evidence cannot and should not be in the form of what witnesses say they had picked up from others.'

'My concern,' said Robert, ' is only to keep the chronology of events alive. If Mr. and West deny that Michelle was at the beginning of April deposited at the police station, was refusing to go home, and that accordingly a foster home was found for her, it would be helpful to know that.'

Said Spratt: 'My learned friend should make no assumptions as to what is agreed and what is not agreed.'

Robert looked down at his note-book. 'Whatever the exact course of events on 1st April this year,' he said, facing the ed psych again, 'when you saw Michelle the next day what happened?'

Townley explained he had seen Michelle in school where she told him that this time she would not go home. She said they had a fight when her father had hit her and she said that she'd had enough. Robert saw Lady Feverel make a note.

'I asked Michelle what she wanted. She said she'd run away if returned home again. I rang her mother, who said she wouldn't let her back through the front door. Foster care followed, I understand.'

Said Robert: 'I think that was for about six days.'

Spratt: 'Is my learned friend giving evidence?'

Robert, again patient, said that so far as he knew the sequence of events was uncontroversial. The curly-headed clerk said nothing.

Townley continued. 'I saw her again a few days after she was back home following the short time in foster care. She told me she was managing at home, but she did express fear about the future.'

Robert: 'I am now jumping forward a few weeks to the 1st of June, when the place of safety order was made. Did you see her that day or very soon afterwards?'

'I will check my diary.' He took a small black diary from an inside pocket, and turned over the pages. 'I saw her two days later, on 3rd June.'

'Did Michelle tell you anything on that occasion about how she came to be moved to a foster home?'

'She said her father had beaten her up. She said she had spilled a bucket of water and got out of the bedroom window, dropping down from the balcony. She said she had hurt herself a bit, and had gone to a friend's for the night. The next day she had been taken to the Social Services office.'

It went through Robert's mind, at this moment, that it would have been difficult to have described this final incident less evocatively. Did the Bench see it as a serious incident?

He noticed Lady Feverel tap her pen softly on her own notes. He put a final question: 'Following the place of safety order, did you have a view as to whether an early return home for Michelle might threaten her development or welfare?'

'Yes. I was concerned that the tension between parents and daughter could become more dangerous, could result in more serious injury to her. Or to others. I was concerned also about the emotional effect on her.'

It was the peak moment in the ed psych's low-key evidence. Robert saw Lady Feverel write something. The female book-end was impassive, and the male seemed again close to dropping off.

It seemed a good moment to finish, but before doing so, Robert, according to approved model advocate behaviour, told the justices he would turn his back to take instructions. He turned to face Jessica. 'Have I missed anything of significance?' She shook her head.

Robert sat down, suspecting that the educational psychologist's evidence, mildly but conscientiously given, would do. Jonathan Spratt stood up. Lady Feverel spoke: 'Are you going to be very long? We are approaching four o'clock. My colleague has another appointment to keep, as you know.'

'Not long, madam.'

Spratt began: 'Mr. Townley, your last answer was that you were concerned that if Michelle returned home following the place of safety order, more serious injury was possible. Have I got that correct?'

'Yes.'

'Would you agree this was speculation on your part?'

'Yes.'

'Would you agree that it was speculation based on partial information?'

'Yes.'

'I suggest to you that Michelle finds it difficult to accept discipline, discipline at home and discipline at school.'

'I accept that may be the case.'

Spratt pursued his advantage, his self-assurance seemingly unbounded.

'Michelle is over-influenced by her friends, and prefers this to the influence of her parents?'

'That seems to be the case.'

'Isn't a serious danger that being in care – with more freedom than she had at home with her parents – is reinforcing her wish to go her own, undisciplined, immature way?'

Townley, without emphasis, responded: 'That may be true.' After a few seconds, he added: 'But it may be true also that Mr. and Mrs. West, through inappropriate and extreme sanctions, and through not accepting Michelle's academic limitations, were making it more likely Michelle would seek alternative sources of guidance.'

Lady Feverel, Robert noted, had listened to this response with attention.

Spratt continued.

'It is a fact, isn't it, that since Michelle has been in foster care, she has truanted from school on a grand scale?'

'Certainly more than she did previously, as I understand it.'

'She hasn't recently been in school for more than fifty percent of the time, has she?'

'I understand that may be correct. I haven't seen the figures.'

'So in considering the risks for Michelle of returning home, it is important to balance against them the very real risks for her of remaining in foster care?' Spratt spoke the words 'very real risks' with slow stress, causing the large and sleepy book-end to move his eyes.

'Indeed.'

'Thank you, Mr. Townley.' Spratt sat down.

Robert rose quickly. 'Just one re-examination question, Madam. Mr. Townley, to dispel any uncertainties, however incomplete your knowledge, what is your view of any risks to Michelle should the court make no order, and should she then have to return home?'

The ed psych said after a few seconds:

'As I indicated earlier, I would be concerned family tensions would result in more serious injury to Michelle or to others, and would be also concerned about the emotional effect on her of returning to an unstable situation.' Lady Feverel made a note.

Mr. Townley's baptism of fire was over. Robert's was not. The battle would recommence on another day. But at least he would have a breathing space before he had to go over the top once more.

It was past four o'clock and the clerk provided dates ahead on which the case could be heard. The first was a week later, and two dates after that, weeks apart, were offered.

'Is there no provision,' asked Robert, 'for a complex care case to be listed on consecutive days?'

'Not in this court,' said the clerk, who had been noticeably quieter during this afternoon session than in the morning. 'Do you want the interim care order renewed?'

'Oh yes,' said Robert, who had quite forgotten about this essential requirement.

Lady Feverel: 'Interim care order renewed until Wednesday next week.'

Said the usher. 'All stand, please.' All stood, and both Spratt and Robert bowed to the risen magistrates.

Lady Feverel and her book-ends made their exit, followed by the clerk.

Mr. and Mrs. West and Spratt and the usher were next to leave, and Robert and Jessica were left with the ed psych, who had, though given permission to leave, remained in the little court room. He said to Robert, anxiously: 'Was my evidence all right? I tried to avoid being dramatic.' Robert reassured him.

'It's always better to under-state than to over-state.'

'Oh, did I under-state?'

'No, not at all,' said Robert.

Graham Townley left, reassured, and Robert asked Jessica a similar question about his own advocacy. 'Was it all right, do you think?'

'I'm impressed,' said Jessica. 'I'm sorry if I told you we needed a barrister. I've had barristers representing us that wouldn't have been as good as you were.'

'And some, I'm sure, that would have been better.'

'We won't quarrel about that.'

'Case not over yet,' said Robert. 'I could make an unholy mess of it next week. We should make a time to sort out your own evidence. I'd prefer to have a proof.'

'A proof? Melanie didn't say anything about that. What's a proof?'

'It's a statement for our use, not the other side's. A proof of evidence. Is now a good time?'

'We could adjourn to the café.'

They did so. They sat with mugs of over-strong tea and had the café to themselves, save for a large and sleepy dog which put Robert in mind of the large and sleepy book-end next to Lady Feverel. Jessica had her file with her, and over the next hour Robert made detailed notes, followed by a promise to put a typed version of Jessica's proof of evidence in the internal post the following day.

At one moment Robert asked what Jessica thought of Mr. West's punishment methods. 'Barbaric,' she said. 'I should guess he was beaten silly by his own father.' 'Has Mr. West been asked about that?' Jessica replied that he had, but had refused to reply, just as both parents had refused to give social workers their dates of birth and other details about their personal histories.

'I do wonder,' she went on, 'whether Mrs. West has mental health issues. Of course I haven't dared to suggest that. A psychiatrist might be able to tease out something. It could shed light on her inability to reflect and change.'

The café was about to close. 'Is it too early for a drink?' he said hesitantly.

'All right then,' she said. They moved, on Jessica's suggestion, and taking their separate cars, to a public house, the Lordship Tavern, nearer to Wood Green. Robert ordered a pint of beer for himself and a half for Jessica, overruling her attempted insistence on buying the drinks. 'Next time,' said Robert, placatory. He resumed talk about the case.

'One thing strikes me. It seems to me that using a belt on a child, male or female, is utterly beyond the pale, but is that how your colleagues see it?'

'Mostly...but we don't really have a clear department policy about physical chastisement. Some social workers, like my senior Derek, are cautious about making a fuss. And some magistrates approve of a good whacking, to judge from some results we've had. On the other hand, in our area office, there is a Team headed by someone who is more critical of parents, much more, than Derek.'

'Who's that.'

'Enid Prosser. She has had a go at Derek more than once. They had an argument about a parental rights resolution passed a few months back.'

'A case of yours?'

'No, not mine.'

Robert did not let on that he had heard about this case. He brought up instead that he'd read in the local newspaper that the cane as a disciplinary instrument was now banned in Haringey schools. He then changed the subject.

'Is there much social life in your office?'

'You mean parties and things?'

'I suppose so.'

'Well, birthdays get celebrated. And' – she hesitated, then carried on – 'at the moment some of us are involved in preparing an entertainment for the delectation of anyone in the department who wants to come.'

'Organised by Social Services?'

'Not by, but for. A few of us are putting it together. Tickets only, if we manage to get it off the ground.'

'Sounds interesting. Can anyone be involved – such as me?'

Jessica hesitated again, then said: 'Why not? We've got a meeting on Friday evening, as it happens. And in this very pub.'

'You're heavily involved?'

'Yes. Up to my neck.'

'Who else – if I might be so bold as to ask?'

'Emily Frost from our office for one. There are a couple of men – Frank Jackson from another office is one.'

'Are you sure I'll be welcome.'

'Of course – so long as a little job can be found for you.'

'Then I'm on.'

'Six thirty here on Friday, then,' she said, gaily.

Though telling himself he should not make comparisons, Robert could not help thinking how attracted to Jessica he was. Her personality was as appealing as her looks; only her wedding ring was a let-down. She had a more stimulating, more outward-going personality than Beth. But Beth had something elusive about her, something unusual which drew him in. He was, in fact, besotted with her.

9

In the Legal Building...

The next day, Thursday, rain returned with a vengeance. As Robert left his flat, running the few yards to the car parked close by, cursing himself for leaving his umbrella inside it the previous day, the downpour dashed at him, wetting his head and shoulders and more, but not dislodging his good temper. He had risen and set off later than on previous days, especially as this was not a court day, taking advantage of the 'flexible hours' work regime which was in place in some borough departments.

The scheme decreed that so long as thirty five hours were worked in every week, the individual staff member had some discretion as to when to start and when to finish. There were, however, earliest allowed start and finish times, and a lunch interval could not be classed as working time. A vital point was that overtime worked could be clawed back by taking time off later.

As Robert's current working week was on track easily to exceed forty hours, he was entitled to take a morning or afternoon off. Once on the second floor of the legal building, he handed to Mary a completed flexi-leave form, which indicated he would be claiming the afternoon next day for his own disposal. Edward Shimble had not yet arrived and George Ballam was speaking with Mary about, Robert gathered, a petty cash difficulty.

He paused, and learned that Pat, the supervisor of a small group of staff who responded to house buyer queries about 'local land charges', was at home unwell; and the key to the petty cash box for which she was responsible was at home with her. The key was now needed to open the cash box.

George to Mary: 'Did Mr. Shimble make any progress getting the petty cash box key back from Pat?'

Mary: "I believe her husband's going to drop it into us this morning. Mr. Shimble rang her at home yesterday to ask for it. She said she had to hold on to it. She said that as she is the person responsible for the key, she could only give it to her senior officer. Then Mr. Shimble said to her – he was being very patient for Mr. Shimble – 'Am I not your senior officer then?' She said, after a second or two, 'Oh yes, you must be.' He said – he was being very patient – 'I'm sure you're right.'"

Mary added, as Shimble entered the office, depositing a full-length dripping umbrella in a stand: 'I think Pat was being a bit slow on the uptake.'

Shimble contributed with a regretful air: 'She is, alas, not the only one in this building who is slow on the uptake,' and entered his office, nodding to Robert. George Ballam said good morning to Shimble's back and left the room.

Soon after, Robert knocked on Melanie Cusack's door and looked in.

'Hello Melanie.'

'Hello Robert.' Her sharp, narrow face produced a slight smile. 'What can I do for you?'

'It's just that I've been asked – well, told – to do a report to the Social Services Committee about parental rights resolutions…'

The disagreeable expression announced its presence.

'Strange it wasn't me that was asked,' she said brusquely.

'Or told.'

'Even told. I'm now number two in our pecking order I suppose.'

Robert had wondered whether this necessary conversation would be a pleasurable one. He dodged bullets as best he could.

'I imagine that Eddie has decided I'd better cut my Committee teeth sooner rather than later.'

He pursued his objective. 'There was a recent resolution which smelt of bad fish or something similar.'

'Bad fish?'

She looked at him uncomprehendingly.

'Sorry. I'm speaking figuratively. I've been told that a recent resolution upset one or two members.'

'The Firth children,' said Melanie, definitively. 'It was a dog's dinner. I had correspondence about it. Enid Prosser was up to no good on that one.'

'So what was the problem?'

Melanie's memory of the case was specific. 'Two children. Twins aged about three. They'd been in voluntary care for a year or eighteen months because of the mother's mental illness, though she wasn't long in hospital. They were fostered out in Lincolnshire. The foster mother wanted to adopt them. She was a personal friend of Enid Prosser's, believe it or not. Then the mother committed suicide.'

'Sounds as if adoption for the twins was a reasonable bet,' Robert offered.

'Only if you forget the father. The parents were divorced, and the father had remarried, but was mainly out of the picture. He hadn't visited the children for a while. A few days after the mother's suicide he heard about it from someone and he rang in to ask Enid Prosser for the twins.'

'Yes. His legal right, wasn't it? Was there anything against him?'

'Yes. Enid Prosser. Because for one thing he hadn't visited the children much, and for another she knew the

Comptroller and Treasurer's department had been after him for contributions.'

'For financial contributions as a parent of children in care?'

'Exactly. Our Treasurer's department is hot on parents paying their dues if they can afford it. And I should think so too. He'd not been answering letters about contributions. Letters asking for information about his means.'

'What about his not visiting them? Was there a reason?'

'He said later he'd been working seven days a week, and he'd been keeping his head down because the mother hated him and was mad.'

'And then she killed herself,' said Robert. 'What a tragedy.'

Melanie went on. 'She'd overdosed a couple of times before that. Anyway, Enid Prosser tried to wrap up the twins' adoption by her friend with an emergency resolution, giving a kind of green light to the adoption plan. The report to Committee damned the father in a few words for persistently neglecting the children, by not bothering to visit them or contribute to their upkeep. Nothing good was said about him. Later he objected to the resolution and so we had to hand the case to the court.'

'The court threw out the resolution?'

'It would have done. He'd kept his head down, but he hadn't persistently neglected them. That was an exaggeration. Enid Prosser backed down when she saw the cards were stacked up against her.'

'And stacked up against the adoption plan.'

'And stacked up, as you say, against the adoption plan. The resolution lapsed by consent.'

'The twins went to the father?'

'They did.'

'Better for them?'

'Maybe,' she said, not very interested. 'Anyway, Enid Prosser came out of it with egg on her face.'

'Figuratively.'

'Figuratively,' Melanie agreed, without a glimmer of a smile. Her cold but precise summary had betrayed no sympathy for anyone involved.

Robert asked to see the correspondence.

Melanie added: 'I was the obvious person to do this Committee report.'

'You could take it up with Eddie.'

'Oh, what the hell. I've got better things to do.'

Robert repeated: 'Would you mind if I looked at the correspondence?'

Melanie, without grace, located in a desk drawer a thin sheaf of papers secured by a pin in the thinnest of cardboard folders and handed this to him without more words.

Back in his room, Robert turned over the pages slowly. Melanie's incisive summary was corroborated, but there was more. There was a note of a meeting with Enid Prosser attended by Melanie. This revealed that the social worker allocated to the family had been off sick for months before the mother's suicide, and before that had not tried very hard to speak with the father about his role in the children's lives. He worked full-time. She would have had to arrange an evening home visit, and had not got round to doing this. The note also showed the father had arranged his visits to the children directly with the foster mother, and that two of these had not got on to the social work record at the time.

Enid Prosser, as supervising senior social worker, had formed the impression, it seemed, on inadequate information, that he was a walking disaster as a father and had concluded in a hurry that the children's adoption by her friend, their foster mother, would be the best way of safeguarding their futures. It was a crude response to a tragic development. No wonder councillors had asked questions.

The unfairness towards the father, Robert concluded, was compounded by his not being notified of the resolution for more than a fortnight. All that said, the resolution had at least staved off a sudden and confusing change in the children's situation from being stably in foster care to an unknown situation with the father and also with the step-mother, whom, it was said, the twins had never met.

What had led to the eventual decision to transfer the children from their foster mother to their father and his new wife – who lived in a south London suburb – was the allocation of a new social worker to the case. She had, between the date of the father's objection to the resolution and the court hearing date a few weeks later, visited him and his wife three times, soaking up information about their situation and viewing their accommodation. She confirmed that the father was working, though badly paid, wished to care for the children with his present wife, who was warmly offering to share the parenting role, and that there was no obvious reason why their offer should not be taken up. A supervised meeting between the couple and the twins had been encouraging.

The new social worker, armed with this substantial information, had managed to persuade Enid Prosser, a few days before the grown-ups were due to be in court, that the children should be moved to the father's care. She had also persuaded the Treasurer's department to write off arrears of contributions.

Melanie had not mentioned a further aspect of the case: that months after the children's move to their father's care he had made a formal complaint which took the form of a letter written by his solicitors, Brady & Co. This letter had denounced the behaviour of Enid Prosser in denying the father his children, following the mother's death, and in promoting their adoption by her fostering friend. There was a note by Melanie of a telephone conversation with Enid Prosser about this. She had written down Enid Prosser's unsympathetic words as follows: 'What's he got to complain about? He's got his children back, hasn't he?'

A perfunctory account of another telephone conversation between Melanie and Director Michael Stone, Robert saw, reported Stone as describing Enid Prosser's work as being her life, and her approach to child care work being 'almost evangelically anti-parent.' She had been admonished by Stone for prematurely writing off the twins' father and proposing the twins' adoption by her friend.

Robert glanced through the pages again, and was struck this time by the name of the social worker in Enid Prosser's team who had resolved matters in favour of the twins' joining their father. It was Emily Frost, the lively and attractive woman whom he had met twice at court, and one of those active, Jessica had told him, in organising the entertainment in which he would himself be taking some part.

It was time to make a start on the parental rights report. By lunch-time Robert had dictated a draft. It began with a bland and neutral explanation of the law establishing the council's powers to pass these resolutions, explaining the procedures that had to be followed and the rights of parents to contest resolutions.

It went on to advise that, before any resolution, full inquiries should clarify whether there were any prospects for the child's return to the family. He proposed too that when resolutions were passed, parents should be informed within seven days. Perhaps that would appease the doubters.

Later he handed the typed draft to Mary for consideration by Edward Shimble. It was now for Eddie to progress the matter further.

The following Wednesday the three-year-old Amy Stewart's case was up for Tottenham juvenile court consideration. As that day was also assigned for the continuation of teenager Michelle's case, Robert was going to have to arrange for someone else to apply for an interim care order on Amy. He had no choice, it seemed but to ask Melanie Cusack if she could stand in. It did not seem unreasonable, as she had previously dumped Michelle's case on him. But it needed readiness to risk rage.

He advanced to her room boldly.

'Hello again Melanie.'

'Hello Robert.'

'As you know I'm handling your Michelle West affair,' he began.

'It's not mine, any more, Robert. You took it. It's yours.'

'Not disputed. I'm handling it,' he said patiently, 'the case that was once yours and is now mine.'

'Isn't that case finished now?'

'No – it could be half-way done, though. The evidence has begun, and will continue next Wednesday.'

'So what slowed it down?'

'Among other things, the barrister for the parents – Jonathan Spratt.'

'You were against Jonathan Spratt? ' Melanie had spoken louder, betraying, Robert surmised, some trepidation about Jonathan Spratt as an adversary in court.

'Yes.'

'That couldn't have been much fun.' After a pause. 'Still, it is a straightforward case.'

'I hope so. Relatively, at least.'

'You're not pushing it back at me, surely?'

'No, of course not.'

'So to what do I owe the honour…?'

'I came to ask you about another case I've been saddled with. It's about a mother medicating a three-year-old child with phenergan – she denies it – when the child needs phenergan like I need prussic acid. Amy Stewart is the child. I was at the case conference, and now we've got a first hearing on Wednesday. I can't do both cases.'

'Oh. You'd better instruct Counsel. I couldn't possibly do it at this short notice. George Ballam has a list of Counsel we use. You'll excuse me, I must get on with other things.'

She reached for a closed envelope of papers and opened it.

The interview was over.

George Ballam was not in his room, so Robert called in to see the square-faced Bill Bowman, who welcomed him with 'Hello then, squire'.

'I've got to instruct Counsel for a case next Wednesday. I gather George Ballam has a list of Counsel we instruct, but he's not in his room at the moment. Do you have a copy, by any chance?'

'Actually, I have the list. I don't think George has one.'

'Melanie told me he has a list.'

'I think, old son, she meant me. For George read Bill. For care cases, I know we often use Sophie Williams at Garden Court. Melanie's used her a few times. Speak to Walter the Clerk. I'll write down the phone number for you.' He did so.

'How long has Sophie Williams been qualified?'

'How many years' call, you mean?' said Bill, shaking his head at Robert's contempt for proper terminology.

'Yes.'

'I think four or five.'

'What's the usual fee for an interim care order application? Half a day at the juvenile court?'

'Probably about £75. But you'll have to negotiate with Walter. He's richer than most of his barristers. Probably earns £25,000 or more a year. He's a rich alcoholic.'

'Walter's easy to negotiate with?'

'So long as you buy him a drink occasionally, preferably a double. I'm joking. He's OK, is Walter.'

Robert returned to his room and his telephone call was soon through to the suave and mellow voice owned by Walter, Clerk to the barristers at Garden Court, Temple. Robert explained who he was and said he looked forward to a fruitful relationship with Walter's Chambers. He went on to book Sophie Williams for the following Wednesday and promised a brief by close of play on Monday.

'Oh, yes,' he added, 'how long has Sophie been at the Bar?'

'Just a year. She's done very well.'

'One year.'

'Yes, one year, completed in the summer.' Robert, amused by Bill Bowman's over-confident and under-accurate estimate of the experience Sophie Williams had under her belt, and torn between staying with her and demanding an unknown but more experienced counsel, took the easy course and stayed with her.

'The fee?' he asked.

'When I have the brief I'll ring you to agree a fee,' said Walter. Robert asked what the maximum would be. Walter replied:

'I shouldn't worry. We won't kill the goose that lays the golden eggs.'

It was time to ring Jessica Palmer. She happened to be in the area office. 'Hello again, Jessica. I'm chasing you about Amy.'

Jessica confirmed that she had given Amy's mother the notice of care proceedings with another copy for Amy's Dad.

'Fortunately,' she added, 'Dad was out or I might have left with a few bruises. She said they were still going on holiday on Saturday for a week and wouldn't give me the address where they were going. She did say it was her mum's.'

'Sounds worrying. Are you going to accept that?'

'No choice, I think. Derek says let it lie till they come back.'

'And Amy? How is she?'

'She's been in nursery this week and the staff haven't had special cause for concern, which is a relief. The health visitor says she's OK too.'

'I assume we still want an interim care order?'

'That's what the case conference ruled and I have to agree with that.'

'Can you cope with giving evidence, if need be, in two cases that day?'

'I can cope.'

'I've lined up a barrister for Amy's case.'

'Who?'

'Sophie Williams. I've booked her on our litigation manager's recommendation. She's one of our regulars.'

'I think she did a case of mine, nearly a year ago. She told me she'd only just been called to the Bar then and it was her second case. All right, but don't you think you should be using barristers with more practice, at least in sensitive cases?'

Robert went wide of the question. 'I'll ask her to be at court early to meet you. You'll need to have with you the details of when you gave the notices to the parents.'

'Noted.'

She had been a bit short with him. She had pressed him for a barrister for Michelle; now she wasn't happy with the barrister he'd got for Amy. Was Jessica doing what Melanie had called getting above herself?

He decided Jessica was justified and Melanie not, before calling at George Ballam's room. He wasn't there, so Robert left a folded note on George's desk. The note simply asked how Albert Clack was. Robert was, in fact, chiefly hoping to be brought up to date with George's situation vis-a-vis Edward Shimble, but he avoided making reference, even indirectly to that in his note, in case wandering eyes – such as those of Bill Bowman – came across it and opened it in his suspected capacity as Shimble's intelligence department.

He was back in his own room, when, after a few minutes, George Ballam entered, politely knocking first. He told Robert that Albert was still critically ill and that if he recovered, it was likely that he would not be able to return to work. Robert nodded sympathetically, and asked if Shimble was still imputing blame to George for Albert's collapse.

'By implication, yes. I've just been with him, and he made some remark about it. I did manage to tell him what had led up to it. The previous Friday – three days before he was ill – Albert's car was stolen from the car park. He reported the theft and the car turned up somewhere in Wood Green minus wheels. So Albert spent the weekend getting new wheels and then putting them on the car himself. And he didn't even have a proper jack.'

'Hardly your fault.'

'Eddie just said that carrying the post to the Post Office can't have helped, although Albert hadn't actually done that. I let that go. But now Eddie wants me to chase solicitors who are down to do committee reports to get them in promptly. He's given me a list. You're on it. I'm chasing you.'

'The parental rights resolution report,' said Robert.

'That's right.'

'But I've done it and passed it to Eddie, so you should be chasing him. Why don't you go and badger him about it right now?'

George Ballam began to laugh, first hesitantly, then more freely. He then queried:

'Did you know the expression Eddie uses for a slap on the wrist?'

'What is it?'

'An arse-welting. I've heard him say it a couple of times about junior staff with a bad timekeeping record.'

'Well, if Eddie doesn't read my report and approve it and get it back to me promptly, that's what I recommend you give him in pursuance of his directive to you.'

'I'll give it serious thought,' said George.

10

A New Relationship?

Robert arrived at Beth's home in Tottenham that Thursday evening at a moment when the steady rain of many hours past was finally faltering. She lived in an improvised two bedroom ground floor flat in a two storey house close to Philip Lane, not very different from the one Robert was sharing, but better furnished and decorated. Beth opened the front door in answer to his ring, greeted him with a simple 'Hello Robert', turned and walked back down the corridor to the kitchen-cum-dining room, where a young man was drinking coffee. Beth introduced him as Paul, her flat-mate. Soon afterwards, Paul withdrew to his own room where, said Beth, he had his own television.

Robert had brought with him a bottle of dry white wine, which he handed over. She thanked him, saying he could open it right away if he liked and that the meal would not be long. He sat down. A curry was evolving in the kitchen and only small talk passed between them until it was served at the modest table which Beth had already laid for two. Robert, who had put off opening the wine, now did so and filled the two wine glasses. He had continued to feel and act as if he were in a rather formal situation.

Said Beth, looking straight at him, above the heaped plates between them: 'You may have thought I was being a bit forward in inviting you round.'

Robert said he hadn't thought of it in that way and that maybe it meant that they had clicked on some level. He said he hoped so.

Beth said she hoped so too, and that she had thought that inviting him round might be an ice-breaker, even if, she added, with a small laugh and without much optimism, the ice froze over again later.

This seemed too wintry an observation, and Robert said that he hadn't thought their friendship had an Arctic feel about it.

'Maybe not, but I'm not really as sociable as most people.'

She went on to say that she hoped he wouldn't draw conclusions from the fact that she'd invited him to her home. She looked at him calmly.

Robert, moved as before by the striking blueness of her eyes, her milky skinned face and the golden mass of her hair, as well as by her unflinching composure, did not shy away from her meaning.

'I didn't assume that a meal meant bed, if that was what you thought I might assume.'

He had, however, thought it might mean that, and was not sure whether to smile or not as she was not smiling.

Suddenly she laughed again, more freely this time, and her face became human sunshine. 'You're right. It doesn't mean that. And I'm throwing you out at ten thirty because I've got to get up early tomorrow. I had a late night last night.'

Tempted to ask, recalling that Beth had told him 'no one serious was around at the moment,' whether this had involved a 'non-serious' man, Robert decided not to, and not to ask how late the night had been. He said: 'Ten thirty it is then.'

They proceeded to eat. For a minute he had nothing to say, other than to congratulate her on the tastiness of the curry, and to refill quickly their empty glasses. Then he began: 'I hope that by ten thirty I will have persuaded you to meet up again. My place is a bit bare at the moment. I only moved in a fortnight ago and I'm not well organised yet.' He explained he had a flat mate too, and asked how Beth got on with Paul.

'Quite well,' she said. He had been a boyfriend, she went on, though it was nothing special and he was involved with someone else at the same time, but they'd become just friends before they decided to flat share. 'I think he's got at least three girlfriends now. *Men,*' she added, dismissively.

'And you?' She brushed aside the question. 'I have a policy of non-involvement.'

So what did that mean? He didn't pursue it. 'You've never been married?'

'No. You?'

'No.'

As they talked, Beth became, in her deliberate way, as readily communicative as on the evening of their theatre outing. Her father had died when she was nine, and she had never got along well with her mother. She had left home in her late teens to live with a boyfriend. She had been the one to exit after two years of cohabitation and her partner had been upset.

'We had become friends more than lovers,' she concluded. 'There wasn't any passion left.' Since then she had had a few relationships, but had not cohabited with anyone.

She went on to say, as if she had not already told him during their theatre visit, that her most recent serious relationship, when still in Bedfordshire, had ended when her boyfriend had gone to live and work in America and, despite earlier promised arrangements, had not, once there, wanted her to follow him. She added that she had become depressed.

'I was sitting in my flat, drinking a bottle of wine a night,' she said. 'It was no good. I needed to move.' So she had changed jobs and come to London. The Social Services administrative job was just temporary. She asked Robert little about himself. He asked her, chiding himself for not having asked earlier, if she'd had the result of her Civic Centre interview.

'I got the job,' she said, without expressing great pleasure.

'I transfer to the Civic Centre in a month's time.' He congratulated her and wished her well with her new post.

They discussed how they liked to spend their spare time, and Beth said she needed quite a bit of time to herself. She liked travel. And reading.

'Me too,' said Robert. 'Ever read Eric Ambler? Thrillers from the 1930s and onwards? Master of atmosphere and suspense and dark deeds?'

'Never heard of him.'

When the deadline set for ten thirty came, it passed, as they were engrossed in conversation. It was Robert who got up and said it was past her chucking out time and that he would phone her to invite her out for a meal. This seemed the right thing to say, and he kissed her on the cheek.

'Mind you do phone,' she said, before the front door closed and he withdrew into the street. He was oblivious to the fact that the rain had now come to a complete halt, that the sky was clear and that the pavement was dry. Driving back to Crouch End, part of his mind was pensive, another part excited.

He had not volunteered telling Beth that he would be involved in the entertainment to be staged by Jessica and others, and would be taking part in a meeting about it next day. He wondered what Beth's opinions were of Emily and Jessica. His social life in London was certainly flowering. As for the future of his relationship with Beth, nothing seemed certain. The more he learned about her, the more uncertain he felt about what sort of person she was.

He was increasingly convinced, on the other hand, that his tenancy partner, the other Robert, was the stereotypical male house slattern. Back at the flat he was horrified to see the kitchen sink overflowing on a grand scale with dirty dishes that were not his own. It was time to say something.

11

A Meeting of Solicitors and Managers

It was Mr. Shimble's practice to have, every two months or so, a meeting of solicitors and managers. Such meetings were intended to hone the department's organisation and procedures, to assist in responses to legislative changes taking place, and to convey Shimble's wishes to his subordinates. Robert's first experience of such a meeting was on the Friday afternoon of his second week at Haringey. He had, after submitting his statement of intention to take the afternoon off, been told belatedly of the meeting, and had decided it would be wrong to miss it.

By two thirty, the scheduled start time, those attending (save for a small number on leave or caught up with other duties they could not escape) were congregated in the meeting room on the first floor of the building. They awaited the borough's 'supremo' solicitor. With them was seated a special guest, none other than Chief Executive 'Smiler' Roland Trask. He had simply asked Shimble if he could attend one of these meetings and Shimble had been unable to think of a satisfactory reason for denying him that opportunity.

Trask, a good looking, tall, friendly, thirty-something man with a mane of dark brown hair tamed for the moment by a neat hair-cut, wished, he told those already present, to get to know legal personnel better. At this point Mary appeared in the doorway. She apologised for Shimble's late arrival, and explained he was on the telephone to the Chairman of the Housing Committee, and would be with them as soon as he could get off the phone.

'That will be Councillor McConnell,' said Trask. 'Councillor McConnell is not known for keeping telephone conversations short.' He smiled broadly.

'I call him Councillor O'Reilly,' said Bill Bowman, not in the least fazed by the presence of the Council's most senior officer and generally ready to practise his expertise in stereotyping people from backgrounds outside his own East End origins.

Said Trask, perplexed. 'But his name is McConnell, not O'Reilly.'

'Bill's always getting people's names wrong,' remarked Colin Masson.

'I think Councillor McConnell,' said Bill Bowman, wisely retreating from the confusion he had caused, 'may be concerned about the judicial review case coming up over someone being refused accommodation as a homeless person. I've been getting together the brief to Counsel on that.'

'Do you do that on the big paper?' asked Trask.

This was an oddly simplistic query from a qualified lawyer, presumably accustomed at some point in the past to prepare briefs on large sheets of paper folded over and secured by a pink ribbon, and Bill Bowman opened his eyes wide. 'Yes, we do,' he said, preparing to say more, but holding his tongue for the present.

At this moment Mary, harassed-looking and breathless, paused in the doorway again, informing the Chief Executive that she was sorry, but had a call for him from the Civic Centre. He got up and followed her.

Said Bill, when the door had shut, as if speaking to a childlike Trask: 'Yes, we do the brief on the big paper. And then we put a nice pink ribbon round it and then we send it to a man called a barrister' (he pronounced the three syllables slowly). 'They're,' he said, enlarging on his explanation with heavy irony and slow solemn emphasis, as if he were educating

Trask in the very basics of the legal profession's activities, 'the men who wear the wigs.'

Said Colin Masson: 'You really should learn to refer to the Chief Executive with respect, Bill.'

'I can guess why they phoned Smiler from the Civic Centre,' said Bill, unabashed and irrepressible. 'One of the toilets has run out of paper, the small paper. He's telling them now to go out and buy a roll. But he can't think of the name of the shop they should go to or tell them how much the roll will cost. Maybe someone should go and help him.'

'Really Bill,' said Colin, while others tittered. A short silence thereafter was broken by the re-entry of Roland Trask, accompanied by Shimble and also Mary, who was tasked on these occasions to take minutes.

Shimble, sitting down with a sigh, as his cannon-ball stomach sank into position, opened the proceedings, wearing as kindly an expression as he could without discomfort achieve. 'I apologise to all of you for the delay. Mr. Trask is our guest today.' Such was the extent of his welcome for his formal superior. He went straight on. 'We must get down to work.'

The much younger Trask, not discouraged and with unreserved friendliness, contributed: 'Could everyone introduce themselves? I'm Roland Trask, for anyone who hasn't met me before.'

'You know me,' said Colin. 'And me,' said Bill. 'And me,' said George. Some introduced themselves by name, including Melanie Cusack, who had not joined in the amusement occasioned by Bill Bowman's derisive remarks about the Chief Executive. When she spoke up, Trask immediately said 'Yes, of course. We've met.' When Robert's turn came, Trask greeted him.

'Ah,' said the Chief Executive, 'the new Social Services Solicitor. Melanie's assistant.'

Said Shimble: 'I think colleague, rather than assistant. Agreed Melanie?' He asked with his little smile, an event which converted his pressed-together equals-sign mouth into a slight curve.

'Certainly, but Robert's presence is certainly assisting me.'

'Now then,' said Shimble. 'First item on the agenda. Oh yes, before we get to that I should mention that I've been told Albert Clack is out of danger and on the way to a degree of recovery. Whether he'll be able to return to work is another matter. I'm sure you, George' (he glanced at George Ballam) 'and in fact all of you will be glad to hear that.' He turned to a piece of paper on the table in front of him.

'First item then. The legal library. There are two issues. One is its untidiness. Two, books borrowed are not always being returned when they should be. The situation has deteriorated, I would say, over the last six months. George, do you have suggestions?'

'Well, keeping the library tidy is one of the jobs of the deeds clerk…'

'Muniments officer, to give him his proper title,' corrected Shimble.

'And unfortunately he's been off sick for three weeks,' said George.

'It's not a large task,' said Shimble.

'I'm expecting him back on Monday.'

'What about the non-return of books?'

Colin Masson, not wishing to empower the Borough Solicitor to turn the knife in George Ballam's body more frequently than could be avoided, interposed: 'I think a number of us are guilty of letting borrowed books outstay their welcome on our desks. Perhaps we should resolve today that all books we are not actually using should be returned to the library promptly. By the way,' he added, looking at Shimble, "I take it the term 'books' includes Acts of Parliament?"

'Yes, of course.'

Colin continued. 'You'll recall the arcana concerning the 1977 Minibus Act?'

'We won't elaborate on that,' said Shimble, guillotining discussion on the topic as neatly as he might have guillotined George Ballam. At that moment his unsmiling lips were tight and straight enough to suggest the edges of a carefully folded sheet of paper.

Said George: 'Perhaps we should also have a simple register – just an exercise book or similar which stays in the library and in which every member of staff borrowing a book records what it is and the date, and enters the date again when returning it.'

Shimble: 'A suggestion of that kind would have been welcome six months ago, but it's still not too late to have it now.'

George: 'I'll see that the deeds clerk…muniments officer… is provided with such a register when he returns to work on Monday.'

Shimble. 'We seem to be agreed on these points. Minuted, Mary?' She nods. 'It's a rather sloppy state of affairs and I don't want to see it continuing. Next item. Quantifying the work we do here. In the light of the reduction of the central government grant to councils, and the council's decision to make savings, I have decided we should carry out an efficiency review. Part of this process will involve providing and assessing numbers of live cases, and hearings over twelve months, and setting these against workloads of individuals and sections.'

Colin Masson interjected. 'The other day, I note, a majority of Labour councillors voted in full Council to refuse to implement cuts against the Leader's wishes.'

'The loony left,' said Shimble. 'I expect they'll soon come to heel.'

'One can understand their frustration, of course,' said Trask, more tolerantly. Shimble paid no heed to him.

'Can you summarise the position for Litigation, Bill?'

Bill Bowman reported that the Litigation section was carrying eighteen hundred current cases – mostly housing possession cases, but also Public Health and Rent Act prosecutions of landlords – and he produced another large figure for the number of court hearings.

Said Colin Masson: 'I'm not sure how reliable a guide those figures are as…'

Shimble swept in with disapproval: 'We don't need to carry out an analysis here and now. It would be a waste of time. I suggest that is done as soon as practicable after this meeting. Minuted, Mary?'

She nodded.

'We should be aware, in passing, too,' Shimble went on, 'that the conveyancing section will almost certainly require expansion as a result of the government's intention to introduce an entitlement by council tenants to buy the accommodation they are presently renting. At a discount.'

Said Colin: 'Dependent on the smooth passage of this legislation, which is certainly controversial.'

Shimble resumed: 'We don't need to get into the politics of that. I'm sure many council tenants will be delighted … delighted…with the opportunity to become owners. I'll mention one other item for information. Venetian blinds. For the last six months I've been requesting these, via George, to prevent sunlight from interfering too much with our work. It's especially a problem in my office. George – is there any more information from the Property Maintenance Surveyor, as to when the blinds are likely to be installed?'

George: 'I've been ringing him weekly.'

Shimble: 'Weekly doesn't seem to be achieving much. What about daily?'

George: 'I don't know about daily.'

Shimble: 'This is becoming increasingly tiresome.' Turning to Trask: 'As you will know from life in the Civic Centre, Roland, minor administrative issues can be utterly intractable. Some Council staff seem more interested in obstruction than facilitation.'

Trask (who nodded, smiling as he spoke): 'I'm sure all staff have the public interest at heart.'

Shimble: 'Does anyone have an 'any other business' item?'

No one did. There was silence while participants in the meeting awaited release.

Said Roland Trask: 'Thank you for inviting me. It's good to see that everything here is going like clockwork, and that everyone gets on with everyone else. I always think that's most important.' There was not the slightest hint of irony in his voice, and he looked around the gathering with open-hearted approval.

The room quickly emptied, leaving Colin and Robert, the slowest to rise, alone together.

Robert: 'The discussion about workload figures was cut short.'

Colin: 'It certainly was. It would have embarrassed Bowman and Eddie to be put under the microscope in the Chief Executive's presence. Bill's figures are fantasy figures.'

'In what way?'

'He was including the dead amongst the living, for one thing. He said there are eighteen hundred live Litigation files. The truth is that a third of these are in fact dead as Diogenes, not live cases, though they have not yet been archived. These cases are finished, done, extinct, archived or not.'

'I see.'

'Again, another big tranche of Litigation files – applications for housing possessions – are only live in the sense that they have been treated as live for six months following the grant of possession, in case an appeal or some other application follows.'

'Two big exaggerations, then.'

'Two mighty falsehoods. And on top of that, the number of court hearings Bill cited was wildly out. You can have as many summonses as thirty in a single Public Health prosecution, all heard at the same time. Bill called each summons a hearing, which is ridiculous.'

'It's like the way,' suggested Robert, 'the count of fish caught got enhanced in Jerome K Jerome's *Three Men in a Boat*.'

'Precisely. Or like the way the electoral voting lists under the Karamanlis government in Greece a couple of decades ago included a fair number of dead people.'

'I got the impression,' said Robert, 'that you don't approve of council tenants having the right to buy their rented accommodation.'

'I'm afraid that it will be a huge bribe to get Tory votes, and that before long there will be a serious shortfall in council houses – and obviously a serious drop in rents received.'

'You're more political than I am,' said Robert.

'I'm more political than most people here.'

'By the way.' said Robert, 'what was that about the Minibus Act? Eddie cut you off.'

'Oh, I was asked a few weeks ago to give advice about it and couldn't find the library copy. Then Mary told me she was sure Eddie had it because he'd commented on it in a memorandum. But she couldn't find it. I asked him for it and he denied point-blank having it. He said someone else must have retrieved it from his desk.'

'Had they?'

'No. When he was out, Mary and I frisked his desk. It was second item down in a pile on the corner. I showed it to Mary. She said she'd been looking for something thicker – the Act was only about six pages. So I explained.'

'Explained?'

'I told Mary,' he continued, without the glimmer of a smile, 'there are two sorts of Acts of Parliament, little ones and big ones. Just like spiders. She laughed. Then Shimble came in and became purple-faced when she told him where we'd found it. That one he couldn't blame on George.'

Robert threw in at this point: "Is there, do you think, any resemblance between Eddie and Richard III? The line comes back to me – 'From forth the kennel of his mother's womb a hell-hound crept – that hunts us all to death.'"

Colin Masson, looking for words which he soon found, questioned the likeness. 'Perhaps less of a hellhound, and more of a neutered tom cat with continence problems.'

'I fear he's more of a hell-hound than that,' said Robert. 'But is Roland Trask always like that? Sunny side up? Thinking the best of everybody? And does he really get involved in toilet roll shortages?'

'Bill caricatures him, of course. I don't know about toilet rolls, but I did hear a while back that when the Civic Centre ran out of paper clips, he popped down to the stationers to buy some more.'

The conversation ended and Robert returned to his room.

12

Preparing for the Revue

In the mild evening of that same day, the select group of social workers who were planning an entertainment for their peers met in the saloon bar of the Lordship Tavern, where a couple of days earlier Robert had drunk beer with Jessica. They were the evening's first customers. When Robert arrived, the four of them already assembled had taken over a corner of the large room. They encircled a table on which glasses of beer, and an ash-tray half-filled with mainly historical cigarette ends, were set. Jessica greeted Robert and introduced him to the others, among whom he already knew, if only slightly, the woman he increasingly thought of as the glamorous Emily Frost.

If the name Emily had been given to her by parents wishing to import a note of decorum into her demeanour from the beginning, the ploy had not succeeded. Emily was loud, flamboyant and productive of both immoderate laughter and a stream of ideas for the entertainment. She smoked cigarettes repeatedly with the help of her large, expressive mouth. She looked like fun, thought Robert, and he wondered, not for the first time, if she might have an Italian or Spanish element in her ancestry.

The idea for an entertainment, a revue, had been born, Robert gathered, of discussion between Jessica and Emily months before. They had agreed that the Social Services department needed a shake-up, was in want of a celebratory event. The pair of them had talked to others and the two initiators had grown to four within a week or two. Humorous sketches sending up their work and some senior personnel had been written and more were in the pipeline.

Emily blamed a degree in English literature and some amateur acting for her suggestions for sketches, which included one based on Oscar Wilde's *The Importance of Being Ernest* and another on the *New Testament*. The trick was to turn phrases and bits of familiar originals into farcical episodes spiced with localised relevance. So Emily, with the help of suggestions from Jessica, had written *The Importance of Being Anorexia*, and a profoundly blasphemous nativity sketch.

'And who, in our revue will take the character of the Virgin Mary?'

'We'll find someone,' said Jessica.

'We'll also have a sketch with someone playing the director. A spoof Michael Stone,' asserted Emily.

'Will he like that?' asked Robert.

'We hope not,' said Emily. 'And it won't be the only thing he won't like. Such as being urinated upon during the interval. The men will have to draw lots for that job. Unless there's a mass urination, which might be better,' she added thoughtfully.

After a moment's bemusement, as Emily had spoken without displaying any sign of levity, Robert laughed and declared that he would prefer not to take on that particular assignment.

'We'll let you off for the moment,' said Emily. 'But you must remember that male lawyers always need taking down a peg.'

'It's not just me, then?'

'No, I've met a few and you're all the same.'

Robert asked where she had worked before Haringey.

'Enfield.'

'You worked with Jack Parnell there?'

'We've met.'

'Come on,' demanded Jessica. 'Let's get on.'

The two sketches so far identified were already in typed form and copies were scattered on the table. Glancing at one, Robert quickly appreciated that a friendly audience familiar with the targets of satire might be pleasantly entertained.

Of the two male social workers present, one, Frank Jackson, lantern jawed, well-built and owner of a resonant speaking voice, spoke of writing a piece about two male social workers taking the parts of early comedy film heroes Stanley Laurel and Oliver Hardy. They would make a visit to a working class household, in response to a report by a neighbour of worries about a baby's welfare, with predictably calamitous and ludicrous results. The idea was applauded and a script was promised for the next meeting.

'We've not been all that quick off the mark with scripts,' said Emily, solemn for a moment, 'but we do need to wrap up the programme soon, if this show is to be on before Christmas.'

Some songs, to be interposed between sketches, had been written (or at least re-written) by the Emily and Jessica writing duo.

The discussion went on to address the question of the venue. Options were put forward and Frank Jackson promised to make investigatory visits to a list of halls and to check out availability and hire charges. Then there was the question of finding a volunteer who would take charge of the wardrobe and stage effects, and of recruiting others who would be responsible for organising a buffet meal. It was envisaged that the audience could sit around tables and eat and drink during the show as they watched.

Conversation floated from one topic to another and hovered above the head of Michael Stone, the Director. 'I've heard he's very good at keeping conversation running at elite dinner parties, the old smoothie,' said Emily. 'A ladies man, without a doubt,' said Frank.

'Do we invite him?' asked Jessica.

'I thought we'd agreed that. It's the only way he'll get the full treatment,' responded Emily. 'We could have a script sending up one of his monthly senior management meetings, with him strutting about and his toadies running scared.'

Said Jessica – 'But he's not really like that.'

'Not the point,' said Emily. 'The further the presentation from the truth the better. We can throw in a few realistic details – such as his Fabianism, toting around pretentiously his copy of that French newspaper – *Liberation,* isn't it? – and the rest can be pure invention.'

Emily was promptly commissioned to write and bring a 'senior management meeting' sketch along to the next meeting. 'If he comes on the night,' said Emily dreamily, 'we'd better have something to throw over him, to cover him with. Custard pies or something. Urinating on him will just be a fall-back option if he's let off the custard pie treatment. Make a note to have a man with a full bladder standing by. Make that two. No, twelve.'

'I suppose it would do something to advance the career progression of the perpetrators,' offered Robert gravely, hesitant to share his true opinion that some of what was being suggested, if seriously intended, might be a bridge too far.

During this talk, he was conscious that he was the only male wearing a suit and not merely a suit, but one which boasted a matching waist-coat. Both Frank Jackson and the other male social worker, Steve Warren, wore jeans and open-necked shirts. At one point Robert adjusted the alignment of his trousers so as to be kind to the neat creases which ran down them, and Frank complimented him on his elegance, and asked for the name of his tailor. Robert countered by asking what male Haringey social workers wore to court.

Not necessarily a suit, he was told, but they did try to be less casually attired on court occasions. Frank explained that in his own area office a court suit and tie was permanently suspended in a corner from a coat hanger and available for any needy male social worker to use whenever the occasion demanded. 'It's more suitable for those of average height than the others,' he added. It had been there for years, like an old theatre prop, but was too small for Frank. In another area office, he said, the shared stand-by court suit was stuffed in a filing cabinet drawer.

The conversation in the group became more general, and Robert described how, during his training, a young male residential social worker had arrived at court for a care proceedings case wearing a T-shirt on which the words were inscribed: 'You're all a lot of fokkers'. The council's lawyer had sent him home to change.

'I know what you're going to say,' said Emily playfully. 'He returned without the T-shirt but with a bare chest covered in a tattoo picture of a pair of bewigged judges having sex with each other.' She added, after a moment's reflection, that a revue sketch could include a male social worker wearing a 'Fokker' T-shirt.

By the time the meeting ended, Robert was feeling he belonged as a member, but was uncertain what his own role in the revue might be. He voiced this. 'We'll find something,' said Emily. 'If nothing else comes to mind, you can wear the Fokker T-shirt outside your three-piece suit.'

Robert looked at her warily, suspecting that Eddie Shimble, were he ever to be informed that one of his solicitors had been so accoutred in public, might well become ill beyond resuscitation.

Driving home, he speculated as to what the state of the shared kitchen would be. He had so far said nothing to the other Robert about sink clearance arrears. His worst fears were on arrival realised. The contents of the sink were piled high, nastily and dangerously. Meanwhile flat-mate Robert was intent on watching television, lifting his eyes in low key greeting before returning them to the set. He had a plate on his lap which contained vestiges of fried eggs and bread. The plate he now lowered to the floor, pushing it back under his arm chair until it clashed with some possibly similar item.

'I'm a bit concerned,' said arriving Robert, 'that the washing-up arrangements are falling short of perfection.'

'I know. I'm a complete slob. I'll wash and dry before I turn in.'

'Including items, there may be several, under your chair?'

'Including items under my chair.'

Arriving Robert became departing Robert, falling back on takeaway food which he went out to purchase and then ate in his room. In the morning, when he ventured again into the kitchen, his relief was palpable. All his flat-mate's kitchen items were back in cupboards, and all china and cutlery items previously resting in the space under the armchair in the living room had joined them.

13

October Begins

Robert's third week had begun. He was not looking forward to the next part of the 'escape from the balcony affair' in the Tottenham juvenile court. His week-end had included a cinema visit, and several unsuccessful attempts during the Saturday to reach Beth by telephone. Eventually, on the Sunday evening, he had got through to her. She was uncommunicative about why she had not been contactable, but showed no reluctance in agreeing to eat out with him on the Thursday of the week to come.

Developments of a different kind had been dropping on his desk or arriving through his telephone receiver. On the Monday morning, with a moody, cloudy day speaking to him through his office window, Robert confronted the first request he had received at Haringey for advice about mental health law. A male social worker based in the south Tottenham office had telephoned, explaining with brisk efficiency that a male client had lately been detained in hospital under mental health legislation and that he, the caller, wished to have clarification as to who was the patient's nearest relative having rights to object to the patient's continued detention. Robert, before asking about the man's known relatives, was curious as to why he had been detained. He received a short answer to his question, and gained the impression that the caller was on the verge of agitation.

'It's not a borderline case.'
'So what were the reasons?'

'The essence of it is that it came into my client's head that he was the ruler of the world.'

'Yes.'

'And then it came into his head as well that the cat in the house – a household pet, I think a tabby, aged ten or twelve, I think, getting on in years, anyway – had taken over the rulership from him.'

'Yes.'

'So he decapitated the cat.' This was spoken flatly.

'Yes.' Worldly as Robert wished to be, the delusion's extremism and power jolted him. For the more experienced and hardened caller, perhaps, it was just another fragment of life's tragic realities.

'Given his hypothesis,' said the caller, impatience beginning to show, 'the internal logic of the sequence is surely impeccable. But we need to be sure about the nearest relative. Can you tell me who it is?'

'I suppose,' said Robert, his mind still fixed on the humanity of the situation, 'that an inference drawn by the psychiatrist was that it might come into the patient's head that a challenge to his world leadership was being made by some other human being, who could be at large risk from what he had done to the cat.'

'That's about it. You're quick off the mark.' The caller, after the sarcasm, mastered his impatience. 'Can you tell me who the nearest relative is?'

A pre-requisite for an adequate response was the provision to Robert of details about the patient's actual close relatives. After making a note of these, and after checking mental health legislation he telephoned back with the advice requested. He promised to confirm this in writing, dictated a couple of paragraphs, and heard nothing more about the patient concerned. When he enquired, some weeks later, about his edgy advice-seeker, he was told that the person concerned had ceased to work in mental health, having decided he was ill-equipped to do so.

Robert now knew the answer to the question recently posed by his Enfield counterpart, Jack Parnell, as to whether Haringey ever resorted to wardship proceedings in the High Court to safeguard children's welfare. Melanie Cusack had informed him that while she had been with Haringey no child had been made a ward of court. Robert telephoned Jack Parnell to tell him this. He was only able to leave a message, but Jack soon returned his call and was as jovial and communicative as before.

He said that Enfield had a policy to date of not making children wards to fill in the gaps in the law as a means of protecting the interests of children, and that he was doing what he could to unhorse that policy. 'But in Enfield,' he said, 'we do quite often intervene in county court proceedings between divorcing parents, when the child's welfare is being severely neglected in the course of squabbling about custody.'

'Edmonton county court?' asked Robert.

'Usually, but sometimes more far-flung county courts too.'

Jack paused a moment, then continued.

'At Edmonton, His Honour Judge Madder is getting madder.'

'Really?' asked Robert.

"That was just a joke, really. He can be cantankerous. I was in court waiting for my own case the other day. A barrister in a case before mine got up and said: 'I wish to ask the court…' and Madder barked out: 'You don't *ask* in my court, you *apply*.' So the barrister, crushed, stammered out that he was 'applying'. Then when that case finished, another barrister, not the crushable sort, got up, and said, 'I wish to *invite* the court, if *invite* is the right word…' Madder just looked po-faced. No laughs in his court."

Robert switched subjects. 'I gather you know Emily Frost.'

'Yes, Emily,' said Jack non-committally. 'I do know Emily. Good social worker. Well, I'd better be getting on. Nice to speak to you.'

Jack, it seemed, was not inclined to continue a discussion of Emily.

After this conversation Robert got down to work on the brief for Sophie Williams 'of Counsel' in the Amy Stewart 'phenergan' case. In preparing this he was now aware – through a phone call to the North Middlesex hospital – that Dr. Alan Pearson was on sick leave and unlikely to be able to attend the hearing on the coming Wednesday.

Before lunch-time the typed version of the brief was on Robert's blotting pad. It contained a summary of the facts and of the position in which the case was likely to find itself (the bad news – probably no parents and no child, probably no paediatrician; the good news – the social worker Jessica Palmer would be not far away). The brief included a bundle of photocopies from Jessica's case records and a report from Dr. Pearson. Robert had not ducked out of explaining how it had come about that the place of safety order obtained had not been acted upon, leaving the three-year-old in the care of her allegedly dangerous parents.

Jessica had been directed by her 'senior', Derek Ivins, not to demand, if the parents did not turn up at court, an interim care order, given that Amy had remained with them and that no further emergency had yet arisen. But Ivins had accepted that, if they did not show, summonses compelling parental attendance at an early further hearing should be obtained.

So it was that on the Wednesday, while waiting in the dull grey-blue-walled corridor of the court building close to the parlour-sized Court 5 for the hearing about teenager Michelle to take wing again, Robert met Sophie Williams, who told him, with more noisy confidence than strictly necessary, that

Amy's case was to be heard nearby in the obscurely situated Court 4.

Soon afterwards Jessica arrived. In discussion Sophie Williams proved to be as full of self-belief a young barrister as Robert expected, but was much less sure about the strength of the case concerning Amy than Robert would have preferred. 'The medication stuff is a bit iffy,' isn't it?' she offered, with a bright smile. 'If that's the gravamen of the case, it could come adrift. Better to put more emphasis on mother's mental health problems and the emotional deprivation.' This analysis did not impress Robert, and it bothered Jessica too, to judge from the expression on her face. And had Sophie Williams used the word 'gravamen' (occasionally heard inside courts, more rarely outside them) to impress?

Robert suggested quietly that the 'gravamen' of the case was the medication abuse, and mentally crossed Sophie's name off the list of his approved barristers, a list which then became entirely blank. But today, he surmised, surely no damage could be done by a barrister whose assessment of the evidence was maverick. He simply urged an adjournment for one week and the obtaining of permission from a magistrate to issue summonses for service on Amy's parents.

Sophie nodded and said to Jessica that if their worships wanted to hear from her, she would coax her out of Court 5. As things were, she expected to manage alone. She seemed, in fact, to know what she was doing.

Soon afterwards teenager Michelle's case was called on. Robert wondered how much the three magistrates remembered of the previous week's hearing, especially of the restrained but surely persuasive evidence of the educational psychologist. Only the clerk had scribbled notes without a pause. Lady Feverel had made some notes, but sporadically. The other two magistrates had seemed to be relying on the excellence of their memories, and, in the case of the large, sleepy male, if Robert's suspicions were soundly-based, this could only apply to his more wakeful episodes.

They would be reminded explicitly, Robert had decided, of the nuts and bolts of Townley's evidence (as well as of its 'gravamen' – he was taking a share in ownership of the word) in his final submission.

'I call Derek Ivins,' he began, when the preliminaries were over. Ivins, once at the witness stand, identified himself, mumbling at first, then speaking more articulately, as a senior social worker who had had a supervisory role over social workers involved since Michelle had come to the attention of the North Tottenham area office.

'When was your first direct contact with the family?' Robert asked.

This, Derek Ivins said, was in March, when he had spoken in some depth with the parents. He had asked Mr. West why he had got into physical confrontations with Michelle. Mr. West had said he had got so frustrated during the rows, that he felt there was nothing left but to use force to make her see reason.

A month later, Michelle's parents had become frustrated at the decision, 'after the next fight' (as Ivins put it) to place Michelle in a foster home rather than in a children's home. A children's home, Mr. West said, would have taught her a lesson.

Regarding the culminating incident in June which had provoked the place of safety order request, Ivins said Mr. West had freely admitted beating Michelle before she made her escape from the balcony, then adding that he had not asked more about 'the alleged beating', explaining that Mr. West must have known it was 'an inappropriate form of discipline for a child of Michelle's age and sex'.

This, however, Robert suspected, was precisely what Mr. West did not know. Ivins, prompted by Robert, went on, with some hesitation, to describe the confrontation he had witnessed between Michelle and her mother on the day of the place of safety order, a confrontation which involved pushing and pulling, he said, more than blows. 'It happened,' he said 'in a very difficult situation.'

At one moment Ivins spoke a few words slowly, and at another, supplied a little rush of them. He gave a novel impression, not altogether to his advantage, or to the advantage of the case. He was attacked little by Jonathan Spratt in cross-examination, who extracted from him the concessions that he could empathise with Mr. West's frustration and that if Michelle returned home he would wish to offer support and guidance to the family. As he did not then volunteer the view that a return home at this time would probably produce further conflict and perhaps another dangerous getaway, after Spratt sat down, Robert 're-examined' Ivins briefly to invite this conclusion, which Ivins then produced limply enough.

When Ivins was allowed to leave the court, Robert announced that the evidence to be called by the Borough was complete, save that if the 'primary condition' were found proved, he intended to call Jessica Palmer in respect of 'disposal' and to submit her social enquiry report. There was no point in calling her to help establish the case, he had decided, as she had not been involved prior to Michelle's move to foster parents in June.

It was now Jonathan Spratt's turn. He called Michelle's father. A well turned-out Mr. West took the oath with dignity, and gave evidence in a down-to-earth manner. He agreed he was a steel erector by occupation.

'How,' asked Spratt, 'did you get on with Mr. Townley?'
'Who is Mr. Townley?'
'The educational psychologist.'
'Why didn't you say so? I disagreed with him. He said not

to over-pressurise Michelle. I just wanted her to rise above the level of illiteracy.'

Spratt soon arrived at the leap from the balcony at the beginning of June which had brought Michelle into care a second time.

'It was on a Saturday. We give Michelle a few chores to do on Saturdays. If she did them and behaved herself she was going to a disco in the evening with her friend. She had to do some cleaning and hoovering. She had to wash the kitchen floor. I got her a bowl of water and she started to wash it. I told her she wasn't making a good job of it. I told her to move the tumble dryer and the dining chairs. She wasn't happy. She threw the cloth into the bowl and she tipped it so it went over me and her little brother. I filled a cup of water and threw it over her. I then told her to mop the water up, and she got abusive.'

'And then?'

'I waved a finger at her. She tried to grab my finger, arguing with me. She thought I was going to hit her and she cowered down by the radiator.'

'Why did she do that?'

'She thought she'd get a back-hander. I tried to get hold of her. I grabbed her wrist. She ran into our bedroom, telling me to f-off. I shouted back at her. I went towards her and she jumped across the bed. I took off my leather belt and gave it her five or six times. She was crying and hysterical. I told her to get into her own room. She refused. I told her if she didn't calm down she couldn't go to the disco. She went into her room and quietened down.'

So it was that Mr. West, Michelle's father unintentionally compensated for the mildness of the ed psych and the lack of bite of Derek Ivins to slap in front of the Bench's eyes the sort of lurid detail which topped up the case for Michelle's continued protection from the care of her parents. Glancing up at the magistrates Robert saw their keen attentiveness. The mouth of the male book-end was half-open, but he did look awake.

'What happened then?'

'After a while her little brother went in there and said she'd gone. The window was open.'

Spratt asked him about punching and kicking.

'I never punched or kicked her. I've given her the belt before when she got hysterical.'

'What did you do when you discovered she'd gone?'

'We assumed she'd come back later. When she didn't, we made phone calls. She was at a friend's, so we left it. Then on the Monday the social rang to say she was at the office.'

'Was that Mr. Derek Ivins who rang?'

'I expect so. They're all the same, aren't they? I told him to send her back. He didn't want to. I told him he must send her back. He was wasting my time. He went on about a cooling-off period.'

West was now talking quickly and Lady Feverel asked him to slow down. 'Please watch my pen, Mr. West.' He continued:

'They said for us to go to Social Services. I said I wanted to see Michelle and get her home. He said he felt she wouldn't come home. When we got to the office he said she was in another room with her friend and her friend's Mum. She did come out then and said she wasn't coming home.'

'What was your attitude to the social workers at that moment?'

'I was angry. They didn't make Michelle come home. We didn't agree to her being in care. It seemed to us the previous time she'd had a holiday. She was the centre of attention and I didn't agree with the area where the foster place was. Undesirable people. You know what I mean.'

'You saw her after she came into care?'

'She came to see us once a few days afterwards, with her

friend. As if nothing had ever happened. She said a few things that made us wonder. She said she was given five quid for being good. She couldn't say what "being good" meant. To me it meant she was giving the foster parents an easy time. She was doing what she wanted.'

'Why do you say she was doing what she wanted?'

'People we know saw her out sometimes – smoking, hanging about with boys. They were all blacks. That bothered me. We had a phone call too from an abortion centre. That turned out to be a mistake. The call wasn't for us. She wasn't doing her schoolwork either.'

Robert rose to cross-examine, satisfied that West had inadvertently doubled the value of the evidence. Robert had few questions for him.

'Have you tried to look at what's happened from Michelle's point of view?'

'I don't know what is her point of view, apart from wanting an easy life.'

'Do you think it's acceptable to hit a 15-year-old?'

'I was at my wits' end. Nothing else was working.'

'Chastising her wasn't working either, was it?'

'Neither was putting her with foster parents. St. Margaret's was her last chance. She's unemployable.'

'Would you agree things had gone wrong at home?'

'No. Nothing was wrong at home.'

'Should she stay where she is?'

'No.'

'If she came home to you would you behave differently towards her?'

'No.'

Robert sat down, content.

Spratt called Mrs. West, who was as neatly dressed as her husband, and whose outfit, it occurred again to Robert, was surprisingly similar to Jessica's. She took the oath confidently, and was clearly more than ready to say her piece. Her manner was somewhere between self-righteous and belligerent.

'It all started at her primary school. The teachers said she wasn't paying attention to anything. Her mind was elsewhere. It was just the same when she went up to secondary school. That was how I got to see the psychologist.'

'You mean Mr. Townley?'

'Yes.'

She was about to run on, but Spratt asked:

'What did you want from him?'

'I asked him if she could have hypnosis treatment to unblock her mind. He said it wouldn't do any good, it wasn't possible. Anyway, I decided she should go to St. Margaret's if we could get a place. Once she was there, there was no difference. I kept trying to get her to do homework, to read books. She got hysterical. I think she's very immature. She's a psychological case.'

'The fights?'

'Mostly verbal fights. She went through a phase of banging her head against the wall. She threw her homework in the bath.'

'Did you or her father ever kick or punch her?'

'Certainly not.'

'Did you disapprove of Michelle's out of school activities?'

'We were happy with her roller skating. But she was obsessed with pop music and boys. She's not old enough for boys.'

It was Robert's turn to ask questions.

'You said in answer to the last question that Michelle's not old enough for boys. On the other hand, isn't she the wrong age for physical chastisement?'

'I don't know what you mean.'

'Ever smack her around the face?'

'Once or twice.'

'So what Michelle called a punch could have been a slap? She must have got the bruise from somewhere.'

'I don't know about that.'

'Many parents might consider it reasonable to smack a four-year-old – but a fifteen-year-old? And repeatedly with a leather belt?'

'I never did that.'

'On the day when Michelle jumped down from the balcony, you've heard that Mr. West gave her the belt. Did you see that?'

'I wasn't in the room. I could hear the lashes.'

'And Michelle's reaction?'

'She was screaming her head off.'

'When you saw her with your husband last Wednesday in the probation rooms here, is it correct that you grabbed Michelle and she pushed you off?'

'I hardly touched her.'

'And she pushed you away?'

'She's worse than she was before she went into care.'

Robert put his final questions.

'If Michelle came home, would you behave differently with her?'

'I'd have to, as she'd be different.'

'Would you and your husband do the same as before?'

'That's all you can do.'

'Those are all my questions, your worships,' said Robert. He had not expected the parents' evidence to put pepper and salt on the case in such quantities. Why had Spratt called them? Robert had glanced over at the justices from time to time. Their undivided attention had been gained while the Wests had given evidence. The family battles had come alive, and the case had become unanswerable.

The time had come for submissions about the 'primary condition', whether Michelle's 'proper development' had been impaired and what-not, and whether she was beyond her parents' control. It was almost lunch-time and the justices directed that submissions would take place at two o'clock. They were back in their seats by ten past and submissions were duly made by first Spratt then Robert. The Bench retired to consider, and returned after a short time.

'We are satisfied that both primary conditions are met,' said Lady Feverel. 'Are there reports?'

Copies of Jessica's report were now handed up. The Bench retired to read it, and once back in court were invited to listen to its author.

All the witnesses so far, before giving evidence, had read the form of Christian oath on the card sitting on the witness lectern. Jessica, however, was determined to be different. She stated she wished to affirm. The clerk, as if making an exception to a general rule, produced a card from his own table containing the standard words for a secular promise to speak the truth, and Jessica read the words aloud.

Robert began his examination-in-chief.

'You've been social worker for the family since the place of safety order at the beginning of June?'

'Since about ten days after that. To be precise from the eleventh of June.'

'You've seen Michelle many times since then?'

'At least half a dozen times, I think. I'd have to check my diary records to be exact.'

'You've discussed with her the problems which led to the place of safety order and her being placed with the Patricks, the foster parents?'

'Yes. Especially at first.'

'I won't ask you about the earlier history as the Court has heard a lot about that. But what has Michelle's position been over the time you've known her in relation to whether or not she should return home?'

'She has been very clear that she was against returning, and that if she did return, she'd run away.'

'How has that been said to you?'

'Wholeheartedly. With determination.'

'And what contact have you had with Mr. and Mrs. West?'

'I visited them very soon after I was allocated the case.'

'On the 13th June?'

Spratt, who earlier might have accused Robert of a leading question, sat mute.

'Yes. I had a discussion with Mrs. West.'

'Was it fruitful?'

'Not in the sense that it opened the way to a negotiated return. She was angry about the foster home, angry about the involvement of Social Services – in fact she blamed Social Services for all the problems.'

'What about Mrs. West's willingness to have contact with Michelle?'

'Well, there was one visit home by Michelle soon after the place of safety order.'

'Was that surprising? Michelle was unaccompanied by a social worker or escort of some kind?'

'A friend was with her. But after that one visit I'm not aware of any more. Mrs. West said to me Michelle was upsetting her young brother. She also said Michelle would have a breakdown if she didn't see her parents.'

'Did Mrs. West blame only Social Services?'

'I got the strong impression that she also blamed Michelle for not complying with her wishes.'

'Was there *any* acceptance by Mrs. West of even part responsibility for the breakdown?'

'No.'

'What would you have liked to happen?'

'I would have liked sessions with Michelle and her parents. To try to reduce disputes. But the situation was entrenched.'

'Did you receive cooperation from Michelle's parents in preparing your report for this Court?'

'Yes, some, but there were difficulties. They did not want to discuss basic things such as their own family backgrounds or even their ages.'

'Did you discuss with them the possibility of some form of family therapy?'

'Yes.'

'The upshot?'

'At first Mrs. West refused consent for a referral. Later she said they'd think about it. They were only prepared to consider a local facility. I told them that the only local facility was Child Guidance. There was a Yes to that at first followed by a definite No.'

'How was Michelle getting on at school?'

'When I first met her she was suspended for being rude and swearing and also for wearing an ear-ring. They are strict at St. Margaret's about ear-rings. Her attendance hadn't been good either.'

'Did you talk to her about that?'

'I did. She was not keen on the school. She said people were picking on her. She said someone's boy-friend was out to get her. Would be waiting for her outside the school gates to beat her up. She believed this. School staff on the other hand said she did have friends at school.'

'Did you also talk with Michelle about her relationship with her parents?'

'Yes. She was tearful at times about that. She felt she was being treated unfairly.'

'You saw Michelle with her parents?'

'Only in the Probation building here last week when we were at Court and there was a physical confrontation. Michelle pushed her mother off her in my presence.'

'Their attitude to each other?'

'The parental attitude to Michelle was hostile and negative. I think that if Michelle were forced home, the consequences would be disastrous, given the lack of compromise.'

'Michelle has had more freedom to go out at the foster home?'

'Yes.'

'How contented has she been there?'

'Happy, overall, I would say. And at first her performance at school did improve.'

'And her attendance?'

'That deteriorated. She said she had headaches, which caused her to stay away from school. I am sure the court process has had a worrying and depressing effect on her.'

'It's intended, I gather, that Michelle be moved from the foster home and placed in a children's home.'

'Yes.'

'Are you satisfied it is a suitable establishment and will provide sufficient structure for Michelle's welfare?'

'That's the Department's view. It also accommodates Mr. and Mrs. West's view to a degree.'

'And is acceptable to Michelle?'

'She's not happy about it – but I'm sure she'll settle in.'

'Suppose a supervision order were made?'

'That would entail her returning home immediately. As I've said, I think the antagonisms between Michelle and her parents are so strong and fixed that returning home would make matters worse and even place her at unacceptable risk.'

Spratt had not interrupted once, and his short cross-examination did not damage Jessica's evidence. Jessica agreed with him that Michelle was living for the moment, not looking to the future. Asked if she had considered that the parents saw her, Jessica, as a hostile force, she agreed. Asked if she agreed that discipline by the Patricks had been lax, she said it could have been stricter, and she hoped that a children's home would provide more structure.

'That isn't likely, is it?' Jessica said only that time would tell. Spratt did not recall either parent to give evidence again. They sat, displeased but wordless.

Final speeches followed. Robert was succinct in arguing for a full care order, and did, as he had promised himself, remind the justices of the brunt of the ed psych's evidence. He even worked in the word 'gravamen'. Spratt was long-winded in opposing a care order outcome. 'It would give Haringey social workers carte blanche to give this irresponsible young girl the easy life that she would like, alienating her even more from the parents who love her.'

Said Lady Feverel, after a retirement of more than half an hour, in a voice which, Robert thought, confirmed very accurately Jack Parnell's mimicry.

'We make a *full* care order to the local authority. We think that Michelle has been having *too* much freedom in the foster home and that she had *too* much pressure in her own home.'

'The judgment of Solomon,' Robert said to Jessica, when they left the court building.

'It'll do,' said Jessica. She had been solemn-faced all day, and now was beginning to relax.

Reviewing mentally the history of this two-day hearing, while Jessica made a telephone call to Derek Ivins from the public booth to inform him of the result, Robert asked himself why Jonathan Spratt, for the parents, had, in calling them to give evidence, been instrumental in sinking their case to the bottom. He surely knew he was doing that. And was it a fact that Haringey had surrendered to the parents' wishes to get Michelle out of the foster home where she was happy and settled, appeasing the parents' racism-influenced preferences. Was Jessica guilty of that? Or was it Derek Ivins? Jessica, speaking carefully when in the witness stand, had said the Department's view was that

Michelle would be better placed in a children's home. She had not said it was her view. Surely committed foster carers would do better than a children's home in which other children would set bad examples and staff would be going off shift repeatedly. If the children's home was not much more than a warehouse, what would become of Michelle?

When Jessica emerged from the telephone booth, Robert asked her pointedly if she had personally disagreed with the decision that Michelle be placed in a children's home.

'I did disagree,' she said. 'I was overridden by Derek who was backed up by the area manager, who didn't want to go against Derek. He also liked the idea of compromising with the parents. But children's homes these days don't have strictness ratings. Maybe Mr. West was brought up in an *Oliver Twist* sort of place.'

'The Wests could turn against the children's home too if they find it doesn't have many rules? Or has black children resident?'

'True. I was supported by Enid Prosser. She was appalled by the plan to move Michelle out of foster care. She gave Derek a real pasting. It was a waste of time, but she tried, as I did. She could have been more diplomatic, though. Derek's views against care may have something to do with his being in care himself as a child. I haven't told you that.'

'So couldn't you have said openly in court that the Department's view wasn't your view?'

Jessica looked at him squarely. 'Maybe I should have. I was worried we wouldn't get a care order if I argued too much against a children's home.'

'So is the battle for a foster home for Michelle lost for ever?'

'I don't know. There's no date set for her move yet. I'll think about it. This is hardly a conversation I would have had with Melanie.'

'Did you fall out with her about anything in a previous case?'

'I disagreed with her about which witnesses were vital. She was most put out. She told me off quite rudely.'

So that was what Melanie had meant, when she had said that Jessica could get above herself.

But Jessica had not finished. 'I do feel a bit sorry for her. After one hearing we chatted together and she revealed personal things. She lost both her parents within two years, first her father and then her mother, and she'd been very close to her mother. And she said she hated most Social Services clients. She said she knew she was in the wrong job.'

'I think she sees herself,' said Robert, 'as intended for better things.'

'Or different things,' said Jessica, more tolerantly. She smiled at him, her first unqualified smile of the day. They said their goodbyes and set off in their respective cars.

The other court hearing, meanwhile, that concerning three-year-old Amy, was now long over, and Sophie Williams was back in her Temple Chambers. In the legal building Robert managed to speak to her over the phone. She was breathy and chatty.

The one surprise, she said, was that she had been approached by a solicitor from Slash & Co who had said he wasn't yet representing the Stewarts, but might well be at the next hearing. Robert asked his name.

'I didn't get that. He was rather an old dodderer. He acted for a couple of juvenile delinquents while I was there and was in between things working his way through the *Times* crossword. I think he'd almost finished it by the time I went.'

'An old dodderer.'

'Yes. He had on an old suit, but if you looked closely – I tried not to – you could see portions of his underwear. His trousers were rather low-slung.'

Robert asked no more about the old dodderer. Amy's case, Sophie Williams continued, had been adjourned for seven days, summonses had been issued and should be received by Robert the following day. 'When,' she added, 'I'm doing a public health prosecution for Bill Bowman.'

'Indian restaurant?' he asked, guessing that it was the case he'd declined.

'Yes. And do you need me next week?' she asked.

'I'll be free myself then,' he said, but thanked her for asking. Once again he was going to put his head in the lion's mouth – or in that of Jonathan Spratt (a stuffed lion to date) or of someone else. He made a note in his diary that he would need to assign a junior member of the litigation team to visit the Stewarts' home for the purpose of serving the summonses.

And he would have to remind that person that the father had a reputation for violence. If the family were away on holiday as they had said they would be, the summonses would have to be served on the Monday, just two days before the hearing.

14

More about Beth and Robert

That Thursday night Beth did not seek to eject Robert from her home at half-past ten, as on the previous occasion, though she ejected him from her bed a while after midnight, saying that she preferred mostly to sleep on her own and asking if he didn't mind leaving her to do so. He complied contentedly enough with her request, considering that it could not easily be disputed that their relationship had progressed, and that Beth's proposal would have the advantage of enabling him more easily to get into the office early.

It had, by inference more than by agreement, become accepted between them during the enhanced evening that they would spend more intimate time together. Robert had not been able to resist asking Beth if a reason for compelling his early departure on the evening she had cooked for him was that she had slept with someone else the night before. He had uttered this query in a teasing way, without at all expecting such an admission.

She had blushed, was candid. It had been part of the reason. But it had been a fact too that she preferred not, at the beginning of a relationship, to leap into bed right away.

'You've always stuck to that principle?' he asked. Beth blushed again. 'You're being very forward,' she said. 'We're not in court.'

'I just want to understand how you think about these things,' he said. 'As for the other guy, I just want to know, if we're going to continue to see each other, if your relationship with him has any future too.'

'Well,' she said, 'are you always monogamous? You seem to be spending time with Jessica and Emily for a start, from what I hear. That could involve complications, knowing what I do about the pair of them.'

'We've been putting together the department's revue. But I'm going on stage with them, not climbing into bed with either of them. I'm sure that anyone can be involved – you've not wanted to be?'

'Not me, no. I'm more of a watcher than a participant. Not that I've been invited to take part, unlike you. Who invited you in – was it Jessica or Emily?'

'Jessica. I didn't really know Emily before going to an organising meeting. But someone must have told you I've been recruited.'

'Oh, it was just that Emily was putting up a notice about it the other day, and I asked her who else was taking part. And your name got mentioned. As an eager volunteer, not a reluctant recruit, I might add.'

'Yes, I think it could be quite a lot of fun. Jessica and Emily have got a lot of ideas.'

'I expect I'll come to see it, then,' said Beth. She added: 'Jessica's marriage is supposed to be rocky, by the way.'

'I didn't know that. Anyway, for what it's worth, I'm not after her.'

'I wasn't implying you were. I haven't got to the jealous stage with you.'

Their talk drifted into other things, and Beth spoke again about the boyfriend she had lived with in her late teens. They had become engaged and Beth had expected the relationship to be for ever, even though passion had waned. Then, when on a week's local government residential training course, she had met someone else to whom she had been strongly, even intensely, attracted. It was, she said, 'an infatuation.' She had put her foot through the relationship with her fiancé and moved out. He, however, had gone into a state of emotional collapse, more profound than she had imagined possible. He was desperate not to end their relationship so suddenly. She had been adamant. She confessed, looking back, that she had been insensitive. But then she had been only twenty.

'I hope he recovered,' Robert commented.

'Oh he did,' she said, even showing relief. 'He met someone else. He's married now.'

'Any regrets?'

'I just don't like to think of it. I shouldn't have told you about it. It brings it all back.'

'And what happened about the guy you met at the party?'

'Who?'

'The one you were infatuated with.'

'Oh, that didn't last five minutes.' Robert left the subject to itself.

Beth had liked the idea of herself and Robert spending the next evening together, but Robert had to explain to her that he was supposed then to meet the entertainment group to progress things, and that he would be letting the side down if he were not there.

'You mean,' said Beth playfully, 'you would be letting Emily and Jessica down. I know my value.'

'Couldn't we meet later that evening? The meeting won't go on for ever.'

What about Saturday, Beth had said, and it was settled they would spend the day together, walking in nearby countryside around Highgate and Hampstead, relying on a map and guide she had for suburban London walkers, and taking with them a lunch-time picnic, whatever the weather.

Their plan came to fruition. Two days later, Saturday arrived and very early Beth arrived at Robert's Crouch End flat. He had been active still earlier, cleaning up the other Robert's kitchen sink washing-up queue, thereby countering any accusations of slobbishness Beth might throw at him. Soon after her arrival, they emerged with sandwiches packed. They took a bus to Highgate, alighting at a point of entry into Queen's Wood. They were greeted there by discarded, redundant yellow and brown leaves on and around the footpath that wanders around the wood's edge, leaves large and small, freshly fallen and old and crushed leaves, soon to be joined by many more.

The sun came out and exerted its magic, and in the clearings blades of grass were gleaming with dew, and not all the wild flowers had disappeared. Joggers often passed them, some too rapidly to be called joggers, and some too slowly to earn the title.

On they went into Highgate village, and downhill to an entrance to Waterlow Park. They drifted through, entering Highgate cemetery on a whim.

'So that's where he lives,' said Robert as the tombstone of Karl Marx rose up in front of them. They had been passing tombstones which denied or under-stated the finality of death. A widow was 'reunited' with her husband, and old men had 'fallen asleep' on such and such a day, and all manner of occupants of ancient graves had 'passed away'. The sight of Marx carrying his head high resisted the notion of mortality with his wealth of rock-hard hair, supported by the great words beneath about the point of philosophy being to change the world, and by the red and white flowers in clusters on the tiny plot in front.

Nearby was the grave of once-famous Herbert Spencer, a lesser nineteenth century thinker. Robert had been told by Colin Masson that it was a rite of passage to visit 'Marx and Spencer's' in Highgate Cemetery, and Robert shared this tired piece of humour with Beth.

Leaving the cemetery, they returned to Highgate village, then moving into Kenwood's green meadows, via the entry point near to the Flask public house. They held hands briefly – though Beth was not a woman much given to holding hands – and advanced into the meadows and around the waters. It was then that the sun decided it had been on duty long enough, while the wind, which had been present in the mildest of forms, became first a friendly presence, then more of a sparring partner, and finally a pugilistic-and-no-mistake enemy, from whom they eventually fled, passing landmark ponds before reaching a coffee shop in Hampstead with near-freezing fingers.

Consumption of the sandwiches had been weather-deterred during the expedition. Ending the 'walk phase' of the day, they took an underground train into central London where in Oxford Street Beth helped Robert choose a desk, and their sandwiches were eaten in a store cafeteria, washed down with tea.

The day they had spent energetically out-of-doors together became a night as well as a day before Beth shooed Robert home to his own devices. At some point she had volunteered, without being interrogated further by Robert, who had thought it wise not to return to the subject, that the unnamed boy-friend with whom she had spent at least some of the night before she had cooked a curry for Robert was no longer 'on the scene'. Robert found her complicated and confusing: susceptible to men, but dismissive of them; calm but capricious; denying jealousy of other women but displaying signs of it; reticent yet revelatory; difficult to read and difficult to resist.

I have run ahead of other events. On the Friday, Robert had been on time at The Lordship Tavern for a meeting to advance the incubating entertainment. Only Emily and Frank Jackson had arrived ahead of him, their pint beer glasses already half empty. Emily was smoking.

'Early birds,' said Robert.

'Ten minutes early at most,' said Emily, definitively, looking at her watch. 'By the way, in case you have suspicions about us, Frank is just my flatmate. Despite that, we get on quite well, don't we, Frank?'

'We get on very well indeed, I think,' said Frank, who was some years older than Emily, well into his thirties, his body as well formed as his jaws. 'Except when I leave the kitchen in a mucky condition. Then there's hell to pay.'

'The same with the lavatory,' Emily contributed firmly.

'Am I right that there's only one other man – Steve – in our group?' asked Robert. Already he was regarding his own membership as secure.

'Apart from you, that's right,' said Emily. 'Steve Warren works with juveniles in trouble with the police at the Intermediate Treatment centre on Green Lanes. Stimulating and lawful activities. But be careful not to upset him. He's pretty thin skinned.'

Jessica, her dark brown eyes shining, was the next to arrive, apologising for being late. Steve Warren came soon afterwards, claiming boldly that as he had arrived, they could now begin. Steve was as thin and wiry as Frank was solid and muscular, and the pair looked a good match as Laurel and Hardy, especially if Frank, as Hardy, were given plenty of quilting around the middle. Steve had knocked out some dialogue for them as inept social workers making a child protection visit, though at this moment he could only circulate a single sheet, handwritten, and not always legible. Read aloud by Steve, using several voices for the several parts, it sounded comic enough, and praise was poured out fulsomely. Robert quickly appreciated that Steve badly needed the compliments that were bestowed, and was sensitive and anxious about anything in his script that might be viewed lacking in quality.

'What about the director's management meeting sketch?' Robert was looking at Emily. 'Can you match Steve's dialogue?'

'I have put down some thoughts, and Jessica has tidied them up. Either we've both made a mess of it or…'

Emily produced sufficient typed copies for all to read. The others decorated their reading with mirth here and there.

'This should do very well,' said Frank who, although Emily's flatmate, had not been privileged to see the sketch earlier. 'I see Michael Stone's French newspaper makes an appearance.'

'Affected bastard,' said Emily. 'We must get one as a prop.'

'Where do the custard pies for him come in,' asked Robert.

'Oh that'll be at the end of the show – a kind of icing on the cake for the whole evening,' said Emily. 'That's when the old smoothie gets his comeuppance.'

'How do we know he's coming?'

'No guarantee, but we're sending him two tickets. We're not sending anyone else complimentaries, and it's really a field social work thing. We're not inviting Day Care.'

'No invite for Charmaine Trickett? The Day Care Manager?' asked Robert.

"Round these parts she's known as the 'Day Care Factor,'" said Emily. 'It would be like inviting Mrs. Thatcher to a Trotskyist wedding. Charmaine Trickett has no sense of humour whatsoever. She runs Day Care like a tyrant.'

More suggestions were made about sketches, and about the songs that were to be slotted between them. A closing song, to be sung in chorus, was borrowed from the musical *Oh What a Lovely War*, but needed re-writing to suit a social work, rather than a war, environment.

'You haven't found a job for me yet,' said Robert.

'What about stage manager unless someone else is desperate to do that?' proposed Jessica.

So the stage manager role was allocated to Robert provisionally, and before long its provisional character was forgotten.

'You're not volunteering to act then?' asked Frank. 'Lawyers are supposed to be natural actors.'

'I'll do what I'm told to do.'

'We need more troops generally,' said Frank. 'We should be putting out feelers for actors – what about that guy in your team, Jessica, who does animal impersonations at parties, even when no-one's asked him to?'

'That's Trevor,' said Jessica. 'I heard him do that once. Another time it was birds. He's always as high as a kite at parties. And he's not very reliable. He dropped out of sight a few weeks ago – no one saw him for three or four days and he hadn't phoned in sick or anything. When he turned up again I asked him out of curiosity where he'd been. He just said he'd been getting his head together.'

'You're being hard on him,' said Steve defensively, as if he, not Trevor, were the subject under discussion.

Jessica continued. 'We need people more solid than Trevor and we don't want police raiding the venue searching for drugs on performance night.'

Robert was shocked. 'I hope you're exaggerating about Trevor,' he said to Jessica.

'So do I.'

'Trevor's an all-right guy,' said Steve Warren, looking as if he meant it.

They went on to agree who was to do what over the next fortnight before a final pre-revue meeting, and to fix the date for the live performance in mid-December.

''If that's the date,' said Frank sagely, 'we'll have to get our skates on.'

'What about,' suggested Emily, 'an evening out together soon as a group?'

Said Frank: 'A group bonding experience. Why not?'

'My other half might want to come,' said Jessica. 'He's feeling marginalised.'

'OK,' said Frank, looking at Jessica for a moment. 'Close connections for other people who don't want to be left out can come too. Are you up for it, Steve?'

'Why not.'

'So what about,' said Frank, 'a meal in a restaurant – Greek, perhaps – and then going on to a dance place. Are you game, Robert?'

Robert said he was.

'Are you,' Frank looked at Robert, 'wanting to bring a girlfriend yourself? Even a new one?'

'I think I could be.'

'It wouldn't be someone called Beth, would it?'

Robert had not expected the question or the knowledge it implied, but did not deny the fact.

Said Jessica: 'News gets round Haringey like wild-fire.'

Said Emily: 'I didn't know lawyers could be such quick workers. They don't chat women up usually, from what I've heard. They just want to take proofs of evidence.'

A chuckle from Robert was swallowed up by general amusement. Before parting, Emily, impulsively, imprinted a kiss on Robert's cheek after first, roguishly, approaching his lips with hers. He returned the salutation. 'I'll tell Beth you did more than that,' said Emily, eyes dancing. 'I'm told she's jealous of me for some reason.'

'No comment,' said Robert.

Good-humouredly, they went their different ways.

15

The Amy Stewart Case Again

The following Monday, an especially cold day, was memorable for a series of communications regarding the case of the toddler Amy. Impatient to know whether she and her parents had returned from their holiday (if indeed they had been truly on holiday), Robert telephoned the day nursery she attended. Was she there that morning? He spoke to the nursery manager, who remembered him from the case conference a few weeks previously and who confirmed Amy had been brought in by her mother. They'd been staying, she'd gathered, with the maternal grandmother in Wolverhampton.

'Amy looks OK?'

'As before, really, though she does have a bruise on her cheek, a small one. I asked her mum where that had come from, but she didn't know. She said I wasn't going to pin that one on her.'

'Does Jessica Palmer know about the bruise?'

'Oh, yes. I spoke to her a few minutes ago.'

Having pocketed this news, Robert went in search of Bill Bowman who was at that moment closeted, so Mary told him, with Mr. Shimble. But a youthful litigation assistant, one of Bowman's 'lads', whom he knew as Errol, was at his desk, eating a beef burger in a bun. Could Errol serve notices and summonses on the child's parents in Tottenham? Errol agreed, shrugging his shoulders, that he was free that morning, so far as he knew. Then he became more engaged and said: 'No problem. I'll be glad to give my bike an airing. Even in this weather.'

'A push bike?'

'No,' Errol grinned, 'a Harley-Davidson.'

This was evidently a means of travel of which Errol was hugely proud. Robert, impatient to convert a need into a deed, but appreciating that he should have Bill Bowman's sanction for any instruction to someone under his command, looked into Mary's office again.

'Any sign Bill might be coming out?'

Mary put up her hands to indicate she had no answer, and then a short burst of merriment could be heard from the inner office, and as the door shielding it opened, Robert heard two words neatly emerging between Edward Shimble's nominal lips. They were 'Gormless George'. Shimble was stretched back in his chair, fully exposing his pot belly, which in this moment of hilarity lacked its customary character of a declaration of war and even that of a provocative ultimatum.

Bill Bowman was still laughing as he came out, while Shimble's mirth was more confined, more Shimble-ish. Bowman looked back and said to Shimble that he'd have his car at the door at two o'clock. 'I'll be there, Eddie,' he added reassuringly.

'Thank you, Bill,' was the reply.

Robert soon explained to Bill, as they both walked back towards Bill's office, why Errol and his motor cycle had to be set in motion that morning.

'We have three main ways of serving summonses on individuals,' said Bill. 'Postal, personal and…' he paused, giving his final word special emphasis, 'rectal'.

Robert passed over the opportunity to enjoy a joke. 'Not by rectum this time. Personal by hand will do.' He asked for Errol's immediate enlistment.

'You can have him with pleasure. Only too glad to get him out of the office. He moans all the time, except when he's on his fucking motor-bike.'

Robert had not seen this less comradely side of Bill Bowman before. He could not resist asking whether Bill was being given special duties by Shimble. 'You're not helping him buy a new car?'

'That was last week. You've not seen his Jaguar in the car park?' Bowman said no more.

Robert had considered asking Bowman, if he could do so casually at a suitable moment, what the joke had been with Shimble about 'Gormless George', but left it, anticipating that Bowman would clam up in response. He learned later from Mary, however, that the amusement was connected with Shimble's inability to forget his annoyance, returned from his summer holiday, about George's in-tray aberration over the inter-Boroughs' meeting that Shimble could not have attended. The passing of time had not excused George. Once such a crime had been entered in the black book of Shimble's mind, it would not readily be deleted. But Mary had said too that at least Shimble was now able to laugh about George's stupidity – if, she said, 'you want to call it that'. Robert had registered too that when Shimble had laughed, although an objective reason for humour was difficult to identify, Bowman had laughed too, as if their respective vocal mechanisms were integrated.

The junior litigator, Errol Staines, duly briefed and in black leathers soon roared off on his Harley-Davidson in the direction of Tottenham, warned to be wary of a physically menacing Mr. Stewart.

Robert's next task was to get on the telephone to Jessica, to ask where she stood regarding the hearing on Wednesday.

'I'm going to visit the family this afternoon. And tomorrow too, after nursery, that is. I can't really say much more, except that I think we probably do need an interim care order and we do have ready a foster home suitable for Amy if the order is granted. I'm really worried about her.'

'Does your senior Derek agree?'

'I'm afraid it's difficult to get much sense out of Derek at the moment. Sometimes he edges this way, sometimes that way. At the moment he doesn't seem to know which way to edge. And he seems agonised about it.'

They agreed that Robert would be informed the next morning how the visit had gone. Before long Errol reported back to Robert that he had handed summonses successfully to Amy's mother. With prompting, he signed a confirmation of this that could be produced to the court. Mr. Stewart, said Errol, had not been present, so he had not needed his self-defence skills, which on his own say-so were considerable.

On the Tuesday morning, just before lunch-time, Jessica telephoned. 'I wasn't allowed in the home. Father's doing. He said I could fucking see Amy at the nursery if I wanted. So I'm going there now.'

Later she phoned again. 'I've seen her. She seems to have regressed. Wetting herself, soiling herself. Miserable and whining. We'll need that order.'

The cold snap which had begun on the Monday had persisted, and showed no desire to move on. That Tuesday evening, before Robert cooked himself a plain dinner (in a kitchen where his partner-in-tenancy's sink accumulation had not quite crossed the criminally intolerable line), he braved the cold for a visit to a nearby launderette, where he watched shirts and underwear monotonously circling into renewed cleanliness before he witnessed their undergoing a tedious water-extraction process. Later, back at the flat, he pressed the trousers of his number one pin-stripe.

Wednesday morning he was at the Tottenham court early, leaving his outer coat in his car in the road outside, as there was nowhere in the building to stow it safely. The waggish male usher remembered him.

'Here again? If you get in the habit you'll never be able to stop.'

Robert was getting to feel more at home in this world of ushers, clerks, magistrates, lawyers, social workers, other 'professionals' and a swirl of other people who would rather be elsewhere.

The usher continued to seek his attention. 'You're Mr. Ford?'

'Fordham.'

'That's right. We've had a message for you to ring a day nursery. They've got the details in the office. By the way,' he added, 'you're in Court 2 today with Lady F.'

Robert delayed not. From the public telephone booth, which fortuitously was free of occupants, he telephoned the nursery manager.

'I thought I should let you know,' she said. 'Mrs. Stewart has been in with Amy. Amy's all right, but Mrs. Stewart told me she had a big fight with her husband last night. She was upset.'

'Visible marks?'

'She showed me a bruise on her neck. Said he'd tried to strangle her.'

'Can you come to court?'

'Now?'

'I'm ever so sorry to put pressure on you, but this could tip the balance between getting an order to protect Amy and not.'

'All right then.' She was resigned. 'I know where the court is, but where do I meet you inside the building?'

He told her. By the time Amy's case was called on before Lady Feverel in Court 2, oppressive with its dark furniture, high ceiling and seats that resembled pews, a number of people had assembled outside. Jessica, Dr. Pearson, Mrs. Stewart and the old dodderer from Slash & Co were all present. The old dodderer's underwear was this time not on view, but it did not escape Robert's eyes that his trousers, unlike Robert's, could do with some attention from an electric iron.

When the hearing began, Robert decided that Lady Feverel was more at ease in a large old-fashioned court room with oak fittings than she had been in the little room that went under the name of Court 5. She was flanked this time by book-ends Robert had not seen before. The clerk was the same curly-headed young man who in the 'escape from the balcony case', without deference had denied Lady Feverel's power to insist that the parents should meet their absconding daughter.

If Robert did not notice that Mrs. Stewart had arrived coatless, despite the cold outside, he did notice that her ill-fitting jumper, of a grey-blue colour matching that of the corridor walls of the court building, was spattered with holes. He felt sorry for her. She was subdued. She told Lady Feverel, when asked, that her husband was at work.

'The application for an interim care order,' said the old dodderer, 'is neither opposed nor agreed by Mrs. Stewart.' Dr. Pearson gave evidence first, removing his spectacles and replacing them, every minute or two, in characteristic fashion, and was thanked as a person of importance by Lady Feverel when allowed to leave. He was replaced by Jessica and then by the day nursery manager, who reported with clarity what Mrs. Stewart had told her that morning. Mrs. Stewart was asked nothing and said nothing. It all, as Robert said to Jessica afterwards, went like the changing of the guard.

A temporary care order for four weeks was made on Amy and arrangements to take her to the foster home direct from the nursery that afternoon were made. Jessica made a point (as she told Robert later) of asking Mrs. Stewart if she wished to leave home, suggesting a women's refuge would accommodate her. Mrs. Stewart's rejoinder, speaking listlessly, was to tell Jessica not to interfere, saying that she had caused enough trouble already. The nursery manager told Robert gloomily that she would now have to phone her boss.

'Charmaine Trickett?'

'We have to keep her informed of everything, and she'll pull me up for not having reported earlier, even though there was no time.'

'Someone you have to keep on the right side of,' Robert suggested.

'If you can,' she sighed. Robert thanked her for her contribution. 'It's made a lot of difference.'

After others had left the court, the curly-headed clerk motioned Robert to remain, and when they were alone, produced a kind of verbal postscript to the previous week's 'balcony escape' case.

'I'd like to give you a tip.'

'Very welcome,' said Robert.

'It's about legal aid. That barrister representing Michelle...'

'Jonathan Spratt.'

'Yes, that's right, Mr. Spratt. He was representing Michelle but taking instructions from her parents.'

'It seemed wrong that he was doing that.'

'You could have pointed something out to Mr. Spratt and the Court. The current legal aid position is that the court *can* enable the parents to be represented separately. You could have raised that and Michelle would have had her own lawyer.'

'I see.' Robert took a chance on falling out with the clerk. 'Couldn't you have raised this?'

'Yes, but my boss doesn't encourage it. He says it's more money for the taxpayer to cough up. He's pretty old-world. He won't even allow a vending machine for drinks in the public area here.'

'Thanks for the tip. Can I ask something else about the West case? It's a bit personal.'

'Well, as personal as I'll allow, as the Queen once said.'

Robert barged ahead. 'There was a moment when Lady Feverel looked cross about your advice – about the court not having the power to direct a meeting between Michelle and her parents.'

'Cross! She was furious, ballistic. Between ourselves, I got a dressing-down. She regards me as a kind of butler in this establishment, and I wasn't behaving like a butler. She said I'd made the court look ridiculous, a laughing stock. I assured her that was the last thing in my mind.'

'Yes, of course,' said Robert.

'The very last.' At which point the curly-headed clerk contorted his features comically.

16

A Social Services Committee Meeting Looms

A fortnight passed after Robert's submission to Edward Shimble of his draft report about parental rights resolution procedure, before it was returned to him. There were no changes, save for the hand-written elimination of two words which, a marginal note indicated, Shimble considered 'otiose', and the replacement of Robert's word 'option' with Shimble's word 'possibility'.

Shimble-approved, however tardily, the report was now dispatched by Robert to Director of Social Services Michael Stone for last-stage endorsement before circulation to the members of the Social Services Committee. Its dispatch coincided with the arrival on Robert's desk of a related report prepared by senior social worker Enid Prosser, but in Stone's name.

This recommended that the Council assume parental rights and duties in respect of a child identified by the initial 'A', a boy approaching his second birthday. 'A' had been conceived, the introduction ran, as a result of rape by an unknown man. The mother, who was still in her late teens, had played little part in the child's care. He had been looked after during the first three months of his life by the maternal grandmother, in whose home the young mother lived too.

Then a crisis had come. The grandmother, not yet out of her forties, said to have a history of volatility, had theatrically opted out of the caring role. She had descended on the Social Services office with 'A' asleep in his pram, insisting first to the receptionist and then to a hurriedly summoned duty social worker, on relinquishing him then and there. She declared that her daughter could not look after him and that she, the grandmother, was 'finished with him'. She was echoing, the report said, her abandonment of one of her own children (not, as it happened, 'A's mother) in similar style some ten years previously.

Social workers visiting the family home hours later managed to speak to 'A's mother, who spoke slowly, using only a handful of words, seemed to have a limited understanding, but told them repeatedly, in tears: 'I said goodbye to him'.

It was, as Enid Prosser said to Robert later, 'a gun-point relinquishment'. There had been no choice but to place 'A' with foster parents, with whom he had remained. He was now a toddler, walking, and beginning to talk. Time was on the wing, and the mother still retained full parental rights and duties for 'A', while having made an exceedingly passive getaway from his life. If the Council assumed parental rights by means of a resolution, a legal basis for him to be in long term foster care or, ideally, adopted, would be built.

The only available ground offered by law for the resolution was that the mother suffered from 'a permanent disability' rendering her unable to care for 'A'. Enid Prosser's argument therefore was that the mother's intelligence, abilities and mental condition fell below the threshold at which she could conceivably care for 'A' herself. In support of this assertion was the fact that a psychiatrist, carrying out a mental health assessment before 'A's birth, had concluded that the mother's difficulties were considerable and innate. Significantly, she had never attempted to shoulder the burden of caring for 'A' herself. Such was the case that the mother was permanently disabled from parenting.

Robert considered this information. It struck him that the mental health assessment of the mother might need review; and he was sure in any event that he should see it, in case the psychiatrist's conclusions were expressed with reservations that Enid Prosser had not thought necessary to mention.

He decided to telephone her to discuss these points, and reached her without difficulty. He introduced himself as a new Social Services solicitor. She was not backward in responding.

'We could do with one.'

Robert explained that he had received the report concerning 'A' for the Social Services Committee.

'Is there something wrong with it?'

He said no, but wondered if it covered the whole territory, bearing in mind that recently another case had not satisfied all the council members.

'You mean the Firth children, I suppose.' She spoke to the point, without demonstrating any desire to please.

'Yes, but I'm only concerned with the fall-out from it, not with that case itself. I want to make sure we get this one through without upset.'

Enid Prosser became more amenable in manner.

'What do you suggest?'

'You say the child was born of rape but you don't say where that information came from.'

'The grandmother. The mother wouldn't talk about it.'

'Can that be added? Again, on the same tack, if the birth was registered, as I assume it was…'

'Yes. I registered it about six months after the birth. The mother didn't get round to doing that.'

'Can it be added, then, that the mother chose not to, or was not able to organise herself to, register the birth, so that this had to be done by Social Services? It could reduce the risk that one or other councillor might say that there is more to this case than meets the eye.'

'Fair enough. What else?'

'The mental health assessment could be a bit out of date or need a second opinion.'

'Yes, but the doctor was clear that the mother's difficulties made it most unlikely she could care for a child.'

'Can I see the report? There's a risk that her difficulties may not be interpreted by a court as amounting to a permanent disability.'

'I think it's a risk we can take. She's not likely to lift a finger to contest this. We can't make her see a psychiatrist again.'

'What about her visiting the child? The information that the mother did not visit her baby in the foster home or seek to do so is put in very general terms. Can that be elaborated a bit?'

'We do have a record.'

'You can add something? I get the impression that members' expectations regarding these reports may be rising. Civil rights awareness is more in the air than it used to be.'

Enid Prosser reverted to brusqueness. 'Always the parents' rights. Never the child's.'

'You could be right about that.'

'Will you put your comments in writing? I'll do what I can once I hear from you. Do you think we'll get it through?'

'There does seem to be an arguable case. Have you informed the mother of your intentions regarding a resolution?'

'No.'

''I think you should do, so that the councillors can be informed of that. And could I have a copy of the letter you send to her?'

'How long have you been in Haringey?'

'A few weeks.'

'I hope you stay.'

It seemed that Enid Prosser's bark was worse than her bite. Robert now converted his comments over the telephone into a typed note which sailed over to the Tottenham Area office with an alacrity which – like Robert's active interest in the case – impressed the not easily impressed Enid Prosser. A copy of the final report soon shot back to him, together with the psychiatric assessment on the mother, which, to his relief, did express the gravest doubts about the mother's capacity to parent.

Things, administrative things, were moving, but while Robert felt satisfied overall with the progress he had so far made in his new life, he was kicking himself for not appreciating at the time how he could have made a fuss in and outside court over the lack of direct legal representation for teenager Michelle. Had he done so, the argument about foster home versus children's home for her might, who knows, have led to a change of plan more in harmony with Michelle's welfare.

He was doubtful about where his involvement with Beth was headed. She had conceded she had no other boyfriend to rival Robert's current status, and she showed willingness to continue the relationship with him. Beyond that, her stance, in Robert's eyes, was ambiguous. He continued to be mesmerised by her.

A few days later he was in the Highgate magistrates court. He had half-forgotten the school attendance cases which had been his introduction there, until he saw in his diary that they were both back in court. He attempted to inquire about the situation regarding each of the boys from the moralistic education welfare officer Shirley, but managed only to leave telephone messages to which there was no response. He was updated only when he arrived in the court building. Shirley apologised for not getting back to him. She had been 'out on visits'.

The eleven-year-old son of the 'over-protective mother', Shirley told Robert with satisfaction, was now back in school and attending regularly, so proceedings could be withdrawn.

Withdrawn they were, though a few months later Robert heard that the boy's attendance had dropped off again.

But what of the mouthy teenager who had been so peremptorily dispatched to a residential assessment centre? Robert skimmed the 'comprehensive' report by the centre staff, and was concerned to see that the 'very lucky boy', in the chairman's phrase of four weeks previously, had had a large share in causing mayhem since. His behaviour in and outside the assessment centre had come close to justifying the extreme step of 'a certificate of unruliness' which, if granted by justices, would have put him behind bars in a secure children's unit. The report's authors were anxious for him to leave the centre as soon as ever possible, and had made no recommendation for an order.

'I feel very sorry for the centre staff and members of the public who have had to put up with you,' said the small and friendly chairman irritably to the youth, who was sitting with his mother, chewing gum and saying nothing.

The chairman announced firmly that the Bench had no choice but to make a full care order. About to utter a few more judicial words, he was then stopped in his tracks, for the teenager's mother, jumping out of her silence, shouted stridently: 'He wouldn't have got into trouble if you hadn't sent him away. He was never in trouble before.' Preferring dignified retreat to answering back, the chairman and his two book-end colleagues rose hastily to their feet and left the court, retiring ceremony leapfrogged.

Robert had already been informed by social workers that if a care order were made there was no proposal for the boy to be placed away from home. The care order would be managed as if it were a supervision order, limited to monitoring and advice for mother and son. (When this was explained to them outside court by a conscientious social worker, the response from the mother was tart. 'We don't want monitoring and we don't want advice.') So the boy would go home and that was that, however little school attendance occurred afterwards, and however much education welfare officer Shirley (whose disapproval was loud in her face) and the justices were put out.

As the magistrates had notified their decision, and had now left the court, it was too late, Robert thought, to advise them impersonally of the social work refusal to adopt an 'away plan' for the teenager. The magistrates had, the second time in a month, shot from the hip, and they, as well as the family and Haringey's Social Services Department, would have to tolerate the fallout, such as it might be.

Outside the court room, he glanced around to see if Jack Parnell was about, but there was no sign of his more experienced Enfield counterpart.

17

Mr. Shimble has a Tantrum

Deep inside the Borough's legal building and the day after the return to Robert of his parental rights resolution report with Edward Shimble's minimal corrections, a grenade exploded. The grenade took the form of the pasting up on the wall adjoining the lift on the second floor of a large notice (designed with the help of thick felt-tipped pens of several colours) of a brash character. It was an announcement of, and indeed an invitation to, a party of an anniversary nature to be staged by the Community Development Team which occupied the ground floor of the building. Details of the time and place of the convivial occasion were given below a large, single, short and eye-capturing word – namely, 'SEX'. It could be inferred that the deployment of this word was intended to draw attention to the rest of the notice, and, indeed, to encourage participation in the party.

Edward Shimble was generally unobservant about the details of his immediate surroundings, but when he emerged from the lift soon after nine thirty, and made his way to his office to commence the day's work, sight of the single and evocative word entrapped his brain and tugged the pin from the grenade. He was horrified and scandalised. This was, after all, the council's legal department, not a hotel specialising in free love weekends. (Later in the week, when legal department cognoscenti reviewed this moment, there was general agreement that Mr. Shimble would not have been more shocked had he received a telephone call from the police station to tell him that the typing pool was functioning as a cover for an escort agency.)

Was somebody in the legal service – his department – responsible? His long face began to purple following a well-established pattern. Was George Ballam the culprit, whether by giving permission for the notice, or by turning a blind eye to its intrusion on to hallowed legal ground, or even by pasting it up himself? Shimble suspected the worst.

'I want to know,' were his first words to Mary that morning, as he passed through her office en route to his own, 'who put up the outrageous notice on this floor next to the lift.'

Mary flushed. 'Somebody in CDT brought it up.'

'I suppose George Ballam told them to go ahead.'

'No, it was me, I'm afraid,' said Mary.

Shimble was astonished and speechless for some seconds. He looked at her.

She went on. 'I was by the lift when the chap who brought it came up and asked if it would be all right. It was only about a quarter of an hour ago.'

'You saw the word on the notice?'

'Yes. I didn't really think about that word.'

'It doesn't give a good impression of this department,' said Shimble. 'It must be taken down forthwith.'

He had not quite finished. 'I should like to make a tour now of the offices to make sure there aren't any more unseemly displays.' So Shimble and an embarrassed Mary set off, first removing the culprit notice, then inspecting all vertical surfaces, giving rise to curious, uncomprehending looks to which Shimble was oblivious. There were no other notices of the Community Development Team party to be seen. Or any other offensive material.

They arrived at the Reprographics room on the first floor, where a giant photocopying machine held pride of place, near the good-sized table used for emptying incoming, and gathering up outgoing, mail. It was there that George Ballam marked out correspondence daily to the various recipients. Neither the morning's post nor George Ballam were yet present in the room; but both would be soon.

Shimble glanced down at a waste paper basket in a corner. It was stuffed with discarded photocopies, and the floor around it was strewn with more, some in the form of torn-up scraps, some screwed into balls, some in pristine condition but abandoned.

'This is disgusting,' he said. 'Odious. I shall have to speak to George about this.'

Mary, whose sympathies lay with George and whose compliant nature forbad the open expression of disloyalty to Shimble, spoke calmly. 'I'm afraid it's the CDT lot again. They share this room and they're not the tidiest of people.'

Edward Shimble's opinion of this particular council unit, as fit only for the heave-ho from council services, was, Mary knew well, no more benevolent than his opinion of the Chief Executive's usefulness, or of the Labour Party's control of the council. He nodded, not being enough in severely investigatory mode at that moment actually to examine the mess on the floor, especially as he hated, for reasons of balance, bending over. Had he done so, Mary knew, it would reveal that the untidiness was not solely the product of the Community Development Team.

She had successfully transferred responsibility for the offence away from Shimble's preferred suspect. Shimble was not, however, quite done. 'Do these people live in filth?' he queried. 'I dread to think what their homes are like.'

'Even worse, I should imagine,' said Mary, shaking her head to share his abhorrence, and relieved she had deflected arrows away from George Ballam. They returned from their tour of two floors of the building to their own office quarters.

While doing so, they encountered Errol, the proud Harley-Davidson rider, who was suffering a minor coughing fit in the corridor. Shimble, always sensitive to indisposition on the part of others, walked passed him quickly, saying to Mary, once back in the safety of his office:

'I'm wondering if I'm going to be ill. My throat feels a bit tickly. Do I look ill?'

Mary's response was her usual one whenever thoughts of personal discomfort were uttered by the borough's senior solicitor. 'I'll make you some tea.'

18

Robert Advises Action

On the day of Edward Shimble's surge of wrath over the Community Development Team's notorious party advertisement, Robert was in his office when he received a call from Emily Frost. He was expecting her to speak about the revue, but was immediately put right. Emily was speaking with total seriousness about one of her families.

She told him the subject was the future of a baby girl born prematurely in the North Middlesex Hospital. The twenty-five-year-old mother, she said, had a history of mental illness, though was currently living in the community. The child was her first. There had been real doubt as to whether she could be trusted to care for her baby, but a decision, in which Dr. Elaine Abrahams had been influential, had been made to discharge the baby from hospital to her mother's care. Emily suspected that care proceedings should be considered, just a week after home care by the mother had begun. The baby was now six weeks old.

'So where do I come in?'

'Legal advice? That's your function, isn't it?' Emily said shortly.

'Yes of course,' Robert said tamely.

Emily went on. 'I visited the mother last Friday…'

'Does she have a name?'

'Yvonne…Yvonne Sircar.'

'Spelt?'

She spelt it for him.

'Asian origin?'

'You'd think so, but her surname is her husband's. They're separated. She's white English. The child isn't his by the way.'

'So you visited Yvonne…?'

'And I was filled with anxiety. I'd welcome help on how strong a case for proceedings is at this moment, and even on how strong the case is for immediate removal. I can send you my notes of that visit.'

Robert welcomed this. He said he didn't know if he'd be much help but he would try. He was, he said, flattered to be asked.

'You can skip that. This is serious.'

'Your senior,' he asked. 'Isn't that Enid Prosser?'

'It was. I'm now in Derek Ivins's team.'

'Ah'

'You may well say 'ah'. He's an idiot. He's over-influenced by Elaine Abrahams and anyway hates taking against parents.'

'I see.' Robert remembered he had been told by Jessica that Ivins had once been in care himself and told to forget he had been told.

Two days later the notes of Emily's visit, together with background information, arrived in Robert's post. He read all this twice through. His conclusion was that if this narrative represented the real picture, for this mother to have continuing care of this baby was likely to be dangerous, perhaps very dangerous, for the baby's welfare.

Emily, when she had visited, had spent more than an hour with Yvonne Sircar and her baby in the rented upstairs flat where they lived. Repeatedly during the visit Yvonne had spoken with bizarre irrationality, while her eyes had darted wildly around the room. Several times she had broken out into semi-hysterical laughter, either hiding her face behind her hands or behind a small cushion snatched up from a nearby chair.

While the baby had been in hospital, Yvonne's visits to the ward had been sporadic and her behaviour there had been worrying. She would absent herself for several days, without explanation, and between these episodes of complete withdrawal would visit late at night, even past midnight and on one of these occasions had been obviously intoxicated. What was more, during these nocturnal descents, she had complained about the crying of other babies, and had worried nursing staff by approaching them in their cots and speaking sternly to them. She had told Dr. Abrahams lately that her baby had said to her, Yvonne, that she did not love her and did not like being poor.

Dr. Abrahams had been able, Emily had written in a covering note, to establish some rapport with Yvonne, but only by treating her as a child.

What complicated the argument was the paediatrician's initial view, based on observation of mother and baby, that there was a real bond between them, and that Yvonne was a committed mother. She had managed, to her credit, to purchase a baby bath, sterilising unit, clothing and nappies. Until now, Dr. Abrahams had been in favour of letting events take their course, with close medical and social work monitoring. She was now not so sure this approach should continue. Emily was frankly inclined to removal.

The note ended with a question: what did Robert say about the appropriateness of care proceedings and urgent removal.
In this material the baby was always referred to as 'baby' as if without a name. But glancing again at the covering note Robert could see a name in the heading – Tania – though her birth was apparently not yet registered.

There was no choice but to reply immediately in writing to Emily. If care proceedings were brought, he wrote, the justification would rest essentially on the neglect of Tania's 'proper development', however unintentional. By visiting irregularly and irrationally at night at the hospital and not engaging adequately with Tania when she was there, there was neglect. It could be inferred from Yvonne's behaviour on the ward and in discussion between her and social workers and other professionals, that the care deficit demonstrated on the ward would probably be replicated away from professional eyes. Now that baby Tania was at home with her mother, unintended neglect of her needs had been observed by Emily and could be inferred to be taking place when witnesses were absent.

The neglect exhibited, wrote Robert, was underlined and enhanced by the indications that Yvonne's behaviour might become dangerous to Tania through, for example, the delusional belief that Tania had said she did not love her mother. It must follow, he continued, that there was a definite case in his view for care proceedings and for Tania's separation from her mother's care, and a place of safety order could be justified. Robert's dictated answer was on its way to Emily within 24 hours. He received a phone call thanking him for his input. And then – silence.

19

A Meeting of the Social Services Committee

It was the habit of Haringey Council's Social Services Committee to meet on Tuesdays at six-weekly intervals in the Council Chamber. By the start time of seven thirty on a cool evening in mid-October, its members, save for one or two who had sent apologies, were ranged around tables aligned to create an oval shape. Several observers, including Enid Prosser, sat on chairs away from the oval, glued to the walls of the grand-up-to-a point setting. On the table in front of each participant was a push-button microphone.

Robert, a pizza contentedly installed inside him earlier in a Wood Green restaurant, sat next to the committee clerk who had not that evening, any more than when they had met weeks earlier, combed his hair or got rid of his freckles. The chairman of the committee was a middle-aged woman of comfortable size and drab clothing, whose voice had a maternal and generous ring to it, save when thwarted. She first drew attention to the significant consequences for local people of the cuts in financial provision imposed by the new Conservative government, a comment which drew approving looks and murmurs from the majority of councillors present, and one dissident and very steely 'Very necessary' from a minority member, who added the more vitriolic remark: 'And the Labour rebels have been sensible enough, after their little tantrum, to accept the reality.'

The chairman ignored this reference to the autumn revolt (now quelled) by some Labour councillors against cuts considered by the leadership to be regrettable but impossible to refuse. She was keen to get down to business.

A sequence of agenda items included day nursery provision, residential homes for the elderly, and the progress achieved in the building of a young people's hostel which had become the subject of a cost overrun. There was also a report for information about the childminding service. The committee clerk, when this item was reached, drew Robert's attention discreetly to a woman in her forties who was sitting next to Enid Prosser. 'That's Charmaine Trickett,' he said, "the one with hair that doesn't move about. She's known as 'the Day Care factor'."

'I've heard that,' Robert whispered back. He took note of her permanently waved dark hair, and her semi-rosebud lips, decorated with dark lipstick. Though her neat face was pleasant enough, its expression was formidably intent.

'Notice the resemblance to Maggie Thatcher?'

'Noted.' There was, indeed, a facial resemblance to Britain's first female Prime Minister, as well as a shared reputation for assertive behaviour. The committee clerk was disparaging. 'She's a dragon.'

The agenda was worked through slowly, more slowly, it seemed, than the chairman would have liked, and she was short with council member comments which she thought unhelpful.

When the hostel building cost overrun issue was reached, a representative of the council's estate management department, who looked tired and sounded miserable, fielded questions. Some soft, generalised answers came from him. No happy solution emerged, and a consensus emerged from the meeting that fire should rain down mercilessly on the building contractor concerned.

The next item was about discipline within the borough's children's homes. Michael Stone, a distinguished-looking man with voice to match and greying hair, speaking with fluent confidence, made explicit that officers in charge had been instructed that physical chastisement was not acceptable as a sanction for bad behaviour at any time.

A Conservative councillor of conservative disposition – in fact the owner of the 'Very necessary' intervention earlier – queried this. 'Are there no circumstances,' he asked, 'such as when a youngster is playing up and being lippy, that staff cannot resort to a clip round the ear?'

'I think not,' smoothed Stone. 'If a staff member resorted to a clip round a child's ear he might find the child – who could be bigger and stronger than the staff member – knocking him into the middle of next week.'

The chairman threw in at this point a reminder that in September the Education Committee had banned corporal punishment in Haringey's schools.

'There's a cost savings there,' the Conservative responded. 'No more purchase of expensive canes,' he jeered, to minority party applause. 'But the children will run rings round school staff and in the children's homes'.

'They may do,' said Michael Stone urbanely. 'But as well as being at risk of counter-attack, we're at risk these days of actions for assault, as I am sure the borough solicitor will confirm.'

Members fastened their eyes on Robert.

'I agree.'

Next to be considered – for the information report on the subject of the childminding service attracted no questions for 'dragon' Charmaine Trickett – was the question of the assumption of parental rights and duties in respect of the child 'A'. For this item the committee went into secret session. A youthful representative of the local press who had been observing languidly, now left the Chamber, while Enid Prosser, a rotund woman aged around fifty, and wearing clothes as drab as the lady chairman's, advanced from her chair by the wall to sit next to Michael Stone. En route she said hello to Robert, smiling at him, as if they had already met.

Stone now introduced the report, explaining that it had been prepared by Miss Prosser, and adding that he had arranged for her to attend in case members had any questions for her. He drew attention to Robert's report explaining the unfortunate need sometimes for these resolutions, and how the procedures which would be followed ensured fairness to parents.

'They've been tightened up, haven't they?' asked a female councillor with a voice exhibiting concern, making a point more than asking a question.

Well spotted, thought Robert.

'And necessarily so,' said Stone.

The resolution was put and passed after only three questions were raised. These were more of an information-seeking character than part of an exercise in scepticism. Enid Prosser rose coolly to the occasion. After a failed attempt to activate the push-button microphone in front of her, an event which did not disconcert her in the slightest, she was successful the second time of trying. Two of the questions were in fact answered in the body of the report, but Enid Prosser answered them anyway. The third went outside it.

'You say,' said the female councillor with the concerned voice, 'that the mother has only visited the child twice since being in care, and not over the last year. Can you expand on that?'

Enid Prosser's customary 'take no prisoners' manner of speaking was not altogether absent. 'Soon after Aaron' – she had forgotten he was to remain anonymous – 'was received into the foster home, his mother visited him with the social worker. She spent an hour with him there, and got on well with the foster mother. She was given the address for future visits. She visited once after that and has not visited since.'

The concerned female councillor said 'I see', and said no more. The fear in the minds of officers of a councillor rebellion against parental rights resolutions in general was put to rest. The committee seemed satisfied and the resolution was passed. It was the last item on the agenda and the meeting was declared closed.

Robert left the Council Chamber, walking a short distance behind Enid Prosser and Michael Stone, noticing how short was the former and how tall the latter. He caught a scrap of dialogue between them.

'Why did you say you'd arranged for me to be present?' asked Enid, in as low a voice as she generally managed in conversation. 'You didn't. I came under my own steam. Nobody asked.'

Stone laughed. 'Really Enid, it's the name of the game. Didn't you know?' He did not listen for an answer, going on, as if talking to himself. 'Oh why is it that I like power so much?'

He strode off towards his car, while Robert caught Enid up. He suggested a drink to celebrate.

'Why not?' she said. They crossed the road to a large public house on a corner. Once inside, Enid refused Robert's proposal that he buy the drinks.

'It's on me,' she insisted. Both soon had pints of bitter in front of them. She thanked him for making the case watertight. 'That councillor who asked about the mother's visiting,' she said. 'It's the same one who made the fuss about the Firth children.'

'Was it just one of them who made a fuss?'

'Just one, unless you count hear-hearing from another one.'

'There could be a battle ahead over Aaron,' he said, 'if the mother objects.'

'I can't see her doing that.'

'Is the plan for Aaron to be adopted?'

'I hope so. If we can find an adoptive home. Though the foster parents are happy to keep him. But will the mother consent to Aaron's adoption? We had one adoption held up when a Danish au pair gave birth and gave up the child for adoption without actually giving written consent. She had to be chased for months and months for her consent when she was back in Denmark.'

'If she was chaste,' said Robert ruminatively, pretending to have got the wrong end of the stick, displaying on his face a mix of innocence and morality, 'she wouldn't have conceived in the first place.'

'My God! What's the man like after he's downed a couple of pints?'

'Oh, a chap's likely to get pretty unruly at that point. But might there be a doubt as to whether Aaron's mother has the legal capacity to consent? I must ask one question – which I should have asked before. Was her second visit to Aaron in the foster home around the time of his first birthday?'

'Yes, it was. Why do you ask? She took him a present.'

'I happened to notice that his second birthday was about a week ago. I wondered if you'd been in touch with the foster mother since then to ask if she'd visited or sent something.'

Enid Prosser was not troubled by this speculation. 'No I haven't, but I'm sure she'd have phoned to tell me.'

'I should have suggested a phone call to check. Too late now.'

'I'd be amazed if anything is different,' said Enid Prosser. She changed subjects.

'I've heard you're one of the bright sparks organising an entertainment for the department.'

'In a small way, yes. Are you thinking of joining in?'

'Good God, no. But I might come to see it.'

They soon made for their respective homes. The desk Robert had lately acquired for home use was now installed in his bedroom. His flat mate was out, and the washing-up accumulated in the sink included a saucepan in which old food encrustation was extreme. Robert left it to its own devices but was determined to say something at a suitable moment. He was still tolerating his antiquated single bed, waiting until more funds were available to buy a new one.

20

Another Shimble Outburst

There came to pass, on a day in the third week of October, the event which in Edward Shimble's view proved beyond all doubt the unsuitability of George Ballam for the task of securing the effective daily routines of the borough's legal service. That day, putting matters shortly, Edward Shimble's copy of the daily *Times,* despite the strictest of instructions to Ballam, had not, by the allotted deadline, reached Shimble's desk; and it was perfectly plain that Ballam was responsible.

Newspapers and legal periodicals were provided to the legal department only after finding their way there through the same channel as the day's post, having first landed at the Civic Centre. It was the Borough Secretary's task – or at least that of one of his staff – to speed them onwards to their proper destination in the legal building downhill and round the corner in Station Road.

The newspaper vital for lawyers was the *Times*, because of its prosaic but space-greedy summaries of judgments in the higher courts. These carried practical implications for local government and therefore for its solicitors, however much passed over with a yawn by the run of readers. Shimble regarded the *Times* as his personal newspaper. Once the paper had passed through his hands – or, if he were on leave, reached Mary – she would cut out relevant law reports and paste them into an album to which the department's solicitors could have ready access. Not all of them, it was rumoured, were said to inspect the album often.

On days when he was in the office – and not out with Bill Bowman on one errand or another, or on holiday, or at meetings, or ill (and his health was sometimes delicate) – Edward Shimble greatly relished sitting in his maroon leather rocking chair, turning over the pages of the paper, sipping tea from a china cup and taking some, though not necessarily meticulous, interest in the legal judgments. Whether he remembered much of what he read, according to Colin Masson, was questionable.

The most important requirement, for Shimble, was that the paper should get to him, and get to him in timely manner each morning. So slips between the Civic Centre offices of the Borough Secretary and those of the legal service could have toxic implications. If the paper had reached the legal department by ten o'clock in the morning, all in the loop could breathe a sigh of relief. If it had not arrived by then, tip-toeing about by those near to Shimble was advisable. Non-arrival triggered action – taut-faced action, so Colin Masson said – by Mary. She would telephone the Borough Secretary's staff to advise them of the *Times*'s absence and of the need for its urgent presence. Although it was on most occasions with Shimble by half past ten, by that time he was, if still waiting, as Mary put it confidentially at home to her husband, 'usually working himself up into a state'.

As a result of two or three late arrivals during a single month, Shimble issued a definitive order to George Ballam. He was to take personal responsibility for early delivery; and if the paper was not in the legal building by ten thirty, he was to arrange for the immediate purchase of a substitute copy from a nearby newsagent.

George's view that it would be difficult for him to take personal responsibility when Mary was well-placed to discover and follow up non-arrival, was waved away; and Shimble took no steps to instruct Mary to transfer her own burden on to George. Better, it seemed, to have the minds of two staff members strapped, as it were, to the local travelling plans of the *Times*.

George, uneasily appreciating that taking personal responsibility would require him to monitor Mary's alertness during the half-hour between ten o'clock and ten thirty when he might have other things to do, decided unilaterally, and therefore dangerously, to decline to share Mary's chasing duty save on any day – a rare phenomenon – when she did not show up for work. Mary, for her part, had devised, in conjunction with him, a simple stratagem to invoke if no Civic Centre copy of the *Times* had turned up by ten thirty, after her telephoned reminder. She would notify a designated junior legal staff member (in fact shoulder-shrugging Errol, whom we have met) of the now-now need to purchase a substitute copy. George had authorised Errol to extract the cost of the paper from the petty cash float kept in his office safe.

Predictably, the common outcome on these anxious occasions was the arrival of two copies of the paper on Mary's desk within a few minutes of each other – a late-comer from the Civic Centre, and a rival from the local newsagent. In these surreal circumstances the first copy to arrive was handed to Shimble by Mary almost as quickly as if she were playing 'pass the parcel', while the second copy, when this had been obtained, stood idly by, if not borrowed by solicitors who happened to be passing through.

Thus the issue seemed to have been comprehensively addressed, though not the underlying insanity of the convoluted arrangement for the delivery of all publications through the Civic Centre.

There came, however, the day of trauma and wrath, which placed George Ballam once more in front of Shimble's notional firing squad. On this particular day the *Times* failed to emerge from the Borough Secretary's office and the substitute copy from the local newsagent also remained unpurchased.

Robert Fordham was later told by the freckled Social Services Committee clerk that, at a moment when daily newspapers were resting on a table in the Civic Centre, already sorted into their various destinations, Chief Executive Roland Trask had paused when passing. The *Times* had caught his eye. Mistakenly assuming this copy was destined for himself, and about to set off for a meeting of council Chief Executives in central London, 'Smiler' had swept it up as handy reading-matter for the train. The reason why no second copy had been obtained was human enough. Errol was that day off sick. Mary, for her part, while aware of this, had optimistically and foolishly assumed the official copy would arrive, and had failed to tell George that the designated fall-back machinery named Errol was that day unable to function.

Once the ten-thirty deadline had passed, Mary had intended to pop out of the building herself to buy a substitute copy, but telephone calls had kept her in her chair and other demands (notably a Shimble call for a teapot-brewed cup of tea) had taken her out of it, but not given her the opportunity to leave the building. George was oblivious that the whole house of cards was tumbling down. He was caught off guard and, in Shimble's eyes, red-handed.

Although Mary confessed to Shimble, when he became agitated over the newspaper's non-arrival, that she should have informed George of the non-arrival both of the *Times* and of Errol, he would have none of it. He was too reliant upon Mary's good offices, and too much offended by George's limitless inadequacies, to criticise her.

Shimble, fuming, allowed half an hour to pass before demanding Ballam's presence. The door between the two rooms was open when George arrived, so that Mary was in no position to warn him that he was on the chopping board again.

George entered, shutting the door behind him, not ready for the sudden descent of an avalanche of rage. The meeting was first cold, then hot.

Shimble opened, his long face journeying slowly from pink towards purple, as he leaned back in his leather chair.

'It's now eleven fifteen. Agreed?'

George agreed.

'And, nevertheless, the *Times,* my newspaper, is not here.'

'The *Times*? Hasn't Mary…?'

George got no further.

'I'm not talking about Mary. I'm talking about you. I specifically allocated you the task – not a task of great complexity, I might say – of making sure my paper reaches here, and not preposterously late.'

'Yes, you did,' agreed George.

'And you have lamentably failed to rise to the occasion.'

'All right, but what about getting a copy from the newsagent now?'

'I think you had better leave this room.' Shimble's nostrils were quivering, he was making a clop-clop sound with his tongue and his face was two thirds through the journey to purple. Mary for her part, while George was being berated, was upset that he was being penalised for her own shortcoming. She had slipped out of the office and bought the newsagent copy of the paper in the hope it would assuage wrath.

George, angry, avoided Shimble for the rest of the day. At home he relieved his feelings by telling the story to his wife in some detail. She said that if he wished to stand up for himself, even if it risked his job, she would be right behind him. She added, after further cogitation: 'Wasn't he making a huge fuss about something amazingly trivial?'

Straightaway George felt better. He would, he decided, in future stand up to the man.

He would have felt better still had he known that within minutes after he had returned to his own room, Shimble had, in vain search of peace of mind, leaned so far back in his flexible chair that it had tipped over and struck the floor behind him, ejecting him messily in the process, giving him a shock and a sore shoulder. Though Mary had supplied medication, soothing words and more tea, Shimble had soon left for home, chauffeured by Bill Bowman.

No-one other than Mary had witnessed the moment of the misadventure, and Shimble was glad of that. Before departing, he had enjoined Mary not to speak of it to anyone, and she sustained her loyalty in keeping mum. But the crash had been heard. When curious colleagues based not far away asked later if there had been an accident, she admitted untruthfully that she had herself knocked over a chair.

Colin Masson had by chance been in the corridor, and, putting his head inside a moment after the fall, had heard groans of pain and observed Mary rush in. He had seen over her shoulder the apparent absence both of Shimble's chair and Shimble himself (both at that moment located invisibly below desk surface level). He had not remained to see Mary's rescue operation and sympathy. A smile played on his mouth off and on during the rest of the day, but he kept what he had seen to himself.

During the afternoon of that day, Robert Fordham visited Colin's office to collect a legal periodical which he needed and Colin needed no longer. He asked, thinking of the autocratic behaviour displayed by Shimble at the recent meeting of solicitors and managers, and knowing nothing of George Ballam's latest humiliation, for any tips Colin had about dealing with Shimble when dark clouds threatened. Colin told him that useful lessons could be learned from his own recent experience of how Shimble had managed his upgrading to the title of senior solicitor. He had faced Shimble down successfully as the negotiation stumbled.

The process had begun without any hint of strife. Colin had been invited in to Shimble's office and had been pleasantly surprised by the beneficial announcement that he was to be lifted to a higher grade; and that there would be a need to update and sign a new job description which would reflect his enhanced status. The advancement promised appeared to be unconditional: a gift.

What followed this later amounted to a catch. Shimble had asked Colin to commit himself to a wider range of tasks than previously considered to be within his remit. As well as general litigation, he was now, it appeared, to be expected to represent the council at planning appeal hearings. His response, collecting himself, was to express doubts that he could commit himself to expanding his current role.

There came a turn of the screw – accompanied by the disappearance of the previous good-humour in Shimble's countenance – the inference drawn by Shimble that unwillingness to 'reach beyond his previously circumscribed functions' might be an obstacle to the upgrading which he had understood to have been promised unconditionally on the basis of his past performance.

'Awkward. So what then?'

'I wrote to him a diplomatically phrased note which declared that I was pleased to have been notified of my planned upgrade, and unequivocally doubted that in view of my current workload I could extend significantly the range of my duties at this time. I said I looked forward to being able to sign my new job description.'

'And then?'

'Nothing. The weeks went by. He dithered. I sent him a reminder and a week after that another. No response. Then he called me in to say he was sorry about the delay, but that my job description should be with me within the week.'

'Was it?'

'Not quite. It arrived two or three weeks later, and when it came there was no inclusion of a wider spread of functions …in truth Shimble really hadn't tried very hard to get his own way.'

'The lesson to be drawn?'

'In summary, if you behave like a mouse he'll act like a cat, and if you act like another cat, he may retract his claws.'

Robert left Colin Masson's office with the periodical he had come to collect.

21

Another Care Proceedings

New appointments were raining down on Robert's diary. A day after the latest Shimble outburst, and not much more than a week after he had advised Emily Frost about possible court action in the case of baby Tania Sircar, he was invited at short notice to a case conference concerning her at the North Middlesex Hospital. This time there was no Beth present to take notes, and the task fell to Emily Frost.

The deliberations took place in an interview room adjoining a children's ward. Dr. Elaine Abrahams, the paediatrician, proved to be a large, robust lady, well into her fifties. She welcomed the visitors and apologised for the smallness of the room. Although she had, Robert knew, at an earlier stage taken an influential role (if spades are called spades 'decisive role' would be more apposite) in discouraging separation of mother and child, this time she took a back seat. Emily Frost, on the other hand, waved the flag without hesitation for urgent resort to the court process. Her 'senior', Derek Ivins, sat silently at the table, as if an observer.

She reported, on the basis of her most recent home visits, a worsened situation. 'Miss Sircar did not seem,' she said, 'to be maintaining much of a hold on reality.' She had been telling Emily of her dreams, during which she could see crowds of people mocking her from the outside of the locked cage in which she was confined. She had lately been sharing her life with Tania's father who, while gentle as a parent, was increasingly the butt of Yvonne's anger. She had been angry, depressed, aggressive.

Emily had lately witnessed in the family home a hair-raising row when Yvonne, anger unbounded, had blown her nose on her hand and had then wiped the contents on the father's sweater. This would have been less concerning had Yvonne not been clasping Tania to herself with her other arm.

More, Miss Sircar was not taking much trouble now with hygiene when preparing or storing milk bottles and teats. She had been leaving the bottle in Tania's mouth, assuming her to be more capable of feeding herself than she was. She was accusing Tania of deliberately provoking her and of saying unkind, cruel things to her. Tania, Emily added unnecessarily, was hardly of an age when she could have said any words, let alone cruel ones.

Two days earlier Emily had requested Yvonne to bring Tania to the hospital for a routine check-up by Dr. Abrahams. Mother's response, said Emily, had been to remove Tania's babygro and nappy, denying the request in a theatrical and childlike gesture.

Dramatic input by a female police officer made the outcome of the conference, Robert thought, highly predictable. She reported that police had, the previous night, taken Tania into police protection after she had been left unattended by her mother in a gaming club on Green Lanes. The officer used the expression 'abandoned'. As police had implemented their own place of safety powers, the emergency, out-of hours duty social worker had been drawn in and had organised Tania's placement in the small hours with obliging foster parents.

Emily spoke again. In her view, Tania should remain with foster parents while court proceedings with a view to a care order should be begun. The silent Derek Ivins remained silent.

Dr. Abrahams, in view of these recent developments, doubted that any other course was possible. Thus the conference adopted Emily's recommendation.

So, another case demanding action was now on Robert's plate. While Emily would now be pursuing a magistrate's authority for Tania's remaining in 'a place of safety', that is, with foster parents, he would have to liaise with Highgate magistrates' court, where care proceedings would be heard, as Yvonne, if only from a recent date, lived in that court's catchment area.

Out of curiosity Robert asked Emily why Yvonne was 'Miss Sircar', when she was married. "Isn't she really 'Mrs. Sircar?'"

"True, but her husband's long gone and she doesn't like to be called 'Mrs.' It reminds her of him. If she wants to be called 'Miss', that's up to her."

'Agreed.'

"Just as some of us prefer to be called 'Ms.' to 'Miss'. You can call me 'Ms. Frost' from now on," said Emily with a grin.

On a Tuesday soon afterwards his application at Highgate for an interim care order was not challenged. Though Tania's mother attended, she was in what Emily described to Robert as a zombie-like state of mind, a condition not previously witnessed by Emily, who had by now met her on a dozen occasions.

Miss Sircar had been given a list of local solicitors known to act for legally aided clients, but so far she was not known to have made any approach to one of these.

'I hope she does,' Emily said to Robert. 'It's only fair.' He could not but agree, and could not resist asking if Derek Ivins was in full agreement with Emily's approach.

'He'll do what he's told or else,' was the laconic answer.

On Emily's oral evidence of the decline in the quality of the care given to Tania in the run up to the police involvement, the magistrates, finding it unnecessary – to Robert's surprise – to hear from Dr. Abrahams, granted a temporary care order for two weeks. Robert then sought to pacify that paediatrician, who was grumbling about having wasted a morning at court, missing a hospital clinic. When he told her she would be needed again in a fortnight's time, she was not at all mollified.

22

An Evening at Dingwalls

More revue planning meetings had taken place before the organisers, Robert Fordham among them, ventured out as a group, first taking on board dinner in a Greek restaurant in Crouch End, and then constituting themselves an expeditionary force for a visit to Camden Lock for a late night at an establishment bearing the name of Dingwalls.

Robert arrived with Beth at the restaurant, and they were joined there by Beth's friend Annie, whom Beth had invited for reasons not explained to Robert. Annie was certainly not as beautiful as Beth, but the deficit in beauty was balanced by other qualities. Her T-shirt had badges affixed to it which denoted precisely the position of her nipples. One read 'Rude Girls', the other 'Rude Boys', and across the front of the shirt below were the words: 'If it ain't stiff, it ain't worth a fuck'. The Greek waiter who greeted each of them as they arrived was momentarily tongue-tied when faced with Annie's frontage on removal of her coat.

Robert concealed his disapproval. 'I didn't realise we needed to dress formally to go to Dingwalls,' he said smiling to Beth, with a glance at Annie's get-up. Emily's comment was more open-hearted. 'I think she's splendid.' Jessica was amused.

Annie plonked herself down on a chair and spoke loudly about the menu, making comical facial expressions and comparing it unfavourably with menus on the Greek island where she had holidayed in the summer.

Jessica's husband had not come. He had preferred, she said, not to come out on this occasion. She said no more about him. He asked her for her opinion of Enid Prosser as a child care social worker.

'I haven't worked with her,' said Jessica. 'Of course I've seen her in meetings. But she has the reputation of not being very subtle or sensitive. She doesn't beat about the bush. She's said to have more sympathy for bad mothering than bad fathering.'

'But on the other hand...' said Robert.

'There is another dimension to her...She's all for the child's best interests and sod the parent's happiness if it means that the child suffers. I agree with that, of course.'

'You're talking about work,' said Emily, interrupting with something near a shout.

A 'hear hear' came from Beth. A 'Fucking hell!' came from Annie.

On to Dingwalls. There was nothing very memorable about the establishment. It was a long one-storey construction of undistinguished appearance, with late night drinking and dancing the only activities on offer. Two suited and shirt-and-tie'd security men stood by the entrance, filtering out unsuitable guests not very successfully. Inside was a lengthy bar at one end of which could be found a small dance floor, near which was planted a nightly changing band, worse in musical quality one night than another, better one night than another. The beer was expensive, the glasses plastic and the music loud. Two or three females present looked no older than fourteen. It was eminently a place to go to in the late evening, and not a place to go to if you had to get up early in the morning.

After some drinking and some dancing, Frank and Robert took refuge at the bar away from the deafening music. Without delay Frank invited Robert to come for a meal the following week with himself and Emily at their flat in Muswell Hill. Just the three of us, he said. He added: 'I'd better warn you now that Emily likes you. But if you'll take a tip from me, she's a bit immature.'

Robert accepted the invitation, and decided not to mention it to Beth, fearing critical comment, while at the same time having no intention of seeking an adventure with Emily.

The night ended very late indeed. Annie disappeared with a member of the band. Just after leaving the nightclub, Robert and Beth passed another Dingwalls' leaver, a young man who, as they walked past him, vomited in profusion, sullying the tip of one of Robert's shoes. Robert quickly crossed with Beth to the opposite pavement, and as they did so the young man called out in a triumphant voice: 'I can reach you from here you know!' He did then vomit a second time on the pavement, and voluminously, but if the pavement was then fuller his boast was empty. For this moment and others it was a night remembered.

A few days later, on the evening appointed for dinner with Emily Frost and Frank Jackson, Robert appeared at their front door with flowers for Emily and a bottle of wine.

'How traditional,' she giggled. 'Nobody brings me flowers.'

Much of the discussion at the dinner table was gossip about friends and colleagues of Emily and Frank, who were both drinking freely, especially Frank. At one point Robert mentioned Jack Parnell, the Enfield council solicitor. Had Emily worked on cases with him when she herself was an Enfield social worker?

'Not just met on care cases, if I remember right,' said Frank meaningfully.

'I don't think so,' she said slowly, sipping at a fourth or fifth glass, and blowing out smoke when not sipping. 'Oh yes,

I remember now. I had a fling with him if you could call it that. Just a post-party night of passion. He's a nice guy', she added, then said: 'There was just one thing he came out with that wasn't on.'

'What was that?' asked Robert.

'He said some people might consider me as rather free with my favours. I told him off for that. I'm free with my desires, that's all. Well, I used to be.'

'It wasn't cricket for him to say that,' said Robert, attracting groans and even a slow hand-clap.

At this point Frank sought, in his convivial way, to put Robert on the spot regarding his own relationship commitments.

'So what are your intentions regarding Beth?'

'She's stunning,' said Emily.

Robert shrank from too much disclosure. 'We're just taking things step by step,' he said.

'What about you?' he looked at Emily. 'Do you have a boyfriend at the moment?'

Frank guffawed. 'She's got three,' he said.

Emily, pouring herself another glass, defended her corner with humour. 'Not true,' she said, 'Out of date. I'll tell you. I had a talk with my number one a few weeks ago. I told him I was fed up with having a lot of part-timers. He agreed with me! He said I should clear this lot out and start anew with a fresh batch.'

She was not alone in her merriment about this and went on. 'So I did get shot of them. All three of them.'

'So have you got a fresh batch now?' asked Robert mischievously.

'Not exactly,' she said. 'I've seen one guy a couple of times but I'm playing my cards differently now. I'm being reserved and mysterious.'

'That doesn't sound like your nature,' said Robert.

Frank, the most intoxicated of the three, clapped Robert on the shoulder. 'What Emily means is she's decided not to be so fucking promiscuous. Before this current phase she wore her vagina on her sleeve.'

Emily, who had until then been consistently merry, was put out.

'You've got a fucking nerve saying that.' There was a pause, before she turned to Robert.

'I'm sorry, Robert, this evening isn't ending too well. Frank can't behave himself when he's had a few drinks.'

'I'm sorry, Emily,' said Frank. 'It just came out.'

When Robert left, Emily hugged him. 'It's great you could come.' He returned the hug.

'It was great to be here.'

He had drunk too much alcohol to drive home safely, and drove home unsafely. Guilt feelings about this were quickly replaced by disgust at seeing the kitchen sink jammed to excess once more with unaddressed dirty crockery and metal. He had one reason, however, for believing in a better kitchen-sink world in the future. The other Robert had confided in him that it was highly likely the Civil Service would soon assign him to another part of the country, in which case he would have to move.

23

A Parental Rights Resolution Looks Iffy

With November barely begun, Robert took a call from Enid Prosser. Her voice was flat.

'Trouble with the resolution on Aaron, I'm afraid, Robert. Aaron's mother has managed to get it together to see a solicitor. We've had a letter from him, wanting more information.'

'Did the mother visit Aaron on his second birthday, after all?'

'No, she didn't. You guessed wrong. But a couple of days after the resolution was passed, she phoned me. She was upset. She'd just had an argument with her mum because her mum had received my letter to say we were taking over her rights and her mum hadn't told her about it till then. She can't read herself, but she got the letter off her mum and took it to a solicitor.'

'So what was she upset about?'

'She thought it meant she could never see Aaron again. That was what got to her.'

'So what did you say to her?'

'I just told her a formal notice of the resolution was being sent out. She said she'd collect it personally. Otherwise her mum would get her hands on it. So she came in this morning. She's got the notice now and she's got a solicitor appointment. She wants Aaron back.'

'Who's the solicitor?'

'A Mr. Brady.'

'Does she say why she didn't argue with her mum about giving up Aaron in the first place?'

'She said her mother had told her Aaron had to go or she'd be kicked out of the home with him.'

'So why has she decided she can have him back?'

'She's just moved out of her mum's place, she's got a boyfriend she's living with now. He could be egging her on.'

'It sounds to me the way forward must be to get a better understanding of her situation before we get to a court hearing. Otherwise we'll be fighting a case with one hand tied behind our back. The permanent disability ground for the resolution looks dicey to me as things are if it gets to court.'

'I'll have to allocate a social worker. Aaron is the important person in all this.'

Enid Prosser promised to send to Robert a copy of the solicitor's letter, to which he would reply. One thing seemed almost inevitable: an objection to the resolution by Aaron's mother, requiring surrender of the question of its continuance to the magistrates. Their worships could, if Enid's evidence failed to satisfy them, strike the resolution down. And that would empower the two-year-old's mother to reclaim him instantly from the only mother – his foster mother – he knew. It looked like a repeat of the Firth children shambles was on its way.

24

Fresh Revelations

Meetings and rehearsals to progress the coming revue were now rapidly succeeding each other. There were no auditions as such for the various parts to be played in the sketches: role allocation seemed to resolve itself. When a particular sequence was tried out during rehearsal and did not come off in the eyes of those performing and watching, re-writing or reconsideration of allocation of roles immediately followed. And consensus soon reached showed the way forward. Sometimes volunteers climbed to a higher level of acting in parts for which earlier they did not seem to be well matched.

The first full week of November was memorable for those navigating their way around the borough in that a strike of electricity workers was periodically blanking out street lamps and plunging rows of shops into darkness. At one planning-cum-rehearsal meeting during this week of reduced public illuminations, a social worker Robert had not previously met, Miriam Fawcett, a cheerful and well-dressed woman in her forties, made her debut as a performer in a rehearsal of *The Importance of Being Anorexia*. It was apparent that she knew as much as anyone else that she was a perfect fit for the part of Miss Bracknell, patrician social worker, a variation on Lady Bracknell from the celebrated Wilde play. The strong-jawed Frank Jackson expressed heartily the view, after spontaneous applause had followed Miriam's first effort, that she *was* Miss Bracknell and should change her surname from that moment henceforth. Miriam Fawcett was amused. She had a loud and infectious laugh.

When Robert introduced himself to her, Miriam announced herself as the only *Daily Telegraph* reader in the Wood Green social services office, and proud of it. 'She's also a magistrate', someone else told him. But conservative as her political outlook was shockingly declared to be, she was not in the least regarded by others more to the political left – there were many such – as letting the side down. She was, in any event, vehemently opposed both to corporal punishment for children and capital punishment for adults.

Her conservatism in practice seemed to amount not to much more than a wish to maintain traditional family and political values, and she held aloof from the new politics of Mrs. Margaret Thatcher's coterie in government. The loss of Edward Heath as leader of the Conservative Party, she was quoted as saying, will be bitterly remembered. At the same time it was understood that she had regrets for the passing of Britain's empire, believing it to have contributed to human progress. Miriam was well-known for putting herself out for the benefit of others, and for never shirking her share of irksome duties. And she was content to remain at the level of social worker. Upward mobility for herself was not in the frame. She did not seem to quite meet the usual specifications for membership of the circle of locally important worthies.

When Miriam Fawcett made her mark in the first rehearsal of *The Importance of Being Anorexia*, another newcomer to the group unhesitatingly selected himself for the part of the young man who had 'lost his parents'. This was Harold Stott, an ex-Rugby schoolboy, also based in the Wood Green office, who told Robert when they fell into conversation that whenever he was due in court, he made a point of wearing his old school tie. Harold was not a man who would consider for a moment the option, on a court day, of borrowing the 'anyone's-for-the-day' court suit on offer in his area social services office. He had, as he told Robert, a number of well-cut suits from which on court days he would make a careful choice.

It was on this occasion of meeting and observing Miriam Fawcett and Harold Stott that Robert got to know Jessica Palmer rather better. The process was facilitated by Jessica's having no car – it was to be collected by her next day after vital maintenance work – and Robert's offer to give her a lift home was gratefully accepted. So was his suggestion of stopping for a drink 'on the way'.

In fact 'on the way' was interpreted as including a detour to Hampstead Heath's Spaniards Inn, which Jessica said she liked, even when it was overpopulated. At this time of year, she thought, it would not be so busy. And so it proved.

Once inside, with beers in front of them, in the warm and ancient hostelry unspoilt by excessive noise or excessive numbers of customers, Robert spoke of his incomprehension that Miriam Fawcett's upper class tones and politics had not succeeded in keeping her out of Haringey as an ordinary social worker.

'She's not an ordinary social worker. She's an extraordinary social worker. By the way, Enid Prosser has taken over supervising me from Derek Ivins. Derek's leaving, going to work in the Child Guidance clinic. I'm sure that's more him than the child protection front line.'

'I'm saying nothing.'

'Also,' said Jessica, returning to the subject of Miriam Fawcett, 'we're a friendly lot. She's not the only one from that background, is she?'

'Harold.'

'And there are more. Maybe you should look at us from another angle, Robert. We're a white middle class majority, aren't we? How many are from ethnic minorities?'

Robert was, so far, aware of only one black social worker in Haringey, and of another of an Asian background.

He acknowledged Jessica's point. She had not finished. With a smile lighting up her oval face, she asked:

'What about the legal department?'

'What about it?'

'All white? Nearly all male?'

He hadn't given thought to this, but agreed. Yes, all of the solicitors, other than Melanie Cusack, were white males, and the only black staff member he'd met was the filing clerk just appointed by George Ballam, having been given the go-ahead to do so by Edward Shimble as if oblivious to the council leader's request for budget belt-tightening. Was there an unconscious assumption in Robert's head that the present weighting of senior appointments in favour of white males was the norm, not to be disturbed?

It was his turn to interrogate, and he dared to do so, shifting the conversational ground to 'personal', and conscious of Jessica's straightforwardness as much as of her attractiveness.

'How is your husband, then?'

Jessica was willing to disclose something of her situation.

'He drinks too much. But I don't think he's happy. For a while we've only been married fifty-fifty, and he's come off worse in this situation, I think. And we don't have much in common now.'

'I'm sorry about that.' He took the plunge, inquiring further. 'Somehow I get the impression ...I could be totally wrong...' (he was wondering if he should be inquiring at all), '...that you might be wishing you were out of it altogether.'

The question did not seem to trouble her. 'Yes, I'd rather be independent now. We've grown apart – were married at University...things were good then – but I no longer feel he's on the same level that we once shared. Our marriage was severely tested a year ago – showed it wasn't working.

Robert forbore to ask how the marriage had been tested. Jessica went on.

'Stephen hasn't accepted it's finished – so things continue to be awkward. Have you been married?'

'No.'

'I'd rather Stephen and I separated by agreement, on an equal basis...But I shouldn't have told you all this.'

'Trouble is,' said Robert, 'you're someone I like, and would like to know better.'

She squeezed his hand, then said, showing sudden curiosity, 'You're still with the lovely Beth?'

'Is that description code for a dangerous woman, a femme fatale, something like that?' he countered.

'I didn't mean that. I don't really know Beth. But...' she tailed off.

'But what? Is that the reputation she has among colleagues? Are they jealous of her?'

'Maybe. She stayed a bit separate from most of us. How is she getting on at the Civic Centre?'

'OK at the moment, I think, though she says her colleagues are as dull as ditch-water. And to answer your question, we are still together.'

They drifted into other topics, talked about films, and Robert told Jessica about his fondness for the novels of Eric Ambler.

'Did he write *The Mask of Dimitrios*?'

'He did.'

'I've got a copy somewhere, but I haven't read it.'

'Maybe you should.'

Their glasses became empty, and the time was late. Robert deposited Jessica outside her front door, having pressed her hand before she left the passenger seat.

'You're a very compassionate person,' he said. 'Let's have another drink together before long.'

'I hope we'll do that.'

25

Chin up in the Juvenile Court

Some days before the commencement of the second phase of the baby Tania story in the Highgate juvenile court, Robert received a telephone call from a solicitor with offices close to Turnpike Lane underground station. It was Mr. Brady of Brady & Co, author of the letter to Enid Prosser about the parental rights resolution concerning Aaron, a letter to which Robert had replied with explanation. He expected at any time to receive an objection to the resolution which could lead to life-transforming consequences for Aaron. It could also blast the professional credibility of Enid Prosser.

But the call was not about Aaron: it was about Tania. Brady spoke courteously, quietly informing Robert that he had been asked by Miss Sircar to act for her.

'To act for Miss Sircar or for Tania?' asked Robert in as disinterested a tone as he could muster.

'Well, the legal aid is in the name of the child, but I am taking instructions – I'm hardly setting a precedent – from the mother. It's not as if the child is old enough to give instructions.'

'No,' agreed Robert, uncomfortably reminded once more that he could have encouraged the appointment of a solicitor for 'beyond control' Michelle precisely because she was mature enough to express her own wishes. He pushed the thought away.

'It's clear to you the mother is able to give instructions?'
'Indeed, yes. There can be no controverting that.'

Robert's face betrayed a doubt that Brady could not see, and undertook to send him the social enquiry report – full and thorough – which had already been prepared by Emily Frost. Emily had imagined that satisfying the magistrates that the 'proper development, ill-treatment and neglect and the rest' condition for making an order would swan through without magisterial misgivings, and that she might as well have a report ready the moment the court called for one.

A letter was soon received from Brady, acknowledging receipt of the report and trusting that this would set a precedent for future cases. This implied, Robert suspected, that the council had not in other cases always been so generous with evidence in advance; but the sentences in the letter which ensued put him on his guard. These informed him that Brady had requested the court to allocate a full day to the next hearing, as he could see every reason for concluding matters then and there. The final sentence, without elaboration, stated that the allegations would be energetically opposed. It was capped by a request for an acknowledgment of receipt of the letter. This Robert supplied. The day of the hearing was now close.

On the eventful Tuesday morning of the hearing, outside the court room before the case was called on, Robert was pleased to be able to greet his witnesses: the female police officer who had been at the case conference, Dr. Elaine Abrahams, and Emily Frost herself. The paediatrician wore a black coat that had seen better days and was not a happy paediatrician, having been dragged to court, as she put it, for a second time in a fortnight, when she should have been at the hospital. The witnesses were thus, as the lawyers' expression goes, tee'd up.

Emily looked tense, despite earlier expressions of confidence. Her natural near-theatricality was offset by the smart but conventional clothes she was wearing.

Robert spoke to Mr. Brady, whom he guessed to be in his later forties. To Brady's neutrally expressed question, 'Not instructing Counsel? Leading the charge yourself?' he replied as neutrally: 'Yes, indeed.' Leading the charge? Was that what he would be doing?

Brady was balding, wore an air of weary professionalism, and was without assertiveness of manner outside court. He spoke mildly, wasted no more words than he had in his letter, and made a refreshing contrast, thought Robert, to Jonathan Spratt 'of Counsel'. Brady simply wished to know which witnesses Robert was calling and in what order. Robert told him. 'I confirm the application is opposed,' said Brady without emphasis. 'By the way,' he added, 'a full day has been allocated.'

'Easier to get than in Tottenham,' said Robert.

'Quite.'

Anxious to get going, Robert was irked by the notification from an usher that the commencement of the hearing would be put back for a short while so that sentence of a juvenile for some offence or other could be heard first. While kicking his heels he found himself face to face with the same Jonathan Spratt of whom he had been thinking, who told him he had his own juvenile crime case to attend to that day. Spratt was relaxed, even jolly. 'I was in the Grimsby Crown Court last week,' he said, using all of his large mouth. 'You know,' he said, bringing a factual detail to light only to share in its absurdity, 'the Grimsby Crown Court has its own particular definition of what constitutes grievous bodily harm.'

'And what's that?'

'In the Grimsby Crown Court,' said Spratt, shaking his head humorously, and almost as if lifting a rabbit from a hat, 'to amount to the offence of grievous bodily harm, the leg actually has to come off.'

Robert chuckled, sharing, as one lawyer with another, the dark humour, and then could not resist asking Spratt something about the case that they had recently shared competitively.

'Thinking back to the Michelle West affair, I was impressed how much you defended the corner of the parents...,' he began.

'You're very kind,' said Spratt. 'Kind words in this place are sometimes followed by sword thrusts.'

'I am just learning my business, and benefiting from examples of advocacy from others,' said Robert, avoiding defensiveness but not pomposity.

'Of course,' said Spratt, tolerantly.

'But the parents' case seemed to me so weak from the beginning, that when all the evidence came out, especially their own, they didn't have a leg to stand on.'

'Sometimes,' said Spratt, 'the weaker the evidence and the more your clients refuse to acknowledge the fact, the more you have to pretend on their behalf.'

'The client is king?'

'The client is king, however off the wall he may be. And sometimes you have to make waves and flap your wings. Simultaneously. They were desperate to tell their stories. And who was I to stop them?'

Robert was left to interpret. So, if Spratt hadn't played to the gallery, and watched his clients condemn their own parenting out of their own mouths, he would have failed in his duty. He decided not to say, finger-wagging, that Spratt should have taken instructions from Michelle, not from her parents. What would be the point? It was a weapon to deploy in the future.

There was a flurry of activity as the sentencing case ended and the actors emerged from the court room. Brady came over towards Robert and Spratt greeted him as 'Bill', to which the latter responded reprovingly – 'William, please'. For some reason Brady looked anxious. As Spratt apologised for the offensive familiarity, the usher urged those associated with baby Tania into court.

'My client,' said Brady, 'seems to have been held up.' Robert, unaware she had not arrived, looked at him enquiringly.

'Ah, there she is.' Brady's anxiety disappeared. Miss Sircar approached them from the building entrance, a small, thin, woman, with a petite, pale face, partly obscured by much loose dark hair.

'Miss Sircar,' greeted Brady, with a smile. 'We're just going into court.' He turned and encouraged her to walk with him. All entered the court room.

As was conventional in the juvenile court in those days, the only witness allowed to sit in court during care proceedings, before being called to give evidence, was the family's social worker in the case, so that the local authority solicitor had present someone from whom instructions could be taken. Dr. Abrahams and the policewoman sat outside, waiting for their respective turns.

Once in the unassuming, modern court room Robert found the justices – two unfamiliar men and one younger woman – already seated. The woman was wearing a navy blue hat from which an artificial flower pointed upwards.

One of the men was the chairman, a clean-shaven man with a brisk but remote manner, perhaps in his early sixties, and without a memorable personality. Robert was told later he was an accountant and also a spare time Territorial army officer. The middle aged male clerk introduced the parties to the Bench. The chairman addressed Miss Sircar, who was sitting expressionless behind Brady: 'The Bench appreciates very much that this hearing is an extremely unpleasant ordeal for you. We will try to make it as painless as we can.'

The sympathetic comment did not trouble Robert, who had no special reason to think large vexations might lay ahead. He was disappointed, though, to see that Tania's father had not arrived as expected, and was not therefore available to be called as a witness as to his own anxieties about Tania's safety.

He began, after supplying a bald description of the case,

by calling the police woman. She had been called to the casino building in Green Lanes on the night Tania's mother had been betting with the help of gaming machines, with Tania close by in her buggy. After a while, having lost money, Miss Sircar had absented herself from the building with a man. So the casino manager had reported. The police evidence primarily consisted of an interview of Miss Sircar and of the police action taken to safeguard Tania's welfare.

She had been unattended at the casino for an hour or more. But by the time that the police witness had arrived, the mother had already returned and had been reunited with Tania, whom she was holding docilely on her lap.

If permitted by the magistrates, which was what Robert expected to happen, the policewoman could have repeated what Miss Sircar had said to her: that Tania was able to look after herself for a couple of hours; that Tania had said that her mother could risk her money if she wanted to; and that Miss Sircar had forgotten where Tania was, thinking she was at home with her father. Her memory had only been jogged by the casino manager, who had picked Tania up when crying, and taken her to Miss Sircar, then preoccupied with a gaming machine and using money apparently obtained from the man with whom she had left the casino.

But when the policewoman was asked what Tania's mother had said to her, Mr. Brady had interposed with tranquil insistence: 'As a matter of law I submit that evidence of what Miss Sircar said to the officer is not admissible in these proceedings.' He proceeded to refer to relevant case law, and to read short passages from reported judgments, providing the clerk and Robert with the references. Robert, taken by surprise, requested, and was granted, half an hour's adjournment to study these points.

He did his best to answer Brady's submissions, arguing,

on the basis of the case law Brady was citing, that 'admissions' by a parent to a witness were unquestionably allowable as evidence, and were routinely accepted as such in his own experience. He asserted that what Miss Sircar had said to the police witness must amount in effect to 'admissions'.

He also had a fall-back argument, which was that even if the police officer's evidence of what Miss Sircar had said might not be evidence of the truth of what she had said, it would at least be evidence of her state of mind.

The Bench retired for a short time to consider the submissions and re-entered the court. They upheld Brady's assertion, rejecting Robert's. Robert asked himself, angry with himself, why he had not requested the casino manager to attend court. And why he was not better armed to counter Brady's submissions. And why he had found himself before a court prepared to apply a crazily narrow view of the law of evidence.

He tried nevertheless to get as much out of the policewoman as he could. He asked her what impressions she had of Miss Sircar's state of mind as a result of speaking to her. Brady surged forward again. He submitted modestly that the answer could not be admitted because it would arise out of answers by Miss Sircar which had already been declared inadmissible. The chairman endorsed Brady's position.

Robert tried another tack. He asked the witness to state what questions she had put to Miss Sircar. Brady again objected. If the witness were allowed to put these questions they could imply the answers given which had already been declared inadmissible.

The chairman again came to Brady's aid. It was almost as if, in Robert's eyes, he was ticking off items in a list provided by Brady, or in any event giving Brady's idiosyncratic interpretation of the law blanket approval. Robert had not assumed the hearing would be plain sailing, and although he had agreed with Brady that he would be leading the charge, he had not anticipated that it would be into the Valley of Death.

Gunned down with such brutality, the case which Robert was putting faced more deadly fire when he called the paediatrician, the solid, mature, even mildly maternal Dr. Elaine Abrahams. The rulings previously pronounced were relaxed to a degree in that the chairman put questions to Dr. Abrahams as to what Miss Sircar had said about her feelings. This more liberal approach, though inconsistent with what the chairman had already ruled out of order, was not the subject of complaint by Brady, who, Robert mused, must have decided, given that the Bench was buttering his bread most generously, that he should hold his tongue when the butter was a little less indulgently applied.

Miss Sircar's damning admission to the paediatrician that she had shaken Tania was not permitted entry into the allowable evidence. Nor were her various disturbing visits to the ward where Tania had been cared for following her birth. (Robert was now telling himself he should have hauled along to court a series of ward nurses who had recorded this information.) It was all, as Brady observed, nodding his head virtuously, in the category of 'hearsay' evidence. It was not direct enough, the court agreed, to deserve the status of material which could properly influence the court.

The result of this was that the greater amount of what Dr. Abrahams was able to say was added to that already banned from the ears of the magistrates by the magistrates themselves.

Emily Frost, sitting in court behind Robert, took all this in with growing consternation displayed in capitals on her face. Robert asked the magistrates, when Dr. Abrahams had finished her evidence and had left the court, for an intermission in which to take instructions from the social worker, and was granted ten minutes. He glanced more than once at Tania's mother, who looked bored, and was yawning repeatedly. He was struck by the contrasts in her dress. She was wearing a low-cut, colourful, dress whose 'party' look was not much subdued by a check patterned maroon waistcoat worn over it.

When Emily gave evidence, once again the 'hearsay' rule, applied with numbing severity, excluded from the permissible much of what she wished to report. She was not permitted to relate what Miss Sircar had told her of her dreams and hallucinations, or of Miss Sircar's admission that she was tempted at times to shake Tania. Nor was she allowed to tell the court what Tania's father had told her of her mother's leaving Tania unattended, or of the moment when he had reason to believe Miss Sircar would throw Tania out of a first floor window, and had rushed down the stairs and outside the building. If she were dropped, her young life at risk, he had been beneath the window, ready to catch her if the threat were activated. None of this was Emily allowed to repeat, though what she had actually observed could not be censored out, such as her account of the frightening row when Miss Sircar had deposited the contents of her nose on her partner's sweater with one hand while holding Tania with the other,

It was no surprise to Robert that William Brady asked no questions of the policewoman, the paediatrician or of Emily, or that he did not offer to put Miss Sircar in the witness box.

The magistrates did not take long – a quarter of an hour of retirement following final representations from Robert and Brady – to find 'the primary condition has not been made out'. The brisk chairman added that he could not help but notice that Ms. Frost was showing perturbation about the outcome, and that he would have expected more professional willingness to accept the considered deliberations of a court of justice. The book-end in the flower-impaled hat, Robert observed, was making mouths in sympathy with the chairman, while the flower was now at an angle. It was not yet lunch-time. Two-thirds of the evidence had been locked-out.

Brady showed no observable reaction to the verdict. He did not, while still in court, make any comment about when he expected Tania to be returned to her mother, nor, once outside, did he seek even to clarify what arrangements would be made for this to happen, other than to suggest that an urgent meeting between social workers and Miss Sircar should take place. He did, however, say, disconcerting Robert, that Robert could have called Tania's mother to testify although he, Brady, had decided not to do so. 'After all,' he added, 'as you know, parents are not parties to these proceedings.' He went on to say that they should speak soon about the 'Aaron' parental rights resolution issue. Robert promised to telephone him. Was another fiasco on the way?

Unaccountably, Miss Sircar had already left the building. Robert was now only too aware that he could have prepared the case better – and perhaps should have put Miss Sircar in the witness box, as Brady conceded he could have done. But conscious too that he could not override history, he spoke to Emily, taking her first to one side. 'My advice,' he said quietly, 'is to make Tania a ward of court immediately. I doubt very much that the High Court will take the same line on what evidence can be served up. This court's position has been extreme.' He was simultaneously cursing himself for not at an early stage seeking to adjourn the hearing to ensure that both Tania's father and the casino manager could be present. Too late.

Emily telephoned her area manager, who, after speaking to Emily, spoke to Robert. The decision to make Tania a ward of court was made.

Robert headed back to his office, where, against likelihood, he managed to extract within a few minutes a cheque for the issue of a wardship summons. He then made for Holborn station on the underground, and walked from there to Somerset House, where a ground floor office supplied the forms he took some time to complete by hand. A complication was the need for approval from a low level judge called a registrar to be sought for a High Court judge appointment to be demanded at short notice. He had to climb to the first floor, where the long thin corridor was sprinkled with little gatherings of lawyers and clients outside a series of smallish court rooms. He located the duty registrar, officially designated the Registrar of the Day, to do this.

He was third in a queue, but once inside the room, where he took up a seat at the large table in front of the overweight and affable registrar, he found no persuasion was necessary to get the permission he needed. This was initialled on the application. By a quarter past four Robert was at the Clerk of the Rules office in the West Green Building of the Royal Courts of Justice and a hearing three days later was fixed and inserted in the court's diary. So far, so good.

That evening – an unremarkable mid-November evening, after a day in which a timid sun, unnoticed by Robert, had occasionally edged itself between clouds – he and Beth were to meet for an Indian meal at a restaurant in Crouch End. Beth was waiting at a table inside when he arrived. 'If you can turn up at court on time without difficulty,' she began, calm but critical, 'you can surely turn up on time to see me. It's embarrassing for a woman to sit by herself in a restaurant.'

He apologised contritely and went on to give an account of the events of his day. 'More exciting than mine,' she said, telling him of the grey and unremarkable people she was working with in the Civic Centre in her new post. She went on to speak of the confirmation she had received of a holiday in Australia she had been arranging for herself for months past.

'You've been saving this up to tell me?' he said lightly.

'I wasn't sure it was going to happen. I'd accumulated some annual leave when I was in Social Services, and I wasn't sure whether transferring it over to my new post would be allowed, but it's now been approved and I must take it. I took the morning off to sort out flights and I'll be going early next month. For two and a half weeks.'

'December. You'll miss the revue.'

'I'm sorry,' she said, looking earnestly at him and clasping his hand on the tablecloth. Her beautiful blue eyes were as candid as ever.

'But why Australia? Where are you going to stay?'

Beth's face showed some embarrassment.

'I'll be staying with an old boyfriend and his parents. Not that I've met his parents.'

She explained that this old boyfriend, an Australian, had been in Bedford a couple of years previously for the summer, staying with relatives. They had spent a lot of time together.

It wasn't what Robert wanted to hear. Obviously, she explained, the relationship came to an end, but they had continued to exchange cards and occasional letters, such as at Christmas. Months ago – before she and Robert had met – he had invited her to come over to stay 'down under'. Of course, she added, she would tell him she had a boyfriend in London.

'By the name of Robert?'

'Yes.'

Robert wished to know nothing more. He became silent, but soon Beth managed to joke him out of his discomposure. His head told him, nevertheless, and persistently, that his relationship with Beth had the kiss of ephemerality about it. She would be back though, Beth said firmly, before Christmas, and hoped to spend time with him then. That was the good news, but it was weak tea enough.

26

In the High Court of Justice

The next day pulsated with activity on Robert's part in the legal building. A sliver of his time was occupied by issuing letters in Edward Shimble's name. These enclosed notices that Tania Sircar had been made a ward of court and of the forthcoming hearing in the Royal Courts of Justice. Robert had them dispatched by hand (and by Errol Staines's Harley-Davidson motor-bike) for delivery to Tania's parents and to the offices of Brady & Co.

The main task was to grow swiftly to adulthood a detailed, comprehensive statement in his own name. The aim was to establish a bank-vault-safe case for a court order which would in the short-term maintain the status quo in Tania's case. This would enable her to remain in foster care until, further down the line on a later date, the giants (in this case Haringey council and William Brady) could do battle, with the help of witnesses and the availability of enough court time, as to whether she should be returned or not to her mother's care. That date could be a month or two hence.

The statement had to be, as Robert told Colin Masson, 'a killer'. It had to present a full picture of the evidence, citing sources of information precisely, displaying prominently and unashamedly the hearsay material which had been condemned as unworthy of judicial consideration by Brady in the first place and by the Highgate magistracy in the second. Included was an impersonal account of the substance of the juvenile court hearing, and, as an 'exhibit', a copy of Emily Frost's social enquiry report. This 'all meat and no veg plateful' (as Robert described it to Colin) was to be in front of a High Court judge two days later, when all concerned would be in court.

When more than half way through his preparation of this paper feast – which he hoped would repel decisively any challenge from Brady – a telephone call from the man himself interrupted Robert.

'You've not wasted time, I see.'

'You've received the notice of wardship then?'

'Yes. I am now applying for emergency legal aid to represent Miss Sircar. I wondered if you were thinking of filing a shred or two of evidential back-up.'

'An affidavit covering the essentials could be with you by tomorrow morning. It should contain no surprises.'

'But a lot of hearsay evidence, I dare say. No barrel-scraping, I trust.'

'As you say. Have you been in touch with your client? We tried to serve her this morning.'

'Not today.'

The conversation was put quietly to death and Robert continued to write. By noon the statement – all forty two paragraphs of it – was dictated and was with one of the department's typists.

Soon after lunch it was in front of Robert in full typed glory. After he had made some small amendments, and after a sigh by the typing pool supervisor ('A pity you couldn't have thought of these changes first time round'), it was soon ready for him to declare it fit for purpose.

Making three neat holes along the margin of the document (with a 'bodger' borrowed from Bill Bowman), Robert sewed it in the approved way with green ribbon, trimming the ribbon's edges symmetrically to achieve neatness and elegance. He recalled a stately remark made by his supervisor during his training, a year or more before. 'An articled clerk,' that person had said, 'if able to do nothing else, should be able to sew.'

An appointment was now made by Robert with a local solicitor – no other than the old dodderer at Slash & Co – to 'do a swear'. He had to bide his time only for a couple of minutes in that firm's waiting room, before he was forwarded into the office of the old dodderer, who was long-practised in the banal business of witnessing sworn statements for a small standardised fee. He did not dispense with formality on this occasion. Robert signed his name where advised to do so (he did not need telling), repeated as uttered to him the standard words of the oath (which he knew), while clutching a Bible (with which he rarely had contact) in his right hand. The signature of the old dodderer, which was not in the least doddery, was inscribed underneath, and the stamp of Slash & Co was applied with aplomb.

By the following morning a ribbonless copy of the sworn affidavit was with Brady, and by afternoon the beautifully dressed original was parked in the Clerk of the Rules office to be added to the court's new-born file, making it judge-ready.

Another copy had been sent off to Emily Frost. There had been no conversation with her since their discussion after the juvenile court's dismissal of the case, save for an agreement for them to meet, on the morning of the hearing, at the Kardomah coffee house occupying the south-east corner of Kingsway, a few minutes' walk from the court complex.

The allocation of a barrister had been negotiated through a telephone call to Walter, the purring and reportedly alcoholic clerk at Garden Court.

'I've got a case on in front of a High Court judge on Friday.'

'Over the road?'

'The Royal Courts of Justice.'

"RCJ? That's what we mean by 'over the road.' Is it in Chambers?" (Walter was verifying that it was a hearing in private, barred from the public and the press, and in which neither judge nor advocates were gowned or wigged.)

'Yes.'

'Who would you like? Sophie Williams?'

'Fervently believing that on this occasion he needed to have the services of someone more wise in the ways of the higher courts, Robert asked for names of those with familiarity with appeal-type cases and wardship.

'I think Miss Byers may be the one you want. Twenty seven years call. In front of High Court judges all the time. She frightens them, I'm told. She frightens me too.'

So purred Walter, and Miss Emmeline Byers was booked. A set of instructions, pink-ribbon-tied, reflectively engineered by Robert and on 'the big paper' (calling to the mind the unsophisticated words of Chief Executive 'Smiler' Trask), reached her early in the evening before the hearing.

Robert was at the Kardomah coffee house by nine thirty on the big day and Emily sailed in only a few minutes later. She was, unlike Robert, anxious, and tensely set about the cappuccino he had bought for her in advance of her arrival.

'What court are we in?' she asked.

'Court 32 in the West Green building. Mr. Justice Steventon.'

He had been given this information by Walter.

'I've only been to the Royal Courts twice,' said Emily. 'Both times it was for the same reason – a straightforward welfare report which wasn't straightforward. Different judges. One of them was pleased with me. He told the parents that I was his eyes and ears outside the court. The other one mainly grunted.'

'And I,' said Robert, 'am a complete novice in the RCJ, apart from walking around it a couple of times and sitting in as an observer once in the Court of Appeal.'

He added that he had instructed Emmeline Byers, of whom Emily had not heard.

'She's said to be very experienced.'

Coffee was swallowed, and soon they were entering the imposing Victorian building and advancing through the vast hall, where staircases on each side led upwards and downwards to remote corridors. They reached the rear of the hall, dominated by a high balcony. 'What a waste of space,' judged Emily.

After turning corners, walking on flagstones and passing through a sequence of doors and a space open to the mild weather, they reached the West Green building, a less grand place, a product of the late Edwardian era. Another corridor led to a corner of the building where narrow stairs and a lift both offered to take them upwards. They chose the lift and were soon in the stub of a corridor which terminated in a door leading to the entrance to Court 32.

Robert could not overlook, lounging near, arms folded, a muscular man, a fringe of greying hair circling his otherwise bald head. He wore a blue shirt without a jacket and a distinctly cheerful facial expression. Nearby stood a tall, angular, prominent-nosed woman in her later fifties, wearing what could be an expensive fur coat. She came up to them with a look of purpose.

'Mr. Fordham?'

'Yes. Miss Byers?' asked Robert, whose eyes had now taken in Brady, who was talking to a male barrister with an ample share of stomach. He could see no sign of Tania's mother.

'Let's speak privately,' said Miss Byers with authority, and they followed her to a spot devoid of people close to the lift. Robert introduced Emily, for whom Miss Byers produced a tolerant smile, before beginning.

'I'm most grateful for such excellent instructions, Mr. Fordham. I think we may have got them on the run now. I cannot imagine Mr. Justice Steventon refusing this application.'

'Is a surrender message coming from Miss Sircar's Counsel?' asked Robert. 'I don't know his name,' he added.

'Andrew Bavington. He's keeping his mouth firmly shut at the moment. Waiting for his client. Whether she comes or not, I doubt this will take Steventon long. But we're third on the list, I'm afraid, and the second case on is a committal application for breaking a court order. That's why the tipstaff is here – no doubt the person under arrest is in the cells at the moment – did you see the tipstaff in the blue shirt?'

Robert acknowledged this, and returned to the matter in hand.

'On the assumption Tania remains in foster care,' he said, 'I've discussed with Miss Frost what access Miss Sircar should have to Tania. We suggest twice weekly for a couple of hours on neutral ground.'

'That sounds reasonable,' agreed Miss Byers. 'I'll put that to Andrew Bavington.'

As it happened, the case soon flew from Mr. Justice Steventon's list. His second case, the committal application, intended not to last longer than two hours, had doubled its difficulties, now threatening to occupy much of the day, and so the parties in Tania's case were shunted over from the old West Green building to the modern Queen's Building, where they took the lift to the second floor. As they entered the extensive waiting area, a broad corridor with a line of court rooms on one side and a series of tables and seats at intervals on the other, with much light welcomed by extensive windows, Robert caught sight of Sophie Williams, at that moment engaged apparently at a semi-detached level in some other case.

He greeted her. Emmeline Byers acknowledged her distantly.

It transpired that Sophie Williams had already been on her feet that morning in front of the judge to whom the Sircar case was now allocated – Mr. Justice Barton.

'What's Barton like?' asked Robert, curious.

233

"Oh, you mean 'Jaws'," responded Sophie.

Miss Byers looked disapproving. 'He's an experienced judge,' she said. She had continued to wear her fur coat, but now removed it, revealing to the world a three row pearl necklace, and a dark, sober suit. She said to Emily: 'Would you mind very much looking after my coat? I don't like to leave it in the robing room.'

Emily, not entirely at home with the role of mobile cloakroom attendant, took the coat with a good enough grace, sure of herself enough to comment gaily: 'Well, we don't want some impecunious female barrister to nick it from there, do we?'

A frown appeared on the face of the fur coat's owner, who said nothing. It was then that Robert saw Miss Sircar, escorted by Brady, who had gone to the Strand entrance of the complex to find her. Soon after that the case was called on, signalled first by the exit of half a dozen people through the entrance doors flanking each side of the court room, and then by a female usher, who asked for parties to come into court.

The judge's place on the podium was above and behind the niche already occupied by his male and severely hair-receding 'associate' – a grand name for a clerk – and was empty for the moment. So, Robert observed, was the front row space to which Miss Sircar's barrister had first advanced and had then as rapidly retreated, leaving the court. A few seconds later, however, he was back, carrying papers. He was saying, not softly, and in a gravelly voice, to Brady: 'I'd left my papers outside on a table. I do think it advantageous, on the whole, to come into court with one's papers rather than without.'

He sniggered at his own drollery. Miss Sircar's voice was then heard. 'Are you laughing at me?' Mr. Bavington, resorting to gravity immediately, disavowed this. At that moment Mr. Justice Barton appeared and all in the court stood, encouraged by the usher. Barton's jaws were decidedly combative in construction, but there was to be no sign of judicial aggression expressing itself through them. Robert was struck by his relative youth – had he reached the age of fifty? The moment after Barton had sat down, his associate, whose forehead, Robert thought, seemed to go on for ever, passed up to him a slip of paper on which, for identification purposes, the barristers had entered their names.

'Yes, Miss Byers,' said Mr. Justice Barton. She had sat down for a few seconds and was now again on her feet. Robert was struck, as he sat there, by the Roman contours of her nose. It was in itself, he decided, a minor court room coup, worth, perhaps, he calculated, three or four weighty legal authorities. She introduced the case in a few dozen words, asking after that if his Lordship had had an opportunity to read the affidavit of Mr. Robert Fordham.

'Yes,' said Mr. Justice Barton, non-committally. 'What I would like to know is whether this affidavit is accepted as setting out with reasonable accuracy the circumstances of the hearing before the magistrates. Mr. Bavington?' He looked over at Miss Sircar's well-girthed Counsel.

That person rose and spoke slowly, measuring each word. 'We don't consider the account in that affidavit complete, my Lord.'

'That said, is there much to argue with in the summary given by Mr. Fordham?'

'Broadly accurate, my Lord. But the view is taken that the justices were entitled to reach the conclusion they did, in the light of the rules of evidence applicable.'

'I can understand that Miss Sircar will have been extremely disappointed and upset by the decision of the magistrates having been put at nought by the commencement of these wardship proceedings, having had her hopes raised one day and dashed the next, but I do have to give priority to the welfare of my ward.'

'Indeed, my Lord.'

'Tania is at the moment lodged with foster parents at the public expense?'

Bavington glanced over at Miss Byers, who rose again, nose to the fore.

'Indeed, my Lord.'

'Then she should stay there for the time being, and the public purse will have to put up with it. I propose, subject to any further comments, to order interim care and control of Tania to the council, pending a hearing on oral evidence.'

Thus the juvenile court decision was, on an interim basis, reversed. The Valley of Death into which Robert and Haringey's Social Services Department had thundered in front of the Highgate justices had been replaced by the Valley of Life. Robert was unable to see Emily without turning his head, but could see, further over to his left, behind Brady, the expressionless face of Tania's mother. Had she understood what had been decided?

Mr Bavington had no more to say, and Mr. Justice Barton went on to ask if directions for the exchange of evidence could be agreed outside court and a date sought from the Clerk of the Rules for a full hearing. 'What is your time estimate?'

Miss Byers confessed she was hopeless about time estimates, but guessed the case could take up to three days.

Mr. Bavington suggested two days.

Miss Byers then rose to mention the frequency of access proposed if Tania remained in foster care, and Bavington explained he had not had the opportunity to discuss that with his client.

Mr. Justice Barton: 'Surely there has been enough time to take instructions about that.'

Bavington: 'My client was delayed in getting here, my Lord.'

'Very well. I will rise for you to take instructions. I agree a time estimate of two days.'

Before retiring, 'Jaws' said again that in this case the interests of the public purse would have to be ignored, and Tania would have to be cared for by foster parents. He also proposed that when agreement was reached as to the directions to be made, a draft order should be handed in. He rose, as did all others in court, bows were exchanged, and the Court emptied. This left in place the associate, who seemed to have little to occupy his attention, and whose hair-line, Robert told Emily later, seemed to have receded further even during this short hearing. Emily returned the fur coat she had been guarding to its mistress, who thanked her absent-mindedly.

'She should thank her lucky stars I didn't race off to pawn it,' were Emily's private words to Robert soon afterwards.

In the broad corridor outside the row of court rooms Robert was consulted as to how long was required for the council's full evidence to be put into sworn form and served on Mr. Brady. Robert offered a fortnight. Miss Sircar was then to have another two weeks to respond.

Somewhere in the midst of this activity Brady came over to Robert. He stressed the importance of their speaking about the parental rights resolution case – 'You know the one I mean,' he added.

The lawyers trooped off to the Clerk of the Rules office and returned some twenty minutes later with a date in January. A sheet of paper –the draft court order – was covered with an agreed plan of what should happen before then, including visiting arrangements for Miss Sircar to Tania – she did not argue with the twice-weekly proposal. Not long after the draft had been submitted, an approving message was received back from the judge.

The business was over, and an arrangement was made for Robert to collect, an hour later, the court order as put in official form by a now more active associate. Robert and Emily made their way to a café outside the building, conversing on the way.

" 'Jaws' was a bit miserable about the public purse," said Emily. 'How much are we paying Miss Byers?'

'£175. I could have done it on my salary,' said Robert, 'but at the cost of raised blood pressure, and I couldn't have taken the risk of being both advocate and a witness. Theoretically I could have been savaged in the witness box.'

Emily was not greatly intrigued by legal niceties. 'What about a discount of her fee for my looking after her fucking coat?'

'I fear,' said Robert, 'that was just one of the small personal services that go with the instruction of such a grande dame.'

'You're the sort that lets women like that get away with murder. If I had my way, I'd have her arrested by the tipstaff for taking a fucking liberty.'

Robert left the subject there, and they sat down for a snack lunch. She noticed his *Guardian* projecting from the outer pocket of his brief-case. 'What else do you read?'

'Eric Ambler.'

'Never heard of him.'

He told her of his good news: that his kitchen-lazy fellow flat tenant would be moving out by Christmas, having definitely been transferred to a new Civil Service posting in Sussex. 'So with him gone,' said Emily, 'you won't be ashamed to invite me round.'

'Exactly.'

27

Tribunal Interlude and More Tottenham Justice

It so happened, a few days after the high excitement of his first High Court mouthful, that the briefest of lulls in Robert Fordham's flow of work enabled him to observe, at Colin Masson's invitation, what Colin described as, by Haringey standards, a major industrial tribunal case Robert would, it was agreed, take the role of note-taker as well as that of observer, and Colin showed him in advance a three-inch high wall of paper – statements and exhibits. The applicant was a Haringey Social Services training officer in the residential and day care sector. She was claiming she had been dismissed unfairly.

The two lawyers arrived before ten o'clock, in colder weather, at the tribunal building at Woburn Place, not far south of Euston railway station. Once inside they were greeted by a male usher – not gowned, as in the magistrates' court or the Royal Courts – who showed them into the room reserved for employer representatives. They were told that the applicant – a Miss Stein – had already arrived and was representing herself. They helped themselves to drinks from a machine.

Colin Masson shook his head mournfully over the fact Miss Stein was not legally represented. 'We could be here for weeks instead of days, but there it is.'

Minutes later suave Director of Social Services Michael Stone joined them, in something near back-slapping mood. 'Do you think it helps our case,' he asked, 'that the lady training officer I have let go, is fucking mad?' 'It could help,' said Colin drily, 'so long as we can demonstrate the council's actions have been sane.'

The usher re-appeared, and Colin told him he would like to speak to Miss Stein before they went in front of the tribunal. She told the usher she agreed and Colin went off to speak to her. Returned, he said he'd asked her if there was a reason why his written request for 'further and better particulars' of her case had not been answered. She had replied that she had no memory of this request and apologised if she had overlooked something. 'She was,' summarised Colin, 'smoking a small cigar and somewhat vague and fluttery.'

'I would have said,' commented Michael Stone, 'that she is vagueness and fluttery personified, and that is why I had to sack her. Oh, why is it that I like power so much?'

Within minutes all were ushered into the spacious tribunal room, where three suited men in the adjudicating role sat at one end of the room, and others sat facing them. Colin Masson opened the case for the council at a steady pace, explaining that Miss Stein had been dismissed as a result of not doing what was expected of her under her contract and job description to a satisfactory level, despite serious and sustained efforts by management to secure improvement. Robert, sitting behind him, was poised to take notes, and was soon doing so.

Miss Stein, a broad-faced woman with greying hair dressed in a blue trouser suit, then took the opportunity to speak. She denied that her work had been sub-standard and asserted that if standards had slipped, this was due to 'factors outside her control': perhaps either her health or not having enough help or both.

During the lengthy session that followed, broken by a lunch interval, Colin duly earned the title of Mr. Thorough in Robert's estimation. Michael Stone, signatory to a lengthy witness statement, answered questions from Colin for several hours, during which Stone referred to, and sometimes illuminated, more than thirty exhibited documents. These bore dates spread over the years of Miss Stein's employment, and particularly over the last year before her dismissal. Steadily, her claim to have carried out her tasks adequately was dented and dismantled. Stone described some of her decisions and behaviour as 'bizarre' or 'arcane'.

Towards mid-day the proceedings were enlivened by Miss Stein's request to interpose a witness on her own behalf. He had travelled, she said, a long way, and needed to leave by lunch-time. Her request was acceded to and the witness was called. He was the head of a college of further education, who declared that he had known Miss Stein since the early nineteen-sixties. He could vouch for her integrity and for her being a first-class teacher. Colin Masson, cross-examining, did not detain the witness long. 'During what period of time did you observe directly Miss Stein's qualities as a teacher?' The answer came back: '1963-4.' 'Fifteen or sixteen years ago, then?' 'Yes.' 'Not since?' 'No.' In short, Miss Stein's witness did not help her case much.

After lunch the examination by Colin of Michael Stone resumed, and no further short-run excitement flowed. But Miss Stein's turn was to come. The next morning she cross-examined the Director. Much said was of limited interest to a spectator. At one moment, however, Miss Stein asked Stone if he knew her married name. He answered that he did not. At another she asked him politely if he remembered saying to her, shortly after he had taken up his post as Social Services Director: 'Why is it that I like power so much?'

Stone replied, maintaining dignity: 'I would not have had such an intimate conversation with you. It did not take place.'

Robert, amused by this particular question and answer, having heard Stone utter precisely the same rhetorical question only a few hours previously, made no show of eyebrow-lifting or of any other demonstration of disbelief.

Another question from Miss Stein was unloaded: 'Did you say, when disciplinary action against me began, that you would bury me under a haystack of paper?' Michael Stone denied he had said this.

During the afternoon the chairman, an alert lawyer sitting with lay colleagues, was patient, as he had been from the beginning. He confined himself to querying the relevance of particular questions from Miss Stein from time to time.

Only occasionally did the heart of the dispute march into the foreground. One example followed Miss Stein's production of a letter from her doctor, which stated that she suffered from an intermittent viral illness. She put to Michael Stone, in her mild way, that this factor had not been fully taken into account. Stone replied vigorously. He said that this defence had been raised only during the third of the in-house disciplinary hearings which had concerned her, and not previously. Moreover, he went on, her work had been, consistently, far below an acceptable standard for years past, not just during short periods when she may have been ill.

That this broadside had struck home was apparent from the demeanour of the tribunal members, not so much from the sharp-witted chairman, but from his flanking colleagues, who had both become more upright in their seats.

For a few seconds after that, Miss Stein appeared irresolute. She then asked Michael Stone if he had been aware of the similarity of their names: Stein and Stone. Stone replied, not as Robert expected he would:

"I was aware that 'Stein' is German for 'Stone', yes; but in a real sense 'Stone', my surname, is an assumed name."

All of the tribunal members were now near-enough ramrod-backed in their chairs. Was the credibility of the council's key witness about to be exploded by a confession that he was an imposter?

Stone continued deliberately: 'My father, whose surname

was Stanislavsky, came over here before the war and took on the name of Stone, which I have inherited.' He would have continued, as if the event in which he was participating was analogous to a dinner party revelatory moment, when the chairman interrupted:

'Miss Stein, what on earth has this got to do with the issue before the tribunal?'

'I just wondered,' she said, 'why the similarity of our names did not enable us to get on better.'

She had one more suicidal question left in her bag. 'Mr. Stone, if you were dissatisfied with my work, why did you appoint me five years ago, and not say goodbye after my probationary period.'

'Perhaps I should have done just that,' he responded. 'I gave you the benefit of the doubt. But over time, the doubts became diamond–hard certainties.'

It was past four o'clock, and the chairman announced that the hearing would continue next morning. Michael Stone, telling Colin and Robert, as the three of them emerged from the building, that his original appointment of Miss Stein must have been one of his better decisions, hailed a passing taxi and was gone in seconds. Robert and Colin, walking towards the underground station, took stock. 'Sadly,' Colin summarised: 'she cannot see the point, get on the point and even if she got on it by accident, cannot not stay on it. And that is why she has no future as a training officer. Could she be, tragically, in the early stages of some form of dementia? If I were advising her, I'd want a medical opinion.'

'At least she's not been a Stone target for Shimble-ish reasons. Contrast the George Ballam situation,' said Robert.

'I must enlighten you,' declared the impressively tall Colin gravely. 'Stone has not been the driving force for her dismissal. He's too much of a playboy. The driving force was Charmaine Trickett.'

'The Day Care Factor.'

'You have it.'

'Still, the George Ballam thing is different.'

'I heard from Mary, the other day,' said Colin, 'that he picked on George for not putting his, that is, Eddie's, clock back. It was an hour out because of the seasonal time change. According to Mary, Shimble said: *The time has changed, George. You don't seem to have noticed. Time is of the essence. Times change.*'

'Did George do the necessary to the clock after that?'

'He did. But from Eddie's point of view he should have done it the first morning after the time changed, although…' – here Colin spoke with a mocking air – 'it was hardly something set down in George's job description, any more than daily checks of Eddie's pulse.'

Robert excused himself from the last dregs of the hearing, the outcome of which – a fair dismissal – was without question a safe bet. He looked at Colin. 'And is employment law your future?'

'Oh yes, but not at Haringey. I'm just getting useful practice. I intend to move on when I have more experience under my belt. I would like to act for the dismissed and the discriminated against.'

'I can offer you something in exchange for today and yesterday,' said Robert. 'You might do worse than attend an entertainment social workers with me as stage manager are putting on.'

'You've been keeping this very dark.'

'I haven't mentioned it around the legal department, true.'

Colin located his wallet and paid for his ticket. He would be Robert's one legal department colleague to be told about the revue and to attend on the night.

Around this time Robert involved himself again in the parental rights resolution concerning the child Aaron which he feared might be thrown out by the court. He telephoned Enid Prosser to ask for news.

'You were going to allocate the case in your team,' he began. 'I wondered what had happened.'

'I changed my mind,' she replied, 'I allocated it to myself. I visited Aaron's mother where she was supposed to be living with her boyfriend, and found that she was already back with her mother. I managed to see her. She was in tears at first, but cheered up when I promised she would be able to visit Aaron at least twice a year. I put it in writing.'

'But she can't read, can she?'

'No, but her mother read it to her, as I did.'

'Can I have a copy for myself?'

'Yes, if you want.'

'I can then send a copy to her solicitor for information.'

'If you think that's necessary.' He received a copy of the visits guarantee a day or two later, and sent a copy to Brady & Co, from whom he heard nothing more. He concluded that Brady, who had at court expressed the wish to discuss the case with him, was now deserted by his client, and consequently immobilised. So whether or not Aaron's mother was permanently disabled from parenting was never to be tested in court. The Firth children fiasco was not repeated.

Robert's thoughts were now concentrated especially on the approach of the final hearing concerning phenergan-drugged Amy on whom, a month before – though it seemed an age – a temporary care order had been made. He was now, without any doubt, blooded.

Had Amy's several hospital admissions really been the result of imbibing unprescribed medication, administered with unpredictable consequences for unknown reasons by her mother? He would have to rely on Dr. Pearson, who seemed unlikely to back-track on his opinion, and who had confirmed he would attend. Robert had no qualms either about the likely performance of Jessica Palmer in the witness stand.

Another medical witness candidate, the family's general practitioner, whose evidence Robert could only guess at, had not been compliant. He had not agreed to give evidence in response to a letter of request. This he had not even acknowledged. When Robert had telephoned him, he replied with heat that giving evidence would 'cut to ribbons' his relationship with the Stewarts as patients, and that if he wound up in court he would not tell the truth and his evidence would favour the parents. Robert had not protested, but did not give up.

He had secured a witness summons from Tottenham magistrates' court against this doctor, and litigation assistant Errol had mounted his motor-cycle in order to serve it, having with him enough petty cash for public transport fares – 'conduct money' – to hand over. There had been light-hearted discussion before Errol set off, as to whether he might have to contemplate queuing in the surgery waiting room with, for example, a pretended gammy leg, in order to get within the necessary yard of the doctor. If need be, faced with refusal to take it, the summons could be dropped at the doctor's feet.

But Errol, without need for subterfuges, had on arrival at the surgery managed to put the ball in the net. He had handed to a resigned general practitioner the summons, a covering letter and the fare money. The doctor had commented, after a grunt substituted for a sigh: 'I expected Mr. Fordham would do this.'

So, in November's third week, on a bleak Wednesday morning, Robert's witnesses gathered in the Tottenham magistrates' court near court room number 2, in which Lady Feverel and two male book-ends would be sitting. Amy's mother, Robert was pleased to see, was less wretchedly dressed than on the previous occasion. She had come in a coat, and the jumper underneath was without holes. Mr. Stewart wore jeans and an old leather jacket. Representing their interests was a female barrister with a cold, angry air and high heels.

When the case was called on, a youthful clerk, whom Robert had not seen before, sat below Lady Feverel, and began, with gauche inappropriateness, by asking the parents if they pleaded guilty or not guilty. He was, from ignorance, treating the proceedings as a criminal prosecution, rather than as a civil application, in which applications are 'Opposed' or 'Not opposed'. Lady Feverel looked heavenwards and tightened her lips. With a contemptuous look, the Stewarts' barrister stated on their behalf that the council's application was opposed.

Robert set out with care the council's case, not limiting it to the medical evidence which, it was difficult to deny, was circumstantial so far as the causes of Amy's sleepy hospital admissions were concerned. Dr. Pearson he called first, and the donnish paediatrician expressed the opinion without hesitation, having removed his glasses several times in five minutes, that one of these admissions was almost certainly due to unprescribed medication, and that it was very likely the others were similarly caused. The angry barrister did not damage the force of this assessment with her questions, which more than once began with: 'So are you, an expert, actually telling this court of law…', to which the answer came tamely as 'Yes'. Dr. Pearson did not stray from answering with patient, qualified, medical explanation, which he was made to repeat a number of times. Lady Feverel flashed a benign glance at Dr. Pearson from time to time.

Then came the general practitioner, who had attempted, outside court, to make his peace with Amy's parents, explaining that his attendance had not been voluntary. When testifying, and asked to refer to case notes, he removed from a briefcase small bundles of medical records, secured with elastic bands which he unpackaged and seemed to be in no chronological order. Lady Feverel patiently watched with an indulgent smile while he found what he wanted with effort and time. When he spoke, in answer to Robert's questions, a troubling picture emerged.

Mrs. Stewart had come into the surgery several times over the months before the council had taken action, telling of her suicidal feelings, and she had, when he had asked whether the injuries to her wrists had been self-inflicted, 'nodded assent'. She had been frequently prescribed medication in her own right – phenergan – for her depressed state of mind. He had prescribed nothing for Amy, who was also his patient.

The general practitioner, after facing very few questions from a barrister constantly on the doorstep of rage, was permitted to leave the court so that he could meet his other patients' needs.

The morning's session ended well before one o'clock on Lady Feverel's command. The reason for the early lunch adjournment was not disclosed. 'A book-end's tummy upset', was Jessica's guess. 'The man on Lady F's left looked distinctly queasy.'

Standing for a minute or two with Jessica and Dr. Pearson in the central foyer of the building, Robert saw Jack Parnell, his Enfield opposite number, enjoying, as Robert was enjoying, respite from forensic labours. He came over just as Jessica was saying farewell to Dr. Pearson, who had remained in court until the end of the GP's evidence. Jack Parnell was soon embarked on his latest anecdote.

'We had a moral danger thing in court today. A 14-year-old girl plus a groping step-father and colluding mother. The step-father proclaimed his total innocence, of course.'

'Difficult to prove, sounds like,' said Robert.

"I got near enough. The step–father, when I cross-examined him, accepted he hadn't been on speaking terms with the girl for the two years he had been living in the household. He agreed that this pattern was broken when he got into bed with her. He said he wanted to show affection to her, to cuddle her. I bowled him a straight one. I said – 'When you got into bed with her, what were you wearing?'"

Jack deferred completing the story, saying: 'You've probably noticed, that when asking questions that reach into the sexual area, the silence of the court becomes deadly. A pin dropping would detonate when it hits the floor. Even the Bench are on the look-out.'

'So what did he say about what he was wearing?'

"No prevarication. He said: 'Just my briefs.' I repeated: 'Just your briefs?' He said yes. I let that sink in and said: 'No more questions.' I could have said: 'How's that?'"

'A care order on the girl?'

'Her feet didn't touch the ground. One of the quickest care orders ever made.'

When the court resumed sitting, Jessica went into the witness box. In response to Robert, she detailed several occasions when she had visited Amy at home, describing her generally miserable demeanour, and contrasting this with the much happier, even blossoming child she had seen recently at the foster home. She spoke too of a visit when Mrs. Stewart had admitted having, in frustration at the combined screaming of Amy and her eight-year-old sister, banged their two heads together until Amy lost consciousness.

The ill-tempered barrister asked Jessica if the Christian name terms on which she had been with Mrs. Stewart were compatible with a professional relationship, and the reply came that building a friendly relationship was likely to be more effective than building a formal one. She was asked another, potentially deadly question: 'And why are you not removing Amy's sister too, to be consistent?'

'We are keeping a close eye on her sister's welfare of course. But she does appear to be less at risk.'

Jessica's written welfare report had previously been supplied to the parents' irascible counsel, who now asked Jessica questions based on its content, a development which caused Lady Feverel to demand copies for the Bench. It was a situation which not so long ago Jonathan Spratt had ensured would not arise in Michelle West's case by not asking the educational psychologist questions about his report. It was clear that the parents' counsel, though high heeled and high tempered, was not as tactically wily as Spratt or Brady. The angry brief had scored a procedural own goal by facilitating the production of a powerful supplement to the evidence for the 'primary condition'.

Robert supplied copies of the report, which the Bench retired to read. On return, her Ladyship graciously complimented Jessica on its clarity and thoroughness.

It was now the turn of the Stewarts to put their side of the story. Mr. Stewart's testimony included memory blanks. He had no memory of attempting to strangle his wife or of putting his hands round her neck a month previously. At one point he said that he could not vouch for what his wife did when he was at work. This produced a hissed interjection from Mrs. Stewart of 'Silly sod!'

While denying that his wife's behaviour was ever violent, he admitted without prevarication that she had knocked a clock off the mantelpiece on one occasion when frustrated, and had thrown objects of various kinds through the windows of their home 'very occasionally' on others.

Mrs. Stewart compromised less than her husband. Asked about his assault on herself, she said it had happened and she didn't want to say any more about it. She denied that she had admitted to Jessica, as Jessica had testified, that she had banged the heads of the children together. She said instead that Amy had banged her head through falling off her bed. She had, it was true, on that occasion taken Amy to hospital to be examined. By then Amy had regained consciousness.

When Mrs. Stewart insisted that a further injury had been

caused to Amy through falling down the stairs, Lady Feverel broke in, asking: 'Was there not a protective gate at the top of the stairs?' There had not been.

The evidence was complete, and the simmering barrister submitted that the heart of the council's case (Robert noted that she did not use the pretentious word 'gravamen') – that Amy had been deliberately medicated to a dangerous degree without medical approval – was unsubstantiated, was precariously circumstantial, and that without it the case fell to the ground. It was, she snapped, even a misuse, however well-intentioned, of protective procedures. (Robert claimed, in conversation later with Jessica, that he had expected his opponent's final submission to be accompanied by sharp taps with one of her stiletto shoes on the pew-top in front of her.)

Lady Feverel, after hearing from Robert, was heard to mutter to her Bench colleagues: 'I'm getting too old for this racket,' before the three of them rose, submitted to bows from the lawyers, and filed out.

When they returned, half an hour later, Lady Feverel was loftily and icily clear: 'We find the 'proper development condition' proved and make a *full* care order to the local authority.'

Tottenham justice, Robert decided, sometimes was justice, while Highgate justice varied in quality as much as Tottenham's. He felt entitled to a self-indulgent evening at home with a book, one to be read by him for a fourth or fifth time. It was another favourite Eric Ambler story – *Epitaph for a Spy*.

28

The Day of the Revue

It was a Friday in mid-December and the day of the stage performance of the revue. Those who had been most involved had taken the day off work to ensure that the hired hall in Muswell Hill was fully primed. The hall was not large, so microphones could be dispensed with. Lighting was another matter. The hired equipment needed installation and checking to ensure it functioned. Backstage arrangements – including improvised curtained-off dressing and changing areas – had to be buttressed by gimcrack structures on which articles of attire could be slung. Many of these were to be donned and discarded in rapid succession.

Setting out tables for the audience was another, if more elementary, chore and was neglected until a late stage. A finishing touch was the decoration of each table with a candle enthroned in a holder. Early in the evening food in quantity and in many dishes arrived and was placed on three long tables ranged together. Another long table for beverages – wine, beer and non-alcoholic – was to one side.

Robert, as stage manager, had lists on a clipboard of the sketches and songs in sequence, and of the performers assigned to each. The cast had been told to be present or else by six thirty. They had, with few exceptions, risen to the occasion, and even the few exceptions were not dangerously late. Outside the hall was cold, cold weather, and the wind had worked itself up into an evil mood.

Just after seven the audience began to trickle in, removing coats, helping themselves to drinks, and chatting to colleagues. Food was to be available from a quarter past the hour so that there was some assurance it would not be consumed too early. Robert was on the look-out for the lady-like Miriam Fawcett (a chronic late-comer). Jessica's husband was pointed out to him, sitting alone. His pint glass was already empty. He looked ruminative, and did not come back-stage to speak to Jessica.

Tables so far without a share of the audience were being commandeered. Several child protection police officers had taken over one table. Enid Prosser was at first seated alone at another, but was soon in company. Colin Masson, wearing casual clothes – a condition in which Robert had not previously seen him – was tenanting another table, and Robert was pleased to see him greeted and joined by several social workers who must have known him for his measured contributions at union branch meetings.

One table only had been labelled 'Reserved'. It was designated for the use of Michael Stone, and he was already seated, together with a lady whose hand he held under the table from time to time as the evening unfolded.

The guests who had arrived by the official start-time numbered well over a hundred. That was the moment when Robert took up a position in front of the curtain and declared the proceedings open, welcoming the guests. He had, besides being stage manager, acquired without debate the additional role of master of ceremonies. The session would be held up for a moment or two, he declared, until those collecting food and drink were in their seats.

Minutes later came the opening message for the audience, written by Emily, delivered by Robert, and punctuated with laughter. 'From one or two chance remarks overheard near the buffet table, I gather some uninformed guests imagine they are going to witness some sort of entertainment.' He paused.

'This idea is entirely misconceived. The sponsors apologise if they have contributed in any way to this misunderstanding. Our presentation is entirely educational. Anyone who is expecting to be entertained should leave now.'

He paused again: 'The price of tickets…is not refundable. This evening's short refresher course about what it means to be a Haringey social worker should be particularly useful for senior managers.' Robert gestured towards Michael Stone's table. 'Including very senior managers indeed.' Laughter and applause.

'I know nothing about the first exercise,' continued Robert, 'but understand it is intended to illustrate how a first child protection home visit, in response to a confidential referral about a baby's welfare, should ideally be conducted, displaying all the knowledge and sensitivity for which this council's social workers are famous across London.'

As Robert retreated into the wings, and the last audience fragments took their seats, Jessica whispered to him 'Well done.' The performance that followed, whatever its amateurish shortcomings, was welcomed by an appreciative audience, and the more telling moments were received with near-rapture.

The curtain opened. Two male social workers, clothed to resemble old-world film legends Stanley Laurel and Oliver Hardy, were sitting at a table drinking tea. Traditional theme music. The actors were a heavily cushioned Frank Jackson as Hardy and a very thin and wiry Steve Warren as Laurel. The telephone rang. After scene-setting antics, the plumped-up Frank took the call. This was from a Mrs. Pottinger, who expressed fears about the welfare of a neighbour's young child.

There were more stereotypical doings before Frank and Steve arrived at the address given. Frank's knock at the address was answered by a formidable man, in braces, extensive tattoos and colourful neckerchief.

'We represent the London Borough of Haringey, sir. We're

here to see your little boy, because one of your neighbours says you are ill-treating him.'

'Who was it who said that? She won't do it again on my oath.'

'Hardy' produced a piece of paper. 'It was Mrs. Pottinger at number 5.' One of the biggest crimes in social work practice had been committed: giving away the name of an informer about a child's welfare. The man went off purposefully; shrieks are heard. He returned, dusting his hands. 'Now it's your turn. Which of you wants it first.' They flew to safety, pursued, before returning alone to centre stage.

The theme music sounded and 'Hardy' closed: 'That's another fine mess you got me into.' Sustained applause.

After another, less memorable sketch, and a song, came *The Importance of Being Anorexia*. This was announced visually by Frank – no longer well padded – and Steve, who together bore a large notice carrying the title from one side of the stage to the other, hovering for a moment mid-stage. The action was set not in an upper class drawing room, but in a Social Services reception area which appeared to serve a peculiarly upper class clientele. The receptionist – identified as 'Anorexia' and played by Jessica – was evidently not from the top social drawer, and a social worker identified as a Miss Bracknell soon materialised. She had an appropriately dignified and even regal manner and was carrying a plate of miniscule sandwiches. It was Miriam Fawcett, serenaded by audience cheers.

'Anorexia, I'll place the cucumber sandwiches here. You are not to touch them.'

'No, Miss Bracknell.'

'They are for clients, do you hear me?'

'Yes, Miss Bracknell.'

'Anorexia', making it obvious she can barely keep her hands off the sandwiches, greeted an exquisitely dressed young gentleman swinging a cane and explaining that he was need of succour and counselling owing to an unfortunate early history. For this part, the ex-Rugby schoolboy Harold Stott was dressed to perfection. 'Anorexia' passed him on to Miss Bracknell, who sized him up through a lorgnette, before interrogating him privately to one side.

The visitor explained, identifying himself as a Mr. Worthing, that he had no parents.

'No parents!' exclaimed Miss Bracknell, going on to utter the immortal lines of her role model: 'To lose one parent may be regarded as a misfortune. To lose both looks like carelessness!'

The young man explained that he had been suddenly orphaned as a four-year-old, and had ever since been searching for his younger sister. His mother had pushed his father under a bus in Trafalgar Square, and had then leaped to her own death from the top of Nelson's Column. 'I believe there was something about it in the newspapers,' he added, flicking non-existent dust from his suit jacket, to a ripple of audience amusement.

Deprived of his parents and a little dazed – so 'Mr. Worthing' revealed to Miss Bracknell – he had wandered into Lyons Corner House nearby, where he was taken up by a short-sighted but kind and well-to-do lady who had imagined that she was in the Savoy Hotel. She had fostered him throughout his childhood, as if her own son, and for this he owed her much. But he had never given up wondering what had happened to his younger sister, from whom he had become separated in a crush of people in the Square. He had advertised for her in vain. At this point 'Mr. Worthing' extended his arms to illustrate this emptiness in his life and the failure of his search.

There was a minor distraction at this point as the spotlight shifted to receptionist 'Anorexia'. She was taking a call from a client who demanded help with locating a diamond necklace. This had vanished from the silver pot which her grandmother had been given by Kaiser Wilhelm II. 'And who is your social worker?' asked 'Anorexia'. It proved, of course, to be Miss Bracknell, who promised to call back. Meanwhile the young gentleman was tucking into the cucumber sandwiches with abandon, while 'Anorexia' stared at them hungrily.

'Mr. Worthing' offered more detail. His only clue to his sister's identity was left in the bag he had been carrying when the well-to-do lady had encountered him: a plain, brown carrier bag. Again, there came from Miss Bracknell, as if to the manner born, an echo from the Wilde play: 'A carrier bag?'

Inside the carrier bag, he went on, was a pair of shoes belonging to his sister, with her Christian name sewn into a label.

The name is then revealed, to theatrical amazement and delight, as 'Anorexia'. Brother and sister were united, though their reunion embrace is interrupted by the entry of a uniformed man who informs 'Anorexia' that Lady Feverel, juvenile court chairman – whose name is met with merry audience acknowledgement – is outside in her carriage and demanding the immediate services of Miss Bracknell. The sketch ends. Furious hand-clapping. The curtains close, though not without technical difficulty this time.

Robert, clip-board held close, based in the wings, could not for a few moments find Emily Frost, who, distracted by the Wilde sketch, had been slow to ready herself for the next stage adventure. 'I'm coming,' she called out over-loudly in response to Robert's stage whisper, causing audience members to cheer.

'That was an intentional double entendre,' she mouthed quietly, as Robert gestured her to go on stage.

'Just go on, Emily,' he murmured.

The curtains opened again, revealing Emily in the guise of

a 'Mrs. Gale', a supposed Social Services client who, shown into an interview room for a discussion about the problems of her son Paul, alighted on the file on the family. This had been left there inadvertently by the family's just allocated social worker, who had been called away to the telephone. 'Mrs. Gale', entranced by discovering that the file concerned her family, was then loudly wrathful. One letter she picked up was from the psychiatrist at the Child Guidance Centre, who – she read out – had declared that he had had a bellyful of the Gale family, and that 'if that woman' showed up again, he would poison her dog's dinner. 'What a thing to say,' said 'Mrs. Gale'. 'That's the last time I go to see that four-eyed Freudian foul-up.'

Jessica, as 'the social worker' re-entered, firm but sympathetic, and relieved 'Mrs. Gale' of the thick folder. Seeking to de-fuse 'Mrs. Gale's' ire, she inquired about her son Paul and said she would like to meet him. 'Mrs. Gale' then launched into her anxieties about the relationship between her son Paul and the family's dog Henry.

'I don't think their relationship is quite natural,' she says.

'Do they…do a lot of…things together?'

'Oh yes. They frisk about together, they eat and drink out of the same dish, do their business by the same lamppost, they chase cats together and they curl up in the same basket at night. It's very nice really.'

'But at the same time,' said Jessica in a concerned way, 'you're troubled about aspects of their relationship.'

'Well, it's when they're in the basket together. They do rude things…'

Their exchanges ended with the revelation – as two dogs trot up to them (they were Frank and Steve in doggy costumes hired at great expense) – that 'Mrs. Gale's' so-called son was actually, like Henry, a dog. 'This is my son Paul. Don't be frightened of stroking him.'

'I shall have to speak to my senior about where we go from here,' says the bewildered Jessica. But a few seconds later, her 'senior', a bearded male social worker, appears in the doorway, wearing a colourful floral dress. 'You called me?' he asks.

Jessica screams, faints, and the curtain closes. Much laughter, much applause. The mid-point of the show has been reached.

During the interval the cast remained back stage. In the wings Robert stood with Emily at a point where they could see the audience through a chink in the curtaining. Robert pointed out to Emily Colin Masson, the only legal department representative present.

'Oh, Mr. Boring Trade Unionist, I presume.'

Robert stood his ground. 'I don't think he's boring at all.'

Emily retreated: 'Then I spoke false.' She switched subjects.

'Look at Mike Stone. Look at the way his lady friend is looking at him. She seems to think he's the bee's knees. Maybe she hasn't been to bed with him yet.'

'And you have, I suppose,' said Robert daringly.

Emily looked at him. 'On a residential holiday for handicapped children at Walton-on-Naze. I was an idiot. He's all show, the most selfish man I ever met.'

'I won't ask for details.'

'Selfish in bed, selfish out of it.'

After the interval came more sketches. Before the next piece of acted nonsense came a news item, articulated with precise solemnity by Robert. 'It has been decided,' he said, 'though not yet announced officially, that each Area Social Services office should have its own consultant astrologist.' He 'quoted' Michael Stone: 'We need to look again at our methods of working, and astrology has a lot going for it.'

'So has palmistry,' Robert went on, 'according to one Area manager, who is reported as having said to a desperate mother who wanted her children out of care, that to judge from her life-line, adverse events would be overtaking her instead. He is now,' said Robert, 'advocating the purchase by each Area office of a crystal ball as an essential social work tool.'

The time had now arrived for the director's management team meeting sketch, which had been put into its final form by Jessica and Emily. This presented Michael Stone as imperious, arbitrary, elitist, hedonistic and a Fabian socialist to boot. Emily, playing the part of a social worker who has supported a parent's request for financial help too vigorously for the Director's taste, was to be the subject of discipline. The senior managers, or senior toadies, as they appeared to be, sipped their wine during the meeting.

The director (from whose jacket pocket a copy of *Liberation* peered out, and who was played by Frank Jackson) invited comment on the wine list he was holding. He admitted blithely to having had difficulty in squaring the Treasurer's department over the last case of Dom Perignon champagne consumed, and said that in future they would have to be more modest in the matter of wine. 'Order a couple of cases of Chablis instead,' says 'Stone' to his assistant.

Several times 'Stone' expressed satisfaction with this assistant, who was repeatedly invited to move his chair nearer the director's, with which requests the assistant sycophantically complied. But then 'Stone' expressed his astonishment with him. 'What on earth are you doing there? You're getting under my feet.' Then, as the assistant picked up the cricket bat required for disciplinary action against Emily, who bent over, short-skirted, 'Stone', his features somewhat contorted with testosterone, decided that the punishment should be for him to deliver personally. 'Oh', said 'Stone', 'why is it that I like power so much?' In the audience Michael Stone put his hands over his face. Noisy appreciation and some stamping of feet.

After several other short items, the curtain opened again to disclose a 'Monty Pythonish' version of the Virgin Mary (played by Frank Jackson, who had changed clothes with astonishing speed and was now wearing a false beard of large proportions). 'Mary' was seated, puffing at a cigarette, with a woman friend close to a manger in which a doll represented a baby. A sign to one side gave the address: 17 Gallilee, Nazareth estate, Tottenham. The female friend appealed to 'Mary' to give the baby a name. First 'Mary' proposed calling the baby 'Mary', after herself. Then she proposed ('after all, 'e is a boy and 'e's got to be someone special, what with that star up there') that he should be called 'Jason'. She was asked about his father, but gave a defensive reply: 'Don't talk to me about 'is father.'

A health visitor came in and cooed while 'Mary' flicked ash over the baby. She claimed: 'I haven't clobbered him yet.'

Said the health visitor: 'I do understand how difficult it must be for you. Bringing up a baby without a father.'

Said 'Mary': 'He's got a father. A very high-up father.'

Three 'social workers from east Haringey' then entered bearing gifts. One brought £5, which 'Mary' said would buy a bottle of gin for her and the baby. A second social worker brought a takeaway curry. A third stated: 'I bring myrrh.'

'Mary': 'Myrrh?'

'Myrrh.'

'Mary': 'I'll have the five quid and the curry. You can stuff the myrrh.'

Left alone with her friend, 'Mary' became angry with the baby's crying.

'That social worker promised to come and take the baby away, but I'm still stuck with it.' She head-butted the doll-baby and then spoke to it firmly with wagging forefinger:

'That'll teach you, Jason, to drag a star round after you and bring all that lot in. Think you're somebody special, do you?' She demanded that social workers take the baby away. (The audience had become much quieter over this gallows' humour development, but the climax of the story was not far off.)

The friend suggested she complained to the Director of Social Services. 'I can't do that. I can't do that...' (the denouement was preceded by a few seconds' pause) '...cause he's...the baby's Dad!' The versatile Frank Jackson as 'Mary' was now pointing at Michael Stone.

For a second time during the show, Stone put his hands to his face, then was revealed to be contriving signs of enjoyment – what else could he do? – and clapping – together with the rest of the audience.

At this point Emily approached Stone from behind, bearing a plate heaped with shaving foam. She called out joyously: 'This is one for liking power so much!' To cackles of delight wrapped up in much audience cheering, she enveloped his face with the foam. Stone's woman friend, meanwhile, alternated between unabashed mirth and embarrassed sympathy. His two free tickets had come at a price.

The performance ends, closing with a sentimental song, the tune borrowed from the play *Oh What a Lovely War*, the words adapted to give social work relevance ('And if they ask us, why social work we do, oh we'll never tell them, oh we'll never tell them...'). Final waves of commendation.

After the audience had gone into the cold and bitter night, there was clearing up to do, and grumbling from some cast members about others who had already made good their escape, submitting excuses for leaving the tidying up to others.

'Very entertaining,' said Colin Masson, having located Robert. 'Dazzling, if you like,' he added, using an un-Masson-like word.

Enid Prosser approached Robert, as short and dumpy as Colin was tall and thin. 'Well done,' she said, 'to all of you. A good show, even if one or two things were below the belt.'

'Such as?'

'Head-butting a baby as a joke. Jokes like that can rebound on you. In this line of work we walk a tight-rope.'

'We got carried away with fantasy. I know you're right.'

'Not long afterwards Robert approached Emily to ask – "That line in the director's management meeting sketch – 'Why is it that I like power so much?' Have you heard him say that?"

'He says it all the time. It's his signature tune. It's supposed to be ironic. Another one is a kind of mock threat when he falls out with someone. He says he'll bury you under a haystack of paper.' So Miss Stein, dismissed and in the employment tribunal, was telling the truth about that. But in her case the threat was carried out.

Jessica, Robert noticed, was as active as anyone in tidying up the hall, and during a break in activity, when they sat together on a corner of the now empty stage, said that he assumed her husband was not waiting for her.

'No, I told him not to waste his time waiting. It was decent of him,' she added, 'to come.'

She said soberly. 'I've not been very good for him. It can't have been pleasant for him – must have aroused memories – to see Frank and me on stage with the others.'

'Memories?'

'Frank's not told you?'

'No.'

'That's Frank. Not one to blurt out private things. He can make obtuse comments, but he can be old-fashioned chivalrous too.'

'What hasn't Frank told me about?'

Jessica looked at Robert squarely. 'I had an affair with him.'

'You told me before that your marriage had been severely tested.'

'The affair didn't have much going for it...Neither does my marriage, sad to say...' She broke off suddenly.

'I'm sorry you're having to go through such a difficult patch.'

'I'll manage, never fear. Was Beth here? I didn't see Beth here tonight.'

'I'm sure she would have come, but she's in Australia. A holiday.' Jessica looked at him.

'You don't sound very pleased about it.'

'I'll survive. I'm not Beth's only priority.'

She changed the subject. 'You must have invited Colin Masson.'

'Yes. You know him.'

'Only from union meetings. I did get talking to him after one meeting. He comes from the same sort of background I come from.'

'Leftie?'

'Yes.'

She changed topics abruptly. 'I've been meaning to tell you something. Michelle West.'

'Escaper via the balcony?' Robert replied with jocularity.

'Yes. Our discussion after the care order was made wasn't a waste of time. I've got her into a more suitable foster home – more hands on and out of London. Long-term. Enid Prosser helped me.'

'White family?'

'Yes. The Patricks were OK, but they were too laid back. The family she's with are middle class, but very nurturing. Derek Ivins' leaving made it easier to argue against a children's home. Especially as the children's homes I looked into couldn't offer what this foster home has.'

'That is something worth celebrating.'

A few days later Robert waited at Heathrow airport for Beth, returned from Australia. As she came through into the arrivals area she was obviously pleased to see him, and immediately kissed him and thanked him for meeting her. Thereafter she was quiet for a while.

Robert, while conscious that she was fatigued, began to ask her what she had seen and done as they made their way towards an exit which led to the underground station. She told him what she had been doing, where she had been, what she had seen, as if she had been unaccompanied. He guessed that her answers were guided by diplomacy. She was also hungry and welcomed his proposal for a Chinese meal.

After the long journey on the underground, they finally reached Robert's car in the parking area by the entrance to Highgate tube station. They were soon at the restaurant. Not far into the meal Robert broached the delicate question, even indelicately.

'I take it that most of these outings were with your ex-boyfriend?'

She nodded, not seeking to shy away from the fact.

'And I imagine you were sleeping with him too?'

'Yes, but not for the first couple of days,' she said levelly.

'It's your life, not mine,' he said. 'But I do get the message that for you our relationship is not especially important.'

'That's unfair. I value our relationship. Maybe I'm not ready yet to settle down. Maybe I don't know what I want.'

'I expect I'm old-fashioned, maybe even ridiculous.'

'I'm sorry to have disappointed you. I know I want to settle down too.'

Lovely as she looked, sincere as was the expression with which she had spoken, there was, Robert thought, something distant about her responses.

'Have you finished with the Australian?'

'Well, I'm not likely to be going back to Australia any time soon,' she said.

'And is every relationship here, other than the one with me, dead and gone and not likely to start up again?'

For a moment he felt a sense of loneliness in her. She said only that she had no plans for seeing anyone else. What grated was that she said nothing to indicate any real commitment to Robert.

She added, with a sudden smile: 'Of course I really enjoy going out with you. How did the revue go?'

Robert told her how it had gone.

29

Christmas Celebrations

The legal people's modest Christmas 'do' was programmed by Edward Shimble to begin at three o'clock on the last working afternoon before the holiday. By a quarter past that hour, the majority of staff who were not already on leave were clustered in an open–plan first floor area around the buffet table, on which light refreshments – mini-sandwiches, cakes, peanuts, wine and soft drinks – were ranged. These delicacies had been prepared by the small all-female local land charges inquiries staff team led by Pat – she with responsibility for a petty cash box and its key. Melanie Cusack was one of the absentees. Edward Shimble had decreed that the ground floor residents, the Community Development Team (from whose filthy party advertisement he had not yet entirely recovered), should not be invited, and his wishes had been respected.

Robert's arrival was late, after a short appearance – his first – in the Edmonton County Court before Judge Madder. It was in support of an adoption application on a four–year-old, and as it turned out, Judge Madder had not found any reason to bludgeon any advocate for using incorrect forensic expressions, despite the inherently provocative 'O.K.' uttered by the young female solicitor representing the adopting couple. He had simply looked at her in disbelief. The couple, during the formal preliminaries in the big court room, had been sitting anxiously with the child elsewhere in the building. All three had then been welcomed into Madder's small private room, where he gave his blessing to the adoption. The process included, with an attempt at a judicial smile, handing the child a sweet.

After this pleasant enough experience, Robert hurried back to the legal building. Almost as soon as he arrived near the buffet table, Edward Shimble, who was, to his surprise, amiably inebriated, wandered over. The paunch which arrived ahead of him had acquired for seasonal reasons a pacific character. Shimble was in a Christmas mood.

'You know, Robert,' he said. 'I'm proud of this department. It's come forward so much since I came here twenty months ago.'

He volunteered that he had had quite a lot to drink, naming the drinks individually (two large whiskeys and now a small glass of dry white wine) and that he and his wife were meeting people for more drinks that evening. He said that the previous Christmas, as a result of too many celebrations, he had acquired a dreadful headache. This time he could already sense the beginnings of such a set-back. Robert suggested, maintaining gravity of demeanour, commonly applied remedies, and threw in the addition of a hot bath when Shimble reached home, to rejuvenate himself for the evening.

'Thank you for that suggestion. I'll take it up.'

Though Robert was sorely tempted to propose another remedy – drawing blood through the application of leeches, adding that as it happened he had some with him, patting a pocket – he resisted the temptation. Though he could pass the thing off as humour, he was not persuaded it would be understood or forgiven.

Mostly consisting of polite conversation around the buffet table, the restrained conviviality would be all over within not much more than an hour. There was no background music or any prospect of the letting down of hair. One post-Robert arrival was George Ballam, who had discarded his tie, a fact for which he was promptly rewarded with some oh-ho! banter from the cluster of suit-and-tie men present. It was exceptional for a male staff member to remove his tie in any circumstances while in the office, almost as exceptional as the removal of trousers; but as George explained to Bill Bowman, he had just emerged from the Civic Centre's typing pool party and had joined in the dancing to pop music there. Bill Bowman responded with ribald innuendos, which George brushed off with geniality, just as Colin Masson unobtrusively joined the group.

'At least I was just celebrating,' said George. 'You remember the star performer at the party last year?'

'Who?' asked Bowman.

'That drunk articled clerk. Pincher of female bottoms. The one who left in September.'

Robert recalled his local courts tour, with Godfrey as guide, in his first Haringey week, and how uncomfortable Godfrey had been when confronted with Emily Frost.

'Godfrey?' asked Bowman.

'That's him,' George responded.

'He shouldn't have got away with it,' commented Colin.

'I remember a few squeals,' said Bowman, nostalgically, undeterred by Colin's intolerance of this behaviour. 'The girls can't have been too cross. He didn't get a slap round the face, did he?'

'Perhaps he should have,' said George.

'Eddie liked him. Said he'd finish up a borough solicitor.'

'Despite the bottom pinching or because of?'

Bill Bowman did not reply.

I recall,' said Colin, 'that he was a proud member of the Conservative Party, which may have gained him favour in some quarters.'

Colin glanced over at Edward Shimble, who was seated a sufficient distance away not to overhear this conversation, and who to all appearances was preoccupied with his own partially disabling condition.

Bill Bowman did not contribute further, and turned away. 'Whatever happened,' Robert asked Colin, 'to the business of collecting figures of court appearances and so on in response to the Leader's call for consideration of possible savings?'

'I presume,' said Colin, 'some sort of departmental workload analysis and conclusions were supplied by Eddie. I would like to think the result was fairly objective.' He raised his eyebrows as he said this, and the conversation moved on.

Edward Shimble, on other occasions highly reactive to the shortcomings of the 'pens and pencils' manager, was on this occasion oblivious to George Ballam's tieless state. He was sitting in a chair with eyes closed, before he rose and approached Bill Bowman, with a movement close to a stumble, to make a request audible only to Bowman. Within minutes both men had muttered seasonal wishes to those nearby, had donned overcoats and were gone from the building. It was manifest that Bill would be driving Shimble home.

Colin, watching them depart, told Robert that Shimble's regime style had marked a revolutionary change from that in place under his predecessor – who had lovingly installed a Rolling Stones poster on one of his office walls and a guitar in a corner. His management approach had been, as Colin put it, 'something less than authoritarian' and his guitar playing, resorted to when he had nothing better to do on Friday afternoons, had been loud but not sophisticated. There was a sense of loss in the minds of some veterans of the legal department for those strange, liberated and quickly passing municipal times.

The gathering contracted, those remaining toasting the now retired Albert Clack (and also 'the ratepayers, God bless 'em'), before Robert left its safe but unstimulating atmosphere. After a change of clothes at home, he made his way to a social workers' party. The venue was an adult Day Centre and before the party went into a decline around midnight, Robert guessed that some fifty or sixty guests – social workers, assistant social workers and some of their 'seniors' had put in an appearance.

Present also, for a short time, and smiling in all directions, Robert noted, was the kindly-uncle-chairman remembered from the Amy Stewart case conference on Robert's second day in action at Haringey, the area manager who had later contributed to the ill-judged (but now thankfully reversed) decision to move Michelle West against her wishes from foster to children's home. At that very moment, Robert took in sympathetically, he was again committing the lesser offence of wearing his sky blue sports jacket (a colour suitable, admittedly, for the covers of the three august volumes of Stone's Justices Manual) above unmistakably brown trousers.

Beth, who could have attended the party with Robert, had declined to do so on the ground that she had arranged to spend the evening with her friend Annie.

If this celebration began sedately enough, it did not continue so. At one point Emily Frost was seen to be borne into the kitchen over the shoulder of Frank Jackson, bearing in one hand a broom for some reason or no reason, while at another she was exuberantly embracing a female social worker she had not apparently met for some time. Not long after that Frank poured beer over Emily's head, an act for which he was punished with several sharp raps on the head by her ring-enhanced hand. These blows, Robert observed, really connected, though at the moment of their delivery his attention was equally drawn to another female social worker who, while dancing alone, was clutching a bottle of wine from which, in a pause between musical renderings from a record-player, she swigged. It was the *Telegraph*-reading Miriam Fawcett.

Soon afterwards, a male social worker Robert did not know, but who was identified to him as 'Trevor' – a name recalled from discussion at an early meeting about the revue

– staggered into the kitchen, intoxicated to the point of incoherence and beyond. He opened the refrigerator door with enough violence to cause a couple of eggs to smash themselves on the floor. The mess thus created he began to clear up in an unconventional way. Instead of hunting for a mop he lay on the floor with his head close to the unsightly and unappetising remains, and began to lick them up. After some seconds he was dissuaded from continuing by sharp words from Jessica. She had appeared on the scene of the crime with a mop, which she applied to the floor with vigour.

From time to time long-playing records were changed by a volunteer disc jockey. Commented Emily when, after the end of one record's sequence of songs, a string of unmusical electronic noises was emitted by the equipment. 'It sounds,' she said coolly, 'as if the record-player's having an orgasm.'

It wasn't the sort of remark likely to have been uttered at the legal department party, had a record player been present and similarly afflicted, and certainly not within earshot of Edward Shimble. Emily remained irrepressible until she left the party. At one moment she proposed a hopping dance, which was taken up by three or four others, and this was followed after a couple of minutes by a jumping up and down dance. She left the party with Robert, who, three quarters sober at best, drove her home and virtuously declined an invitation for coffee.

'The very last thing I had in mind,' insisted Emily, 'was to shag you. For a start, I am a reformed woman.'

Robert made a conversational detour. 'I've been intrigued by your darkish complexion. Where does it come from?'

'According to my mother, it's from my Romany grandmother, who I never knew. But I'm not Carmen. Just a child of my generation. These are changing times.'

'You must miss sketch writing with Jessica,' he said, throwing in her name hoping to hear of any fresh developments in Jessica's marital life.

'I know I will miss that. And sharing the downfall of her marriage with her.'

'Downfall? Is it definitely finished?'

'Dead as Queen Victoria. They split up a few days ago.'

'He's OK about it?'

'I gather he is, sort of. Nice enough bloke. She's on her own now. She's staying at Miriam Fawcett's place in East Finchley.'

Robert said nothing to Emily about Beth, and Emily did not ask him about her.

Days earlier Robert had spent the evening – and indeed the night – with Beth at her flat. She was, he thought, in an odd mood. They had a take-away Indian meal which Robert had collected, purchasing in an off-licence a couple of escorting bottles of beer. All had seemed well, at first. They had gossiped about every-day things and had got on to the subject of Beth's friend Annie, of whom Robert struggled with himself entirely to approve. Beth had known Annie since childhood, he gathered, and she alternated between criticism of her and expressions of loyalty.

Beth had met with Annie on the evening of the social workers' Christmas party, and now referred to her in uncomplimentary terms. She spoke of Annie's expressive, but in Beth's view, unfortunate, facial mannerisms, and, disparagingly, of Annie's 'groupie' sexual behaviour with members of obscure male rock bands, and of her public confession of an experiment in lesbianism ('I screwed a woman in Newquay – thought it would never get back to anyone'). And then there was Annie's self-centredness...

And now, she said, Annie was planning to train as a social worker, a profession for which Beth thought her singularly ill-suited.

'She seemed a good-hearted person when I met her on the Dingwalls night out,' Robert said lamely. 'Whatever her personal life-style,' he went on, 'you must have things in common with her. And if she wants to be lesbian, why not.'

Robert had, in saying this, been provoking, so far as Beth was concerned. 'I know what I don't have in common with Annie. I don't make ridiculous facial expressions, I've never been the slightest bit inclined to be a groupie, or into lesbian experimentation. And I hope I'm not unduly self-centred. Am I guilty of any of that in your view?'

Robert was confused by this mini-tirade. 'I think you're very different from Annie. I'm not sure why you have got wound up by what I said.'

Beth seemed mollified, but was palpably nettled a short time later when Robert confessed that he had to finish preparing for a court hearing the following morning. 'Shouldn't you have done that in the office?' she complained. 'I was hoping you'd watch something on TV with me.'

Robert apologised, while saying that at times too much was going on to keep it within office hours. That, too, was the wrong thing to say, though later Beth softened. But in the morning, when he had left the flat, his thoughts were clearer. There was something in Beth's personality that would always jar with his, whatever their level of commitment to each other. He decided the relationship would have to end, while suspecting some of the time that Beth could well be on the point of ending it too.

30

Into the High Court Again

The end of year break had come and gone, without featuring snow or even rain, and Robert had taken advantage of the time off to visit his parents in rural Somerset. He returned to London in early January at a moment when snow was promised. The new and comfortable bed which he had recently purchased was now in place and its austere and narrow predecessor had gone. So had Robert's flat-mate, the other Robert, taking with him his kitchen primitivism. Winter would now be more bearable, so long as he, as surviving tenant, could pay the full rent or, much better, find a less messy flat-sharer.

But what was expected to be the decisive phase of the wardship proceedings concerning baby Tania was now just a few days away, and Robert's preparations took on a sometimes frantic character. One demand for action on his part arose from a last-minute police notification that a police witness was permitted to give evidence in the High Court only if a subpoena were received first.

Through a visit to the Strand buildings by bored litigation assistant Errol, Robert procured this elite form of witness summons, but not in time to deliver it to the police officer who, however, conceded that so long as she received it at court, she could enter the witness box.

There was another development in Tania's case. Her mother, so Emily informed Robert a couple of days before the hearing, had been arrested and in police custody overnight. She had eaten an Indian meal in a restaurant without paying and her behaviour when police arrived had contributed to her arrest. Emily was in a position to name the particulars of the food consumed by the vegetarian Miss Sircar (a poppadom, a vegetable samosa and a vegetable biriani).

That afternoon a conference took place in Miss Emmeline Byers' chambers in the Temple. Robert attended with Emily Frost, who defied Miss Byers' assumption of full organizational command, when they were seated around the long oak table in the book-lined conference room, by insolently (or charmingly, whichever it was) asking: 'Where's the coffee, then?'

Use of the internal telephone by a not very good-humoured Miss Byers soon produced a tray with china cups and saucers, portered in by one of the junior clerks.

Strict chairing caused steady progression through the obstacles that could rise up at the hearing. Among these, Miss Byers suggested, was the absence of plans for Tania's future, save for the most general words about it, in the council's statements. 'So what access by Miss Sircar to Tania do you have in mind?' she asked of Emily. 'The prospects of maintaining a maternal relationship of value to Tania do not look good, do they?'

Emily had no immediate answer, and it was decided she would take advice from the council's adoption adviser. All weaknesses in the case were the subject of scrutiny to the satisfaction of Miss Byers, who termed them 'lacunae'.

Then, on the afternoon before the hearing, Robert received a telephone call from Walter. 'I'm most sorry, sir, but Miss Byers is part-heard today in another case which goes over to tomorrow. She won't be available.'

'Oh, my God!' said Robert. 'What do we do?'

Walter had the solution: 'I have no other suitable Counsel on tap, and have had to sign up another Chambers: 5 King's Bench Walk, in fact. Giles Springett is your man.' A telephone number for Springett's Chambers was provided, and Robert immediately called to confirm the nomination. It seemed, on inquiry, that Giles Springett did have the requisite credentials for a sensitive wardship case as well as being at a loose end next day. Not only that, but the brief had already been walked over to him by one of Walter's juniors.

The next morning Robert met Emily again at the Kardomah coffee house where Kingsway meets Aldwych, and they strolled from there in decidedly chilly weather conditions to the Royal Courts. Outside their allocated battleground on the second floor of the Queens Building they encountered Springett, a personable, clean-shaven man in his mid-thirties, who spoke crisply and without condescension, and seemed to have internalised the essentials of the case.

They were soon joined by Dr. Abrahams, who was wearing the ancient black coat she had worn in the juvenile court and which, around the collar, was speckled with dandruff. Robert identified her as she approached.

'Dr. Abrahams,' Giles Springett greeted her. 'I'm rent-a-brief.' She took to him without hesitation, and did not grumble on this occasion about having to be at court.

Soon, moments after ten thirty had arrived, the case was called on. Places in court were taken, but although Miss Sircar's barrister, again the portly Andrew Bavington, and solicitor William Brady were in their places, Miss Sircar was not in hers. 'I think that's fifteen love to us,' said Springett nonchalantly over his shoulder to Robert.

The judge this time was Mr. Justice James, who, after short observation, Robert marked down as both near to retirement and as the most gentlemanly judicial figure he had so far encountered. 'Oh dear,' he said, when told Miss Sircar was late.

The case was put back for half an hour. The judge's associate this time was a man with a full head of dark hair and a vague smile on his lips. All left the court room.

Waiting outside, Robert recognised Jack Parnell among a knot of people outside the next court room along the broad corridor, and went over to speak to him.

'A right shenanigans this morning,' said Jack. 'We've applied to commit a mum for repeatedly breaking injunctions.'

'Where is she?' asked Robert, looking round.

'In the cells. The tipstaff will go and get her' (and as Parnell said this Robert observed that relaxed and blue-shirted official, arms folded, leaning against the outer wall of the court room) 'when the case gets called. The judge ordered her arrest when we applied – that was three days ago – and the tipstaff arrested her yesterday with police help.'

'She didn't struggle then?'

"I don't suppose so. I asked him just now if he ever got into a fight with people he arrests. He said: 'No sir, they're always as good as gold. I once had a chap who tried to jump out of the car. I restrained him.' That's his story, anyway."

Emily came over to join them and exchange a friendly greeting with Jack. Robert continued (considerately putting a question in a way which would enable Emily to make sense of the conversation):

'So what did this mum do to get herself arrested for breaching an injunction?'

Parnell was specific: 'Weeks ago she went to the children's home. She managed to get in. She was screaming for the children. After that she was banned from going there. Then it got worse. One night she put a brick or something through the window, hit the manager of the home, and snatched one of her kids.'

'Wouldn't it be simpler to move the children to an undisclosed home?' asked Emily. 'It sounds as if there is no hope of containing this mum.'

'Good point,' said Jack. 'I'll ask about that, but I must tell you about another case too…'

The telling was interrupted by Giles Springett calling Robert over for a word. Emily remained with Jack Parnell. A few minutes later she rejoined Robert, who was standing alone. 'An Enfield child has died,' she said, her face clouded with shock. 'A mum with two children at home lost control of herself with the younger one, bashed its head against the cooker. They've warded the older one – the uninjured one – who's now in care. It's Enfield's first wardship. Jack said the case conference on the survivor following the death – that was yesterday – was the largest by far he's been to – around thirty professionals present.'

'We can do without that sort of thing in Haringey,' said Robert.

'That won't stop it happening.'

Tania's case was called on again, as half an hour and more had passed. Mr. Brady's office, it transpired, had received a telephone call from his client, explaining she would arrive later in the morning. The judge withdrew again, saying this time that if the mother should turn up before the lunch interval, the hearing would be reconvened, but if not, the sitting would resume at two o'clock. As the court cleared again, the word was passed to Springett by the usher, who had spoken to the judge's dark haired associate, who had heard it murmured by the judge that 'Miss Sircar would probably be pissed by then'. It was the one ungentlemanly remark that day which he heard from, or was attributed to, Mr. Justice James, whom Springett referred to as 'Gentleman Jim'.

In fact Miss Sircar arrived before noon, giving the explanation that she had to wait for her delayed Giro benefit cheque before setting out. As before, Tania's father was invisible.

The hearing now began in the proper manner. 'Gentleman Jim' asked to know the names of all who were in court, including whether, in the case of women, the title was 'Miss' or 'Mrs.'

Giles Springett opened the case with cogency, explaining how it was that the magistrates had refused to consider various categories of evidence on the grounds that they were 'hearsay inadmissible'. 'Gentleman Jim' shook his head slightly, as if perplexed. Springett's opening ended with the information that, since the previous hearing, Miss Sircar had made no attempt to see Tania, although she could have done so regularly, and had not sought either to speak to her social worker.

When Dr. Abrahams went into the witness stand, wearing her dandruff-speckled antique coat, 'Gentleman Jim' early on assumed the controls. He asked her particularly about the list of occasions following Tania's birth when Miss Sircar had visited the ward nocturnally, exhibiting irrational behaviour. The list, originally compiled by Dr. Abrahams, was extracted from Robert's papers, and the judge proposed that each separate visiting occasion of concern should be put to the mother when her turn came as a witness.

Rather late in the day, as Springett said later to Robert, 'Gentleman Jim' asked the advocates to comment upon the status of the list as evidence. Mr. Andrew Bavington, once again Miss Sircar's barrister, did not challenge the introduction of the document, saying only that the rules of evidence in the juvenile court were somewhat more restrictive than those in the High Court.

'That appears to be so,' said 'Gentleman Jim'. 'But not, perhaps, for ever.'

During the paediatrician's evidence, Miss Sircar walked out on one occasion, having lit up a cigarette first, saying 'I'm bloody fed up', and on other occasions she interrupted with dissatisfied comments.

At the witness lectern at last, she again lit a cigarette which 'Gentleman Jim', curtly for once, told her to extinguish.

'Why should I?' she said.

'Because I say so, Miss Sircar,' he rejoined. He then directed others in court, without specifying anyone in particular, to remove the offending item from her. No one tried very hard. She walked out, returning a short time afterwards, cigarette-free.

Attempts by the lawyers and judge to put to her, singly, the events in Dr. Abrahams' list of her night-time ward visits were fruitless. Soon it was time for Emily's testimony. Scrupulously fair and without condescending words for Miss Sircar, Emily evidently impressed 'Gentleman Jim' who, Robert suspected, found her expressive, Romany-influenced face as attractive as her words.

The outcome was never in doubt. Judicial concern was expressed in the judgement, given orally late that afternoon, about the off-the-wall decision-making (though kinder phrases were employed) that had taken place in the Highgate juvenile court. Legal care and control of Tania was given to Haringey council, and judicial praise was given for 'admirable foster parents', while nothing was said about the expense to the public purse. No access between Tania and her mother was to be permitted without the agreement of the court or of Haringey Social Services.

Once the court had been evacuated, in the spacious corridor outside, Miss Sircar sat smoking and breathing heavily. Emily was concerned for her, but her offer to sit and talk was refused. After a while, Miss Sircar walked away.

'Are you doing anything this evening,' Robert asked Emily, as they left the court. 'I am not suggesting a celebration of the result, just a celebration of relief that it's over. Do you fancy eating out?'

Emily showed pleasure. They settled on a Chinese restaurant in Soho which Emily had patronised once before, and ate early there, after which Emily invited Robert back to the flat she continued to share with Frank Jackson. On the way Robert bought a bottle of wine which they – joined by Frank – soon emptied. It was then that their cheery conversation was savaged by a telephone call.

Frank, after a moment, passed the receiver to Emily: 'It's Jessica, for you.'

Emily took the call and became very still as she listened. 'Oh God,' she said, 'I can't believe it. He was on top of the world after the performance.'

Frank broke in: 'It's Steve Warren, isn't it?'

Emily took the receiver from her ear, asking how he knew without waiting to hear a reply, before resuming conversation with Jessica. Soon she hung up, turning to both Frank and Robert. 'Steve Warren killed himself last night. Jessica's just been told. He cut his wrists in the bath and bled to death.'

There was silence for a few seconds. 'It was over a girl, wasn't it?' asked Frank.

'That's what Jessica said. He'd started a relationship with someone at Alexandra House, the children's home. She didn't want to carry on with it. It was apparently his first relationship with a woman, even though he is – was – in his early twenties.'

'I knew of his wonderful highs and terrible lows,' said Frank. 'He was on a high weeks ago when I saw him, and he told me he'd met somebody and she was great. Then it went sour and the dark clouds enveloped him. I spoke to him a couple of days ago over the phone, and urged him to see his doctor. I should have gone to see him.'

'The girl must feel terrible,' said Emily, who had held an unlit cigarette between her fingers since she had taken the call. 'So must Miriam Fawcett. Jessica said Miriam was called out last night – she was doing out-of-hours duty – and visited Steve at the Intermediate Treatment place. She stayed with him for hours there – he was there overnight in the sleeping quarters they have. She didn't leave until he told her he was OK and was in bed. After she'd gone, he did it.'

The funeral service for Steve Warren came sooner than some expected, and was attended by dozens of his colleagues. That day snow lay in quantities on the ground, silently supporting the wintriness of the occasion. Afterwards Robert went for coffee with Jessica. He told her that his relationship with Beth, which had continued, but more mechanically than before, was now finished.

'You feel OK?' she asked, as if the dark clouds which had descended upon Steve might have descended upon him too.

'Yes,' he said, noticing that a wedding ring had gone from her finger. 'I feel sad, but I feel OK. I hope Beth does too.'

'Emily will cheer you up,' said Jessica.

'As a friend.'

What he didn't say was that he had not told Beth yet. That was left until that evening, when he telephoned her. She answered.

'I know why you're ringing. You don't want to carry on seeing me.'

'And do you want to carry on seeing me?'

'Not if you don't.'

She always seemed to Robert to be one step ahead of him. The conversation tailed off. Beth replaced the receiver with so little warning that he imagined the call's ending to be accidental, and rang again. This time she didn't answer, and he gave up. All good and some mixed quality things come to an end.

A few weeks later Beth was seen in a Muswell Hill restaurant having lunch with Director of Social Services Michael Stone, and not long after that they were spotted together somewhere else.

31

George Ballam Says Enough

Throughout the borough of Haringey, the day after Steve Warren's funeral, snow and ice were largely gone from the pavements, but showed more reluctance to depart from hedges, walls and roofs. Late in the morning, Robert was in his office and trouble was abroad elsewhere within the legal department.

Robert's door was wide open when George Ballam looked in, pausing in the doorway. He was obviously agitated, though spoke with his voice hardly raised. His tie's relationship to his collar was insecure, Christmas festivities not being this time the cause and justification. Without preliminaries he advised Robert that he was going to tell Shimble he could stuff his job.

Robert, alarmed for George, invited him in to talk about what was happening. George closed the door behind him.

'Here I am,' he said, 'a man of thirty eight, and I'm nearly in tears. I can't face working for him anymore. This morning was it.'

'So what happened? You were on the carpet?'

George, standing at first in front of Robert's desk, ignoring the vacant chair close by, explained that he had been called in to see Shimble, and that this was just one more of a series of occasions when he had been blamed for something outside his control. This time it was the disappearance, days previously, of £5 in cash from a locked box in a locked drawer in the local land charges section. 'The senior girl', Pat, George explained, looked after the cash box (as Robert knew) and she was completely trustworthy. The disappearance remained unexplained. Shimble had asked George repeatedly that morning if he agreed that this made the legal department's management look foolish, a laughing stock.

'Repeatedly?'

'Four times in about five minutes.'

'Why would it be your fault?' Robert was mystified, while a remarkably similar dressing-down from Lady Feverel for one of the clerks in the juvenile court floated into his mind.

'He was insisting that the money should have been in the safe in my office, not in a desk drawer. Maybe it should have been, but as long as I've been working here and longer than that, it has been in that drawer and money has never gone missing before. Eddie has always known about the arrangement. The theft was a one-off. I've reported it to the police. Obviously now that float will be put in the safe.'

George further explained that he had informed Shimble what steps he had taken, and had asked him what else he should do. Shimble had replied, said George – and he took a few seconds, relaxing a trifle, to describe Shimble's rocking back in his maroon leather chair to a safe degree, pressing the fingers of each hand together meditatively, and looking at George fixedly, without expression. He had with care pronounced the words: 'I want you to buck your ideas up'. George had got up and said 'That's it', and had walked out. He looked at Robert. 'I'm pitiful. I'm completely at a loss. That man has got me on the run.'

Expressing sympathy as George finally sat down, Robert proposed that they track down Colin Masson for a consultation. As the department's trade union representative, he was definitely the person to see. Robert urged George not to blame himself for what had been happening. It was about Shimble's management style, his preference for reliance upon favourites, his arbitrary pickiness, his unreasonable expectations. It was agreed that George would wait, while Robert checked whether Colin was around and accessible. If not, the consultation would have to be postponed. George agreed limply.

As fortune would have it, when Robert appeared in Colin's open doorway, Colin was seated grumpily at his desk, staring at a stack of paper. He was to be in the employment tribunal next day, was in the midst of preparation, and said to Robert. 'This borough employs some dodgy staff, you know.'

As Robert spoke to him, Colin put down his Waterman fountain pen. He was a traditionalist, scorning the use of the ball-point and followed Robert to his room. George had not moved. His facial expression was now more glum than tearful.

The pair were left together. Robert made tea for the three of them in the corridor niche nearby. When, a few minutes later, he brought in and deposited the steaming mugs, he caught remarks about pressure George had been put under from Shimble for big changes in his job alongside the gripe about the £5 theft in that morning's head to head, or, more accurately, foot to buttocks. He decided he should leave them for longer and took a file with him to read elsewhere. He found Melanie Cusack's room empty and took up residence at her desk, on which sat neatly arranged the materials for writing and the usual in and out trays, but nothing on which she was working. She likes tidiness and order, and not very much work, he thought. And she hated courtroom advocacy, despite her readiness with brusque and succinct sentences. He made several phone calls.

Melanie walked in when Robert was speaking into the mouth-piece. He got up to leave her chair free for occupation, while she stood impassively. Completing his call, he returned the receiver to its rest and apologised for borrowing her room and desk, explaining that his own was occupied at that moment and that he had been stuck for a working base and telephone access. She didn't smile, but didn't protest at her room's invasion either. It was evident that something else was on her mind.

'I'm leaving, Robert,' she said, 'In fact you're the first to know. As you know, this job isn't one I'm over the moon about. How I've stuck it for this long I don't know.'

'So where are you bound?'

'Civil service. Education,' she summarised, then returning to the subject of Robert's presence in her room so seamlessly that he had to defer his congratulations.

'Who is occupying your office?'

Not wishing to speak of George's present awkward predicament, Robert evaded the question, and said it was just a meeting that should end soon. He apologised again, suspecting that resentment was afoot, however unspoken, and left, after congratulating Melanie on her new post, while she looked at him as if he should have answered her question properly.

George and Colin were reaching the end of their discussion when Robert returned. 'Do you agree that I speak to Eddie now to clarify his position?' George nodded. Colin rose and went out. He returned after a few minutes. He reported that Shimble had told him he 'appreciated' – Colin emphasised and grinned at this word – Colin's involvement. He had said he was concerned about George's 'lack of initiative'. Colin summarised: 'In everyday terms, if we can resort to a wretched phrase, he's pissed off with you, George.'

George commented gloomily that Colin was telling him nothing new. 'So what do we do? A memo from you to him as you suggest?'

'I think that would be the best way forward,' said Colin, whose spoken and written language often suggested a public school classics master as much as a trade union representative.

'Eddie Shimble,' he continued, 'is too much used to getting

his own way with staff members' – Robert reflected that this generalisation did not seem to apply to Colin himself – 'and a line needs to be drawn in your case. He needs to be shunted back from it. He must be made to retreat, and such retreat will be his defeat. I suggest you return to your room, George, and if asked to see Eddie, you should respond that you will do that with your union representative present. In the mean-time I will evolve a memorandum to him which you must correct, as far as it is necessary to correct, and approve before it smacks into his in-tray. Then the ball is in his court. He could back-track, come out of his corner fighting, or just – who knows – dither. He has been known to dither at difficult times. Can you stay around until I have filled a page with handwriting?'

George agreed. 'All this,' he said in a weary tone, 'over a squirt like Shimble.'

'That's the spirit,' Robert threw in.

'The intention is,' said Colin, "that my memo will appear to have been written by an angel of reasonableness and discretion, and we will have to wait to see whether a gladiatorial answer comes back. However, I am not persuaded that 'gladiatorial' is the first word that comes to mind when considering the personality of our esteemed borough solicitor."

George, much less anxious and upset, expressed the hope that this strategy would be successful.

'By the way,' Robert contributed, 'Melanie's going,' and he passed on the details he'd been given. Neither commented, as if Melanie's departure would not be an occasion for sorrow for either of them, any more than it was for Melanie herself. Both left Robert's office.

The next morning George returned to Robert's room, now regarding him as a confidential ally, and showed him the memorandum as composed in Colin's dark and flowing ink.

'Do you think this is all right?'

Addressed to the Borough Solicitor, from Colin Masson, as NALGO representative, it was set out on the borough's internal memorandum paper. Robert read it quietly aloud:

'This note has been prepared with the unqualified approval of Mr. George Ballam, who asks that you consider its contents most seriously. It arises from your meeting with him yesterday' (here the date was punctiliously inserted), "when you advised him that he lacked initiative (in your words to him 'should buck up his ideas'). Mr. Ballam considers this criticism of him to be objectively unfair and that it is but the latest in a series of unfair rebukes extending over several months. The compilation, in his view, includes your having put to him, as recently as a week ago, verbally and without prior notice, major suggested changes to his current job description, followed by your insistence that you receive an immediate acceptance in the face of his reluctance to provide this, telling Mr. Ballam that he was 'moving into a dispute situation' and could be considered to be 'thwarting management's right to manage'."

'Very much to the point,' said Robert, before continuing:

'Mr. Ballam requests, so that an effective working relationship can be restored, your acknowledgement that he has to the present date performed his duties conscientiously and to a satisfactory level.'

'Again to the point,' said Robert. George went on: 'Given the importance of a swift resolution not only in the interests of both parties but for the effective running of the Legal division, I trust that you will reply, with brevity if need be, within the next few days. Meanwhile I have advised Mr. Ballam that it would be preferable for me to be present during any further meetings with you. I look forward to hearing from you in the hope that a positive outcome will emerge.'

Colin Masson, at this moment, joined them, while Robert told George that he had not known of the proposals to change the nature of his job. 'That in itself nearly took me over the edge,' confessed George. 'When he said that, I was looking at a volume of the Supreme Court Practice on his desk. It's pretty hefty...'

'Oh, the White Book,' murmured Robert...

'I was contemplating hurling it at him.'

'If he had taken that in the chest area while he was rocking back,' said Robert, 'I think he might have rocked back beyond the point of no return.'

'It wouldn't be the first time such a calamity has occurred,' said Colin, 'though on the last, possibly just the most recent, occasion when that happened, the damage was self-inflicted, and he became for an interval invisible from his doorway.'

'Now you see him, now you don't,' George completed the picture, humorous in his turn. 'Was that the time when Mary told everybody who heard the crash that she'd knocked over a chair?'

Colin nodded.

George added, holding out the note in front of him – 'Do you approve, Robert?'

Robert did. But George said too that he felt unable to work in his own room, just along the corridor. He intended to camp in the open-plan area on the first floor for the time being.

He returned Colin's handiwork to its author, who would place it in the hands of Mary who would deliver it to Edward Shimble. Robert was a passive trade union member and for him George's problem was the first of its sort he had known. But he had admiration for Colin in wishing to push forward George's claim to just treatment. How events would pan out he could not guess.

Clues were soon provided. Less than an hour later, Robert's own duties required him to visit Mary's office, and through the open doorway he saw Edward Shimble at his desk.

Shimble's face suggested – unless the effect was

coincidental – that he had received and read Colin's memorandum. His long face was a study. The usually pink facial skin tones had been replaced by a pastier colour, and he was sitting bolt upright. If the memorandum was the cause, the effect was startling. Shimble was not angry, but neither was he contented. Not contented at all. The stuffing had been removed, metaphorically, from his insides, it appeared. Robert slipped away.

Early the next day, with snow now more comprehensively absent from the scene, but shivery conditions continuing, Robert was invited inside Edward Shimble's den for a word with 'the Man', as Bill Bowman liked to call him. From his manner, in which irritability was absent, Robert deduced that he might be looking for friends and allies in a hostile world.

'I'm hoping, Robert,' Shimble began, with a trace of a smile, 'that you could help us out with a rather silly employment-related issue. Can you make room in your busy life for a meeting with the Principal of Tottenham Technical College? I'm sure it's trivia, but there it is.'

'Is a date and time for the meeting already fixed?'

'Yes, it's as early as this afternoon, I'm afraid. Melanie was due to go, but she's reported in sick this morning. She was well enough yesterday, when she gave me her resignation. But in this weather, we may easily all go down with something. I've a tickly throat myself.'

Robert had no fixed appointments that afternoon and could find no credible reason to excuse himself. So he took the Tottenham College memorandum Shimble handed to him and read it in his room, treating himself first to coffee. It was signed by the College's Principal.

There wasn't much of substance to the document beyond the story it told of a female lecturer having complained about questions put to her during an interview for a more senior post. Robert was left to guess that the inference was that she had been discriminated against because of her sex, an inference which might be embarassing enough not to be overtly acknowledged on paper. Advice as to how to respond to the complaint was requested. The memorandum had been copied to an adviser in the council's education department.

At the appointed time that afternoon Robert, having parked his ageing Ford Escort in a south Tottenham side road, where tiny front garden hedges still carried occasional blotches of snow, shook hands with the Principal, a humourless man in late middle age, and also with the educational adviser, a much younger man. The three of them sat down in the Principal's office.

The two advisers listened to a ponderously circumstantial account of what had happened. Applications for the senior post had mostly been from outsiders, but two had been internal, one from a male and one from the complainant, a Mrs. Platt. Mrs. Platt and the male internal candidate, plus two of the external candidates, both males, had been interviewed. Mrs. Platt had not been selected, and subsequently complained of sex discrimination because of some questions she had been asked.

Her original letter of complaint was extracted by a tight-lipped Principal from a desk drawer and it was read in turn by Robert and the educational adviser. There had been a remarkable reluctance to make copies, as if copies added to the discomfort of the situation. Light was finally shed on the core of the grievance. Mrs. Platt had been asked what her 'child care responsibilities are', and if, as she had young children, 'there could be an impact on her work in consequence'.

'Were the other three candidates asked such questions?' asked Robert.

'No, but really.'

Robert and the education adviser exchanged glances, and

Robert said: 'I'm afraid that this is discrimination under the legislation.'

'If these questions had been left out, she still wouldn't have been appointed, I'm sure of that,' said the Principal, adopting a defensive posture. 'The successful external candidate was better qualified and shone at the interview. He is,' he said, unsmiling but with complacency, 'our first Oxbridge man in living memory.'

'An apology is due to Mrs. Platt,' said the education adviser. 'A smoking gun, I'm afraid. Your dabs are on this one. The times they are a-changing,' he said repeating the words of the song, in a semi-sing-song fashion.

'That's an odd thing to say,' said the Principal, who appeared not to know of the song.

'Bob Dylan,' the educational adviser declared. 'I grew up with him.'

Not apparently aware of the Principal's incomprehension, he went on, in a worldly way: 'Did you know that Mrs. Platt is a left-winger, involved with the International Socialists?'

'No,' said the Principal, taken aback again. 'I didn't know that. She's a nice little thing.'

The education adviser looked at him as if his worst fears had been confirmed.

Terms were agreed, after anxious hesitation by the Principal, for a letter of apology to Mrs. Platt, and the education adviser added that he hoped it was accepted that a candidate from a superior university was not necessarily superior to a candidate with an academic background associated with a more humdrum establishment.

'Oh, indeed,' said the Principal. 'I was myself from such a hum-drum establishment.'

January had been shooting past, for Robert, at startling speed. Then, as February came into play, the rush of work slowed, despite his having taken over from Melanie Cusack what proved to be a remarkably small case-load; and there was time to draw breath. An otherwise unmemorable Social Services Committee meeting was an occasion for the expression of anger against further planned cuts in the central government grant necessitating a smaller allocation to services for those in need; and it was then that Robert heard that there would be a march followed by a protest demonstration on Ducketts Common near Turnpike Lane. 'These idiots need a kick up the arse,' averred a Conservative member. It was he who had, months before, suggested that a clip round the ear might be desirable as a sanction in a children's home.

It was during this transitional period that Robert encountered directly, at first over the telephone, the feared Day Care Factor, Charmaine Trickett – manager of the Day Care sub-division of the Social Services Department. The occasion was the imminent prosecution of a woman – a childminder who was not formally approved and registered by the local authority – for illegally minding a little boy, almost a baby. The council was the prosecutor, and Robert was to be its agent in the court arena.

The misdemeanour had come to light through the little boy's emergency admission to hospital, after drinking excessively hot milk given him by the childminder.

Hospital staff had informed Social Services, and a childminding enforcement officer had been sent out by Charmaine Trickett to interview first the mother and then the minder. This revealed that the minder had been employed for just seven successive days, and for the sum of eight pounds for the whole week.

A day before the defendant was due to face her accusers in court, Charmaine Trickett telephoned Robert. Her manner exuded exaggerated respect and implied a demand for close attention to her words.

'I know you will make sure,' she said, 'that this prosecution succeeds. It is vital that it does.'

Robert decided not to say what flitted outrageously into his mind, possibly as a result of associating with Emily in the pre-Christmas revue. This consisted of the following brisk lines: 'Well, if the witnesses come up to proof, it'll be a breeze. If they make a hash of it, it won't be down to me, Charmaine baby.'

Instead he said, fully alert to the need for diplomacy, that the case did seem to be a strong one, and he asked if she had any personal contribution to make. In particular, had she spoken with the defendant at any stage?

'She did phone me to say she'd just been doing the parent a favour. I told her I trusted the court wouldn't do her any favours, and put the phone down.' She ended this, to Robert's bemusement, with a girlish giggle. The Day Care Factor, he concluded, had investments in the just retribution industry.

The hearing was on a Tuesday before the Highgate magistrates. Unusually one of the court rooms usually set aside for juvenile court cases had been assigned to adult court prosecutions. This one was listed to be heard first.

While waiting, Robert stood together with Charmaine Trickett and her colleague in the foyer. The childminder, a haggard, sad-looking woman, sat not far away with the old dodderer from Slash & Co, who was dividing his attention between his client and the *Times* crossword, giving more attention to the latter than the former. The childminding officer was an anxious young woman in whom Charmaine Trickett (whose dark permanently waved hair, Robert remembered, was as rigid as castle battlements) appeared to be inducing fear. She had not given evidence before, and her boss was giving her strict instructions about how to maximize her ability to impress the justices. 'Make no concessions,' Robert heard. 'No sign of weakness, please.'

Opening the case, Robert explained to the three magistrates that the prosecution was on seven counts, one for each day of illegal, unregistered minding.

The child's mother gave evidence first, and convincingly, about the financial arrangements and about her distress over the hot milk incident. Then came the young day care officer, who in a nervous rush (unresponsive to the chairman's appeal for her to slow down) told the court among other things that the childminder had avowed – 'I know it's illegal to do this for money.'

When the minder was in the witness stand and had finished answering questions put to her gently by the old dodderer, who had laid the crossword aside, Robert asked her: 'If the mother was a complete stranger to you, as you have agreed in your evidence, why would you have minded her child without any payment?'

Her answer – 'That was just how it was,' did not stir the court to find in her favour. The justices fined her £20 for each day of illegal minding, and added another sum towards the costs of prosecution.

Afterwards Robert, who was thanked earnestly and excessively for his achievement by the Day Care Factor, heard her moments later admonishing her colleague: 'Your interview with her should have been more vigorous. I would have extracted a full confession from her. If only I could be duplicated.'

As Robert listened, he saw Jack Parnell, the Enfield solicitor, emerge from the other court room, in which juvenile cases were taking place. Robert greeted him, expecting the circumstances of his own presence that day to be capped by a far more exciting story.

'Something of interest today, Jack?'

'Not really. Just an application for the court's permission to withdraw care proceedings. The only weird thing is the length of time the magistrates took to agree. They were out for well over half an hour. If they hadn't agreed, we'd have offered no evidence and then they'd have had to dismiss it with nothing to discuss.'

'On the other hand,' offered Robert, 'magistrates don't want to be rubber stamps, and I doubt you want them to be.' Jack Parnell looked at him thoughtfully. 'You have a point.'

Robert told him something about the baby Tania wardship affair, and then Jack spoke again.

'I had a real nasty in Tottenham last week.'

'What was that about?'

'A mother with three children who decided her husband – the children's step-father – was out of order. She told the eldest boy to stab him with a knife, told him to go into the kitchen to get one...And when the children told the social worker what she'd said, and she got to hear about this, she told them she'd chop them up for that, for grassing on her. Anyway, that's what the children said to the social worker when they were sitting in the probation building at Tottenham, waiting for the case to come on. They were terrified.'

'Did the mother deny she'd said that?'

'No, that's what got me. When I asked her if it was correct that she'd threatened to chop them up – believe it or not she said, as if I was making a fuss about nothing, that it was *just an expression*. In a way, she may have been right. So, have you thought again about playing cricket for us?'

32

A Revue Reunion

A few days into February, in continuing inhospitable weather, the select group responsible for putting on December's 'dazzling' stage entertainment – if Colin Masson's praise can be cited again – met up once more, and in the flat of Emily Frost and Frank Jackson in Muswell Hill. The group had put into a pot enough money to cover the cost of food and drink. Frank demonstrated his ability on this occasion, urged on by Emily, to take the main responsibility for arranging a selection of aromatic items lodged in outsize dishes. From these all helped themselves, returning with their plates either to austerity chairs commandeered from the kitchen or to upholstered seating in its own location. A record-player supplied traditional jazz music, with the sound low enough not to inhibit conversation.

Before the lion's share of the eatables had disappeared, Frank applauded the efforts of everyone involved in making the revue a success, 'not excluding,' he said, 'my own little efforts.'

He had referred to absent friends and spoke movingly of the loss of Steve Warren. Robert found an empty hard-seated chair next to another occupied by Jessica. He had decided that she was at least as lovely as Beth. Perhaps lovelier, he thought, concluding for the first time that her eyelashes were longer than Beth's, if only marginally.

'How have you been,' he asked. 'Are you more settled now?'

'I hope so,' she replied, sounding more positive than her words suggested. 'Did you know I've been lodging with Miriam?'

'I heard that. She couldn't come tonight?'

'There was a jamboree for magistrates which took priority. I don't think it would be much of a fun occasion. Miriam loves events of that sort, partying with the nobs, though I've never seen a sign she wants to be one.'

'But magistrates are usually not nobs,' said Robert. "I was in Tottenham the other day, buying my *Guardian* at a newsagents, and the large man behind the counter asked if I recognised him. I didn't. I said not. He announced, quite proudly, and maybe a bit disappointed, that he was 'local Bench'. Then I remembered seeing him sitting next to Lady Feverel, half-asleep, and not taking a single note."

'You didn't tell him off for that?'

'I'm a coward. And not a nob.'

'I grew up in a family,' said Jessica, 'which regarded the powerful as people to be suspicious of, not to be deferential towards. It was a socialist working class family. Mrs. Thatcher would not have approved. So I shall be going to the protest demo against the cuts on Ducketts Common.'

'My family is more boring. I'm the son of a Conservative-voting municipal accountant.'

'Are you leaving out the female line?'

'Only because they were traditional housewives.' He hardly paused before adding: 'Could you bear the thought of coming out with me one evening?'

'That would be nice. And I promise I won't try to turn you into a hard-line leftie. Or make you come to the protest.'

'But I, on the other hand,' said Robert, 'will try to persuade you to read Eric Ambler.'

'Not much persuasion needed. I'll begin with *The Mask of Dimitrios.*'

Their first evening out together was not the last.

33

More George Ballam

Edward Shimble's accumulated dissatisfaction with George Ballam, which had come to such an unhappy pass, had resulted, as we have seen, in a hammer of a riposte on George's behalf.

Now, in February's second week, the weather was warmer, and some days had short meetings with sunshine. No answer had come to the memorandum Colin Masson had sent, requesting in effect from Shimble a confession that he had wronged George and would not wrong him again. Shimble kept out of George's way, and did not try to speak to Colin about the matter. It seemed possible, even likely, that Colin Masson's memorandum had blasted a large hole in Shimble's complacency. He was known to have called Bill Bowman in for a consultation within hours of receiving the pen and ink communication.

Robert had learned of this the next day, when, during a discussion of a prosecution case, Bill let fall the fact that 'the Man' and George had fallen out. Self-importantly Bill told Robert that he wished to do what he could to end the deadlock.

'Eddie asked for my advice yesterday about it,' said Bill.

'Oh, he called you in to discuss it?'

Had Bill said too much? He reflected for a moment, considered the option of muteness on the subject, and then said that he had advised Eddie not to be too hard on George. He went on.

'I told him that a few weeks ago George told me he'd been feeling very low and had been in tears one morning. Eddie said that perhaps George should be transferred to another post on health grounds.'

'He asked for your view about that?' Robert struggled to exclude indignation from his voice.

'Not specifically.' Bill was wishing he had not begun the discussion.

'Surely you didn't give advice as to whether that would be a good idea or not?'

'I said I could see Eddie's point. I'm not taking sides in this,' he added, ill at ease.

Robert pressed him. 'Not even if Eddie has been getting at George without a shred of justification?'

'You sound like Colin Masson,' Bill answered. 'It's upset Eddie, you know...' Then he stopped, before going on, while Robert stared at him, to say: 'It could end, you know, if Eddie leaves.'

'Leaves?'

''He's been applying for other jobs. I've been carting him about to interviews since November. I won't say more.' He added, anxiety on his face: 'Don't spread it around, will you?'

Robert felt unable to give that guarantee.

'So Bill has grassed on George,' was Colin's comment. 'I will remind Bill of his duty, as a union member, in the course of a dispute involving a fellow union member, to show solidarity to that fellow member, and not to rat on him.'

From Shimble himself, however, silence remained the order of the day and the order of the week. Was he, as Colin had anticipated, just dithering?

A few days after George had deserted his own room to camp on the first floor, he felt confident enough to return. Necessary communications between him and Shimble were terse and either in writing or oral via Mary.

Colin saw Shimble again. He said that he was concerned he had not yet received any reply to his memorandum.

Shimble gave no ground, while betraying no anger. He said he had been troubled by George's 'indifference' to his concerns about a number of administrative issues. Colin promptly invited the precise reasons for Shimble's dissatisfaction with George, whether orally (in George's presence) or in writing.

'Certainly, Colin,' said Shimble. 'But I have had many other matters taking up my time and I will do it as soon as I can.' He spoke mechanically. His face, reported Colin later, betrayed apprehension, or something near it.

More days passed. George used this time to put on paper the fullest history of the persecution in readiness for further action.

When Robert was asked in passing by Bill Bowman 'if it had all blown over', he said he was sure things would be resolved in time. He added, pointedly: 'I take it you're keeping out of it?' Bowman looked at him, saying nothing.

Fourteen days exactly after George had walked angrily out of Shimble's office saying 'That's it', a further memorandum from Colin – this time typed and occupying three complete pages – walked in to Shimble's office and, grim-faced, found a resting place in Shimble's in-tray. The step-by-step history backed up the conclusion that Shimble had behaved unacceptably towards a colleague. The memorandum, ratified whole-heartedly by George, wound up, using a polite formula of words, by declaring that a grievance procedure would be initiated in the absence of a satisfactory response.

'Are we pushing him into a corner?' George queried.

'I hope so,' was Colin's reply. 'If Eddie Shimble has a heart attack in consequence, though, we will jointly share the guilt. You were not directly or indirectly responsible for Albert Clack's collapse. We both could, on the other hand, be blamed in the present circumstances more justly for a health crisis on the part of the Borough Solicitor. Let us see if he continues to dither.'

Another week passed without a response to Colin's second salvro. But during that week further pointed expressions of Shimble's displeasure were funnelled towards George, though not directly. During one otherwise uneventful discussion between Shimble and Colin about something unrelated – Shimble's wish to withdraw flexi-leave privileges from a junior staff member for persistently bad time-keeping – Shimble fumed about George. He complained first that George had forwarded to his incoming post tray – and not for the first time – brochure material about forthcoming training events which had no relevance to his own training needs. Days later Shimble marched, or at least walked more quickly than usual, into Colin's room waving a sheet of paper, this time expressing wrath about a memorandum on the subject of staff car parking which, like the aforementioned training material, had made a burglarious visit to his desk.

'His tongue was clop-clopping,' reported Colin. 'He was close to apoplexy.' Shimble had managed to get the words out: 'My in-tray is not a refuge for irrelevance.' He had followed this up, calming down a little, by asking Colin, with a pained facial expression: 'Does George have an animus towards me?'

Colin's stiff and sober reply had been: 'It would not be proper for me to comment,' but he took the opportunity to ask if a response to his memorandum on George's behalf could be expected soon.

'I have it very much in mind,' said Shimble. 'It would have been with you already had it not been for a pressing Council issue over threatened industrial action by dustmen. This has taken up much of my time.'

'I look forward to receiving your response,' Colin had said, telling George when reporting these developments: 'Eddie's been showing a pathetic, bumbling aspect of his personality that is not pretty to observe.'

Another five responseless days passed.

'He has been,' remarked Colin to George, 'supreme in the art of dithering. A ditherer supremo, to adapt a Shimble phrase. Time to launch the grievance procedure.'

George's notice of grievance, another stately miniature art-work from Colin's fountain pen, specified with precision the factual basis. It listed chronologically and dispassionately the events which had upset George. Set out neatly were the humiliating comments from Shimble in the cost-cutting discussion in which George had participated, the unjustified frustration with George in respect of the delivery and collection of legal service post, and more concerning the invitation for solicitor attendance at the Inter-Boroughs housing meeting while Shimble was on holiday. Included too was the blame for Albert Clack's collapse, for the missing £5 from the petty cash float, and for the omission to update with alacrity the time on Shimble's clock. Petulance over the non-arrival of the *Times* was given close attention, as was, most important of all, the vague and menacing manner in which major changes to George's job description had been proposed.

'Now all this is in the grievance pipeline,' pronounced Colin, 'Eddie has no more scope for fence-sitting. He will have to respond or look both absurd and incompetent. It hardly looks well for him that he has been silent during the prelims.'

'There is the question of how the notice of grievance should be served,' said Robert playfully. 'Bill Bowman has said to me there are three sorts of service available for legal documents: personal, postal or rectal.'

'I think rectal in this case,' said Colin Masson, as if weighing the option seriously, 'would in all probability be counter-productive.' He added: 'As the notice of grievance is being copied to the Chief Personnel Officer, Shimble is now in very public view. He has no choice but to buckle on his sword and respond.'

March had come, by which time Melanie Cusack had made her departure from the legal service, destined for a new legal role within the Civil Service. She refused the usual goodbye ceremony, and arranged no farewell drinks with any of her colleagues.

Shimble's composite reply to Colin's memorandum and the notice of grievance arrived. Seven pages of it.

When George read this, he was nervous in face and body. Might Shimble's causes for dissatisfaction add up to something convincing in the eyes of the personnel department?

'What do you think?' he asked Colin, who had already ingested it.

Colin spoke as he would have written. 'On the one hand,' he said, 'Eddie maintains his original stance in relation to the various issues, and attempts to reinforce his position by saying that he made a mistake in not instituting disciplinary proceedings against you earlier, throwing in some additional minor grouses to give that more body. On the other hand this little treatise is rife with implausibilities and evasions. For example he still attributes blame to you for Albert Clack's collapse although you had nothing to do with it – he didn't collapse as we know as a result of carrying a sack of post or anything else for this office and you had advised him not to do so on any account. Besides, Albert broke down at home, not here. Again, in relation to the question of the collection of post and the delivery of newspapers and the like he ignores the fundamental consideration that your arms were tied by the Borough Secretary's office. You weren't free to press the override button.'

Colin paused, lifting his eyebrows and resumed, in full flow: 'It hasn't dawned on him that he needed to make concessions in relation to the least plausible of his complaints if his response to the grievance in other respects were to carry credibility. George,' completed Colin, staring out of the window, 'his position is untenable, and our response should rock him right out of his chair. We do not need either or both volumes of the White Book propelled with force in his direction to achieve that.'

'Pity,' said George.

Unknown at that moment to the three legal musketeers, the grievance procedure now on the conveyor belt was overtaken by another development, in Edward Shimble's own life. He had, with Mary and Bill Bowman sworn to secrecy, put in for the position of borough solicitor in another London local authority, and a decidedly Conservative one – Barnet. Not only that: he had been interviewed and appointed, and his resignation from Haringey employment was already with the Chief Executive, 'Smiler' Roland Trask.

Almost right away, however, the information blackout was lifted, and Bill Bowman was spreading the word to all he encountered that Edward Shimble was on the move.

Colin Masson took steps to achieve a resolution of George's grievance while Edward Shimble remained in post. He pointed out to Shimble that it would be most unfair and inappropriate if a paper war of conflicting allegations were left technically alive after Shimble had left for a successor to address. He asked for a letter to confirm he regarded George as having always carried out his duties competently and conscientiously.

Unexpectedly, such a letter – astonishingly, in the terms requested – quickly arrived, in part because Shimble accepted that he had gone too far. He may have been influenced by Bill Bowman, who told Robert later, to his credit, that he had suggested to Eddie that his leaving celebration would not be a happy event if he did not end the war. Surrender was thus complete, taking George Ballam's breath away. He was, delighted and relieved, returning rapidly to his pre-persecution former self.

Robert Fordham, bringing Jessica up to date with these developments, explained that the campaign to rescue George from an impossible situation had proved, because of Shimble's exit from Haringey, a waste of time. She had disagreed, and with heat. That campaign, she insisted, had sent out serious messages which would not be forgotten: a message to George that he should not doubt himself and should resist unfair treatment; a message to those around George that what could protect George could protect others; and a message to Shimble, and to any that might offer him support, that there were limits to his powers and punishment for their misuse. Robert accepted the lesson with good grace and growing love. He had accepted too Jessica's invitation to attend with her the mid-February protest meeting on Ducketts Common against the government's cuts to the local government grant. This proved to be a noisy, peaceful and rained-on affair attended by hundreds of politically-minded, community-minded people, including a young and bearded Labour councillor, who had been described in the local newspaper in early February as a spokesman of the protest campaign.

By this time Robert was absorbed in fresh children cases. One concerned a baby boy who had suffered bleeding in the brain which a doctor attributed to an inappropriate 'shaking'. Another was a mother's agonised resort to the court process, years after her child had been placed with a family with a view to adoption, her 'access' suspended, to see her child again. Another arose from the abandonment, in the grounds below Alexandra Palace, on a public bench, of a just-born baby, the result of what must have been a 'Do-it-yourself' birth. He had also received information that an application to the Highgate magistrates was on foot for the discharge of the care order made on the cheeky teenage school absentee the previous autumn by exasperated justices. Though the youngster was still not going to school, the social workers were supporting the care order's discharge, given the lad's probably extreme behaviour should he be placed again away from home.

Over the telephone Shirley, the moralistic education welfare officer still involved, told Robert: 'These kids think they can get away with anything.' Would the justices display self-righteous rage, directed at teenager and social workers alike, when they heard the application? Might they, he fantasised, laughing like hyenas, and in insane and impotent fury, be tempted to impose a care order on the London Borough of Haringey itself?

The Shimble leaving event in the legal building was better attended than some had expected. The Borough Solicitor's long thin face on this occasion suggested a state of mind close to relaxed cheerfulness, and his cannon-ball stomach struck Robert (who had respectfully put in an appearance) as bearing a disarmingly docile expression. In attendance, of course, was 'Smiler' Trask, for whom Shimble had nothing but derision, but who delivered thanks and good wishes on behalf of the council in his open and friendly way. Bill Bowman expressed open contempt of Trask's public completion, during a quiet moment, of his own 'flexi-leave slip'. Did he not realise it demeaned his status as Chief Executive?

George Ballam attended too. 'No hard feelings, I hope, George,' said Shimble to him at a convenient moment, even shaking George's unenthusiastic hand. A leaving collection had raised enough for a fountain pen of less than sterling quality for the departing Borough Solicitor.

Colin Masson did not attend the leaving celebration and sent no apologies. Asked later by Robert as to whether he had contributed to Eddie's leaving gift he said simply, or not so simply:

'Robert, I have always considered, in this type of situation, that the amount of a donation made should bear a relationship to the view the donor has of the donee. In this particular case, having regard to all the circumstances, I would consider half of one penny not to be excessive.'

Colin was not quite done. Meditating for a few moments, he added: 'By the way, you were with Jessica at the Ducketts Common demonstration despite the rain. I gather you and Jessica are an item. Congratulations.' They shook hands.

Jessica had, in fact, accepted Robert's invitation to move into his half-empty flat. But her acceptance was subject to a condition. 'If our relationship ends,' she insisted, 'I leave first.'

'If you say so.'

'I do.'

Spring was arriving: not far from the legal building slightly stooping daffodils could be seen on a narrow grass verge, their youthful yellow faces brightly serene.

Postscript

This story, imitating life, ends with changes, continuations and loose ends. George Ballam remained in his office manager post during the more avuncular reign of a successor to Edward Shimble, while Colin Masson, a year or so after the events recounted, was to fulfil an ambition to join a well-established firm of solicitors with trade union clients.

Robert Fordham was to move on from Haringey not long after Colin's departure, first to become a barrister specialising in family law (on occasion finding the likes of Jonathan Spratt, Sophie Williams, Giles Springett and even the close to retirement Emmeline Byers, as his opponents). Robert did, incidentally, succumb to Jack Parnell's urgings to join his cricket team, for which he played for some summers.

The three, George, Robert and Colin, having become friends at Haringey, were to exchange Christmas cards and meet together annually as the years advanced, and reminders of life at Haringey under the querulous rule of Edward Shimble naturally found a place in their conversations.

Robert Fordham and Jessica Palmer, having 'got together', stayed together, loved each other, married and had children whom they also loved. Along the way – in fact earlier rather than later – Jessica read, and even enjoyed, Robert's favourite Eric Ambler novels, just as Robert was beginning to tire of re-reading, but not of admiring, them. Occasionally they had political disagreements, but they were generally resigned to each other's positions. Beth, the beautiful Beth, also became more settled, to the extent of marriage with the much older Michael Stone, though it was considered by Emily Frost (who had no such plans, but did before long give up smoking), that bets could reasonably be taken as to how long the marriage would last.

Edward Shimble's post-Haringey life need not detain us. Bill Bowman remained at Haringey, where he did not acquire a special relationship with Shimble's replacement. What happened in the lives to come of the children whose lives crossed those of Robert, Jessica, Emily and Enid Prosser, including the 'beyond control' Michelle, the drugged Amy, the 'at risk' Tania and a little boy called Aaron, if it were known, cannot be reported. Those who worked for Haringey council and for their welfare certainly hoped they would benefit in the long as well as the short run from the interventions in their lives which had taken place, while retaining compassion for the distress and difficulties of the parents.

As for Lady Feverel, she retired as chairman of the Tottenham juvenile bench soon after her role in this story ended. A justices' clerk – the curly-headed young man who had become a familiar face – said to Robert, announcing the news: 'I'm not pleased.' He then configured his face into a series of gurneyisms which perversely contradicted his words.

Less than a decade later dramatic cuts in services caused Haringey council to offer voluntary redundancy to many. Swathes of experienced and able social workers and their 'seniors' accepted the offer, and the previous practice standards in the social services department came under threat. In a less happy work environment, there were no more in-house entertainments.

Incidentally, the young and bearded Labour councillor who took part in the rained-on gathering of more than five hundred at Ducketts Common in mid-February 1980 to protest against cuts in the central government grant to councils, was to come to national prominence thirty five years later when elected leader of the Labour Party. This was Mr. Jeremy Corbyn.

Afterword

The preceding narrative is the product of imagination, and it is reliant on imagined characters. It is much more about what could happen than about what did happen. The child care cases presented are not 'actual cases with the names changed', though features of such cases and of the dilemmas arising derive from my own pre-Children Act working life and knowledge over a span of many years. Still, the narrative as a whole is intended to be more or less consistent with a realistic time and place setting; and it is hoped that the characters and their interactions, professional and social, are not so outlandish that they would seem to a reader impossible to slot into such a remote municipal environment.

The legal context underpinning social work concerning the welfare of children was in the late 1970s rather different from what it is now. The statutes, court rules, and rules of evidence are all much changed – and for the better.

'Place of safety orders' (authorizing the emergency removal of children from their carers) were usually applied for unilaterally by social workers to magistrates, so that parents had no right to attend and object. Again, in care proceedings, parents were not technically 'parties' with a full right to participate in their own right, while the child's own voice was much less heard than is the case today. When care proceedings were begun, and parents approached solicitors to obtain legal aid so that they could be represented, the legal aid granted would routinely be 'for the child', in many cases allowing the child's interests to be under-protected when the legal representative took instructions from parents. Again, the statutory grounds for care proceedings were unduly narrow, compelling local authorities on occasions to consider other procedures (notably the crude device of parental rights resolutions in some cases, and the more sophisticated device of wardship in the High Court in others). There was not much scope for independent welfare reports.

One antiquity was that the child in care proceedings (at least if aged five or over) had to be physically produced, happily or not, to be seen by the justices at the first hearing. Another curiosity was that police officers and juveniles in crime cases waited for their cases to come on outside the same courtroom doors as did social workers and parents concerned only with a child's welfare. The lumping together in the juvenile court of criminal and care cases had an impact on the way civil care cases were heard. Thus in civil care cases, as if guilt or innocence, rather than probabilities, were to be explored, professional witnesses (such as doctors, health visitors and teachers) were expected to wait outside the court until called. More substantially, a serious blurring between criminal and civil cases arose from the rules of evidence in care cases, which when strictly interpreted, were far too close to those in criminal proceedings, and potentially in conflict with welfare considerations.

Magistrates in those far-off days were required to distance themselves from what local authorities planned for children under care orders. Though magistrates could make care orders, they were not to give reasons for their decisions (unless appeals followed), and they were not required to approve local authority plans for children, should care orders be considered. Planning for the futures of children made subject to care orders could then be woefully primitive, not helped much by central government guidance of the time.

In summary, the overall legal environment for child welfare management was, compared with today's arrangements, ramshackle and confusing, making outcomes less predictable, while planning for the futures of children in care was undeveloped. Much of the reform, including the establishment of the 'civil only' family proceedings magistrates court, and an improved statutory expression of the grounds for care proceedings, was the consequence of the Children Act 1989. Improvements in the rules of evidence, and the routine introduction of an independent social worker – the guardian ad litem – to represent the child's best interests, came earlier.

In the narrative, the dangerous medication of Amy with phenergan by her mother was an example of what was already being labelled as Munchausen syndrome by proxy and later, less obscurely, as fabricated illness, generating a substantial literature.

Professional assumptions have also undergone advances. In the 1970s social workers were social workers for the family, not, as these days, social workers for the children. The Enid Prosser 'almost evangelical' approach, applied more subtly, became mainstream.

Sadly, there is a dark side to this story of progress. Over time there has been a significant reduction in the supply of human and financial resources to support families struggling to parent their children. Yet over these welfare-state-shrinking decades, not least in recent, recession-blasted years, the demand for such support has grown. Concurrently, the content of child protection social work has been transformed, driven by bureaucratic obsessions. A generation ago, the priority was human contact and 'early intervention' wherever possible, and record-keeping, though important, came second. Today the priority is reported to be vast and repetitive record-keeping, while human contact and 'early intervention' come a poor second. Meanwhile, the arrangements for care proceedings have regressed to a degree, such as through some trimming of the formerly generous remit of the guardian ad litem – these days labelled the children's guardian.

I confess to importing an element of greyness through not shirking some explanation of the law which underpins the narrative. I have been able to find no way to avoid this.

John Ellison